Saardam 1634 – My Lord, as requested

1	Mizzenmast	14	Capstan wheel
2	Poop deck	15	Staircase
3	Animal Pens	16	Mainmast
4	Passenger cabins×8	17	Orlop deck sailor half
5	Governor general's cabin	18	Cargo hold
6	Great cabin	19	Wycks' cabin
7	Helm	20	Sailmaker's cabin
8	Gunpowder Store	21	Forecastle deck
9	Orlop deck passengers	22	Foremast
10	Cargo hold	23	Sailmaker's store
11	Bilgepump	24	Pipps's cell
12	Quarter deck	25	Beak prow
13	Compartment under half deck	26	Compartment under forecastle

THE
DEVIL
AND THE
DARK
WATER

ALSO BY STUART TURTON

The Seven Deaths of Evelyn Hardcastle

THE
DEVIL
AND THE
DARK
WATER

STUART TURTON

RAVEN BOOKS

LONDON · OXFORD · NEW YORK · NEW DELHI · SYDNEY

RAVEN BOOKS
Bloomsbury Publishing Plc
50 Bedford Square, London, WC1B 3DP, UK

BLOOMSBURY, RAVEN BOOKS and the Raven Books logo
are trademarks of Bloomsbury Publishing Plc

First published in Great Britain 2020

Typeset by Integra Software Services Pvt. Ltd
Printed and bound in Great Britain by CPI Group (UK) Ltd, Croydon CR0 4YY

To find out more about our authors and books visit www.bloomsbury.com
and sign up for our newsletters

To Ada.

Right now, you're two years old, asleep in your cot. You're very strange and you make us laugh a lot. By the time you read this, you'll be somebody else entirely. I hope we're still pals. I hope I'm a good dad. I hope I don't make too many mistakes and you forgive the ones I do. Truth is, I have no idea what I'm doing. But I'm always trying hard.

I love you, kid. This is for you. Whoever you've become.

PROLOGUE

In 1634, the United East India Company was the wealthiest trading company in existence, with outposts spread across Asia and the Cape. The most profitable of these was Batavia, which shipped mace, pepper, spices and silks back to Amsterdam aboard its fleet of Indiaman galleons.

The journey took eight months and was fraught with danger.

Oceans were largely unmapped and navigational aids were rudimentary. Only one certain route existed between Batavia and Amsterdam and ships that strayed beyond it were often lost. Even those that kept between these 'wagon lines' remained at the mercy of disease, storms and pirates.

Many who boarded in Batavia would never make it to Amsterdam.

Manifest of notable passengers and crew sailing aboard the Saardam *bound for Amsterdam, as compiled by Chamberlain Cornelius Vos*

Dignitaries
Governor General Jan Haan, his wife Sara Wessel &
his daughter Lia Jan
Chamberlain Cornelius Vos
Guard Captain Jacobi Drecht
Creesjie Jens & her sons Marcus and Osbert Pieter
Viscountess Dalvhain

Notable passengers
Predikant Sander Kers & his ward Isabel
Lieutenant Arent Hayes

Saardam's senior officers
Chief Merchant Reynier van Schooten
Captain Adrian Crauwels
First Mate Isaack Larme

Notable crew
Boatswain – Johannes Wyck
Constable – Frederick van de Heuval

The prisoner
Samuel Pipps

Arent Hayes howled in pain as a rock slammed into his massive back.

Another whistled by his ear; a third striking his knee, causing him to stumble, bringing jeers from the pitiless mob, who were already searching the ground for more missiles to throw. Hundreds of them were being held back by the city watch, their spittle-flecked lips shouting insults, their eyes black with malice.

'Take shelter for pity's sake,' implored Sammy Pipps over the din, his manacles flashing in the sunlight as he staggered across the dusty ground. 'It's me they want.'

Arent was twice the height and half again the width of most men in Batavia, including Pipps. Although not a prisoner himself, he'd placed his large body between the crowd and his much smaller friend, offering them only a sliver of target to aim at.

The bear and the sparrow they'd been nicknamed before Sammy's fall. Never before had it appeared so true.

Pipps was being taken from the dungeons to the harbour, where a ship waited to transport him to Amsterdam. Four musketeers were escorting them, but they were keeping their distance, wary of becoming targets themselves.

'You pay me to protect you,' snarled Arent, wiping the dusty sweat from his eyes as he tried to gauge the distance to safety. 'I'll do it until I can't any more.'

The harbour lay behind a huge set of gates at the far end of Batavia's central boulevard. Once those gates closed behind them, they'd be beyond the crowd's reach. Unfortunately, they were at the tail end of a long procession moving slowly in the heat. The gates seemed no closer now than when they'd left the humid dampness of the dungeon at midday.

A rock thudded into the ground at Arent's feet, spraying his boots with dried dirt. Another ricocheted off Sammy's chains. Traders were selling them out of sacks and making good coin doing it.

'Damn Batavia,' snarled Arent. 'Bastards can't abide an empty pocket.'

On a normal day, these people would be buying from the bakers, tailors, cordwainers, binders and candlemakers lining the boulevard. They'd be smiling and laughing, grumbling about the infernal heat, but manacle a man, offer him up to torment, and even the meekest soul surrendered itself to the devil.

'It's my blood they want,' argued Sammy, trying to push Arent away. 'Get yourself to safety, I'm begging you.'

Arent looked down at his terrified friend, whose hands were pressing ineffectually against his chest. His dark curls were plastered to his forehead, those high cheekbones swollen purple with the beatings he'd received while imprisoned. His brown eyes – usually wry – were wide and desperate.

Even maltreated, he was a handsome sod.

By contrast, Arent's scalp was shorn, his nose punched flat. Somebody had bitten a chunk out of his right ear in a fight, and a clumsy flogging a few years back had left him with a long scar across his chin and neck.

'We'll be safe once we reach the docks,' said Arent stubbornly, having to raise his voice as cheers erupted ahead of them.

The procession was being led by Governor General Jan Haan, who was stiff-backed on a white stallion, a breastplate fastened above his doublet, a sword clattering at his waist.

Thirteen years ago, he'd purchased the village that had stood here on behalf of the United East India Company. No sooner had the natives signed the contract than he'd put a torch to it, using its ashes to plot out the roads, canals and buildings of the city that would take its place.

Batavia was now the Company's most profitable outpost and Jan Haan had been called back to Amsterdam to join the Company's ruling body, the enigmatic Gentlemen 17.

As his stallion trotted along the boulevard, the crowd wept and cheered, stretching their fingertips towards him, trying to touch his legs. Flowers were thrown on the ground, blessings bestowed.

He ignored it all, keeping his chin up and eyes forward. Beak-nosed and bald-headed, he put Arent in mind of a hawk perched atop a horse.

Four panting slaves struggled to keep pace with him. They were carrying a gilded palanquin with the governor general's wife and daughter inside, a red-faced lady's maid scurrying alongside it, fanning herself in the heat.

Behind them, four bow-legged musketeers gripped the corners of a heavy box containing The Folly. Sweat dripped from their foreheads and coated their hands, making it difficult to hold. They slipped frequently, fear flashing across their faces. They knew the punishment should the governor general's prize be damaged.

Trailing them were a disorderly cluster of courtiers and flatterers, high-ranking clerks and family favourites; their years of scheming rewarded by the opportunity to spend an uncomfortable afternoon watching the governor general leave Batavia.

Distracted by his observations, Arent allowed a gap to form between himself and his charge. A stone whistled by, hitting Sammy on the cheek, bringing a trickle of blood and jeers from the crowd.

Losing his temper, Arent scooped up the stone and hurled it back at the thrower, catching him on the shoulder and sending him spinning to the ground. The crowd howled in outrage, surging into the watchmen, who struggled to hold them back.

'Good throw,' murmured Sammy appreciatively, ducking his head as more stones rained down around them.

Arent was limping by the time they reached the docks, his huge body aching. Sammy was bruised, but mostly untouched. Even so, he let out a cry of relief as the gates swung open ahead of them.

On the other side was a warren of crates and coiled ropes, piled-high casks and chickens squawking in wicker baskets. Pigs and cows stared at them mournfully, as bellowing stevedores loaded cargo into rowboats bobbing at the water's edge, ready to be transported to the seven Indiaman galleons anchored in the glistening harbour. Sails furled and masts bare, they resembled dead beetles with their legs in the air, but each would soon teem with over three hundred passengers and crew.

People rattled their coin purses at the ferries rowing back and forth, pushing forward when the name of their ship was called. Children played hide and seek among the boxes, or else clutched their mothers' skirts, while fathers glared at the sky, trying to shame a cloud out of that fierce blue expanse.

The wealthier passengers stood a little apart, surrounded by their servants and expensive trunks. Grumbling under their umbrellas, they fanned themselves futilely, sweating into their lace ruffs.

The procession halted and the gates began to close behind them, dimming the sound of the braying mob.

A few final stones bounced off the crates, bringing the assault to an end.

Letting out a long sigh, Arent bent double, hands on his knees, sweat dripping from his forehead into the dust.

'How badly are you hurt?' asked Sammy, inspecting a cut on Arent's cheek.

'I'm fair hungover,' grunted Arent. 'Otherwise, I'm not too bad.'

'Did the watch seize my alchemy kit?'

There was genuine fear in his voice. Among his many talents, Sammy was a skilled alchemist, his kit filled with the tinctures, powders and potions he'd developed to assist his deductive work. It had taken years to create many of them, using ingredients they were a long way from being able to replace.

'No, I stole them out of your bedchamber before they searched the house,' replied Arent.

'Good,' approved Sammy. 'There's a salve in a small jar. The green one. Apply that to your injuries every morning and night.'

Arent wrinkled his nose in distaste. 'Is that the piss-smelling one?'

'They all smell like piss. It's not a good salve if it doesn't smell like piss.'

A musketeer approached from the direction of the wharf, calling Sammy's name. He wore a battered hat with a red feather, the floppy brim pulled low over his eyes. A tangle of dirty blond hair spilled down his shoulders, a beard obscuring most of his face.

Arent examined him approvingly.

Most musketeers in Batavia were part of the household guard. They gleamed and saluted and were good at sleeping with their eyes open, but this man's ragged uniform suggested he'd done some actual soldiering. Old blood stained his blue doublet, which was dotted with holes made by shot and sword, each one patched time and again. Knee-length red breeches gave way to a pair of tanned, hairy legs riddled with mosquito bites and scars. Copper flasks filled with gunpowder jangled on a bandolier, clattering into pouches of saltpetre matches.

Upon reaching Arent, the musketeer stamped his foot smartly.

'Lieutenant Hayes, I'm Guard Captain Jacobi Drecht,' he said, waving a fly from his face. 'I'm in charge of the governor general's household guard. I'll be sailing with you to ensure the family's safety.' Drecht addressed himself to the musketeers escorting them. 'On the boat now, lads. Governor General wants Mr Pipps secured aboard the *Saardam* before the –'

'Hear me!' commanded a jagged voice from above them.

Squinting into the glare of sunlight, they craned their necks, following the voice upwards.

A figure in grey rags was standing on a pile of crates. Bloody bandages wrapped his hands and face, a narrow gap left for his eyes.

'A leper,' muttered Drecht, in disgust.

Arent took an instinctive step backwards. From boyhood, he'd been taught to fear these wasted people, whose mere presence was enough to bring ruin to an entire village. A single cough, even the lightest touch, meant a lingering, dreadful death.

'Kill that creature and burn it,' ordered the governor general from the front of the procession. 'Lepers are not permitted in the city.'

A commotion erupted as the musketeers peered at each other. The figure was too high up for pikes, their muskets had already been loaded on to the *Saardam* and none of them had a bow.

Seemingly oblivious to the panic, the leper's eyes pricked every single person gathered before him.

'Know that my master' – his roaming gaze snagged on Arent, causing the mercenary's heart to jolt – 'sails aboard the *Saardam*. He is the lord of hidden things; all desperate and dark things. He offers this warning in accordance with the old laws. The *Saardam*'s cargo is sin and all who board her will be brought to merciless ruin. She will not reach Amsterdam.'

As the last word was uttered, the hem of his robe burst into flames.

Children wailed. The watching crowd gasped and screamed in horror.

The leper didn't make a sound. The fire crawled up his body until he was completely aflame.

He didn't move.

He burnt silently, his eyes fixed on Arent.

2

A s if suddenly aware of the flames consuming him, the leper began beating at his robes.

He staggered backwards, falling off the crates, hitting the ground with a sickening thud.

Snatching up a cask of ale, Arent covered the distance in a few strides, tearing the lid free with his bare hands and dousing the fire.

The rags sizzled, the smell of charcoal singeing his nostrils.

Writhing in agony, the leper clawed at the dirt. His forearms were terribly burnt, his face charred. Only his eyes were still human – the pupils wild, thrashing against the surrounding blue, driven mad with pain.

A scream wedged his mouth open, but no sound passed his throat.

'That's impossible,' muttered Arent.

He glanced at Sammy, who was straining against his chains, trying to see better. 'His tongue's been cut out,' Arent hollered, struggling to be heard over the din of the crowd.

'Stand aside, I'm a healer,' came an imperious voice.

A noblewoman pushed past Arent, removing a lace cap and shoving it into his hands, revealing the jewelled pins glittering among her tight red curls.

No sooner was the cap in Arent's possession than it was snatched away again by a fussing maid, who was trying to keep a parasol over her mistress's head, while urging her to return to the palanquin.

Arent glanced back towards it.

In her haste, the noblewoman had yanked the curtain off its hook and spilled two large silk pillows on to the ground. Inside, a young girl with an oval face was watching them through the torn material. She was black-haired and dark-eyed, a mirror of the governor general, who sat stiff on his horse, examining his wife disapprovingly.

'Mama?' called out the girl.

'A moment, Lia,' replied the noblewoman, who was kneeling beside the leper, oblivious to her brown gown piled up in fish guts. 'I'm going to try to help you,' she told him kindly. 'Dorothea?'

'My lady,' responded the maid.

'My vial, if you please.'

The maid fumbled up her sleeve and removed a small vial, which she uncorked and handed to the noblewoman.

'This will ease your pain,' the lady said to the suffering man, upending it above his parted lips.

'Those are lepers' rags,' warned Arent, as her puffed sleeves drifted perilously close to her patient.

'I'm aware,' she said curtly, watching a thick drop of liquid gathering on the rim of the vial. 'You're Lieutenant Hayes, are you not?'

'Arent will do.'

'Arent.' She rolled the name around her mouth, as if it possessed an odd flavour. 'I'm Sara Wessel.' She paused. 'Sara will do,' she added, mimicking his gruff response.

She gave the vial a slight shake, dislodging the drop into the leper's mouth. He swallowed it painfully, then shuddered and calmed, the writhing ceasing as his eyes lost focus.

'You're the governor general's wife?' asked Arent disbelievingly. Most nobles wouldn't leave a palanquin that was on fire, let alone leap out of one to aid a stranger.

'And you're Samuel Pipps's servant,' she snapped back.

'I –' He faltered, wrong-footed by her annoyance. Unsure of how he had offended her, he changed the topic. 'What did you give him?'

'Something to ease the pain,' she said, wedging the cork back into the vial. 'It's made from local plants. I use it myself from time to time. It helps me sleep.'

'Can we do anything for him, my lady?' asked the maid, taking the vial from her mistress and putting it back up her sleeve. 'Should I fetch your healing sundries?'

Only a fool would try, thought Arent. A life at war had taught him which limbs you could live without and which nicks would wake you in agony every night until they killed you quietly a year after the battle. The leper's rotting flesh was bad enough, but there'd be no peace from those burns. With constant ministrations he could live a day, or a week, but survival wasn't always worth the price paid for it.

'No, thank you, Dorothea,' said Sara. 'I don't think that will be necessary.'

Rising to her feet, Sara gestured for Arent to follow her out of earshot.

'There's nothing to be done here,' she said quietly. 'Nothing left except mercy. Could you ...' She swallowed, seemingly ashamed of the next question. 'Have you ever taken a life?'

Arent nodded.

'Can you do it painlessly?'

Arent nodded again, earning a small smile of gratitude.

'I regret I have not the fortitude to do it myself,' she said.

Arent pushed through the whispering circle of observers towards one of the musketeers guarding Sammy, gesturing for his sword. Numb with horror, the young soldier unsheathed it without protest.

'Arent,' said Sammy, calling his friend closer. 'Did you say the leper had no tongue?'

'Cut out,' confirmed Arent. 'A while back, I reckon.'

'Bring me Sara Wessel when you're finished,' Sammy said, troubled. 'This matter requires our attention.'

As Arent returned with the sword, Sara knelt by the stricken leper, reaching to take his hand, before remembering herself. 'I have not the art to heal you,' she admitted gently. 'But I can offer you a painless escape, if you'd have it?'

The leper's mouth worked, producing only moans. Tears forming in his eyes, he nodded.

'I'll stay with you.' She looked over her shoulder at the young girl peering at them from inside the palanquin. 'Lia, join me, if you please,' said Sara, holding out a hand to her.

Lia climbed down from the palanquin. She was no more than twelve or thirteen, already long-limbed, her dress sitting awkwardly, like a skin she hadn't managed to quite wriggle out of.

A great rustling greeted her, as the procession shifted to take her in. Arent was among those curious onlookers. Unlike her mother, who visited church each evening, Lia was rarely seen outdoors. It was rumoured her father kept her hidden out of shame, but as Arent watched her walk hesitantly towards the leper, it was difficult to know what that shame could be.

She was a pretty girl, if uncommonly pale, like she'd been spun from shadows and moonlight.

As Lia drew closer, Sara flicked a nervous glance at her husband, who was sitting rigid on his horse, his jaw moving slightly as he ground his teeth. Arent knew this was as close to fury as he'd come in public. By the twitching of his face, it was obvious he wanted to call them back into the palanquin, but the curse of authority was that you could never admit to losing it.

Lia arrived by her mother's side and Sara squeezed her hand reassuringly.

'This man is in pain,' she said in a soft voice. 'He's suffering and Lieutenant Hayes here is going to end that suffering. Can you understand that?'

The girl's eyes were wide, but she nodded meekly. 'Yes, Mama,' she said.

'Good,' said Sara. 'He's very afraid and this isn't something he should face alone. We will stand vigil; we will offer him our courage. You mustn't look away.'

From around his neck, the leper painfully withdrew a small charred piece of wood, the edges jagged. He pressed it to his breast, squeezing his eyes shut.

'Whenever you're ready,' she said to Arent, who immediately rammed the blade through the leper's heart. The man arched his back, going rigid. Then he went limp, blood seeping out from underneath him. It was glossy in the sunlight, reflecting the three figures standing over the body.

The girl gripped her mother's hand tightly, but her courage didn't falter.

'Well done, my love,' said Sara, stroking her soft cheek. 'I know that was unpleasant, but you were very brave.'

As Arent cleaned the blade on a sack of oats, Sara tugged one of the jewelled pins from her hair, a red curl springing loose.

'For your trouble,' she said, offering it to him.

'Aint kindness if you have to pay for it,' he responded, leaving it sparkling in her hand, as he returned the sword to the soldier.

Surprise mingled with confusion on her face, her gaze lingering on him a moment. As if wary of being caught in such naked observation, she hurriedly summoned two stevedores who'd been sitting on a pile of tattered sailcloth.

They leapt up as if stung, tugging a lock of hair when they were near enough.

'Sell this, burn the body and see his ashes receive a Christian burial,' commanded Sara, pressing the pin into the nearest calloused palm. 'Let's give him the peace in death he was denied in life.'

They exchanged a cunning glance.

'That jewel will pay for the funeral with enough left over for any vices you seek to indulge this year, but I'll have somebody watching you,' she warned pleasantly. 'If this poor man ends up in the undesirables lot beyond the city walls, you'll be hanged – is that understood?'

'Yes, ma'am,' they muttered, tipping their hats respectfully.

'Can you spare a minute for Sammy Pipps?' called out Arent, who was standing next to Guard Captain Jacobi Drecht.

Sara glanced at her husband once again, obviously trying to weigh his displeasure. Arent could sympathise. Jan Haan could find fault in a bold table arrangement, so watching his wife dash through the dirt like a harlot after a rolling coin would have been unbearable to him.

He wasn't even looking at her. He was watching Arent.

'Lia, return to the palanquin, please,' said Sara.

'But, Mama,' complained Lia, lowering her voice. 'That's Samuel Pipps.'

'Yes,' she agreed.

'The Samuel Pipps!'

'Indeed.'

'The sparrow!'

'A nickname I'm sure he adores,' she responded drily.

'You could introduce me.'

'He's hardly dressed for company, Lia.'

'Mama –'

'A leper's quite enough excitement for one day,' said Sara with finality, summoning Dorothea with a lift of her chin.

A protest formed on her daughter's lips, but the maid stroked her arm, encouraging her away.

The crowd melted from Sara's path as she approached the prisoner, who was busy straightening his stained doublet.

'Your legend precedes you, Mr Pipps,' she said, curtsying.

After his recent humiliation, this unexpected compliment seemed to take Sammy aback, causing him to stumble on his initial greeting. He tried to bow, but his chains made a mockery of the gesture.

'Now, why did you wish to speak with me?' asked Sara.

'I'm imploring you to delay the departure of the *Saardam*,' he said. 'Please, you must heed the leper's warning.'

'I took the leper for a madman,' she admitted in surprise.

'Oh, he was certainly mad,' agreed Sammy. 'But he was able to speak without a tongue and climb a stack of crates with a lame foot.'

'I noticed the tongue, but not the lame foot.' She glanced back at the body. 'Are you certain?'

'Even burnt, you can see the impairment clearly within his bandages. He would have needed a crutch to walk, which means he couldn't possibly have climbed up on those crates without help.'

'Then you don't believe he was acting alone?'

'I don't, and there's a further cause for concern.'

'Of course there is,' she sighed. 'Why would concern want to travel alone?'

'Do you see his hands?' continued Sammy, ignoring the remark. 'One is very badly burnt, but the other is almost untouched. If you look carefully, you'll notice a bruise under his thumbnail and that his thumb itself has been broken at least three times in the past, rendering it crooked. Carpenters accrue such injuries as a matter of course, especially shipborne carpenters, who must contend with the unsteady motion of the boat while they're working. I noticed he was bow-legged, another common trait of the sailing class.'

'Do you believe he was a carpenter on one of the boats in the fleet?' ventured Arent, examining the seven ships in the harbour.

'I don't know,' said Sammy. 'Every carpenter in Batavia likely worked on an Indiaman at some time. If I were free to inspect the body, I might be able to answer the question more definitely, but –'

'My husband will never free you, Mr Pipps,' said Sara sharply. 'If that's to be your next request.'

'It's not,' he said, his cheeks flushing. 'I know your husband's mind, as I know he will not hear my concerns. But he would hear them from you.'

Sara shifted her weight uncomfortably, staring at the harbour. Dolphins were playing in the water, leaping and twisting in the air, disappearing back beneath the surface with barely a ripple.

'Please, my lady. You must convince your husband to delay the fleet's departure while Arent investigates this matter.'

Arent started at that. The last time he'd investigated a case had been three years ago. Nowadays, he kept out of that side of things. His job was to keep Sammy safe and trample underfoot whatever bastard he pointed his finger at.

'Questions are swords and answers are shields,' persisted Sammy, still staring at Sara. 'I'm begging you: armour yourself. Once the *Saardam* sets sail, it will be too late.'

3

UNDER BATAVIA'S BURNING SKY, Sara Wessel walked the length of the procession, feeling the scouring eyes of the courtiers, soldiers and sycophants upon her. She went like a condemned woman: shoulders square, eyes down and fists clenched by her sides. Shame reddened her face, though most mistook it for heat.

For some reason, she glanced over her shoulder at Arent. He wasn't hard to spot, standing a clear head and shoulders taller than the next man. Sammy had put him to work inspecting the body, and he was currently picking through the leper's robes with a long stick that had previously been used to carry baskets.

Feeling Sara's gaze upon him, he glanced at her, their eyes meeting. Embarrassed, she snapped her head forward again.

Her husband's damnable horse snorted, kicking the ground angrily as she approached. She'd never got along with this beast. Unlike her, it enjoyed being underneath him.

The thought drew a wicked smile, which she was still wrestling from her face as she came upon him. His back was to her, his head bowed in hushed conversation with Cornelius Vos.

Vos was her husband's chamberlain, foremost among his advisors and one of the most powerful men in the city. Not that it was obvious by looking at him, for he managed to carry his power without charisma or vigour. Neither tall nor short, broad nor thin, his mud-coloured hair topped a weathered face devoid of any distinguishing features, beyond two luminous green eyes that always stared over the shoulder of whoever he was speaking to.

His clothes were shabby without being ragged, and there hung about him an air of such potent hopelessness one would expect flowers to wilt as he walked by.

'Is my personal cargo boarded?' asked her husband, ignoring Sara.

'The chief merchant has seen to it, my lord.'

They didn't pause, didn't acknowledge her in any way. Her husband couldn't stand being interrupted and Vos had served him long enough to know that.

'And matters have been arranged to ensure its secrecy?' asked her husband.

'Guard Captain Drecht attended to it personally.' Vos's fingers danced at his sides, betraying some internal calculation. 'Which bring us to our second piece of important cargo, my lord. May I ask where you wish to store The Folly during our voyage?'

'My quarters seem appropriate,' declared her husband.

'Unfortunately, The Folly's too large, sir,' said Vos, wringing his hands. 'Might I suggest the cargo hold?'

'I'll not have the future of the Company packed away like an unwanted piece of furniture.'

'Few know what The Folly is, sir,' continued Vos, momentarily distracted by the splashing oars of an approaching ferry.

'Even fewer know we're bringing it aboard the *Saardam*. The best way to protect it might be to act as though it is an unwanted piece of furniture.'

'A clever thought, but the cargo hold remains too exposed,' said her husband.

They fell silent, puzzling the matter over.

Sunshine beat at Sara's back, thick beads of sweat gathering on her brow and rolling down her face, clogging the white powder Dorothea applied so liberally to conceal her freckles. She yearned to adjust her clothes, to remove the ruff around her neck and tug the damp material away from her flesh, but her husband hated fidgeting as much as being interrupted.

'What about the gunpowder store, sir?' said Vos. 'It's locked and guarded, but nobody would expect something as valuable as The Folly to be housed in there.'

'Superb. Make the arrangements.'

As Vos walked towards the procession, the governor general finally turned to face his wife.

He was twenty years older than Sara, with a teardrop head, which was bald except for a tonsure of dark hair connecting his large ears. Most people wore hats to shield them from Batavia's harsh sunlight, but her husband believed they made him look foolish. As a result, his scalp glowed an angry crimson, the skin peeling and collecting in the folds of his ruff.

Under flat eyebrows, two dark eyes weighed her, as fingers scratched a long nose. By any measure, he was an ugly man, but, unlike Chamberlain Vos, he radiated power. Every word out of his mouth felt like it was being etched into history; every glance contained a subtle rebuke, an invitation for others to measure themselves against him and discover the ways in which they were wanting. By merely living, he thought himself an instruction manual in good breeding, discipline and values.

'My wife,' he said in a tone that could easily be mistaken for pleasant.

His hand jerked to her face, causing her to flinch. Pressing a thumb to her cheek, he roughly wiped away a clot of powder. 'How unkind the heat is to you.'

She swallowed the insult, lowering her gaze.

Fifteen years they'd been married and she could count on one hand the number of times she'd be able to hold his stare.

It was those ink-blot eyes. They were identical to Lia's, except her daughter's glittered with life. Her husband's were empty, like two dark holes his soul had long run out of.

She'd felt it the first time they'd met, when she and her four sisters had been delivered overnight to his drawing room in Rotterdam, like meat ordered specially from the market. He'd interviewed them one by one and chosen Sara on the spot. His proposal had been thorough, listing the benefits of their union to her father. In short, she'd have a beautiful cage and all the time in the world to admire herself in the bars.

Sara had wept all the way home, begging her father not to send her away.

It hadn't made any difference. The dowry was too large. Unbeknown to her, she'd been bred for sale and fattened like a calf with manners and education.

She'd felt betrayed, but she'd been young. She understood the world better now. Meat didn't get a say on whose hook it hung from.

'Your display was unbecoming,' he rebuked her under his breath, still smiling for his courtiers. They were edging close, wary of missing anything.

'It wasn't a display,' she muttered defiantly. 'The leper was suffering.'

'He was dying. Did you think you had a lotion for that?' His voice was low enough to crush the ants crawling around their feet. 'You're impulsive, reckless, thick-headed and soft-hearted.' He flung insults the way rocks had been thrown at Samuel Pipps. 'Such qualities I forgave when you were a girl, but your youth is far behind you.'

She didn't listen to the rest; she didn't need to. It was a familiar rebuke, the first drops of rain before the fury of the storm. Nothing she said now would make any difference. Her punishment would come later, when they were alone.

'Samuel Pipps believes our ship is under threat,' she blurted out.

Her husband frowned, unused to being interrupted.

'Pipps is in chains,' he argued.

'Only his hands,' she protested. 'His eyes and faculties remain at liberty. He believes the leper was a carpenter once, possibly working in the fleet returning us to Amsterdam.'

'Lepers can't serve aboard Indiamen.'

'Perhaps the blight showed itself when he reached Batavia?'

'Lepers are executed and burnt by my decree. None are tolerated in the city.' He shook his head in irritation. 'You've allowed yourself to be swayed by the ramblings of a madman, and a criminal. There's no danger here. The *Saardam* is a fine vessel, with a fine captain. There isn't stouter in the fleet. That's why I chose her.'

'Pipps isn't concerned about a loose plank,' she shot back, quickly lowering her voice. 'He fears sabotage. Everybody who boards today will be at risk, including our daughter. We already lost our boys, could you really stand to …' She took a breath, calming herself. 'Wouldn't it be wise to talk to the captains of the fleet before we set sail? The leper was missing his tongue and had a maimed foot. If he served under any of them, they would certainly remember him.'

'And what would you have me do in the meantime?' he demanded, tipping his chin towards the hundreds of souls sweltering in the heat. Somehow the procession had managed to edge within eavesdropping distance without making a sound. 'Should I order this procession back to the castle on a criminal's good word?'

'You trusted Pipps well enough when you summoned him from Amsterdam to retrieve The Folly.'

His eyes narrowed dangerously.

'For Lia's sake,' she continued recklessly. 'Might we take quarters aboard another ship, at least?'

'No, we will travel aboard the *Saardam*.'

'Lia alone, then.'

'No.'

'Why?' She was so confounded by his stubbornness she failed to take heed of his anger. 'Another ship will do well enough. Why are you so intent upon travelling –'

Her husband slapped her with the back of his hand, raising a stinging welt on her cheek. Among the courtiers there were gasps and giggles.

Sara's glare could have sunk every ship in the harbour, but the governor general met it calmly, retrieving a silk handkerchief from his pocket.

Whatever fury had been building inside of him had evaporated.

'Fetch our daughter, so we might board together as a family,' he said, dabbing the white powder from his hand. 'Our time in Batavia is at an end.'

Gritting her teeth, Sara turned back towards the procession.

Everybody was watching her, tittering and whispering, but she had eyes only for the palanquin.

Lia stared out from behind the tattered curtains, her face unreadable.

Damn him, thought Sara. Damn him.

4

OARS ROSE AND FELL, sunlight sparkling in the falling drops of water as the ferry made its way across the choppy blue harbour to the *Saardam*.

Guard Captain Jacobi Drecht was in the centre of the boat, a leg either side of the bench on which he was seated, his fingers absently picking out flakes of salted fish from his blond beard.

His sabre had been unhooked from his waist and laid across his knees. It was a fine weapon, with a delicate basket of metal protecting the hilt. Most musketeers were armed with pikes and muskets, or else rusted blades stolen from corpses on the battlefield. This was a noble's sword, much too fine for a humble soldier, and Arent wondered where the guard captain had come upon it – and why he hadn't sold it.

Drecht's hand lay lightly on its sheath, and now and again he would cast a suspicious glance at his prisoner, but he was from the same village as the ferryman, and the two of them were talking warmly of the boar they'd hunted in its forests, and the taverns they'd visited.

At the prow, chains coiled around him like serpents, Sammy fingered his rusted manacles wretchedly. Arent had never seen his friend so dejected. In the five years they'd worked together, Sammy had proven himself vexing, short-tempered, kind and lazy, but never defeated. It was like seeing the sun sag in the sky.

'Soon as we board, I'll talk to the governor general,' vowed Arent. 'I'll put sense before him.'

Sammy shook his head.

'He won't listen,' he responded hollowly. 'And the more you defend me, the harder it will be to distance yourself once I've been executed.'

'Executed!' exclaimed Arent.

'That's the governor general's intention once we reach Amsterdam.' He snorted. 'Assuming we make it that far.'

Instinctively, Arent sought out the governor general's ferry. It was a few strokes ahead of them, his family sheltered beneath a curtained canopy. A breeze pushed at the gauzy material, revealing Lia's head in her mother's lap. The governor general sat a little apart.

'The Gentlemen 17 will never let that happen,' argued Arent, recalling the esteem in which the rulers of the United East India Company held Sammy. 'You're too valuable.'

'The governor general sails to take a seat among them. He believes he can convince the rest.'

Their ferry passed between two ships. Sailors were hanging from the rigging, firing bawdy jokes at one other across the gap. Somebody was pissing over the side, the yellow torrent narrowly missing them.

'Why is this happening, Sammy?' demanded Arent. 'You recovered The Folly, as you were asked. They held a banquet in your honour. How is it a day later you walked into the governor general's office a hero and were dragged out in chains?'

'I've thought on it and thought on it, but I don't know,' he said despairingly. 'He demanded I confess, but when I told him I didn't know what I was confessing to, he flew into a rage and had me tossed into the dungeon until I reconsidered. That's why I'm begging you to leave me be.'

'Sammy –'

'Something I did during this case brought his wrath upon me, and without knowing what it is, I can't hope to protect you from it,' interrupted Sammy. 'But I swear, once he's finished with me, our good works will count for nothing and our standing in the United East India Company will be undone. I'm poison to you, Arent Hayes. My conduct was reckless and arrogant, and for that I'm being punished. I won't compound my failure by dragging you into ruin.' Leaning forward, he stared at Arent fiercely. 'Go back to Batavia, let me save your life for once.'

'I took your coin and made my promise to keep you out of harm's way,' responded Arent. 'I've got eight months to stop you from becoming a crow's banquet, and I mean to see it done.'

Shaking his head, Sammy fell into a defeated silence, his shoulders slumping.

Their rowboat approached the creaking expanse of the *Saardam*, its hull rising out of the water like an enormous wooden wall. Only ten months had passed since she left Amsterdam, but she was already ancient, her green and red paint flaked, the timbers warped from her passage through the freezing Atlantic into the steamy tropics.

That something so large could float was a feat of engineering akin to devilry, and Arent felt immediately diminished in its presence. He stretched out a hand and dragged his fingertips along the coarse planks. There was a dull vibration in the wood. He tried to imagine what was on the other side: the warren of decks and staircases, the stray beams of sunlight piercing the gloom. A ship this size would require hundreds of souls to sail her and would carry that many passengers again. They were all in danger. Even chained, even beaten and maltreated, Sammy was the only one who could help them.

Arent conveyed this thought as eloquently as he was able. 'Somebody's trying to sink this boat, and I swim like a bag of rocks. Any chance you can pull your head out of your arse and do something about it?'

Sammy grinned at him. 'You could lead an army over a cliff with that tongue,' he said sarcastically. 'Did your search of the leper's body turn anything up?'

Arent withdrew a piece of hemp he'd hacked off a sack on the docks. Wrapped inside was the charm the leper had been holding when Arent killed him. It was too charred to make out any detail.

Sammy leant forward, eyeing it intently. 'It was snapped in half,' he said. 'You can make out the jagged edges still.'

He pondered it a moment, then swivelled towards Guard Captain Drecht. His voice was filled with authority despite the chains. 'Have you ever served upon an Indiaman?'

Drecht squinted at him, as if the question were a dark cave he didn't want to enter.

'I have,' he answered, at last.

'What's the fastest way to sink one?'

Drecht raised a bushy blond eyebrow, then nodded towards Arent. 'Get your mate to ram his fist through the hull.'

'I'm serious, Guard Captain,' said Sammy.

'Why?' he asked suspiciously. 'Not a pleasant thing you're going to, but I'll not let you drag the governor general into hell with you.'

'My future is in Arent's hands, which means I'll fear for it no longer,' responded Sammy. 'However, a threat's been made against this ship. I'd like to ensure it comes to nothing.'

Drecht looked past Sammy to Arent. 'Is that truly his intent, Lieutenant? On your honour.'

Arent nodded, causing Drecht to stare at the ships surrounding them. He frowned, adjusting the bandolier slung over his shoulder, the copper flasks rattling.

'Put a spark to the gunpowder store,' he said, after a long pause. 'That's how I'd do it.'

'Who keeps watch on the gunpowder store?'

'A constable behind a barred door,' responded Drecht.

'Arent, I need you to find out who has access to that room and any grievances our constable may hold,' said Sammy.

Arent was encouraged to hear the eagerness in his friend's voice. For the most part, they investigated thefts and murders, crimes long committed and easily understood. It was like arriving at the theatre after the performance had ended and being asked to work out the story using pieces of discarded script and the props left on stage. But here was a crime not yet undertaken; a chance to save lives rather than avenge them. Here, at last, was a case worthy of Sammy's talents. Hopefully, it would be enough to distract him until Arent secured his freedom.

'You'll need to get permission from Captain Crauwels,' interrupted Drecht, flicking a drop of seawater off his eyelash. 'Only his good word will get you inside. Not that his good words are easy to come by.'

'Then start there,' Sammy told Arent. 'Once you've spoken to the constable, see if you can identify the leper. I'm treating him as a victim.'

'Victim?' scoffed Drecht. 'He was the one raining curses down on us.'

'How? His tongue had been cut out. All he really did was give us something to stare at while another voice issued the threat. We have no idea whether the leper shared its malice or not, though I'm certain he didn't climb those crates by himself or ignite his own robes. His hands didn't move from his sides until he hurled himself off the crates, and we all saw his panic as the flames consumed him. He didn't know what was going to happen to him, which makes his death a murder – and a heinous one at that.' A small spider was scurrying along Sammy's chains and he made a bridge of his hand, letting it crawl on to the bench. 'That's why Arent's going to find the name of the leper, then talk to any friends he had and piece together his final weeks. From those fragments, perhaps we'll understand how he came to be on those crates, whose voice we heard and why it harbours such hate for those aboard the *Saardam*.'

Arent shifted sheepishly. 'I'm not certain I can do any of those things Sammy. Maybe we can find –'

'Three years ago, you asked me to teach you my art and I made you my apprentice,' said Sammy, irritated by his reticence. 'I believe it's time you acted as such.'

Old arguments rose up between them like noxious bubbles in a swamp.

'We gave up on that,' said Arent heatedly. 'We already know I can't do what you do.'

'What occurred in Lille wasn't a failing of intellect, Arent. It was a failure of temperament. Your strength has made you impatient.'

'I didn't fail because of my strength.'

'That was one case, and I understand that it dented your confidence –'

'An innocent man nearly died.'

'Innocent men do that,' said Sammy, with finality. 'How many languages can you speak? How easily did you collect them? I've watched you these last years. I know how much you observe. How much you retain. What was Sara Wessel wearing at our meeting this morning? Boots to hat, tell me.'

'I don't know.'

'Of course you do,' he said, laughing at Arent's instinctive lie. 'You're a stubborn man. I could ask you how many legs a horse has and you'd deny having ever seen one. All that information, what do you do with it?'

'I keep you alive.'

'And there you are again, leaning on your strength when it's your mind we need.' He lifted his heavy chains. 'My resources are limited, Arent, and until I'm free to pursue my own enquiries, I'm expecting you to protect the ship.' Their boat bumped into the hull of the *Saardam* as the ferryman brought them alongside. 'I'll not have some bastard drown me before the governor general hangs me.'

5

FERRIES SWARMED THE *SAARDAM*, crossing the water in a long chain, like ants attacking a dead ox. Each one teemed with passengers clutching the single bag they were allowed to bring. Hollering for the rope ladders to be thrown down, they found themselves mocked by the sailors high above, who made great show of being unable to find the ladders, or of simply not hearing the requests.

They were forgiven their sport by the *Saardam*'s officers, who were waiting for Governor General Haan and his family to finish boarding at the aft of the ship. No other passengers would be allowed up until they were comfortably housed.

A plank attached to four pieces of rope was currently hoisting Lia serenely upwards, with Sara watching below, hands clasped, terrified that her daughter might spill, or the rope would snap.

Her husband had already ascended, and she would follow last.

In boarding, as all other things, etiquette demanded she be the least important thing in her own life.

When her time came, Sara sat on the plank and gripped the rope, laughing in delight as she was raised into the air, the wind plucking at her clothes.

The sensation was thrilling.

Kicking her legs, she stared across the water at Batavia.

For the last thirteen years, she'd watched from the fort as the city spread like melting butter around her. From that vantage, it had felt huge. A prison of alleys and shops, markets and battlements.

But, at this distance, it seemed a lonely thing: its streets and canals clinging tight to one other, its back to the coast, as if afraid of the encroaching jungle. Clouds of peat smoke hung above the rooftops; brightly coloured birds circled overheard, waiting to descend on the scraps of food left behind by the market traders, who'd soon be packing up for the day.

With a pang, Sara realised how much she was going to miss this place. Every morning Batavia screamed itself awake, the trees shaking as thousands of parrots came screeching out of their branches, filling the air with colour. She loved that chorus, as she loved the strange, lyrical language of the natives and the huge spicy pots of stew they cooked on the street of an evening.

Batavia was where her daughter had been born and where her two sons had died. It was where she had become the woman she now was, for better and for worse.

The seat delivered Sara to the quarterdeck, which lay under the shadow of the towering mainmast. Sailors were climbing the rigging like spiders, tugging ropes and tightening knots, while carpenters planed warped planks and cabin boys threaded caulk and slopped tar, trying to keep from a scolding.

Sara found her daughter at the railing overlooking the rest of the ship.

'It's remarkable, isn't it?' said Lia in admiration. 'But there's so much unnecessary effort.' She pointed to a group of grunting sailors lowering cargo through a hatch into the hold, as if the *Saardam* were a beast that needed feeding before the voyage could begin. 'A better pulley and joist and they'd need half the labour. I could design one, if they'd –'

'They won't, they never will,' interrupted Sara. 'Keep that cleverness in your pocket, Lia. We're surrounded by men who won't take kindly to it, however well intentioned.'

Lia bit her lip sulkily, staring at the unsatisfactory pulley. 'It's such a small thing. Why can't I –'

'Because men don't like being made to feel stupid, and there's no other way to feel when *you* start talking.' Sara stroked her daughter's face, wishing she could ease the confusion she saw there. 'Cleverness is a type of strength, and they won't accept a woman who's stronger than they are. Their pride won't allow it, and their pride is the thing they hold dearest.' She shook her head, unable to find the right words. 'It's not something to be understood. It's just the way it is. You were sheltered in the fort, surrounded by people who loved you and feared your father, but there's no such protection on the *Saardam*. This is a dangerous place. Now heed me and think before you speak.'

'Yes, Mama,' said Lia.

Sara sighed and pulled her close, her heart aching. No mother wanted to tell their child to be less than they were, but what use was it encouraging a child into a thorn bush. 'It won't be like this for very much longer, I promise. Soon we'll be safe, and we'll live our lives as we wish.'

'My wife!' hollered the governor general from the opposite side of the deck. 'There's somebody I wish you to meet.'

'Come,' she said, linking her arm through Lia's.

Her husband was talking to a fleshy, sweating man with a face overrun by veins. His eyes were bloodshot and watering.

Evidently he'd risen late and attended his toilet carelessly. Though dressed to the fashion, his ribbons were dishevelled and his cotton shirt only tucked into one side of his belt. He was unpowdered and unperfumed, and in dire need of both.

'This is Chief Merchant Reynier van Schooten, the master of our voyage,' said the governor general.

Dislike squirmed beneath his words.

Van Schooten's glance put Sara on a scale, weighing and evaluating, pinning a price to her ear.

'I thought the captain was in charge of our ship,' said Lia.

Van Schooten stuffed his thumbs in his belt and puffed out a perfectly round belly, summoning whatever dregs of pride were left to him. 'Not on a merchant vessel, my lady,' he explained. 'Our captain's role is merely to ensure our ship arrives safely in Amsterdam. I'm responsible for all other matters.'

Merely, thought Sara. As if there could be some grander ambition for a ship than to keep it from sinking.

But, of course, there was.

This was a merchant vessel flying United East India Company colours, which meant profit went before every other consideration. It wouldn't matter if the ship made it back to Amsterdam if the cargo had spoilt, or if the trade at the Cape had been handled badly. The *Saardam* could drift into port full of bodies and the Gentlemen 17 would still call it a success so long as the spices weren't damp.

'Could I show you around our ship?' asked Reynier van Schooten, extending an arm to Lia and making sure every one of his jewelled rings were on display. Unfortunately, they couldn't distract from the sweat patch under his armpit.

'Mama, would you like a tour?' Lia asked, turning her back to the merchant and screwing her face up in revulsion.

'My wife and daughter can acquaint themselves with the vessel later,' interrupted the governor general impatiently. 'I'd like to see my cargo.'

'Your cargo?' Confusion became realisation. 'Ah, yes. I can take you directly.'

'Good,' he said. 'My daughter, you're in cabin three.' He waved vaguely to a small red door behind them. 'My wife, you're in cabin six.'

'Cabin five, my lord,' corrected the chief merchant apologetically. 'I had it changed.'

'Why?'

'Well …' Van Schooten shifted uncomfortably. The shadow of the rigging made it appear he'd been thrown under a net. 'Cabin five is more comfortable.'

'Nonsense, they're all identical.' The governor general was infuriated that any order of his – however small – should be so overruled. 'I specified cabin six.'

'Cabin six is cursed, my lord.' The chief merchant spoke quickly and blushed with embarrassment. 'In our eight months from Amsterdam, it had two occupants. The first was found hanging from a hook on the ceiling and the second died in his sleep, eyes wide with fright. Steps sound from inside at night, even when it's empty. Please, my lord, it's –'

'I care not!' interrupted the governor general. 'Take whichever cabin suits you, my wife, and consider yourself at your liberty. I'll have no further need of you until this evening.'

'My husband,' acknowledged Sara, inclining her head.

Sara watched Reynier van Schooten lead him down the steps, then she clutched Lia's hand, dragging her as quickly as their cumbersome skirts would allow towards the passenger cabins.

'Mama, what's the rush?' fretted Lia, almost tugged off her feet.

'We need to get Creesjie and the boys off this ship before it sets sail,' she said.

'Father will never allow it,' argued Lia. 'Creesjie told me she wasn't meant to leave Batavia for another three months but Father wanted her here. He demanded it. He even paid for her cabin.'

'That's why I'm not going to tell him,' said Sara. 'He won't even know Creesjie's disembarked until we've set sail.'

Lia planted her feet, clutching her mother's hand with both of her own, forcing her to stop.

'He'll punish you,' said Lia fearfully. 'You know what he'll do, it will be worse than –'

'We have to warn Creesjie,' interrupted Sara.

'You couldn't walk last time.'

Sara softened, cupping her daughter's cheek. 'I'm sorry, dear heart. That was … I wish you hadn't had to see me like that, but I can't allow our friend to be put in danger because your father is too stubborn to hear reason from a woman.'

'Mama, please,' pleaded Lia, but Sara was already tearing her ruff off and ducking through the low red door.

On the other side lay a narrow corridor lit by a solitary candle, guttering in an alcove. There were four doors on either wall, each marked by a Roman numeral scorched into the wood. Trunks and furniture were being delivered by grunting stevedores, cursing the weight of wealth.

Sara's maid harried them, pointing and arranging on behalf of her mistress.

'Which cabin is Creesjie in?' asked Sara.

'Seven. It's opposite Lia's,' said Dorothea, before stopping Lia to enquire about some small matter, leaving Sara to press on alone.

A harp twanged under its protective cloth as Sara pushed through the confusion, only to find herself blocked off by a large rug tied with twine, which was being manoeuvred into a cabin far too small to house it.

'It won't fit, Captain,' whined one of the sailors, who had it on his shoulder and was trying to bend it around the door-frame. 'Can't we put it into the cargo hold?'

'Viscountess Dalvhain won't be without her comforts,' came the captain's vexed voice from inside. 'Try standing it up.'

The sailors strained. There was an audible crack of wood.

'What in the seven hells have you done?' barked the captain angrily. 'Did you break the doorframe?'

'Wasn't us, Captain,' protested the nearest sailor. A thin rod slid out from the centre of the rug, clattering on the floor. One end was snapped.

One of the sailors hastily kicked it away with his heel. 'It's only to keep the rug straight,' he explained, a small grimace betraying his uncertainty.

'Bugger this,' growled the voice inside the cabin. 'Just lay it corner to corner. Dalvhain can find a place for it when she comes aboard.'

As the rug was swallowed by the cabin, a broad-shouldered, well-muscled man stepped into the corridor, coming face to face with Sara. His eyes were ocean-blue, his hair lopped short to fend off lice. Ginger whiskers covered his cheeks and chin, leaving a face that was sun-browned and angular, fadingly handsome, much like the ship he commanded.

Seeing Sara, he bowed floridly, as if at court. 'I apologise for my language, madam,' he said. 'I didn't realise you were out here. I'm Adrian Crauwels, captain of the *Saardam*.'

The corridor was narrow and busy, forcing them to stand awkwardly close.

His pomander draped him in the smell of citrus, and his teeth were unusually white, his breath suggesting he'd been chewing on water mint. Unlike the chief merchant, his clothing was expensive, his doublet dyed rich purple, golden embroidery catching the candlelight. His sleeves were paned, and his trunk hose tied above cannions with silk bows. The buckles of his shoes shone.

Such fine dress suggested a successful career. Fleet captains earned a percentage of the profits they safely delivered. Even so, Sara wouldn't have been surprised to discover Crauwels was wearing his entire fortune.

'Sara Wessel,' she said, introducing herself with a dip of the head. 'My husband speaks highly of you, Captain.'

He beamed in delight. 'I'm honoured to hear it. We've sailed together twice before, and I've always enjoyed his company.'

He nodded to the ruff clutched in her hand. 'The tight quarters of the *Saardam* aren't best suited to fashion, are they?' From somewhere outside, a coarse voice hollered for the captain. 'I'm afraid my first mate requires my attention. Will you be attending my table tonight, my lady? It's my under-standing the chef has prepared something special.'

Sara's smile was a brilliant thing, trained by endless, unwanted social engagements.

'Of course. I'm looking forward to it,' she lied.

'Excellent.' Raising her hand, he kissed it politely, then took himself into the light.

Sara rapped on the door to cabin seven. Behind the wood, she could hear her friend's laughter and the squeals of delight coming from her two sons. The sound was like a breath of wind carving through a pestilent fog, her mood lifting immediately.

Footsteps approached from within, a young boy opening the door carefully, his face brightening when he realised who it was.

'Sara!' He threw his spindly arms around her.

Creesjie Jens was rolling around on the floor with her other son, oblivious to her silk nightgown. Both boys were in their undergarments, their skin clammy and hair wet, sopping clothing discarded on the floor. Evidently some mishap had befallen them on the crossing, which didn't surprise Sara at all.

Marcus and Osbert were mishap bloodhounds. Marcus was ten, older than his brother by two years, though not nearly so quick-witted. It was Marcus who was clinging to Sara, forcing her to shuffle into the cabin.

'You've raised a barnacle,' she said to Creesjie, stroking the boy's hair affectionately.

Creesjie pushed Osbert away from her face, examining them from the floor. Her hair formed a messy blonde halo on the wood, and her deep blue eyes sparkled in the sunlight, her face soft and round, her pale cheeks blushed with exertion. She was the most beautiful woman Sara had ever seen. It was the only thing she and her husband agreed upon.

'Hello, Lia,' said Creesjie to the dark-haired girl, as she trailed her mother into the cabin. 'Are you keeping Sara out of trouble?'

'I'm trying, but she seems terribly fond of it.'

Creesjie tutted at Marcus, who was still pressed to Sara's skirt. 'Leave her be. You'll soak her through.'

'We went over a wave,' explained Marcus, ignoring his mother's instructions as usual. 'And then –'

'The boys stood up to greet the next one,' supplied Creesjie, sighing at the memory. 'They nearly tumbled over the edge of the boat. Thankfully, Vos caught hold of them.'

Sara raised an eyebrow at the mention of her husband's chamberlain. 'You travelled with Vos?'

'More like he travelled with us,' said Creesjie, rolling her eyes.

'He got very upset,' supplied Osbert, who was still lying on his mother, his naked belly rising and falling. 'But the wave didn't hurt, really.'

'It hurt a bit,' corrected Marcus.

'A little bit,' re-corrected Osbert.

Sara knelt down, passing her gaze between their earnest faces.

Watery blue eyes, guileless and merry, fixed upon her. They were so alike. Sandy hair and red cheeks, their ears waving to the world from either side of their head. Marcus was taller and Osbert broader, but otherwise there was little to separate them. Creesjie said they took after their father, her second husband, Pieter.

He'd been murdered four years ago, something Creesjie didn't like to talk about. From the stumbled-upon stories, Sara knew that he'd been loved dearly and mourned fiercely.

'Boys, I need to speak with your mama,' said Sara. 'Would you go with Lia? She wants to show you her cabin, don't you, Lia?'

Irritation wrinkled Lia's brow. She hated being treated like a child, but her fondness for the boys was enough to drag a smile out of her.

'More than anything.' She became deadly serious. 'I think there's a shark in there.'

'No, there isn't,' protested the boys in unison. 'There are no sharks on land.'

Lia feigned bafflement. 'That's what they told me. Shall we find out?'

The boys agreed readily enough, dashing out in their undergarments.

Sara closed the door as Creesjie got to her feet, dusting her nightgown off. 'Do you think they'd let me wear this around the ship? I had to put it on after the wave soaked –'

'You need to get off the *Saardam*,' interrupted Sara, tossing her ruff on to the bunk.

'It usually takes at least a week before people start asking me to leave places,' said Creesjie, frowning at a dirty spot on her sleeve.

'The ship has been threatened.'

'By a madman on the docks,' replied Creesjie sceptically, walking over to a rack on the wall that held four clay jugs. 'Wine?'

'There isn't time, Creesjie,' said Sara, exasperated. 'You need to get off the ship before we set sail.'

'Why are you giving the ravings of a madman any credence?' replied her friend, filling two cups and handing one to Sara.

'Because Samuel Pipps does,' said Sara.

The cup stopped halfway to Creesjie's lips, her face showing interest for the first time. 'Pipps is onboard?' she asked.

'In manacles.'

'Do you think he'll attend dinner?'

'He's in manacles,' stressed Sara.

'He'll still be better dressed than most of the other guests,' said Creesjie, thoughtfully. 'Do you think I can visit him? They say he's exceptionally handsome.'

'When I saw him, he looked like he'd climbed out of a midden.'

Creesjie made a disgusted face. 'Perhaps they'll clean him up.'

'He's in manacles,' repeated Sara slowly, putting down her untouched cup. 'Will you consider departing?'

'What does Jan say?'

'He doesn't believe me.'

'Then why is he letting me go?'

'He isn't,' admitted Sara. 'I ... wasn't going to tell him.'

'Sara!'

'This ship is in danger,' exclaimed Sara, throwing her hands in the air and smacking them into the beamed ceiling. 'For your sake and the boys', please go back to Batavia.' She tried to shake the sting from her pained fingers. 'There'll be another voyage in four months. You'll be home in plenty of time for your marriage.'

'Time isn't the problem,' argued Creesjie. 'Jan wanted me on this ship. He bought my berth and had my ticket delivered by the household guard. I can't depart without his blessing.'

'Then talk to him,' she pleaded. 'Ask for it.'

'If he won't listen to you, why would he listen to me?'

'You're his mistress,' said Sara. 'He favours you.'

'Only in the bedroom,' replied Creesjie, draining her wine and starting on Sara's. 'It's the curse of powerful men to heed only their own voices.'

'Please! At least try!'

'No, Sara,' she said softly, dousing Sara's passion with calm. 'And not because of Jan. If there's danger on this ship, do you truly think I'd abandon you to it?'

'Creesjie –'

'Don't argue with me, two husbands and a court full of lovers has taught me stubbornness. Besides, if there's a threat to the *Saardam*, surely our duty is to stop it. Have you told the captain?'

'Arent is doing it.'

'Arent,' she cooed lasciviously. Sara suspected that somewhere on the ship Arent suddenly started sweating. 'When did you get on first-name terms with the brutish Lieutenant Hayes?'

'On the docks,' said Sara, ignoring her suggestive tone. 'How am I supposed to save the *Saardam*?'

'I don't know, I'm not the clever one.'

Sara scoffed at that, snatching her wine back and taking a big gulp. 'You see a great deal more than most.'

'That's a polite way of calling me a gossip,' responded Creesjie. 'Come now, stop being a worried friend and play at being Samuel Pipps. I've seen you play-act his cases with Lia and try to solve them.'

'They're games.'

'And you are very good at them.' She paused, peering intently at her. 'Think, Sara. What do we do?'

Sara sighed, rubbing her temple with her palm. 'Pipps believed the leper was a carpenter,' she said slowly. 'Possibly on this ship. Somebody must have known him. If so, they might have more information on this threat we're facing.'

'Two ladies won't be safe tromping into the depths of the *Saardam*. Besides, the captain's forbidden any passengers from going beyond the mainmast.'

43

'What's that?'

'The tallest mast, halfway along the ship.'

'Oh, we don't need to go that far,' replied Sara. 'We're nobility. We can make the information come to us.'

Flinging open the door, she gathered her voice and hollered imperiously, 'Somebody fetch me a carpenter, I'm afraid this cabin simply won't do!

6

S AMMY PIPPS DANGLED IN the air, hands and feet poking through the cargo net hoisting him on to the *Saardam*.

'If you try to leap out, the weight of those manacles will drown you,' warned Guard Captain Jacobi Drecht, squinting up at him from the boat below.

Sammy smiled tightly. 'It's been a long time since anybody mistook me for stupid, Guard Captain,' he responded.

'Desperation makes us all stupid from time to time,' grunted Drecht, removing his hat and leaping on to the rope ladder.

Arent followed him up, though much more slowly. Years at war had taken more than they'd given and each rung caused his knees to crack and his ankles to pop. He felt like a sack of broken parts clattering together.

Eventually he dragged himself over the gunwale and on to the waist of the ship, the largest and lowest of its four weather decks. His eyes swept left and right, searching for his friend, but there was far too much commotion. Clusters of passengers waited to be told where to go, while sailors poured buckets of water into the yawls and stuffed the cannons with hemp to keep the weather out. Hundreds of parrots were screeching on the yard, cabin boys waving their arms, trying to chase them off.

Cargo was being lowered into the hold through hatches in the deck, as insults were traded, blame assigned for tasks gone awry. The loudest voice belonged to a dwarf dressed in slops and a waistcoat, who was spitting names from the passenger manifest held in the crook of his arm. He put Arent in mind of a lightning-blasted tree stump, such was his stature and width, the roughness of his weathered skin and the strange sense of disaster he carried about him.

As each passenger identified themselves, he blotted their name in his manifest and barked them to their berth in a heavily accented voice, flinging a hand generally in the direction they were supposed to go. Most he ordered down to the orlop deck, a stinking hotbox where they'd be crammed in shoulder to shoulder, feet to scalp, making them easy fodder for malady, sickness and palsy.

Arent watched them go pityingly.

On his voyage to Batavia almost a third of everybody berthed down there had died, and it made him heartsick to see children trotting gaily down the stairs, excited for the trip ahead.

Wealthier passengers who still couldn't afford the cost of a cabin were being shown through an arch on his right into the compartment under the half deck, where hammocks were strung alongside supplies and carpentry tools. They'd have space enough to stand and lie down – so long as they didn't stretch out – but, more importantly, they'd have a curtain for privacy.

After a month at sea, such a simple thing would feel like a luxury.

Arent had been berthed in this compartment on the voyage out and would be travelling the same way back. He could already feel his back grumbling. He fitted a hammock the way an ox fitted a fishing net.

'Your man's over here,' hollered Drecht from the far end of the waist, waving his hand to be seen over the heads of the crowd. He needn't have bothered. The jaunty red feather in his hat was impossible to miss.

Two musketeers were wrenching Sammy out of the tangled net, laughing coarsely at what they'd caught and wondering aloud whether they should throw him back.

Outwardly, Sammy was bearing this humiliation stoically, but Arent could see his eyes flickering across their clothing and faces, pulling them apart for secrets.

He wasn't sure what he'd find.

He knew these two from Batavia. They were an unsightly pair, their uniforms grease-spotted and their faces filthy. The taller of the two was called Thyman. He had green teeth and a patchy ginger beard. The shorter man was Eggert; he was bald, with scabs covering his scalp. He picked at them when he was nervous, which was unfortunate because he was nervous most of the time.

'Where to, Guard Captain?' asked Thyman, as Arent and Drecht approached.

'A cell's been built in the bow of the ship,' said Drecht. 'We'll take him through the forecastle, and down into the sailmaker's cabin.'

Passengers and sailors parted to let them through, their whispers rising like a swarm of disturbed flies. Nobody knew why Samuel Pipps was in manacles, though they all had theories. Arent felt partially responsible for that. For the last five years, he'd written reports on each of Sammy's investigations. At first, they'd been for the eyes of their clients, who'd wanted to ensure their investment was paying dividends, but, over time, they'd become popular with clerks, then merchants and, finally, the public. Now copies of the reports were scribed and dispatched to every port that flew a Company flag. They were performed on stage; bards even set them to music. Sammy was the most famous man in the Provinces, but so fantastical were his adventures, so incredible his deductive methods, that many thought him a charlatan. They accused him of being responsible for the crimes he'd unravelled, believing it was the only way he could have solved them. Others accused him of conspiring with dark forces, trading his soul for supernatural gifts.

As Sammy shuffled across the deck towards his cell, they pointed and whispered, believing their petty suspicions vindicated.

'Finally caught,' they said.

'Too clever by half.'

'Struck a devil's bargain and come undone.'

Arent's glare silenced them momentarily, but the whispers simply sprang up again when he passed, like grass trampled underfoot.

Annoyed by Sammy's slow pace, Eggert shoved him forward, causing him to trip on his chains and fall. Giggling, Thyman aimed a kick at his rump, but before he could swing his leg, Arent grabbed hold of the musketeer's shirt and hurled him into the railing with such force the wood cracked.

Snatching up his dagger, Eggert swung wildly at Arent.

With a quick step, the mercenary manoeuvred around the musketeer, catching hold of his arm and twisting it upwards, forcing the point of the dagger to his jaw.

Guard Captain Drecht moved even faster, unsheathing his sabre and thrusting it forward, touching the tip of the blade to Arent's chest.

'I can't have you laying hands on my men, Lieutenant Hayes,' he warned calmly, lifting the brim of his hat to meet Arent's eyes. 'Let him go.'

The sword bit into his chest. A little more pressure and he'd be dead.

A MID THE CLAMOUR OF Arent's stand-off with Jacobi Drecht, nobody noticed Sander Kers climb aboard, which was impressive given his stature. He was tall, thin and stooped, his tatty purple robes hanging from his limbs like rags blown into the boughs of a tree. His wrinkled face was the same shade of grey as his hair.

Behind him, a second, smaller hand emerged over the side, strong fingers trying to find something to grip on to.

Reaching down, the elderly man ineffectually tried to help, but the hand swatted him away, as a panting mardijker woman with curly brown hair appeared. She was much shorter and many years younger than Sander, with the broad shoulders and thick arms of a farmer. Her cotton shirt was rolled up to her elbows, her skirt and apron stained.

A cumbersome leather satchel was hanging across her back with a brass buckle fastening it shut. Afraid the splashing water might have wormed its way inside, she checked it hurriedly, offering a small prayer of relief to find it sealed.

Whistling to the boat bobbing below, she nimbly caught the wooden cane thrown up by the ferryman and held it out to Sander. He didn't immediately take it from her for he was transfixed by a fight happening nearby. Craning her neck, she peered through a gap in the crowd, recognising the bear and the sparrow from the stories. They were evocative nicknames, but they concealed more than they revealed. In the flesh, Arent Hayes wasn't merely large, he was monstrous, like a troll come stamping down from the mountains. He was holding a knife to the throat of a squirming musketeer, while a bearded soldier pressed the tip of a sabre to his chest. Given Arent's immensity, it was difficult to believe the sabre would even pierce him, let alone kill him.

Samuel Pipps was trying to get up, his efforts reminding her of a bird with a broken wing. In this case, it was the manacles keeping him from rising. The stories described him as handsome, but it was a fragile beauty. His cheeks were sharp, his brown eyes glistening atop them like glass orbs held on altars. He was even smaller than she'd imagined, and as delicately built as a child.

'It's already started,' muttered Sander Kers, disturbed.

He touched her arm and pointed at the quarterdeck where the governor general had boarded earlier. 'The ritual will work well enough from up there,' he said, resting his weight on his cane. 'Come along, Isabel.'

She went reluctantly. She enjoyed a good fight and was eager to see if Arent lived up to his fearsome reputation.

Glancing over her shoulder, she helped Sander slowly up the staircase, every step an agony for him.

The sky was darkening above them. It was monsoon season, and the afternoon frequently delivered violent storms, so Isabel wasn't surprised to see clouds elbowing their way across the bright blue sky, obscuring the sun before unveiling it again. Shadows drifted across the water, raindrops beginning to patter on the deck as the grand flags of the United East India Company snapped in the wind.

On the quarterdeck, Sander clumsily undid the buckle on the satchel Isabel was carrying, sliding out the huge book contained within.

As drops of rain splatted on the sheepskin wrapping protecting it, he reconsidered.

'Hold up your apron,' he commanded. 'We need to shelter it from the rain.'

Frowning, she did as he asked, prickling at the sharpness in his voice. He was afraid, she realised.

Fear nipped at her like the first embers of fire.

For over a year, he'd taught her his craft, but his stories of their enemy were passionless things – horrifying but distant, the way somebody else's tragedies always were. Compared to the torments she'd endured before meeting Sander, the labour ahead seemed to have a fairy-tale quality. Foolishly, she'd thought of it as a grand adventure.

But watching Sander's hands trembling, she now felt the knife to her throat.

Her eyes darted towards Batavia.

It wasn't too late to flee. By nightfall, she could have the hot dirt beneath her bare feet once again.

'Your arms, girl!' scolded Sander, removing the wrapping to reveal the leather-bound cover. 'Keep the apron above the book. It's getting wet. There isn't time to daydream.'

Doing as he bid, she dragged her gaze from the distant rooftops. Whatever danger lurked on this ship, she would not allow cowardice to convince her there was safety in Batavia. She was poor, alone and a woman, which meant every one of its alleys had teeth. God was offering her a better life in Amsterdam. She simply had to hold her nerve.

Resting the heavy book partially on the railing, Sander began turning the vellum pages as quickly as reverence would allow. On the first was a creature with a goat's body and a haggard human face sitting on a throne of snakes. The next page showed a fanged torment digging its claws into the pile of screaming bodies it was climbing. After that came a three-headed monstrosity with a spider's body leering at a blushing maid.

On and on, horror after horror.

Isabel turned her face away. She hated this book. The first time Sander had shown her some of its contents, she'd emptied her stomach on the floor of his church. Even now the gleefulness of its evil made her queasy.

Sander finally found the page he wanted: a naked old man with spiny wings riding a monstrous creature that had a bat's head and a wolf's body. The old man had claws instead of hands and was using them to stroke the cheek of a young boy being pinned down by the wolf. The creature was snarling, its tongue lolling, as if laughing at the terrified boy's predicament.

On the opposite page was a symbol that resembled an eye with a tail. Beneath it was a strange incantation.

Pressing his palm against the image, Sander returned his attention to the fight.

Samuel Pipps had started talking and all eyes were upon him. It was like in the stories. Despite being on the ground, despite being manacled and belittled, his authority was absolute. Even the giant seemed cowed.

Rain was falling harder now, running down pulleys and collecting in puddles, seeping through the apron. The sky was soot, cracks of golden sunlight riddling the clouds.

Something made Guard Captain Drecht tense, the sword pressing harder against Arent's chest.

'Do it,' urged Sander Kers under his breath. 'Do it now.'

8

HOLDING HIS DAGGER TO Eggert's neck, a sword pressed to his chest, Arent had to admit that boarding hadn't gone as well as he'd hoped.

'Easy,' he said, gripping the squirming musketeer a little tighter.

He eyed Jacobi Drecht, perfectly steady on the other side of his sabre.

'I've no quarrel with you,' said Arent. 'But Sammy Pipps is a great man and I'll not have him treated ill by piss-stains like this.' He nodded to Thyman, who was staggering to his feet in a daze. 'I want the word to go out that Sammy isn't sport for bored soldiers. From this point on, anybody who lays hands on him won't live long enough to regret it.'

Arent's words betrayed none of his uncertainty.

There wasn't a fouler individual alive than a musketeer in the United East India Company. The job paid poorly and so attracted only the blackest hearts, those content to pursue a reckless course far from home because home was where the hangman was. Once away, their only concerns were amusement and survival, and woe betide anybody who came between them.

The only way to command such men was through fear. Drecht would have to know which offences to turn a blind eye to and which insults required blood. If Drecht didn't kill him, if he didn't defend the honour these men didn't have, they'd call it weakness. For the next eight months, he'd be fighting to get back even a pinch of the authority he'd boarded with.

Arent tightened his grip around the dagger, a drop of Eggert's blood rolling down the edge. 'Put the sword down, Drecht,' he demanded.

'Release my man first.'

They stared at each other, the howling wind whipping rain at their faces.

'Your mate cheated you at dice,' declared Sammy, breaking the tension.

Everybody looked at him, having entirely forgotten he was there. He was talking to Eggert, the musketeer being held by Arent.

'What?' demanded Eggert, the movement of his jaw forcing Arent to lower the dagger lest he accidentally put a spare hole in his mouth.

'Earlier, while you were freeing me from the net, you were scowling at him,' said Sammy, grimacing with effort as he got to his feet. 'He annoyed you recently. You kept casting glances towards his coin purse and frowning. I heard it rattling under his jacket as we walked. Yours didn't, because yours is empty. You've been wondering if he cheated you. He did.'

'He can't have,' sniffed Eggert. 'They were my dice.'

'He suggested you use them?'

'Yeah.'

'Then you took a few rolls, but your luck soured after he won his first pot. Isn't that so?'

The musketeer picked at the scabs on his bald head in agitation. He was so taken with Sammy's accusations he hadn't noticed Arent had released him.

'How can you know?' he demanded suspiciously. 'Did he say something?'

'He had another set of dice in his hand,' explained Sammy. 'He switched them when he scooped up your dice with his winnings. At the end of the game, he handed yours back.'

The crowd watching them murmured their surprise at this insight. More than one hushed voice accused him of devilry. It was always the same way.

Sammy ignored them and nodded at Thyman, who was leaning weak-kneed against a wall. 'Open his coin purse, they'll be in there,' he said. 'Roll them five times and you'll win five times. They're weighted in his favour.'

Seeing Eggert's anger growing, Drecht sheathed his sword and put himself between the two musketeers.

'Thyman, that way,' he ordered, gesturing towards the mainmast. 'Eggert, down there.' He pointed at the stairs on to the orlop deck. 'Keep away from each other today, or you'll have me to answer to.' His gaze suggested very clearly they wouldn't enjoy that. 'And you lot can see yourselves away, as well. I'm sure you've something else to be doing.'

Grumbling, the crowd broke apart and wandered off.

Drecht made sure Eggert and Thyman were truly done with each other, then turned his attention to Sammy.

'How did you do that?' He was filled with that curious mixture of awe and alarm that Sammy's gifts often provoked.

'I judged the character of the men and the relative heft of their coin purses,' said Sammy, as Arent dusted him off.

'I knew one was angry at the other, and money seemed a simple motive, so I led his anger where it wanted to go.'

The implications of the statement moved across Jacobi Drecht's face with impressive speed.

'You guessed?' he exclaimed disbelievingly.

'I know the game,' said Sammy, spreading his hands as far as the chains would allow. 'I used it myself in my youth. It requires quick fingers, lots of practice and somebody stupid enough not to realise they're being cheated. I saw all of those qualities before me.'

Drecht barked with laughter and shook his head, marvelling at the audacity of it.

'*You* cheated people at dice?' he said. 'Where does a noble learn to cheat people at dice?'

'You mistake me, Guard Captain,' said Sammy, becoming uncomfortable. Sammy didn't speak much of his past, but Arent knew it was something he'd worked hard to escape. 'I wasn't born to nobility. My father died when I was a boy, and my mother was the poorest widow you ever saw. I grew up with the dirt for a pillow and the wind for a blanket. I had to take any coin that came my way, even if I had to put my hand in somebody else's pocket to get it.'

'You were a thief?'

'And a dancer, and an acrobat, and an alchemist. For the most part, I was a survivor, and I still am, which is why I hired Arent to keep the murderers I investigate from adding me to their tally. He's good at this labour, Guard Captain, and he won't stand by if somebody threatens me.' Sammy raised an eyebrow. 'You see our dilemma, of course.'

'Aye,' said Drecht thoughtfully. 'That's why I'm going to guarantee your safety. I'll put somebody I trust on your door.

Anybody who bothers you will answer to me, and everybody onboard will know it.' He thrust his arm towards Arent. 'On my honour, Lieutenant Hayes. Will you accept it?'

'I will,' said Arent, shaking his hand.

'Then it's past time I showed Pipps into his cell.'

They exchanged the open air of the ship's waist for a large, gloomy compartment in the bow, where the thick trunk of the foremast speared through the roof and into the floor. A solitary lantern swayed on the ceiling, momentarily revealing the scattered faces of the sailors sitting in the sawdust, before taking its light elsewhere. They were playing dice and complaining.

'This is where the crew take their recreation when the weather's bad,' explained Drecht. 'Reckon it's the most dangerous part of the ship, but that's just me.'

'Dangerous?' queried Arent.

Sammy kicked at the sawdust, revealing the bloodstains beneath.

'Once we're out to sea the front half of the ship is given over to the crew, while the rear half is reserved for the passengers and senior officers,' explained Drecht. 'Neither will be allowed to cross into the other half unless they have duties there, which means the front half of the ship is basically lawless.' He lifted a hatch to reveal the ladder beneath. 'We're down here.'

Descending, they arrived in a small room housing great rolls of sailcloth suspended in hooks on the walls. A workbench had been nailed to the floor, behind which a sailmaker was stitching together two pieces of hemp with an iron needle the size of Arent's hand. He glanced at them without interest, then returned to his work.

Sammy examined the compartment. 'I'll admit, I expected much worse.'

A door opened behind them, a tremendous mass of gut and shoulders ducking through. He was bald, with mangled ears and pitted skin that resembled sand crossed by a small animal. A leather patch covered his right eye, but there was nothing to be done about the spiderweb of scars surrounding it.

He sneered at Pipps's manacles.

'You the prisoner?' His tongue roamed his cracked lips. 'I heard you were coming aboard. Been looking forward to some company.'

The sailmaker snickered over his stitching.

'He's under my protection, Wyck,' warned Drecht, touching his sword. 'There'll be a musketeer keeping watch. Any harm befalls either of them, I'll have you flogged. Doesn't matter if there's a dozen sailors who'll vouch you were elsewhere.'

Wyck stepped forward, his face darkening. 'What's a soldier' – he almost spat the word – 'doing telling me anything? You don't have any authority over the crew.'

'But I have the governor general's ear, and he's got the ear of anybody he damn well pleases.'

Wyck scowled and stomped to the ladder. 'Keep him quiet then. I'll not have him wailing in the night, keeping me awake.'

With a nimbleness that belied his size, he leapt up the ladder and disappeared through the hatch.

'What was *that*?' asked Sammy.

'The boatswain.' Drecht's tone was grim. 'He keeps the crew in line.'

'You're not putting Sammy in with him,' warned Arent.

'No, that's Wyck's cabin in there,' replied Drecht, pointing to the door he'd emerged from. 'The cell is beneath us.'

He heaved open another hatch. This ladder was so narrow Arent's shoulders got jammed halfway down, forcing him to wriggle to dislodge himself.

At the bottom was the sailmaker's storeroom, offcuts of material piled on the ground, where they'd been dropped from above. It sat at the waterline, the gentle slaps of waves becoming the blows of a battering ram down here. A solitary finger of grubby light poked through the hatch, leaving all else in darkness. It took Arent a moment to realise Drecht was drawing the bolt on a small door at the rear.

'This is the cell,' he said.

Arent held Sammy back, then stuck his head inside. It was pitch black, windowless and fetid, and cut in half by the trunk of the bow mast. The ceiling was barely high enough for Sammy to sit upright.

'What is this place?' Arent demanded, barely able to hold his temper. Officers captured on the battlefield were entitled to treatment equal to their rank, which meant respectable quarters for the duration of their imprisonment. He'd expected the same for Sammy.

'I'm sorry, Hayes, those are the governor general's orders.'

Sammy's face fell, panic showing for the first time. He backed away from the door, shaking his head.

'Guard Captain, please, I can't …'

'Those are my orders, sir.'

Sammy turned his wild eyes on Arent. 'It's too small, I'll …' He eyed the ladder, clearly considering fleeing.

Drecht tensed and gripped the hilt of his sword. 'Calm him down, Lieutenant Hayes,' he warned.

Arent took his friend by the shoulders, staring him full in the face.

'I'm going to talk to the governor general,' he said sooth-ingly. 'I'll see you're moved, but I can't do that if you're dead.'

'Please …' pleaded Sammy, clutching his friend desper-ately. 'Don't let them leave me here.'

'I won't,' said Arent, surprised to discover Sammy's aversion to small spaces. 'I'll go to the governor general now.'

Quivering, Sammy nodded, only to shake his head a moment later. 'No,' he croaked, then more firmly, 'No. You have to save the ship first. Talk to the captain, then the consta-ble. Find out why somebody would threaten us.'

'That's your job,' argued Arent. 'I save you; you save every-body else. That's the way it's always been. I'll talk to the governor general. He'll see sense, I'm certain of it.'

'We don't have time,' said Sammy, as Drecht took hold of his shoulder, walking him towards the cell.

'I can't do what you do,' said Arent, almost as panicked as Sammy had been.

'Then you better find somebody who can,' responded Sammy. 'Because I can't help you any more.'

'In you go,' said Drecht firmly.

'Strike his manacles for pity's sake,' demanded Arent. 'He'll not know a moment's peace with those on.'

Drecht considered it, staring at the rusted links. 'The governor general didn't give any specific orders regarding the manacles,' he admitted. 'I'll send somebody down first chance I get.'

'It's up to you now,' said Sammy to Arent, getting down on his hands and knees and crawling into the cell.

A moment later, Drecht closed and bolted the door, casting him into absolute darkness.

9

S ARA PACED HER CABIN from wall to wall, stopping occasionally to stare out of the porthole, relieved to find Batavia exactly where she'd left it. The *Saardam* hadn't weighed anchor, which meant she still had time to uncover information on the plot threatening the ship. If she could find something solid before they set sail, she might yet be able to convince her thick-headed husband of the danger.

Unfortunately, the carpenter hadn't arrived and she was growing impatient.

'You'll sink the ship pacing the way you do,' chided Dorothea, who was kneeling on the floor, arranging Sara's clothes in drawers.

The maid was forgiven such bluntness, for she'd been with the family so long Sara couldn't remember life before her. She'd been part of her husband's household when they wed, a comforting, bickering presence who'd been her only counsel in those vile early days.

Grey had overrun her plaited hair, but in every other way, she remained the same. She rarely smiled, never raised her voice and kept her past under her tongue. Despite this, they had grown close over the years for she was quick-witted, occasionally wise and unapologetic in her hatred of the governor general.

Three knocks sounded on the door, causing Dorothea to rise painfully – her knees were a constant frustration – and open it with a frown.

'Who are you?' she demanded through the gap.

'Henri, the carpenter,' said a sullen voice. 'Your lady wants shelves building.'

'Shelves?' queried Dorothea, over her shoulder.

'Show him in.'

Sara felt silly at the grandeur of the proclamation, as there wasn't a great deal of showing to be done. This cabin would fit inside her changing room in the fort. Under a low-beamed ceiling, a single bunk had been built into the wall, two drawers beneath it. There was a desk near the porthole, one rack for storing drinks and a chamber pot pushed discreetly into an alcove built for the purpose. A rug had been thrown down to make it more comfortable and she'd been allowed to bring two paintings, along with her harp.

After years of living in the roomy fort, the interior of the *Saardam* felt like a coffin she'd been cast adrift in.

She intended on spending as much time as possible outside.

Henri slouched into the room, carrying a toolbox and several planks of wood under his arm.

He was terribly thin, his skin pulled taut across his ribs, his arms corded with muscle. Spots crowded around his nose like worshippers at church.

'Where should the shelves go?' he asked sulkily.

'There and there,' said Sara, pointing to the space above and below the existing rack. 'How long will it take?'

'Not long.' He ran his hand across the uneven surface of the wall. 'Boatswain wants me back to my duties before we cast off.'

'Fine work deserves reward,' said Sara. 'A guilder for your trouble, if I like what you've done.'

'Yes, ma'am,' said Henri, perking up slightly.

'Yes, my lady,' rebuked Dorothea, neatly folding one of Sara's light dresses.

Sara considered sitting on her bunk, but hated the implication of intimacy, and pulled the chair out from the desk instead, placing herself primly on its edge.

'You seem young for this work,' she said, watching as he measured the length of the existing rack with his forearm and hand.

'I'm a carpenter's mate,' he said distractedly.

'Are you young for a carpenter's mate?'

'No.'

'No, my lady!' corrected Dorothea angrily, causing the boy to blanch.

'No, my lady,' he muttered.

'What does a carpenter's mate do?' asked Sara pleasantly.

'All the jobs the master carpenter doesn't want to.' A hundred grudges peeked out from beneath his words.

'I think I've met the master carpenter,' said Sara, trying to keep her tone bored and distant. 'Lame foot, yes? Missing a tongue?'

Henri shook his head. 'That's Bosey you're thinking of,' he said, marking a piece of wood with a stick of charcoal.

'He isn't the master carpenter?'

'Can't get up the masts with a maimed foot,' he scoffed, as if the responsibilities of a master carpenter were common knowledge.

'I suppose not,' agreed Sara. 'Did this Bosey serve aboard this ship, or am I thinking of somebody entirely different?'

He shifted his weight uncomfortably, and flashed her a nervous glance.

'What's wrong, young man?' she asked, becoming flint-eyed.

'Boatswain said we shouldn't talk about him,' he muttered.

'What's a boatswain?'

'He's in charge of the crew on deck,' he said. 'He doesn't like us talking about ship business with strangers.'

'And what's the name of this boatswain?'

'Johannes Wyck.'

He spoke it reluctantly, as if the words themselves could summon him.

Henri picked up one of the planks and went into the corridor, where he began sawing it down to size, offcuts clattering on to the ground.

'Dorothea,' said Sara, her gaze on the carpenter. 'Fetch two guilders from my coin purse, will you?'

Greed dragged Henri's eyes upward, though he kept on sawing. Sara doubted he earned much more than this a week.

'Two guilders, plus the one already promised, if you tell me what Wyck doesn't want me to know about Bosey,' said Sara.

He fidgeted, his will faltering.

'Your shipmates will never know,' said Sara. 'I'm the governor general's wife. I likely won't speak to another sailor for the rest of the voyage.' She gave that a minute to sink in, then held out the coins. 'Now, did Bosey serve aboard this ship?'

He snatched them from her palm and jerked his head towards the cabin, indicating they should speak privately. She followed him in, closing the door as much as propriety would allow.

'Aye, he served aboard the *Saardam*,' said Henri. 'Got the maimed foot in a pirate attack, but the captain liked him, so kept him on. Said nobody knew the ship like he did.'

'An innocent story,' said Sara. 'Why doesn't Wyck want me to know it?'

'Bosey never shut up,' said the carpenter, looking nervously at the slightly open door. 'He'd brag about anything. If he beat you at dice, you'd have him in your ear for a week. If there was a whore he'd been' – he blanched in the face of Dorothea's glare – 'well, he was always talking. Latest thing was some bargain he'd struck in Batavia that was going to make him rich.'

'He was always talking?' Sara frowned. 'When I met Bosey, he was missing his tongue.'

For the first time, the carpenter appeared ashamed. 'Wyck did that,' he said quietly. 'Cut it out about a month back. Said he was sick of listening to him squawk. He did it on the waist of the ship. Made us hold him down.'

Sara felt a great swell of pity. 'Did the captain punish him?'

'Captain didn't see, nobody saw. And nobody will say anything against Wyck. Even Bosey wouldn't.'

Sara was beginning to get an understanding of how life worked on an Indiaman.

'If you held him down, I'm assuming he didn't have leprosy,' she said.

'Leprosy?' The boy shivered with disgust. 'Aint no lepers allowed on an Indiaman. Could have got it after we docked. Once we're in port, Captain lets us come and go as we like. Most of us took our leave in Batavia, but Bosey hid away on the ship after we took his tongue, kept to himself.'

'Before his lost his tongue, did Bosey say anything else about this bargain he'd struck, or who it was with?' asked Sara.

The carpenter shook his head, obviously desperate to have the questions over with. 'Only that it was the easiest coin he ever made,' he said. 'Few favours here and there. When we'd ask what they were, he'd smile this horrible little smile and say "Laxagarr".'

'Laxagarr,' repeated Sara, confounded. She could speak Latin, French and Flemish fluently, but she'd never heard a word like that one.

'What does it mean?'

The carpenter shrugged, clearly disturbed by the memory. 'I don't know, none of us did. Bosey was Nornish, so it was probably something from his own tongue, but the way he said it … it scared us.'

'Does anybody on the ship speak Nornish?' she asked.

The carpenter laughed grimly. 'Only the boatswain. Only Johannes Wyck, and it'll take a lot more than three guilders to make him talk to you.'

10

A RENT HAD BARELY STEPPED out of the sailmaker's
cabin when a bell rang amidships, the dwarf standing
on a stool to work the clapper.

'Up, you dogs!' he hollered, spittle flying from his lips. 'Up
on deck, all of you.'

Hatches burst open, sailors swarming up from below decks
like rats fleeing a fire. Clogging the waist, they clambered over
and atop one another, scurrying up the rigging and sitting
on the railings, throwing themselves on to any available lap,
bringing laughter and shoving.

Arent was pushed back towards the bow of the ship, until
he was jammed against the very door he'd just walked out
of, the air growing thick with the smell of sweat and ale and
sawdust.

Guard Captain Jacobi Drecht flicked the brim of his hat,
welcoming him back.

He hadn't moved, except to lean against the wall, one sole
flat against it, foul smoke rising from a carved wooden pipe
gripped between his teeth. The sabre, which only moments
ago had been pressed to Arent's chest, was propped up beside
him, like a friend keeping him company.

'What's happening?' asked Arent.

Drecht removed his pipe, scratching the corner of his lip with his thumb. Between that large hat and the bird's nest of his blond beard, his squinting eyes were surprisingly blue in the sunlight.

'This is a ritual of Captain Crauwels,' said Drecht, thrusting his chin towards the quarter deck, where a squat man with square shoulders and thick legs stood with his hands folded behind his back. A turned-down mouth suggested a grim disposition.

'That's the captain?' said Arent, surprised. He was better dressed than many generals Arent had met. 'Pretty as a predikant's wife, isn't he? What's he doing sailing an Indiaman? He could sell his wardrobe and retire comfortably.'

'You always this full of questions?' asked Drecht, looking at him askew.

Arent grunted, annoyed at being revealed so easily. This constant curiosity was Sammy's doing. It happened to everybody who spent time with him.

He changed them.

He changed the way they thought.

Arent had been a mercenary for eighteen years before becoming Sammy's bodyguard. Back then, his only concern had been with sabre and shot and whatever was trying to imminently kill him. He wasn't one to fret idly; he couldn't afford it. The mercenary who saw the spear, then thought about it too long, ended up with half of it buried in his chest. Nowadays, he'd see the spear, wonder who made it, how it had come to be in the soldier's hands, who the soldier was, why he was there … on and on and on. It was a wretched gift, that had left him neither one thing nor the other.

Crauwels swept his gaze across the assembled crew, taking in every detail of every man under his scrutiny.

Rain pattered around them.

One by one, conversations were snuffed out, until there was only the slap of waves and the screech of birds circling above.

He left it a second more, letting the silence congeal.

'Every man aboard this ship has cause to see land again,' he said, his voice rich and deep. 'Mayhap it's a waiting family, mayhap it's a favourite brothel or just an empty purse as needs filling.'

Subdued laughter met the declaration.

'To see our homes, to fill our purses, to draw one more breath, we must keep this ship afloat,' he continued, placing both hands flat on the railing before him. 'There's plenty as would see it otherwise. Pirates will stalk us, storms will lash us and this damn restless sea will try to deliver us into the rocks.'

The crew murmured fervently, standing a little straighter.

'Trust in this, if you trust in nothing else.' Crauwels raised his voice. 'Behind every bastard there'll always be another bastard, and to get ourselves home, to wrap our hands around whatever's waiting there, we'll need to be bigger bastards than they are.' The crew cheered, his words spreading like flame. 'If pirates attack us, they'll live long enough to see their comrades slaughtered and their ship brought under our flag. A storm's naught but wind in our sails, and we'll ride whatever waves bear down on us all the way back to Amsterdam.'

Cheers rang out as the sandglass was tipped and a solitary bell rang, scattering the sailors to their labours. Four burly men began turning the capstan wheel, the mechanism screeching as they hoisted the *Saardam*'s three anchors off the ocean floor. A course and speed were ordered, the instruction handed down from the captain, to the first mate, to the helm.

Finally, the mainsail was unfurled, good cheer turning to shock.

Rippling in the wind, on the great white expanse, an eye with a tail had been drawn in ash.

11

ALL EYES WERE ON the symbol on the sail, so nobody saw Creesjie Jens grip the railing of the quarterdeck, the colour draining out of her cheeks.

Nobody saw Sander Kers close the huge book held in Isabel's hands, hiding the picture of the eye drawn there.

Nobody saw the boatswain, Johannes Wyck, touch his eyepatch in memory.

And nobody saw Arent stare incredulously at the scar on his wrist, which was exactly the same shape as the mark on the sail.

12

CAPTAIN CRAUWELS BELLOWED INSTRUCTIONS down to the helmsman, who was sighting their course through a small window in the helm, setting the rudders by adjusting the whipstaffs. Slowly, like an ox dragging a plough across a field, the *Saardam* picked up speed, bouncing over the waves, sea spray splashing on to the deck.

The crew had dispersed to their duties, leaving Arent to stare at the symbol already being washed away in the rain.

The captain had ordered the sail inspected for holes and loose stitching, but nothing had been found and the sheet had been declared wind-worthy. If anybody else was troubled by the symbol, they gave no indication. Most seemed to think it was the result of some strange jest, or an accident in storage.

Arent ran a troubled finger across his scar. He had to stare to see it, as it was hidden beneath a dozen other worse injuries. He'd received it as a boy, not long after the first hairs had sprouted on his chin. He'd gone hunting with his father, the family expecting them back that evening, as normal. Three days later, a merchant caravan had found Arent wandering alone on the road. His wrist was badly gouged and he was sodden, as if he'd fallen in a stream, though there were none nearby and it hadn't rained. He couldn't speak, couldn't remember what had become of him, or of his father.

He still couldn't.

That scar was the only thing that had returned from the forest with him. For years, it had been his shame. His burden. A reminder of unremembered things, including the father who'd disappeared completely.

How could it be on the sail?

'Oi, Hayes,' said Jacobi Drecht.

Arent turned, blinking at the guard captain, who was pressing his hat on to his head as the wind picked up across the water.

'If you still want to talk to the captain, he'll be in the great cabin,' he said, the red feather in his hat twitching like an insect's antenna. 'I'm going over now, I'll introduce you.'

Arent dropped his hand self-consciously behind his back, and followed Drecht across the waist towards the rear of the ship.

He felt as if he were learning to walk again.

Even at this slow pace, the *Saardam* was unsteady underfoot, sending him lurching from side to side. He tried to mimic Drecht, who was on the balls of his feet, anticipating the movement of the ship and balancing himself accordingly.

That's how he'll fight, thought Arent. Light-footed, circling. Never stopping. You'd swing at where he'd been, while he put his sword where you would be.

Arent was lucky the guard captain hadn't run him through.

Luck. He hated that word. It was an admission, not an explanation. It was what you depended on when good sense and skill deserted you.

He'd been lucky a lot recently.

These last few years he'd started making mistakes, seeing things too late. As he got older, he was getting slower. For the first time in his life, he felt the weight of his body, like a bag of rocks he couldn't put down. Near misses were getting nearer, close calls closer. One day soon, he wouldn't see his killer's feet, wouldn't hear their shuffling or catch their shadow drawing up the wall.

Death kept flipping a coin and Arent kept taking the odds. Seemed like madness, even to him.

He should have quit a long time ago, but he didn't trust anybody else to protect Sammy. That pride seemed ridiculous now. Sammy was in a cell aboard an imperilled ship and Arent had nearly got himself killed before they'd even left Batavia.

'Shouldn't have reacted the way I did earlier,' said Arent, catching hold of a rope to steady himself. 'Put you in a bad position with your men. I'm sorry for that.'

Drecht's eyebrows reached for each other in thought.

'You did right by Pipps,' he said, at last. 'Did what you were paid to do. But it's my duty to protect the governor general and his family, and I can't do that without the loyalty of these musketeers. Put me in that position again and I'll have to kill you. I can't seem weak, because they won't follow me. You understand that?'

'I do.'

Drecht nodded, the matter settled.

They passed through a large arch into the compartment under the half deck. It was the width of the ship and ran back like a cave. Hammocks were strung wall to ceiling on the starboard side, curtains hanging between them for privacy.

Arent was berthed in the one closest to the helm, a small, gloomy room where the whipstaffs working the rudders finally emerged after their long journey through the ship. Having set their course, the helmsman was now squatting on the floor with his mate, rolling dice for ale rations.

'How do you know the captain?' asked Arent.

'Governor General Haan's sailed aboard the *Saardam* a couple of times before,' he said, puffing on his pipe. 'Crauwels has a flatterer's tongue and managed to put himself the right side of him, which aint a feat most manage. That's why he chose this ship to sail home on.'

Drecht ducked through the door into the great cabin, leaving Arent to stare at it in dismay.

The doorway was half his size.

'Should I fetch a saw?' asked Drecht, as Arent contorted his huge frame through the gap.

After the dim helm, it took his eyes a moment to adjust to the dazzling glare of the great cabin. It was aptly named, for it was the largest room on the *Saardam* outside of the cargo hold. The whitewashed walls were bowed and the ceiling beamed, four lattice windows revealing the other six ships in the fleet spread out behind them, sails billowing.

A huge table took up most of the room, its surface covered in scrolls, ledgers and manifests. A navigational chart had been unrolled over the top, the four corners pinned down by an astrolabe, a compass, a dagger and a quadrant.

Crauwels was using the chart to plot a course. His jacket was folded neatly over the back of a nearby chair, revealing a crisp cotton shirt, clean enough to suggest it was new from the tailor that day. As with the rest of his attire, it was expensive.

Arent couldn't make sense of it. Sailing was dirty work. Ships were kept afloat by tar and rust and grime. Clothing was sweated through, then stained, then torn. Most officers wore their clothes to rags, replacing them grudgingly. After all, why waste coin on finery, when it wouldn't survive the voyage? Only nobles were so frivolous, but no noble would ever lower themselves to this profession. Or any profession, come to think of it.

The dwarf Arent had seen on deck, directing the passengers to their berths, was now standing on a chair, his hands pressed flat on the table, either side of a ledger which described the state of the ship's stores. His downturned mouth and furrowed brow suggested it made for ill reading. He tapped the captain's arm, drawing his attention to the source of his displeasure.

'The dwarf is our first mate, Isaack Larme,' whispered Drecht, following Arent's stare. 'It's his job to manage the crew, which means he's got a vile temper, so stay away if you can.'

Crauwels glanced up from the ledger as they entered, then immediately turned his attention to the chief merchant, Reynier van Schooten, who was slumped in a chair with his feet on another, drinking from a jug of wine. His jewelled hand lay across his round belly, which resembled a rock that had rolled into a ravine.

'Tell me how I'm feeding three hundred souls when we left port with provisions for one hundred fifty,' demanded Crauwels.

'The *Leeuwarden* has taken on extra supplies,' said Van Schooten lazily, his voice already slurred with drink. 'Once we consume ours, we'll have space to bring them aboard.'

'What happens if we lose sight of the *Leeuwarden*?' asked the first mate in a thick Germanic accent that immediately put Arent in mind of cold winters and deep forests.

'We call out very loudly?' suggested Van Schooten.

'Now's not the –'

'We'll ration and resupply at the Cape,' interrupted Van Schooten, scratching his long nose.

'Half rations?' asked Crauwels, dragging another ledger in front of him that listed the victuals in their hold.

'Quarter,' said Van Schooten, earning a dark look from the captain.

'Why did we put to sea without sufficient rations for the voyage?' asked the first mate angrily.

'Because we needed space for the governor general's cargo,' responded Van Schooten.

'That box the musketeers carried aboard?' replied Larme, confused. 'Vos ordered us to make room in the gunpowder store.'

'That box wasn't his only cargo,' replied Crauwels irritably. 'There was something much bigger, as well. Van Schooten organised for it to be brought aboard in the dead of night and he won't tell me what it is.'

Van Schooten took a long, fortifying gulp of his wine. 'Ask the governor general if you're curious, see where it gets you.'

The two men glared at each other, their dislike warming the air.

Jacobi Drecht coughed uncomfortably, gesturing to Arent when the captain raised his eyes.

'Captain Crauwels, I'd like to introduce –'

'I know him well enough, I've heard the stories,' interrupted Crauwels, immediately returning his attention to Isaack Larme. 'Tell me about the cabins? Where am I sleeping now the governor general's in my quarters?'

'Port quarter,' said the first mate. 'Cabin two.'

'I hate that cabin, it's beneath the animal pens on the poop deck. Every time anybody goes near it, the sows squeal for an hour to be let out. Put me starboard bow.'

'I've already claimed it,' said the chief merchant, shaking his empty jug of wine disappointedly, then peering inside.

'Aye, because it's a favourite of mine and you know it,' growled Crauwels, the cords in his thick neck flaring. 'You're a petty bastard, Reynier.'

'A petty bastard who won't be kept awake by squealing sows all night long,' agreed the chief merchant pleasantly, waving his empty jug in the air. 'Somebody summon the steward, I'm out of wine.'

'Who else has a cabin?' asked the captain, ignoring him.

The first mate searched for the passenger manifest on the table, then turned to the page listing the nobility. He read the names with difficulty, running a grubby finger underneath each one. 'Cornelius Vos. Creesjie Jens. Her sons Marcus and Osbert. Sara Wessel. Lia Jan. Viscountess Dalvhain.'

'Anybody we can move?' asked the captain.

'Nobles all,' responded the first mate.

'Like vipers in their damn baskets,' sighed Crauwels, rapping the table with his knuckle. 'Sows it is.'

For the first time, he looked directly at Arent, but his attention was immediately diverted by the clack of a cane hitting wood, followed by hobbling footsteps. Glancing over his shoulder, Arent saw an elderly man in the doorway, surveying them like they were something foul slipping off a wagon wheel. He had gaunt cheeks, grey hair and yellow bloodshot eyes. Ragged purple robes hung from his thin body and a huge cross was dangling around his neck. A splintered wooden cane seemed to be the only thing keeping him upright.

Arent would have put his age at seventy, but appearances were deceptive this far from Amsterdam. A difficult journey to the East Indies could easily put ten years on a body, which was then assaulted by Batavia's never-ending cycle of disease and recovery, each time regaining a little less of what had been lost.

Before any of them could speak, a young, broad-shouldered native woman rustled in after him. She was a mardijker, if Arent had to guess. A slave freed by the Company because she was a Christian. She was dressed for the fields in a loose cotton shirt, her curly brown hair tucked into a white cap, a long hemp skirt trailing along the floor. She wore a sodden apron and a large satchel hung across her back, but she seemed untroubled by its weight.

Her face was round, with heavy cheeks and large, watchful eyes. She offered the assembled company neither deference nor greeting, simply turning her gaze to her companion and waiting for him to begin.

'May I speak with you, Captain Crauwels?' asked the elderly man.

'Every other bugger has today,' grunted Crauwels sourly, glancing at the splintered cross. 'Who are you?'

'Sander Kers,' said the stooped man, his firm voice betraying none of the weakness evident in his trembling body. 'And this is my ward Isabel.'

The sun momentarily dipped behind the clouds, darkening the room.

From his chair, Van Schooten twisted his body towards them, leering suggestively. 'Oh, aye, your *ward*, is she? How much does a *ward* cost these days?'

Evidently Isabel didn't understand the comment because she wrinkled her brow and looked to Sander for an explanation. He contemplated Van Schooten through narrowed eyes, his gaze as fierce as holy light. 'You are so far from God's sight,' he said, at last. 'What drove you into the dark, my son?'

Van Schooten blanched, then became angry, waving him away. 'Off with you, old man, there's no passengers allowed up here.'

'God brought me here; it isn't for *you* to send me away.'

Such was his conviction, even Arent believed him.

'You're a predikant?' interrupted Isaack Larme, nodding to the cross.

'That's right, dwarf.'

The first mate stared at him with misgiving, while the captain plucked a small metal disc from the table, flicked it into the air and caught in his palm.

Arent shifted uncomfortably, conflicting urges demanding he hide or flee. His father had also been a predikant, making it a profession he instinctively associated with malevolence.

'You'll find precious little welcome here, Sander Kers,' said Captain Crauwels.

'Because Jonah was cursed by God for sailing against his divine will, and now sailors believe all holy men bring ill fortune,' said Sander, his tone suggesting he'd heard the warning more than once. 'I have little patience for superstition, Captain. God's plan for each of us is writ in the heavens long before we're born. If this ship flounders, it's because He has chosen to close His fist around it. I will welcome His will and go before Him with humility.'

Isabel murmured in agreement; the rapt expression on her face suggested they'd all be lucky to drown so devoutly.

Crauwels sent the metal disc spinning into the air and caught it again. 'Aye, well, if you've come to complain about your quarters, then –'

'I've no quarrel with my accommodations, my needs are few,' said the predikant, who'd obviously taken umbrage at the presumption. 'I wish to discuss your rule prohibiting me from travelling past the mainmast.'

Crauwels regarded him warily. 'Everything afore the mainmast is the domain of the sailors, everything aft is kept for the senior officers and passengers unless the crew have duties there,' he explained. 'Any sailor crosses the mast without permission gets flogged. Any passenger goes the other way is at the mercy of the crew. It's that way on every ship in the fleet. Even I don't often venture down that end of the ship.'

The predikant raised an eyebrow. 'You fear these men?'

'Isn't one of them who wouldn't slit your throat for a free drink, then rape your ward while your blood was still warm,' interrupted Reynier van Schooten.

His tone was meant to shock, but the predikant gazed at him levelly, while Isabel's hand tightened around the strap of her satchel. Whatever she thought of the declaration, it didn't show on her face.

'Fear is the curse of the faithless,' said Sander. 'Upon my brow, a sacred duty has been placed. I mean to fulfil it and I will trust God to protect me while I do so.'

'You mean to go amongst the crew?' asked Isaack Larme.

'Yes, dwarf, and deliver God's word.'

Larme bridled. 'They'll kill you.'

'If that is God's plan for me, then I welcome it.'

He did, thought Arent. He really did. He'd come across a few pious men in his time and learned to spot the fakers. Piety, true piety, came at a savage cost. God was the only flame that gave them light, the only source of warmth and direction. They saw the rest of the world as a dull grey thing they'd ecstatically set alight to spread their flame. Sander Kers spoke every word as if he were striking the flint.

A silent conversation passed between Crauwels and Larme, a question asked through twitches and small movements of the head, the answer delivered with pursed lips and a slight shrug. It was the language of those who worked at dangerous occupations in close quarters. Arent communicated with Sammy the same way.

The predikant's gaze bore into Captain Crauwels. 'Now, do I have your blessing to go about my ministrations?'

Crauwels threw the metal disc into the air again, only to immediately snatch it back down in frustration. 'My permission, aye. Not my blessing. And it extends only to you, not your ward. I'll not risk a mutiny over lust.'

'Captain –' protested the young woman.

'Isabel!' Sander interrupted sternly. 'We have what we came for.'

She glared from one face to the other, her expression indicating quite clearly that while *they* had what they had come for, she did not. Sucking her lips in irritation, she stamped out of the cabin.

Sander Kers hobbled after her on his cane.

'Well, there's a spot of trouble I had no use for,' said Crauwels, scratching his eyebrow. 'Now, you, thief-taker, what do you need from me today?'

Arent bristled at the title. Sammy had always hated being called a thief-taker. He said it was the profession of brawlers and gutter dwellers, fit only for small mysteries easily solved by fists. He preferred to be called a problematary; a title entirely made up and entirely his own, yet one kings had emptied treasuries to employ.

'Did you have a maimed carpenter aboard?'

'Bosey, aye. Knew the name for every nail and plank holding this ship together. Didn't turn up for roster, though. Why?'

'Sammy Pipps thinks he was the leper who threatened us on the docks.'

Isaack Larme flinched, then tried to cover it by rolling up his chart and hopping down from his stool. 'I need to check our speed, Captain.'

'Take the jug of ale out of the helmsman's hand while you're out there,' he said gruffly.

Arent watched Larme leave, resolving to talk to him later, once he had everything he needed from the captain.

'Can you think of any reason this Bosey would be threatening the *Saardam*?' asked Arent.

'I know he fell afoul of the crew somehow, though I couldn't tell you how. A captain has to keep his distance from the men much as he can, else there's no way to govern them. Larme would know more.'

'On the docks, he mentioned having a master? Know anything about that?'

'There's one hundred and eighty sailors on my crew, Hayes. You're lucky I know his name. Honestly, it's Larme you need. He's closer to the rabble than I am.' He was growing impatient. 'Is there anything else? I've still got a dozen other nuisances to attend.'

'I need permission to speak with the constable guarding your gunpowder store,' said Arent.

'Why?'

'Sammy Pipps is worried somebody's planning to blow it up.'

'Good enough,' grunted the captain, throwing the metal disc towards Arent, who caught it in his palm. It was heavy and engraved with a double-headed bird. Arent might have mistaken it for a wax stamp, except for the hole in the middle.

'Show the constable that token and he'll know you go with my good word,' he said.

'A moment,' said Reynier van Schooten, making a grand show of rising from his chair and going to the table.

He pulled a quill from an ink pot and began scrawling a series of numbers on a piece of vellum. 'I'm the master of this voyage, and all doors will remain closed to you until I say otherwise. Unfortunately, I can't give you what you ask until you settle a debt,' he said, tossing a handful of pounce on the ink to dry it, before handing it to Arent.

'What this?' asked Arent, staring at it.

'It's a bill,' responded Van Schooten, his eyes shining.

'A bill?'

'For the cask.'

'What cask?'

'The cask of ale you broke open on the dock,' he said, as if it were the most obvious thing in the world. 'It was Company property.'

'You're charging me for sparing a man's suffering?' demanded Arent incredulously.

'The man wasn't Company property.'

'He was *on fire.*'

'Be glad the Company didn't own the flames,' said Van Schooten, with that same infuriating reasonableness. 'I'm sorry, Lieutenant Hayes. As per Company policy, we may not render you any service until prior debts have been settled.'

Crauwels growled, snatching the vellum from Arent's hand and shaking it in the chief merchant's face. 'Hayes is trying to help, you dark-hearted wretch. What's become of you these last two weeks? It's like you're a different man.'

Doubt flashed on Van Schooten's face, but it was no match for his arrogance.

'Perhaps if he'd come to me first, we could have been spared this unpleasantness, but' – he shrugged – 'here we are. My authority must –'

'Your authority is worth salt!'

The voice had come from an adjoining doorway, where Governor General Jan Haan was red-faced and shimmering with rage. 'How dare you treat Lieutenant Hayes with such disrespect,' he hissed, disgust pouring out of him. 'From this point forwards, you will address him as "sir" and you will show him the same deference you show me, or I'll have Guard Captain Drecht cut out your tongue. Do you understand?'

'My lord –' Van Schooten stammered, glancing between Arent and the governor general, desperately trying to draw some line between them. 'I ... I ... no offence was –'

'Your intentions couldn't be less important to me,' snapped the governor general, dismissing Van Schooten with a wave of his hand.

His gaze found Arent, a sudden smile brightening his face.

'Come, Nephew,' he said, inviting him inside. 'It's time we talked.'

13

THE GOVERNOR GENERAL HAD taken the captain's cabin. It was twice as large as the others, with its own privy. Furs were piled on the bunk and a rug laid on the floor. Hanging on the walls were oil paintings of famous scenes from the governor general's personal history, including the siege at Breda.

Arent was in that one. He was the giant covered in blood, carrying his injured uncle over his shoulder, while single-handedly fighting hordes of Spanish soldiers. It hadn't happened that way, but it was close enough to make him feel sick with the memory. Truth was, they'd hidden under bodies and clambered through middens, holding their breath all the way through the enemy line. He could understand why his uncle hadn't commissioned that for his wall, though. It was a difficult thing to capture magnificently in oil.

A harried clerk was transferring clothes from a sea chest into drawers, while Cornelius Vos, the governor general's chamberlain, was arranging scroll cases very precisely on a shelf. It took Arent a couple of glances to really notice him. With his muddy hair and brown clothes, it was difficult to distinguish him from the pillars supporting the roof.

'I appreciate your intervention, but I can fight my own battles, Uncle,' said Arent, closing the door behind him.

'This battle was beneath you,' responded Jan Haan, waving an agitated hand in the direction of the great cabin. 'Reynier van Schooten is weak and venal and grasping. That there's any place for him in this Company I love makes me love this Company a little less.'

Arent examined his uncle. They'd last seen each other a month ago, when he and Sammy had first arrived in Batavia. They'd eaten a large dinner and drunk a great quantity of wine, then reminisced, for it had been eleven years since they'd met last.

He hadn't changed a great deal. Over the years, that hawk-like face had become more hawkish, perhaps, and there was now an island of sunburnt baldness on top of his head. About the only significant change was his weight. He'd lost the coating of fat that was the privilege of wealth, growing thin as any beggar on the street.

Eerily thin, thought Arent. The way a sword was thin. Sharp, rather than frail, as if age were a whetstone. Could it be worry that had remoulded him? A breastplate sat snugly atop his clothes, the metal gleaming. Despite its obvious quality, it must have been uncomfortable. Even generals at war took their armour off once they returned to their tents, but his uncle showed no such inclination.

The governor general peered around his nephew's body, finding Guard Captain Drecht waiting patiently behind him, his hat pressed respectfully to his chest.

'You look like you're attending my funeral, Drecht. What do you want from me?'

'To request permission to offload some of our musketeers to another ship, sir. We've got them crammed into every empty space we can find, but there just isn't enough room on the *Saardam*.'

'How many did we bring aboard?'

'Seventy.'

'And how many do you want to offload?'

'Thirty.'

'What do you make of it, Vos?' the governor general asked his chamberlain.

Vos glanced over his shoulder, his ink-stained fingers twitching as he considered the details. 'Your protection would be adequately served by the number we'd retain, and the extra rations would be welcome. I can see nothing against it,' he declared, before returning to his work.

'Then you have your permission, Guard Captain,' said the governor general. 'Now if you gentlemen would excuse me, I'd like some time alone with my nephew. We have much to discuss.'

With a regretful glance at his pile of unordered scrolls, Cornelius Vos followed Jacobi Drecht into the great cabin, shutting the door behind him.

'Curious fellow,' said Arent.

'None finer with figures, but you'd have more fun talking to the figurehead,' he said, running his fingers along the jugs in his wine rack. 'He's loyal, though. As is Drecht, and that counts for a great deal these days. Do you want a drink?'

'Is that your famous wine cupboard?'

'As much as would fit,' said Jan. 'I have something French that I'd be glad to waste on those wretched taste buds of yours.'

'I'd be glad to have it wasted on me.'

Jan took down a jug, blowing the dust away. Tearing the cork loose, he poured out two mugs, handing Arent one. 'To family,' he said, raising his mug.

Arent clinked it and they drank heartily, savouring the taste.

'I tried to see you after your soldiers took Sammy, but I wasn't even allowed into the fort,' said Arent, trying to keep the hurt from his voice. 'They said you'd summon me when you had a free moment, but I didn't hear anything.'

'That was cowardice on my part.' The governor general lowered his eyes, shamefaced. 'I've been avoiding you.'

'Why?'

'I was afraid if I saw you … I was afraid of what I might be forced to do.'

'Uncle?'

The governor general rolled the wine around his mug, staring deeply into the red liquid as if some great truth would shortly reveal itself.

Sighing, he stared at Arent.

'Now you're standing in front of me, I realise my oath to the Company is not greater than my oath to your family,' he said quietly. 'So tell me, without fear, did you know what Samuel Pipps was doing?'

Arent opened his mouth, but the governor general silenced him with a hand.

'Before you answer, understand fully there will be no recrimination from me,' he said, his eyes scouring Arent's features. 'I will do everything in my considerable power to shield you, but I must know if Samuel Pipps intends to name you as a' – he searched for the word – 'conspirator when he goes before the Gentlemen 17.' His face darkened. 'If that's the case, additional measures must be taken.'

Arent had no idea what 'additional measures' meant specifically, but he could hear the blood dripping from them.

'I never saw him do anything underhand, Uncle,' he said stridently. 'I never have. He doesn't even know what he's accused of.'

'He knows,' scoffed the governor general.

'Are you certain? He's a better man than you give him credit for.'

The governor general went to the porthole, his back to his nephew. Only an hour at sea and the fleet was already beginning to disperse, the white sails leaving the black monsoon clouds behind.

'Do I strike you as a stupid man?' asked the governor general, an edge in his voice.

'No.'

'Reckless, then? Cavalier, perhaps?'

'No.'

'Pipps is a a hero to this noble Company we all serve. He's a favourite of the Gentlemen 17. I would not manacle him, nor treat him with such disregard if I had any other choice. Believe me, the punishment befits the crime.'

'And what is that crime?' asked Arent, vexed. 'Why keep it a secret?'

'Because when you face the Gentlemen 17, this bafflement will be your greatest defence,' said the governor general. 'They'll believe you were involved. How could they not? They know how close you and Pipps are. They know how he leans on you. They will not believe you were ignorant. Your outrage, your confusion; this is how we'll sway them.'

Arent picked up the wine jug, refilling his mug and his uncle's.

'His trial is eight months away, Uncle,' he said, joining him at the porthole. 'But while we're worrying about the sword, we may miss the spear. Sammy believes there's some threat to this boat.'

'Of course he does. He thinks he can use it to parlay his freedom.'

'The leper had no tongue, yet he spoke. He had a maimed foot, yet he climbed a tower of crates. These peculiarities alone are worth Pipps's attention. And then there's the symbol that appeared on the sail.'

'What symbol?'

'An eye with a tail. It was exactly the same as the scar on my wrist. The one I got after my father disappeared.'

Suddenly, Arent had his uncle's full attention. Going to his desk, Jan Haan plucked a quill from its well, drawing the symbol on to a sheet of parchment and holding it in front of Arent's face.

'This one?' he demanded, the ink dripping down the sheet. 'You're sure?'

Arent's heart hammered. 'I'm sure. How could it be here?'

'How much do you remember of that period after your father disappeared? Do you remember why your grandfather came for you?'

Arent nodded. After he'd returned alone from the hunting trip, he'd been shunned. His sisters had treated him with scorn and his mother had kept her distance, leaving his care to the servants. Everybody had hated his father, but nobody seemed glad he was gone. Nor were they happy that Arent had come back. It was never spoken aloud, but their accusation was obvious. They thought he'd put an arrow in his father's back, then feigned memory loss.

Soon enough, the rumour was the truth, spreading amid his father's congregation, poisoning them against him.

At first, they accused him quietly, the other children whispering vile insults whenever they saw him on the road. Then one of the villagers had cursed him after Mass, screaming that the devil danced behind him.

Trembling with fear, Arent had clutched his mother for protection, only to find her staring at him with the same loathing.

That night he'd crept out of their home in the dead of night and carved the shape of his scar on to the villager's door. He couldn't remember why he'd done it, or what dark impulse had inspired him. Nobody would have recognised the mark, but there was something malevolent about it, he'd thought. It frightened him, so he assumed it would frighten others.

The next morning it was the marked villager who was being shunned, his denials for naught. The devil came to the door of those who invited him, they claimed.

Thrilled by his victory, Arent crept out the next night, and the next, carving the symbol on the door of anybody who'd ever offended him, watching as they became the targets of suspicion and fear. It was such a small thing, the only power he had, the only revenge he could summon.

The symbol was a jest, but the villagers poured their terror into it, giving it life. Before long they burnt any house branded by the mark, driving its occupants out of the village. Terrified of what he'd created, Arent stopped his nocturnal visits, but the mark kept appearing, settling old feuds and inspiring new ones. For months, the village tore itself apart under the weight of its grudges, people accusing and being accused until, finally, they found somebody to blame.

Old Tom.

Arent's thoughts strained. Was Old Tom a leper? Was that why they all had hated him?

He couldn't remember.

It didn't matter. Unlike Arent, Old Tom was a poor man without powerful kin, or walls to hide behind. He certainly wasn't a demon, though he'd always been strange, sitting in the same spot in the market, come rain, sun or snow, begging for alms. Nothing he said made sense, but most had thought him harmless.

One day a mob circled him. A little boy had disappeared, and his friends claimed Old Tom had led him away. The villagers hurled accusations and demanded a confession. When he didn't provide it – when he couldn't – they beat him to death.

Even the children joined in.

The next day, the symbols stopped appearing.

The villagers congratulated themselves on driving the devil from their homes and went back to smiling and laughing with their neighbours, as if nothing had happened.

Arent's grandfather, Casper van den Berg, had arrived in his carriage a week later. He removed Arent from his mother's care, taking him back to his estate in Frisia on the other side of the Provinces. Casper claimed it was because his five sons had all disappointed him and he needed an heir. They both knew it was because Arent's mother had summoned him. She knew the truth about the scar and the marks he'd drawn on the doors.

She was afraid of him.

'After you were taken to Frisia, we heard tales of that mark spreading across the Provinces.' The governor general touched the parchment to the candle flame and watched the foul thing burn. 'Woodcutters noticed it first, etched in the trees they were felling. Then it began appearing in villages and, finally, carved into the bodies of dead rabbits and pigs. Wherever it appeared, some calamity followed. Crops were blighted, calves delivered stillborn. Children disappeared, never to be seen again. It went on for almost a year, until mobs started attacking the houses of the noble families who owned the land, accusing them of conspiring with dark forces.'

As the flame reached his fingertips, the governor general threw the scrap of parchment out of the porthole and into the sea.

'Why didn't you tell me any of this?' demanded Arent, staring at his scar. It was barely visible, but he could feel it underneath, trying to dig its way out.

'You were young.' There was a shine to his face, an old fear taking hold again. 'It wasn't your burden to carry. We assumed one of the mark's foul servants had come upon you in the woods, killed your father and branded you in some perverse ritual, but you showed no ill effects. Then we heard a witch-finder had chased the mark over from England, where his order had been battling it for years. He claimed it was a devil's work and set to scouring the land of its followers, slaughtering the lepers and burning the witches who'd appeared in its wake.'

Lepers, thought Arent. Like Bosey.

'The pyres burnt across Frisia for months, until it was finally banished,' continued his uncle. 'Your grandfather was worried the witchfinder would mistake you for one of its servants, so he hid you away.' A dark shadow passed across his face, the wine trembling in his hand. 'That was a terrible time. The devil twisted itself tight around the great and powerful, leading

96

them into perversity. A few of the old families couldn't be saved. They were already too enthralled by its evil.'

Lost in thought, the governor general's fingernails rapped the side of his mug. They were buffed to points, a style long out of fashion and somehow unsettling. They looked like talons, thought Arent. As if his uncle were slowly transforming into the bird of prey he'd always resembled.

'Arent, there's something else you should know. According to the witchfinder, the devil called itself Old Tom.'

Arent's legs felt weak beneath him, and he had to steady himself against the desk.

'Old Tom was a beggar,' he protested. 'The villagers murdered him.'

'Or maybe they found the right creature by accident. If you throw enough stones, occasionally you hit somebody deserving.' The governor general shook his head. 'Whatever the truth, those events were almost thirty years ago, why would the mark appear again now? Half a world away?' He turned his dark eyes upon Arent. 'Do you know my mistress, Creesjie Jens?'

Arent shook his head, confused at this new line of questioning.

'Her last husband was the witchfinder who saved the Provinces. The man we hid you from. It's through him I came to know Creesjie. If he confided in her about his work, she may know more about Old Tom, why it threatens this ship and what that mark on your wrist represents.'

'If you believe there's some threat, wouldn't it be wisest to return to Batavia?'

'Retreat, you mean?' The governor general snorted his contempt for the idea. 'There are almost three thousand souls in Batavia and fewer than three hundred aboard this ship. If Old Tom is here, it will be trapped. Do this for me, Arent. Any resource' – he spotted Arent's objection – 'aside from Pipps shall be yours.'

'I can't do what he does.'

'You stormed a stronghold to save me from the Spanish army,' balked the governor general.

'I didn't go there expecting to succeed; I went there knowing I would die.'

'Then why go at all?'

'Because I couldn't have lived with the guilt of not having tried.'

Overcome by the weight of love he bore his nephew, the governor general turned away to disguise it. 'I never should have taught you about Charlemagne when you were a boy,' he said. 'It's rotted your mind.'

Uncomfortable around any feeling that didn't end in profit, he went to his table and sifted through some papers. 'You've served Pipps for five years,' he said, once his documents were thoroughly reordered. 'Surely, you've observed his method.'

'Aye, and I've observed squirrels running up trees, but I can't do that either. If you want to save this ship, you need to free Sammy.'

'I know I'm not your uncle by blood, but I feel our kinship keenly. I've watched you grow up, and I know your capabilities. You were your grandfather's heir, chosen above his own five sons and seven grandsons. He did not offer you that honour because you were stupid.'

'Sammy Pipps isn't simply clever,' argued Arent. 'He can lift up the edges of the world and peek beneath. He has a gift I'll never understand. Believe me, I've tried.'

The face of poor Edward Coil flitted through his thoughts, followed by the usual shame.

'I can't free him, Arent.' There was a strange expression on the governor general's face. 'I *won't* free him. I'd rather let this ship sink and know he drowned in that cell.' Draining his mug, he thumped it back on to the table. 'If Old Tom's on this boat, then you're the best person to hunt it down. The safety of the *Saardam* is in your hands.'

14

A RENT STARED AT HIS uncle, feeling queasy. He'd not truly reckoned with the idea that this task would fall to him – alone. He'd been convinced that his uncle's affection for him would sway the matter, but it was the same affection that now doomed them.

Jan Haan's faith in him was absolute and it always had been. As a boy, he'd taught him swordplay by pitting him against full-grown men. First one, then two, then three and four, until servants would stop in their duties to watch him practise.

In his teenage years, when the clinking of the abacus replaced the clanking of swords, Jan had convinced Casper to send Arent to negotiate contracts with merchants so cunning they would have had the hands off Arent's arms if he hadn't been careful.

Emboldened by those distant successes, his uncle now courted failure, because there could be nobody less capable of protecting the *Saardam* than Arent.

'If I'm to do as you ask, I'll require Sammy's counsel,' he said desperately.

'Talk to him through the door.'

'Can we not move him to a cabin, at very least?' pleaded Arent, hating how weak he sounded. 'Does he not deserve that for the service –'

'My family is in those cabins,' said the governor general tightly, on the verge of insult.

'If we don't give him air and exercise, disease will ravage him,' said Arent, changing the point of attack. 'He'll be dead long before we reach Amsterdam.'

'No more than he deserves.'

Arent gritted his teeth, his temper rising at his uncle's stubbornness. 'Will the Gentlemen 17 not object?' he demanded. 'Will they not want to hear the accusations first-hand and render their judgement?'

The governor general's certainty wavered.

'If I'm not allowed to free him, then at least allow me to exercise him,' said Arent, sensing a crack in his uncle's fortitude. 'Even the passengers on the orlop deck walk the deck twice a day. He could join them.'

'No, I'll not have his taint spreading any further than it already has.'

'Uncle –'

'Midnight,' he countered. 'You may walk him at midnight.' Before Arent could press, he swept on sternly. 'Don't test my patience any further; I've already given more ground than I expected to, and it's only because you're the one asking.'

'Then I take it gratefully.'

The governor general slapped the back of his hand into his other palm, obviously annoyed at himself. 'Will you breakfast with me tomorrow?'

'Are you not attending the captain's table tonight?'

'I prefer to be asleep before dusk and awake before dawn. By the time the captain hosts the simpering idiots and belli-cose fools sailing aboard this ship, I will be abed.'

'Breakfast it is,' agreed Arent. 'Though I'd appreciate it if we could keep my family name secret.'

'You walk around in rags and yet it's your name that shames you?'

'It isn't shame, Uncle,' disagreed Arent. 'That name runs ahead of me. It straightens crooked paths, and it's the crooked paths I wish to walk.'

The governor general examined him admiringly. 'You were a strange boy and you've grown into a stranger man, but a unique one, I think.' He blew out a breath. 'Have it your way, your true name will not pass my lips. As your past should not pass yours. Does Pipps know about your scar and your father's disappearance?'

'No. Grandfather made me keep what happened in those woods a secret, and the lesson stuck. I don't speak about it. I rarely even think about it.'

'Good. Keep it that way, even from Creesjie Jens when you meet her. She's a fine woman, but still a woman. She'd believe the worst.' He rapped the desk with his finger. 'Now, as much as it pains me, I have duties to attend.' He opened the door, revealing Cornelius Vos and Guard Captain Drecht talking on the other side.

'Vos, escort my nephew to Creesjie Jens. Tell her that despite appearances he's a fine fellow, and he comes under my instruction.'

'I'd like to start with the gunpowder store first,' countered Arent. 'We need to know how this leper's master intends to attack us.'

'Very well,' he agreed. 'Take my nephew down to the gunpowder store and see the constable answers his questions.' He leant close, whispering into the chamberlain's ear, 'And then send Creesjie Jens to me.'

'Thank you, Uncle,' said Arent, inclining his head respectfully.

Jan Haan held out his arms, drawing him into an embrace. 'Don't trust Pipps,' he whispered. 'He's not the man you think he is.'

Cornelius Vos led Arent out of the great cabin and back through the helm into the compartment under the half deck. Every stride was perfectly equal, his arms held close to his sides, as if he were wary of taking up more space than he had to.

'I'll confess I thought I knew every root and branch of my master's genealogy, back to its ancestry.' Vos spoke slowly, blowing the dust off each word before it passed his lips. 'I apologise for not recognising you as family immediately.'

He sounded genuinely regretful, thought Arent. His grandfather's older servants had been the same way. The family was their life and being in service was their pride. His grandfather could have put collars around their necks and they would have polished them to a shine.

'I'm not related to the Haans; the governor general calls me nephew as a mark of affection,' explained Arent. 'His lands are next to my grandfather's in Frisia. They're great friends and raised me between them.'

'Then who are your people?'

'That's a matter I prefer not to speak on,' said Arent, making sure nobody was listening. 'And I'd take it as a kindness if you didn't mention my connection to the governor general to anybody else.'

'Of course,' said Vos frostily. 'I would not have this position if I struggled for discretion.'

Arent smiled at Vos's disgruntlement. Clearly, it vexed him that anybody should wish to distance themselves from the privilege of the governor general's friendship.

'Tell me of yourself, Vos,' he said. 'How did you come to be in service to my uncle?'

'He ruined me,' said Vos, without ire. 'I was a merchant once, but my company came into competition with the governor general. He spread scurrilous rumours about me to my customers, putting my business to the sword, then offered me a job as his chamberlain.'

He spoke in the fond tones of somebody recounting their Christmas feast.

'And you accepted?' said Arent, aghast.

'Of course,' said Vos, frowning at Arent's confusion. 'It was a great honour. If it hadn't been him, it would have been somebody else. I had no talent for business, but your uncle recognised my talent for figures. I'm exactly where I belong, and I thank God for His wisdom each night.'

Arent studied his bland face for some suggestion of wounded pride or repressed resentment, but there was nothing. He seemed grateful to have been crushed and added to his uncle's collection.

Vos took a small lemon from his pocket and dug his sharp fingers into the peel, spraying zest into the air. The mercenary watched him a moment, the boat rocking beneath them.

'Do you know why Sammy Pipps is imprisoned?' he asked abruptly, hoping to catch him off guard.

Vos's body stiffened. 'No.'

'Yes, you do,' disagreed Arent. 'Is it as bad as my uncle says?'

'Yes,' said Vos, biting into the lemon, bringing tears to his eyes.

The word was dropped across the conversation like a rock in front of a cave mouth.

The staircase down to the orlop deck was located opposite Arent's berth, and an almighty commotion was rising up the steps.

Descending into the gloom, Arent felt like he was being swallowed whole.

A ribcage of thick beams held up the low ceiling, drops of humidity falling like bile. Six cannons were spaced at regular intervals along the bowed walls and the centre of the deck was taken up by the huge capstan wheel, its four long handles used to hoist the anchors off the seabed.

It was swelteringly hot, with passengers expected to bed down wherever they could find space. At a guess, Arent suspected there were around fifty people down here. A few experienced travellers were stringing their hammocks between the gun ports, where they'd at least have a breeze, but the rest would have to settle for mats on the floor, and the feel of rats scurrying by their bodies in the night.

Arguments raged, sickly passengers coughing, snorting, spitting and vomiting, as they complained about their berths. Sander Kers and his ward, Isabel, were standing at the centre of them, listening sympathetically and offering God's blessings.

'The gunpowder store is this way,' said Vos, nodding towards the aft of the ship.

They hadn't gone three steps when they were thronged by passengers hurling complaints over each other. An irate man tried to prod Arent in the chest, then realised how far he'd have to reach, so prodded Vos instead.

'I sold everything to buy this' – he pointed at his hammock disgustedly – 'berth. There isn't even room for my possessions.'

'Fascinating,' said Vos, plucking the offending finger away like a piece of dirt. 'But I have no say over your accommodations. I had very little say over my own …'

He trailed off, distracted by something.

Following his gaze, Arent saw two sandy-haired boys with prominent ears darting across the deck, trying to tag each other. They were dressed identically in yellow hose and brown breeches, pressed tunics and short capes.

This was noble attire. Compared to the worn-out boots and faded clothes the rest of the passengers wore, it was painfully conspicuous. Their pearl buttons alone would have paid for one of these families to take quarters upstairs.

'Boys!' hollered Vos, bringing the two young nobles to an immediate halt. 'I'm certain your mother doesn't know where you are, and I'm certain she wouldn't approve. Up to the cabins with you.'

The boys muttered, but trudged up the stairs as ordered.

'They're the sons of Creesjie Jens,' explained Vos. He spoke her name with such yearning, he was momentarily rendered human. At short acquaintance, Arent had assumed Vos's heart was a ball of parchment, but evidently there was warm blood in there somewhere.

A weeping woman broke through the crowd, tugging Arent's sleeve.

'I've two children,' she complained, sniffling into a handkerchief. 'There's no light, no air. How will they endure eight months of this?'

'I'll talk to –'

Vos slapped her hand away, earning an annoyed glance from Arent. 'Lieutenant Hayes cannot help you any more than I can,' he said officiously. 'We're passengers like you. Harangue the first mate, or the chief merchant.'

'I want to talk to the captain,' demanded the irate man, pushing the woman out of the way.

'And I'm certain he'd like to talk to you,' said Vos blandly. 'Perhaps you should try hollering to him.'

Rather than wait for a response, he strode purposefully towards the gunpowder store and rapped on the door with the authority of a man for whom doors were always opened. Steps thudded on the other side, a panel sliding open, revealing suspicious blue eyes under wild white eyebrows.

'Who's that?' rasped an old voice.

'Chamberlain Vos, representing Governor General Jan Haan. This is Arent Hayes, the companion of Samuel Pipps.' He gestured for the metal disc Crauwels had given Arent in the great cabin, which Arent handed to him. He held it up to the slot. 'We're here with the blessings of your captain.'

Something scraped, the door swinging open, revealing a weathered sailor with only one arm, bent double like an overdrawn bow. He was shirtless, in slops that reached his knees. A twisted lock of blond hair hung from a cord around his neck, his own hair springing off his head like sparks from a grey bonfire.

'Come in, then,' he said, gesturing them inside. 'But bar the door after you, if you please.'

The gunpowder store was a windowless compartment with tin plates nailed to the walls and dozens of small casks of gunpowder laid flat in racks. There was a hammock in the corner and a privy pail beneath it that, thankfully, was empty.

A thick wooden beam scraped back and forth above Arent's ducked head.

'Connects the rudder to the whipstaff in the helm,' said the constable, who'd noticed Arent noticing. 'You get used to the squeaking after a while.'

At the centre of the room was the huge box containing The Folly. It was being used as a table by the constable, who sat down and swung his feet on top of it, sending a pair of dice skittering to the floor.

He was barefoot, like every other sailor Arent had seen.

Arent stared at the box in bafflement, wondering how something so precious had ended up being treated so carelessly. The Folly was the reason they'd been called to Batavia all those months ago. Only a handful of people knew what it was, and even Sammy wasn't one of them. It had been quietly built, quietly tested, quietly stolen, then quietly retrieved. They'd spent an hour in its company after recovering it and had examined it from top to bottom.

Even so, they couldn't make head nor tail of its purpose.

It came in three pieces which locked together. Once assembled, a brass globe lay inside a circle of wood, surrounded by rings of stars, a moon and a sun. Whenever you tilted it, cogs spun and everything shifted, such that trying to keep track of even one piece had given Arent a headache.

Whatever it was, it was important enough for the Gentlemen 17 to send their most valuable agent to find it, knowing full well the journey from Amsterdam might kill him first.

Fortunately, Sammy had not only survived, but succeeded in his errand, uncovering four Portuguese spies. Arent had been tasked with bringing them before the governor general's wrath, but two had taken their lives before he laid hands on them and two had spotted his approach and escaped.

The failure still embarrassed him.

'What brings fine sirs like yourselves down to the arse end of the ship?' asked the constable, putting a dried piece of fish into his mouth. Far as Arent could tell there wasn't a single tooth waiting for it.

'Has anybody approached you about putting spark to this room?' replied Arent, finding no better way to frame the question.

The constable's old face collapsed in confusion, like an orange that had just had all the juice sucked out of it.

'Why would anybody want to do that?' he asked.

'A threat's been made against the ship.'

'By me?'

'No, by –' Arent faltered, aware of how ridiculous the answer was. 'By a leper.'

'A leper,' repeated the constable, looking to Vos for confirmation of this foolishness.

The chamberlain bit a chunk out of his lemon, but said nothing.

'You think a leper's convinced me to take part in a plot that drowns me along with everybody else?' The constable munched his fish noisily. 'Well, let me think on that a minute. I get so many lepers down here, it's difficult to keep them straight.'

Arent kicked at the floor.

Investigation wasn't his work, and he wasn't comfortable doing it. They'd tried once before. Sammy thought he saw the sparkle of some talent in Arent, and a quick way to retire. He'd trained him, then given him a case. It went well enough until they nearly hanged the wrong man on Arent's good word. Only caught the mistake because Sammy put his bottle down long enough to peer hard at the facts, spotting something Arent had missed.

Until then, Arent had been arrogant. He'd seen Sammy's talents and thought them magnificent, but only in the way a fine display of horsemanship was magnificent. They were something admirable, but learnable.

He was wrong.

What Sammy did couldn't be trained or taught. His gifts were his alone.

Sensing Arent's discomfort, Vos took pity on him and turned his hard gaze on the constable.

'Know that Arent Hayes comes at the behest of Governor General Jan Haan himself,' he said. 'Whatever his questions, you will answer them thoroughly and with courtesy, or we'll see you flogged. Do you understand?'

The old man blanched.

'I'm sorry, sir,' he stumbled. 'I didn't mean no offence.'

'Answer the question.'

'No lepers, sir. No plots, neither. And I'll tell you this, if I wanted to kill myself, I'd spend a night whoring and drinking with the bastards out there,' he continued, pointing past the barred door. 'I don't because I've got coin enough and family waiting; plenty of reasons to go home.'

Arent had none of Sammy's gifts, but he had his own talent for spotting lies. People had been trying to deceive him his entire life, whether to persuade him into a bad deal when working for his grandfather, or to convince him that the dagger held behind their back wasn't meant for him. Upon the old man's wrinkled face, he saw hope and nervousness, but nothing to suggest he was lying.

'Who else can get in this room?' asked Arent.

'Nobody most days; everybody when battle stations are called. Crew would be in and out collecting gunpowder for their cannons. Only folks with a key are myself, Captain Crauwels and the first mate, though,' he said, wriggling his toes.

'Do you know a carpenter called Bosey. Had a lame foot? Might have a grudge against the *Saardam*?'

'Can't say I do, but I'm new to the crew. Only joined in Batavia.' The constable chewed more fish, saliva running down his chin. 'You worried somebody wants to sink the ship?'

'Aye.'

'Then you're seeing this all wrong,' he said. 'This room's got bread either side, and tin all around.'

'I don't –'

'Bread is packed in the compartments either side,' he clarified. 'Even if a spark did ignite it, the explosion would be snuffed out by the tin and the bread. Wouldn't put a hole in the hull. The fire wouldn't be a charm, but we'd have time to douse it before it ate us up. That's why they build them this way.'

'You understand I'll be putting this same question to Captain Crauwels?' asked Vos sternly.

'And he'll say the same, sir,' replied the constable.

Arent murmured. 'Can you think of a better way of sinking the *Saardam*?'

'Few ways,' said the constable, fingering the dirty twist of hair around his neck. 'Another ship could turn cannon on us, sink us the honest way.' He mulled it over. 'Could leave us be and trust pirates, storms or pox to finish us. That happens more often than not, or ...' He became troubled.

'Or?' prompted Vos.

'Or ... well, if it were me, and it aint me, I'm just talking.' He looked up at them for acceptance that he was 'just talking'.

'Tell us your idea,' demanded Vos.

'Well, if it were me, I'd try and put the captain out of the way.'

'Crauwels?' said Arent, surprised.

The old man picked at a splinter on the table. 'How much do you know about him?'

'Only that he dresses like he's at court and hates the chief merchant,' responded Vos.

The constable slapped his thigh in mirth, stopping when he noticed that Vos's blunt assessment hadn't meant to be humorous.

'True words all, sir, but Captain Crauwels is the finest sailor in the fleet, and everybody knows it, including that whore's son of a chief merchant, Reynier van Schooten. Could sail a longboat back to Amsterdam and arrive safe with his cargo, could Crauwels.' There was awe in his voice, but it was gone when he spoke again. 'Company pays poorly, which means the *Saardam* crew is comprised of malcontents, murderers and thieves to a man.'

'Which are you?' asked Vos.

'Thief.' He tapped his stump. 'Once. But here's what matters. Bad as this crew are, every one of them respects Captain Crauwels. They'll grumble, they'll plot, but they'll never move against him. He's fierce, but he's fair with the whip hand, and we know he'll get us home, so these animals bow their heads and accept the leash.'

'What would happen if he died?' asked Arent. 'Could the first mate keep this crew together?'

'The dwarf?' spat the constable scornfully. 'Not likely. If the captain dies, this boat burns, you mark me.'

15

S ARA AND LIA WERE standing on the poop deck at
the very rear of the ship watching Batavia recede into the
distance. Sara had expected it to disappear by degrees, like a
blot being scrubbed out of cotton. Instead, its chimneys and
rooftops had simply vanished between blinks, leaving no time
for goodbyes.

'What's France like, Mama?' asked Lia, for the hundredth
time that week.

Sara could see the trepidation in her eyes. Batavia was the
only home her daughter had ever known. Even then, she'd
rarely been allowed to venture beyond the walls of the fort. As
a child, she'd pretended it was Daedalus's labyrinth, spending
hours fleeing the minotaur in the maze. Her father had filled
the monster's role nicely.

Now, after thirteen years surrounded by stone walls and
guards, she was being shipped off to start an entirely new life
in a grand house with gardens.

The poor girl hadn't slept soundly for weeks.

'I don't know it well,' admitted Sara. 'I visited last when I
was very young, but I remember the food being exquisite, and
the music delightful.'

A hopeful smile crept on to Lia's face. She loved both of those things, as Sara well knew. 'They're talented inventors, scholars and healers,' carried on Sara wistfully. 'And they build miracles – cathedrals that touch the heavens.'

Lia rested her head on her mother's shoulder, her dark hair falling down her arm like black water.

The running lantern creaked on its long pole above them, the ensign flag snapping in the wind. In the animal pens, chickens clucked and sows grunted, trying to communicate their displeasure at the deck heaving beneath them.

'Will they like me there?' asked Lia plaintively.

'Oh, they'll love you!' exclaimed Sara. 'That's why we're doing this. I don't want you to be afraid of who you are any more. I don't want you to have to hide your gifts.'

Lia clutched her tightly, but before she could ask the next question on her list, Creesjie came hurrying up the stairs, her blonde hair flying. She'd changed out of her nightgown, and was now wearing a high-necked chemise, with ribbon-tied red sleeves and a broad-brimmed hat with plumes. She was holding her shoes in her hand, sweat standing up on her brow.

'There you are,' she said breathlessly. 'I've been searching everywhere.'

'What's wrong?' asked Sara, concerned.

Creesjie had arrived in Batavia two years ago at the governor general's request, falling on their drab lives like sunshine. Creesjie was a natural flirt with a gift for tall tales, and the skill to tell them well, something she practised daily. Sara couldn't ever remember her being in a bad temper, or anxious. Her natural state was delight, and there was always some suitor around to provoke it.

'I know what's threatening this boat,' said Creesjie, panting. 'I know what Bosey's master is.'

'What? How?' exclaimed Sara, her questions all elbowing out at once.

Creesjie rested herself on the railing, catching her breath. Directly beneath them were the square portholes of the passenger cabins and inside they could hear Crauwels continuing to bicker with Van Schooten about his cabin.

'Did I ever tell you about Pieter Fletcher, my second husband?' asked Creesjie.

'Only that he was the father of Marcus and Osbert,' replied Sara eagerly. 'And he knew my husband at one time.'

'Pieter was a witchfinder,' said Creesjie, speaking his name painfully. 'Thirty years ago, long before we were married, he arrived in the United Provinces from England investigating a strange symbol that was spreading across the lands of the noble families like a plague.'

'Was it the symbol that appeared on the sail this morning?' asked Lia.

'Exactly the same,' said Creesjie, glancing anxiously at the billowing white sheet. 'When he was investigating the mark, my husband freed the souls of hundreds of lepers and witches, and they all told the same story. In their worst hour, when their hope was exhausted, something calling itself Old Tom had whispered to them in the darkness, offering to fulfil their heart's desire in return for a favour.'

'What kind of favour?' asked Sara, unable to conceal her excitement.

She felt the way she did whenever a new Pipps case arrived in Batavia. She would play-act them with Lia, refusing to read the ending until they had devised their own theory. She was right more often than not, though she usually got the motive wrong. Jealousy and spurned passion weren't concepts Sara could understand, let alone comprehend somebody murdering for.

'My husband wouldn't speak in detail of his work. He believed it wasn't for a lady to hear.'

'Wise counsel,' said Vos, climbing the staircase. 'My master requires your presence immediately, Mistress Jens.'

Creesjie acknowledged him with distaste.

Arent loomed up behind him, bowing his head to Sara. Something had changed since she'd seen him on the docks, she thought. He carried his body heavily, as if some fresh weight had fallen upon it.

'Abide, Creesjie,' said Sara, as the men joined them. 'Have you met Lieutenant Hayes? He assisted me with the leper on the docks.'

'Arent,' he corrected in a low rumble, smiling at her. She found herself returning it.

Creesjie's eyes shimmered as she took him in. 'I hadn't, but I'd hoped to,' she said, curtsying. 'The stories of your size aren't overstated, are they, Lieutenant Hayes? It's like God forgot to stop making you.'

'Seduce him later, Creesjie,' chastised Sara gently, before addressing Arent. 'Apparently the mark on the sail belongs to a devil called Old Tom.'

Recognition flashed across Arent's face.

'You know the name?' she asked, cocking her head.

'The governor general gave me the story.'

'Well, I spoke with a young boy today, who told me the leper on the docks had been a carpenter on the *Saardam* named Bosey,' she said. 'Before he died, he'd bragged that he'd struck a bargain with somebody in Batavia that would make him rich, and all he had to do in return were a few favours.'

Creesjie shook her head sadly. 'Whatever favour Old Tom asked of this Bosey, its only end would have been suffering.' She wiped sea spray from her face. 'Once you bargain with Old Tom, you become its servant. You're never free of it. It feeds on our pain, and those who don't serve it a banquet are made to suffer themselves. Pieter was possessed of formidable will, but even he baulked at recounting the depravities he'd witnessed.'

If it was grievances Old Tom sought, it would have no want of them here, thought Sara. Everybody on this ship had cause for complaint. Everybody felt mistreated. Everybody wanted what somebody else had. She could only imagine the price these people would pay for a better life.

Look at the price *she* was willing to pay.

'Plenty of grievances on the *Saardam*,' rumbled Arent, echoing her thoughts. 'Did your husband say what Old Tom actually was?'

'A devil of some sort, but he never confronted it directly. Not until ...' Creesjie faltered, her eyes flooding with tears. 'Four years ago, Pieter came home in a panic. We were living in Amsterdam, in a grand house filled with servants. He rushed us into a carriage leaving for Lille without any explanation, or any of our possessions –'

'Lille?' interrupted Arent, startled.

'Yes.' She tried to make sense of his discomfort. 'Does that mean something to you?'

'No ... I ...' He shook his head, his expression that of a man who'd seen an awful shape flit across the window. 'We investigated a case there once. I have bad memories of the place. I'm sorry to have interrupted your account.'

Sara knew all their reports by heart, so she knew he'd never written about Lille. She wondered what this lost case could be, and why it so unsettled him, but she had too many other concerns to linger on it.

'My husband told me Old Tom had found him and we had to flee,' continued Creesjie, a throb in her throat. 'I begged him to tell me more, but he wouldn't say another word. We travelled for three weeks to arrive at our new home, and two days later he was dead.' She swallowed. 'Old Tom tortured him and left its mark on the wall, so we'd know exactly what was responsible.'

Sara clutched Creesjie's hand. 'Do you have strength enough to tell my husband this?' she asked. 'It may be enough to convince him to turn back for Batavia.'

'It won't,' said Arent. 'The governor general already knows what that symbol represents. He's asked me to investigate, but he won't turn the ship around.'

'That damn stubborn fool,' cried Sara, glancing at Lia in concern.

'It's unbecoming to speak of your husband in such a manner,' scolded Vos, earning a venomous glance from Creesjie.

The chamberlain wrung his hands, speaking quickly to disguise his embarrassment. 'If it's a devil we face, might I suggest we consult the predikant. Surely, this would be closer to his realm than our own.'

'*You* believe in demons, Vos?' asked Lia. 'I wouldn't have thought it. You're so ...'

'Passionless?' supplied Creesjie.

'Rational,' clarified Lia.

'I have seen them first-hand,' he said. 'My village was beset when I was a boy. Only a handful of homes survived the assault.'

Sara addressed Arent. 'I'll speak to the predikant, if you wish,' she said. 'I need to arrange confession, anyway.'

'That would be a help, thank you,' said Arent. 'I'll keep asking around after Bosey. If his master really is Old Tom, one of his friends may know how they became acquainted.'

'I may have some useful information on that also,' replied Sara, who relayed to Arent what she'd learned about the carpenter that morning, including his last words before his tongue was cut out.

'Laxagarr?' mused Arent, when she was finished. 'I know a handful of languages, but I've never heard a word like that.'

'Neither have I,' agreed Sara, gripping the taffrail as the ship smacked into a large wave. 'The boy I spoke to thought it was Nornish and the only person onboard who speaks the language is the boatswain Johannes Wyck and he was the one responsible for cutting out Bosey's tongue, so I doubt he'll be amenable to our questions.'

'He won't be,' agreed Arent. 'I've met him already.'

'I've sent Dorothea to ask around among the passengers on the orlop deck, just in case any of them can help.'

Arent looked at her in admiration, drawing a confused half-smile in response.

'If Old Tom feeds on suffering, why would it leave Batavia?' interrupted Vos in his usual monotone. 'There's thousands of souls in the city, and only a few hundred aboard the *Saardam*. Why trade a banquet for a snack?'

'It's here for me,' said Creesjie, her voice frail. 'Don't you see? Pieter freed its followers and banished it from the Provinces.

Old Tom butchered him in revenge but I fled before it could finish its work. I kept moving, so it would never find us, but I thought we'd be safe this far from the Provinces. I became complacent, but now it's come for the rest of his family.' Her desperate gaze found Sara. 'It's here for me.'

16

A s the day drew to a close, sailors sang, danced and played their fiddles on the waist, heeding the occasional barked order from the quarterdeck. Up in the rigging, they laughed at ribald jokes and called down insults to those below. They were so boisterous that their sudden silence was louder than a thunderclap.

Arent was striding past the mainmast.

Up on the quarterdeck, Captain Crauwels cursed under his breath and considered calling out a warning, immediately realising it would be no use. Even on short acquaintance, it was obvious Arent Hayes went where he wished.

Sailors stopped fast in their labours, watching him pass. Once out to sea, everything afore the mainmast belonged to them. Any passengers who ventured into their half of the *Saardam* surrendered themselves to whatever torments the sailors devised. That was the way it had always been, but Arent showed nary a concern. Even so, nobody moved. A few crew members squinted at him as he passed, weighing the chances of theft or intimidation, but his size swiftly put aside any uncharitable ideas. Cowed, they returned to their duties, leaving Arent to climb the stairs on to the forecastle at the bow of the ship.

The foremast towered above him, the sails casting everything in shade. The beakhead stretched out over the sea, the golden lion figurehead seeming to leap from wave to wave.

He was momentarily blinded by the molten orange sun. Its light was drawing across the white sails of the fleet, setting fire to them.

Blinking, he heard cheers, then the soft, wet slaps of a fist fight. Peering through a crowd of sailors and musketeers, he caught sight of two shirtless bodies circling each other. They were bruised and bloodied, swinging wild, tired punches. Most missed, a few landed. The loser would be whichever one of them fell down first from exhaustion.

Peering over the heads of the crowd, Arent sought out Isaack Larme.

The first mate was sitting nearby on the railing overlooking the beakhead, his short legs swinging as he whittled a piece of wood with his knife. Occasionally, he'd glance up, eyeing the proceedings with the scowl of a professional fighter watching a very unprofessional fight.

Arent hadn't taken two paces towards him, when Larme shook his head.

'Cark off,' he warned, still intent on his whittling.

'Captain told me you might know something about a carpenter called Bosey. Who his friends were? What he did before joining the Company?'

'Cark off,' repeated Larme.

'I saw your reaction in the great cabin when I mentioned Bosey. You flinched. You know something.'

'Cark off.'

'The *Saardam*'s in danger.'

'Cark. Off.'

Laughter rang out from the surrounding sailors. The fight had stopped and everybody was watching them instead.

Arent balled his fists, his heart a jackrabbit. Ever since he was a boy, he'd hated being the centre of attention. Most of the time he walked with his shoulders slouched and his back bent, but he was much too large to go unremarked. That was why he enjoyed working with Sammy. When the sparrow was in the room, nobody paid attention to anything else.

'I come with the governor general's authority,' tried Arent, hating himself for having to invoke his uncle's name.

'And I come with the authority of being the only man keeping this rabble from slitting your throat in the night,' said Larme, flashing Arent a vicious grin.

The sailors jeered. This was clearly a much better fight than the one they'd been watching.

'We think Bosey has a master called Old Tom who's trying to sink this boat.'

'And you think he needs some clever scheme to do it?' retorted Larme. 'Best way to sink an Indiaman is to leave her be. If a storm doesn't get us, pirates will. If it aint pirates, it'll be disease. This ship's damned, leper or no.'

The crew murmured their agreement, their hands instinctively reaching for their good-luck charms. Each one was as distinct as the soul that owned it. Glancing around, Arent saw a burnt statue and a curiously knotted length of rope. There was a twist of bloodied hair and a strange vial of dark liquid; a melted scrap of iron and a colourful chunk of mica, the edges seared by flame.

Larme's was a strange thing. Half a leering face, carved out of wood.

'Will you answer my questions?' flailed Arent.

'No.'

'Why?'

'Because I don't have to,' responded Larme, brutally hacking a chunk from the block he'd been whittling. He tossed it into the ocean.

After waiting for the laughter to die down, he pointed towards the bloodied fighters with the tip of his knife. 'You should fight,' he said.

'What?' replied Arent, confused by the sudden shift in conversation.

'Fight,' repeated Larme, as the sailors murmured uncertainly. 'This is where we settle disputes, but there's good coin if the odds are right.'

Everybody in the crowd looked at each other, trying to work out which one of them would be foolish enough to fight this giant. Johannes Wyck could do it, suggested somebody, bringing muttered assent.

'I don't fight for fun,' said Arent. Being fundamentally honest, he added. 'Any more.'

Larme wiggled his knife, yanking it free of the block of wood. 'They're not fighting for fun; they're fighting for money. We're the ones having fun.'

'I don't do that either.'

'Then you're up the wrong end of the ship with no reason for being here.'

Arent stared at him helplessly. He had no idea what to say next. Sammy would have noticed something or remembered an important fact. He would have found the key for the human lock before him. Arent could only stand there and feel foolish.

'If you won't answer my questions, at least tell me how I can get the boatswain to answer them,' he tried desperately.

Larme laughed again. It was a vicious, terrible thing.

'A nice dinner and some soft words in his ear should do it,' he said. 'Now cark off, so we can finish this fight.'

Defeated, Arent turned his back and walked away, the jeers of the sailors following him.

17

Dusk arrived in ribbons of purple and pink, a few stars puncturing the sky. There was no land in sight. Only water.

Captain Crauwels ordered the sails furled and anchors dropped, bringing their first day of sailing to an end. The governor general had demanded to know why they couldn't continue their journey at night, for he knew captains who made good time sailing by moonlight.

'Is your skill not equal to theirs?' he'd said, trying to needle Crauwels into rashness.

'Skill's no use when you can't see the thing trying to sink you,' he'd responded calmly, before adding, 'If you tell me the names of the captains who sail by night, I'll tell you the names of the ships they've sank and the cargo they've lost.'

That had put a swift end to the argument, and now Crauwels was listening to Isaack Larme ringing eight bells, summoning a new watch.

Crauwels loved this time of evening, when his duties to the crew had ended and his duties to the damned nobility had not yet begun. This was his. One hour, around dusk, to smell the air and feel the salt on his skin and find some joy in this life forced upon him.

Going to the railing, he watched the weary crew pass on orders, rub their charms and say their prayers, tapping whatever part of the hull they could reach for luck. Superstition, he thought. It's the only thing keeping us afloat.

From his pocket, he removed the metal disc he'd given to Arent. Vos had returned it to him earlier, obviously annoyed that he was treating a gift from the governor general so carelessly. He rubbed its surface with his thumb and forefinger, then examined the sky, a troubled frown on his face.

For the past few hours, he'd felt that familiar itch on his skin telling him a storm was building beyond the horizon. The air was growing prickly, the sea subtly changing shade. Opening his mouth, he'd tasted the air. It was like licking a piece of iron dredged up from the seabed.

It would be here in a day, maybe less.

A cabin boy walked past him, carrying a flaming torch to the back of the ship, stretching on his tiptoes to light the huge lantern hanging there.

One by one, the other ships in the fleet followed suit until seven flames burnt in the endless dark, like fallen stars adrift on the ocean.

18

D INNER THAT NIGHT WAS a torment for Sara, who
was much too full of worry to settle to small talk with
the other passengers.

Guard Captain Drecht had stationed a musketeer outside
the passenger cabins, easing her mind a little, but that had
been her last success. Dorothea hadn't been able to find a
passenger who knew what Laxagarr meant, which left only
Johannes Wyck to translate. Much as she wished to summon
the boatswain to her cabin and interrogate him, she couldn't
risk her husband finding out. Calling for the carpenter
had been risky enough, and she'd had a good excuse for
doing that.

It was infuriating.

She was the highest-ranking noblewoman onboard, and
yet she had less freedom than the lowliest cabin boy.

At least this interminable dinner was almost over, she
thought.

The food had been eaten and the cutlery cleared, aside from
a great silver candelabrum, its dripping candles casting every
face in a sinister light. The leaves of the table had been dropped,
making room for the diners to scatter around the great cabin
and engage in trivial, mostly tedious, conversations.

Sara had taken herself to a chair in the corner, begging a few minutes' rest to overcome a headache. It was a ploy she'd used before at social engagements and it usually yielded at least twenty minutes of solitude after the initial barrage of concern had waned.

Sitting silently in the shadows, she tried to make sense of the strange gathering before her. Mostly it was senior officers Sara didn't recognise, aside from Captain Crauwels, who was resplendent in a red doublet and crisp white hose, his silk ribbons immaculately tied and buttons polished, each one catching the candlelight. It was a different outfit from the one he'd worn during the day, but equally well tailored.

He was talking to Lia, who was peppering him with seafaring questions. Initially, Sara had worried that her daughter was letting her cleverness slip. She often did when she was excited, but Lia was wearing her best disguise – the vacuous expression of a dim noblewoman trying to impress a suitor.

Crauwels seemed to be enjoying it. In fact, it was the most comfortable he'd appeared all evening.

He was a peculiar man, she thought. Caught at the crossroads of his own contradictions. For all his fine clothes, he was a ruffian at heart. Honeyed words greeted the nobles, but he was coarse and short-tempered with everybody else. His feast was lavish, and yet he ate very little of it. He drank from his own bottle of ale rather than the wine served, and urged on the conversations around him, even while speaking little, and becoming impatient when anybody else spoke to him. There was no doubt he wanted to impress, and equally no doubt that he was uncomfortable with the people he was trying to impress.

Her eyes drifted to Sander Kers, who was lurking near the windows with Isabel, scrutinising their fellow diners.

He'd been avoiding her all evening.

At first she'd thought him merely awkward – happier to observe conversation than participate in it – but as the hours had gone by, she'd begun to discern a pattern. He wasn't interested in people; he was interested in their arguments. At every raised voice, he would lean forward eagerly, his lips parting, only to sag in disappointment when the argument dissolved into good-natured laughter. He would then mutter something to Isabel, who'd nod her agreement.

As far as Sara could tell, his ward had said nothing all night, but she wore her silence comfortably. For some, such as Creesjie, being quiet was the loudest thing they could do. It demanded investigation.

Isabel was the opposite. Those watchful eyes were filled with candour. They did the work her mouth would not, admitting every moment of doubt and fear and surprise.

There was a noise from the doorway and Sara's heart leapt, hoping to see Arent finally arriving. But it was only the steward bringing more wine.

She shook her head, annoyed at her own eagerness. She wanted to know what he'd discovered, but his chair had remained empty, as had that of Viscountess Dalvhain, who hadn't been able to attend because of ill health.

This, at least, had given the diners something to gossip about.

After trading theories on the imprisonment of Samuel Pipps for a full hour, they'd moved on to discussing Dalvhain's wealth and lineage, but it was all speculation. Nobody in the room had ever met her, aside from Captain Crauwels, who spoke gruffly of a sickly woman with a cough that could knock the leaves off a tree.

'Dalvhain,' murmured Sara, worrying at it.

As a girl, she'd been forced to memorise reams of heraldry, ensuring she'd never shame her father by not immediately knowing who a wealthy stranger was at a party, but she didn't recognise the name Dalvhain.

Creesjie's laughter rose above the chatter. She wasn't capable of sitting in her cabin and moping. She thrived on good cheer, which was handy because it was Creesjie's great gift to be able to convince people that her day had been a wretched grey thing before their arrival.

Currently, she was talking with Chief Merchant Reynier van Schooten, her fingertips resting lightly on his forearm. By the rapt look on his face, the chief merchant's heart was already twisting itself in knots.

Sara couldn't understand why Creesjie was bothering. Van Schooten was a vexatious creature, permanently drunk and apparently incapable of conversing without spite. It was a measure of this evening that everybody else kept the table between themselves and him.

As ever, Cornelius Vos was standing a little way away, hands behind his back, watching Creesjie with the expression of pained longing he always wore in her company.

Pity mixed with frustration in Sara's breast.

Vos was a decent sort, with a great deal of power and, presumably, wealth. There would be plenty of suitors happy to share his life, but he pursued the one impossible choice.

Creesjie Jens was the most desirable woman in the Company.

Aside from her beauty, she was a fine musician, a witty conversationalist and, by her own admission, talented in the bedchamber. Such women came around rarely, and their value was considerable.

Her first husband had been a staggeringly wealthy merchant and her second the world's foremost witchfinder. Jan had summoned Creesjie to Batavia to be his mistress after he'd heard of the witchfinder's unsolved murder, and now she sailed back to wed a duke in the French court.

Poor, dull Vos, writhing in his adoration, might as well have fallen in love with the moon itself. It would have been easier to talk into his bed.

Spotting Sara in the chair, Creesjie begged a moment from her companion and flounced over.

'What a wonderful company,' she said gaily, her eyes watering with wine. 'Why are you skulking in the shadows?'

'I'm not skulking.'

'Brooding?'

'Creesjie –'

'Go find him.'

'Who?'

'Arent Hayes,' she said in exasperation. 'He's the one you want to talk to, so go find him. You can lock eyes and talk chastely of lepers and demons and other dreadful things. It would do my heart glad to think of you two battling this evil together.'

Sara reddened, earning a sly laugh from Creesjie, who took her hands and hoisted her out of the chair. 'It's my understanding that he's staying in the compartment under the half deck,' her friend said. 'That's two walls away, on the other side of the helm.'

'I can't go,' protested Sara half-heartedly. 'I'm the highest-ranking noble here.'

'Of course you can.' Creesjie adopted a pompous tone. 'As the highest-ranking noble here, you can do what you wish. Besides Jan is in bed, so it really doesn't matter. I'll tell everybody you felt faint.'

Sara touched her friend's cheek in gratitude. 'You are marvellous.'

'I know.'

'Keep Lia away from the chief merchant,' she said, taking a step towards the door. 'He makes me queasy.'

'Oh, leave Reynier be. He deserves pity, not scorn.'

'Pity?'

'Can't you see the pain that beats where his heart should be? He's hurt, so he's hurting others.' She mulled it a second. 'Besides, he's drunker than a king on his wedding night. He couldn't carry himself back to his bed, let alone Lia, but I'll do as you wish.' Anticipating Sara's next question, she added, 'And I'll ensure somebody of merit escorts us both back safely. Now, go find your brute.'

From the candlelit brightness of the great cabin, Sara entered the darkness of the helm, where she heard a distant fiddle being played, accompanied by somebody singing in a low, rough voice. At first, she mistook it as coming from the bow of the ship, but she realised it was drifting down from the quarterdeck.

The captain had warned the women not to move around by themselves at night, but curiosity was ever her vice.

Hitching her gown, she climbed the staircase and walked straight into the song.

Arent was playing the fiddle by the light of a candle melted to a cask. His eyes were closed, those large fingers moving deftly across the strings. Guard Captain Jacobi Drecht sat opposite, singing a maudlin song. He was slouched forward, his clasped hands dangling between his knees, his magnificent sabre laid at his feet. Two empty jugs of wine lay on the floor and there was a third on the cask, suggesting they'd been here for some time.

Seeing Sara, Drecht leapt up, knocking his stool backwards.

The music stopped immediately. Arent peered at Drecht, then over his shoulder at Sara. He smiled with genuine pleasure. She mirrored it, surprised by how pleased she was to see him.

'My lady,' stumbled Drecht, who was obviously drunk and obviously trying not to be. 'Did you need assistance?'

'I never knew you could sing, Guard Captain,' she said, clapping her hands delightedly. 'All these years you've protected my family, how did I not know?'

'The fort's a large place, my lady,' he said. 'And I sing very quietly.'

She laughed at his jest, before turning her attention to Arent.

'And you, Lieutenant Hayes.'

'It's still Arent,' he corrected gently.

'You play beautifully.'

'Only useful thing I brought back from war,' he said, stroking the neck of his fiddle. 'Well, this, and an excellent recipe for mushroom stew.'

'Are you returning to your bedchamber, my lady?' wondered Drecht. 'May I escort you?'

'I actually came to speak with Arent,' she said.

'Then you should sit,' said Arent, pushing a stool towards her with his foot.

'I'll help you, my lady,' said Drecht solicitously.

'Very kind, Guard Captain, but sitting down is one of the few things I'm still allowed to do for myself, so I'm reasonably skilled at it.'

Eyeing the low stool, Sara cursed her pride. Her petticoat was made of red brocade and inlaid with pearls, and her bodice was covered in a waterfall of lace. The entire outfit was only slightly lighter than a suit of armour. Very awkwardly, she lowered herself on to the stool, the candle's golden light washing over her. Amid the waves and twinkling stars, the formal chatter of the great cabin felt like a very distant life.

'Drink?' asked Arent, passing her a jug.

'I'll find you a mug,' said Drecht.

'The jug will be fine,' she said soothingly. 'Just don't tell my husband.'

Tipping it to her lips, she braced herself for the dreadful taste of whatever swamp water soldiers drank, but it was wonderful.

'It's from Sammy's stash,' explained Arent, who was plucking the strings of his fiddle experimentally. 'If you want to try real soldier swill, you'll have to wait until next week when we've run out of this.'

There was that smile again. It started in his eyes, she realised. They were green with golden centres, strangely delicate considering the brutal face surrounding them.

'Have you told the guard captain about Old Tom?' asked Sara, handing the jug back.

'Didn't need to,' said Drecht. 'The governor general's already had a word. Told me about the symbol on the sail and how it ravaged the Provinces thirty years back. Can't say I believe any of it, but he's afraid. He's demanding I personally escort him whenever he leaves his cabin.'

'Lucky you,' said Sara sarcastically.

'You don't believe in devils, Drecht?' asked Arent, holding his fiddle to his ear as he tightened one of the strings.

'Don't see the use of them,' he said, picking a trapped moth out of his beard and crushing it in his fingers. 'I've never seen one standing over a dead child. I aint ever seen one ravage a woman or set fire to a hut with a family still inside. You've been on the battlefield, Hayes. You know what men are when there's nobody ordering them to be better. They don't need Old Tom whispering suggestions in their ear. Evil comes from in here' – he hammered his chest – 'it's born in us; it's what we are when you take away the uniforms and the ranks and the order.'

Sara hadn't needed a battlefield to teach her that lesson. Her entire life had been spent in study of men. Not from love or admiration, as was the proper way for a woman, but from fear. Men were dangerous. They were fickle of mood, liable to lash out when disappointed, and they were frequently disappointed – most often by their own shortcomings, though only a fool would tell them as much.

'If you don't think a devil's prowling this boat, what's responsible for that mark on the sail?' prodded Arent.

'I reckon one of the crew's got hold of the story and is playing tricks on his betters.' Drecht flung his hand towards the waist of the ship. By the reaching flame of the running light, Sara could just about see the crew singing and dancing to flutes and drums. The shrieks, laughter and sudden eruptions of violence made Sara's skin crawl. 'Nothing but spite and boredom at work on this boat, you mark me.'

'I'm not saying it aint, but your theory still leaves plenty of questions Sammy won't be happy without answers to,' replied

Arent, taking a swig of wine. 'Not least how the ship's lame-footed carpenter became a leper, then ended up climbing a stack of crates to doom the *Saardam* without a tongue.'

'He wasn't a leper,' said Sara. 'At least not in the traditional sense. Leprosy is a dreadful thing that worsens over years. If he'd had it on *Saardam*, the crew would have known. If he developed it in Batavia, it wouldn't have been advanced enough to require those rags.'

'Do you think it was a disguise?' asked Arent.

'Or a uniform,' suggested Drecht. 'Every army has one.'

'Johannes Wyck probably knows,' said Sara, picking at a loose pearl on her dress. 'He must have cut out Bosey's tongue to stop him saying something, and he likely knows what favours were asked in return for the riches Bosey was promised. And he definitely knows what Laxagarr means.'

'Laxagarr?' queried Drecht. 'Is that a name?'

'Could be. Or a place,' Sara shrugged, her dress rustling. 'Apparently, it's Nornish.'

'I'll ask my musketeers. Somebody might recognise it. Everybody's from everywhere down there.' He finished off his wine. 'What about you, Arent? Do you believe we've a devil onboard?'

'I've seen Sammy pick apart too many ghost stories to believe there's one happening here,' said Arent, the flame reflected in his eyes.

Drecht yawned and stood up stiffly. 'I best relieve the musketeer on the governor general's door.' He offered an arm to Sara. 'May I escort you to your cabin, my lady?'

'I'd like to stay in the fresh air a little while longer, Guard Captain,' she demurred. 'I'm certain Arent will escort me when I'm ready to leave.'

Drecht flashed him an enquiring glance, earning a nod.

'Very well,' he said a little uncertainly. 'Goodnight, my lady. Goodnight, Arent.'

Arent nodded and Sara waved, both of them watching in amusement as he stopped halfway down the stairs and glanced over his shoulder.

'Is it me he doesn't trust, or you?' wondered Sara.

'Oh, you, certainly,' said Arent. 'Me and Jacobi Drecht are the best of friends now.'

'I can see that,' she said. 'Didn't he have a sword to your chest this morning?'

'And he will again if I cross him,' replied Arent cheerfully. 'Most cold-blooded man I ever met.'

'Strange sort of friendship.'

'Strange sort of day.' He plucked at his fiddle, clearly itching to play. 'Would you like a song?'

'Do you know "O'er the Gentle Water"?'

'I do,' he said, finding those first notes.

Some songs weren't mere songs. They were memories curled tight and set alight. They made you heartsick. 'Gentle Water' did that for Sara. It carried her back to childhood, to her parents' grand house and her sisters, the five of them coming home bone weary and shivering cold after a day's riding, creeping into the kitchen to eat stew under the table with the dogs.

Her own daughter had never had that innocence, she thought sadly. Nor that happiness. Her father had jailed her behind the fort's stone walls for fear she'd be accused of witchcraft if she were allowed into the world. Once they were free of him, Sara intended on giving Lia every childhood experience she'd been denied.

Arent played his fiddle softly.

'Why didn't you come to dinner tonight?' she asked him, surprising herself with her candour.

Arent flicked her a glance, then returned his attention to his playing.

'Did you want me there?'

She bit her lip, only able to nod.

'Then I'll come tomorrow,' he said softly.

Sara's heart was beating furiously. For something to do, she started tugging the jewelled pins out of her hair, allowing her red curls to come tumbling free, easing the pressure on her scalp.

'Is that one of the pins you offered me on the docks?' asked Arent.

'I had thirteen of them,' said Sara, moving one of them around to catch the firelight. 'They were a wedding gift from Jan.' She smiled slightly. 'After fifteen years I finally found a use for them.'

'Those pins must be worth a fortune,' he said. 'But you traded one for a funeral that would have cost three guilders.'

'I didn't have three guilders on me.'

'But –'

'I haven't worn these pins since my wedding day,' she interrupted, still staring at the one in her palm. 'My husband asked me to wear them today, so I fetched them from the treasury this morning, blew the dust off and put them in my hair. Tonight, they'll go back into their case and I won't wear them again for another fifteen years.' Sara shrugged, placing the pins near the candle on the cask. 'Perhaps you see some value in that, but I don't. I saw value in putting them to a Christian purpose and treating an unfortunate soul with dignity and respect, however late it may have come.'

Arent stared at her admiringly. 'You're the wrong kind of noble, Sara.'

'I certainly hope so. Oh, that reminds me.' From her sleeve, she withdrew a vial of the sleeping draught she'd given the leper on the docks. The viscous brown liquid glittered in the candlelight. 'Here,' she said, handing it to him. 'I meant to give you this at dinner, but here will do well enough. It's for Pipps.'

He stared at it uncomprehendingly, the vial tiny in his scarred palm.

'It will help him sleep,' she explained. 'My cabin is a coffin, so I can't imagine how dreadful his cell must seem. A drop of that and he'll sleep all day or night. Two drops and he'll sleep half of the next.'

'What happens if he takes three drops?'

'He'll make a grand mess of his breeches.'

'Three drops it is.'

Her rich laughter became a yawn, which she swiftly covered with her hand. She wanted to stay there all night, talking and listening to him play, and that alone was reason enough to leave. 'I should sleep,' she said, annoyed by how formal she sounded.

Arent carefully leant his fiddle against the keg. 'I'll escort you.'

'There's no need.'

'I promised Drecht,' he said. 'And it would put me at my ease. Besides, I don't think you can get up without help. That dress looks heavy.'

'It is!' she exclaimed. 'Why don't tailors ever think of these things? And you know, amidst all this brocade, it doesn't even have pockets. Not one.'

She tugged at the material where the pockets should have been.

'It's a scandal,' said Arent, taking her hands and helping her stand. His skin was coarse. She reddened at his touch, then marched ahead to hide it.

Arent scooped up the discarded hairpins from the cask and went after her.

It was a beautiful night full of stars, all of them reflected on the still water. Among them were the seven fleet lanterns, their golden flames strangely comforting in the black.

They slowed on the staircase to admire the view.

'You didn't answer Drecht's question about whether you believed in demons,' said Arent, glancing at her.

'If you'd listened carefully, you would have noticed he didn't actually ask me,' she said, smiling slightly.

'Well, I'm asking,' he said. 'Do you believe there's a demon on this boat?'

Her hands curled around the railing. 'Yes,' she said.

Growing up, she'd been taught that demons walked the earth to torment sinners. Off forked tongues came alluring promises, but they were tricks with only hell waiting at the end. Those who trusted in God's love would see through their deceits and be sheltered from harm. She believed that, as she believed that those who fell prey to the wickedness of demons were somehow deserving of it, but that hadn't saved Creesjie's husband. And if Old Tom was willing to sink the *Saardam* to hurt Creesjie, it wouldn't save anybody else.

'My mother was a healer, and that often brought her into conflict with devils,' continued Sara. 'She told me stories about children dragging their own parents into the woods to be slaughtered. She told me about possessed adults whose skin would tear, because the demon could barely fit inside them. We're mice to them, to be played with and ripped apart. That mark on the sail is how is starts. It's meant to scare us because scared people will do anything to stop being scared, and they'll do it to almost anybody.'

Arent murmured his agreement and became thoughtful. Sara looked at him shyly from the corner of her eye. It was rare she spoke so freely to anybody aside from Creesjie and Lia, and she was surprised – and pleased – to see how deeply he was considering what she'd said. Side by side, they admired the night's beauty in silence for a few moments, then continued on.

Eggert – the musketeer whose throat Arent had nearly slit this afternoon – was guarding the entrance to the passenger cabins and he glared at the mercenary, touching his neck self-consciously.

'I shouldn't have taken hold of you the way I did,' said Arent, stopping in front of him. 'It weren't right, and I'm sorry about it.'

Sara cocked her head, impressed. She hadn't heard a lot of apologies in her life, certainly not from those who had no compelling reason to offer them.

Eggert's expression very clearly suggested that he believed this was a trick.

'Is all right,' he said nervously, shaking Arent's proffered hand.

Fearing some assault, he turned his face slightly away and braced himself. The mercenary smiled at him good-naturedly, then followed Sara through the red door, leaving Eggert blinking after them in bewilderment.

Arent escorted Sara a little way down the corridor, though not to her door.

She was glad of that. Those final few steps would indicate an intimacy she was keen to avoid. A solitary evening in his company and she already felt a strange tangle of emotions twisting in her breast.

She promised herself she would take shears to this tangle over the next few days. She had a purpose aboard the *Saardam* and she wouldn't compromise it for a childish infatuation. No matter how much she had enjoyed his company tonight.

'Goodnight,' said Arent, returning her hairpins.

'Goodnight,' responded Sara.

He obviously wanted to say something more, but, in the end, he inclined his head and walked back up the corridor, his hulking figure blocking the view outside.

Sara watched him depart, then opened her cabin door. She screamed.

Staring at her from the porthole, covered in the same bloody bandages she remembered from the docks, was the leper.

19

'Nerves?' repeated Sara, batting the word back at Reynier van Schooten with icicles on it.

Van Schooten and Captain Crauwels had come clattering into the cabin after hearing her scream, finding Creesjie and Lia comforting her. Arent had been the first to arrive, but he'd stuck his head out of the porthole, then run up on deck hoping to catch sight of the leper, taking the musketeer guarding the cabins with him.

Sara hadn't stopped shaking. Before Van Schooten had arrived, it had been fear. Now it was anger.

'It's been a gruelling day,' interjected Crauwels, in a pacifying tone that would make an angel throw its cloud at him. 'No one would blame you for having weary eyes, my lady.'

'You think I imagined it?' she said incredulously. Nobody else had seen the leper. Even Arent had been too slow. It had scrambled away when she screamed, frightening the animals in the pens above them, which were making an unholy din.

'Of course not, my lady. I simply think you mistook the …' Crauwels crouched a little, putting his head at the same level as Sara's, and stared through the porthole. 'The moon!' he declared triumphantly, seeing it outside.

'Does the moon wrap itself in bloody bandages?' demanded Sara witheringly. 'How strange I've never noticed that before.'

'My lady –'

'I know the difference between a face and the moon,' she yelled, furious at having to defend herself against so ridiculous a charge. If the leper had appeared at her husband's porthole, the *Saardam* would already be sailing back to Batavia.

'The only thing out there is a long drop,' grunted Van Schooten, his breath thick enough to make her eyes water. 'There's no ledge to stand on, and no way to climb down from the poop deck.'

Creesjie laid a gentle arm on Sara's. 'Calm now, dear heart,' she soothed.

Sara took a breath.

It wasn't the done thing to shout at a man in public, especially not high-ranking Company officers. Deference was something she was supposed to put on every morning, along with her cap and bodice.

'Please understand, my lady,' said Crauwels ingratiatingly, 'Indiamen sail on superstition as much as wind and waves. Won't be a man onboard who doesn't have a piece of the hull he kisses for luck, or a token he swears saved him from some catastrophe on his last voyage. If word gets around you saw a leper, whether it exists or not, these men will create it.

'Every dead bird as hits the mast, every broken arm, every bit of blood spilt on a crooked nail, they'll collect in a pile and claim it's the work of something malign. Next thing you know, sailors are getting their throats slit because they babbled in their sleep and it sounded like devilry.'

Dorothea bustled into the cabin with a mug of spiced wine for her mistress. She'd gone down to the galley to fetch it.

Sara had tried to dissuade her, but Dorothea believed spiced wine was the best thing for a nasty shock and wouldn't be dissuaded from her errand.

'Whatever you *think* you saw, keep it in this cabin,' demanded Van Schooten.

Dorothea handed the mug of spiced wine to Sara, then turned her iron glare on van Schooten. 'Know your place, merchant,' she warned. 'This is a high-born lady you're addressing. My mistress knows what she saw. Why do you think you know better?'

Van Schooten bore down on her. By his expression, it was obvious he thought that indulging the nonsense of a spoiled noble was intolerable enough without being ridiculed by an insolent servant.

'Listen to me —' he said, pointing.

'No! You listen to me, Chief Merchant,' interrupted Sara, stepping between them and jabbing her finger into his chest. 'Bosey threatened the *Saardam* in Batavia. That strange symbol appeared on the sail and now he's peering in port-holes. Something's happening on this ship and you need to take it seriously.'

'If the devil wants to sail aboard the *Saardam*, he buys a ticket like everybody else,' snapped van Schooten, his jaw clenched. 'Speak with your husband. If he tells me to investigate, I will. Until then, I've got real problems to attend to.'

He stalked out. Crauwels bowed courteously and followed.

Sara tried to chase after them, only to be held back by Lia and Creesjie.

'It won't do any good,' advised Creesjie. 'Anger makes good men stubborn and stubborn men petty. They won't hear you.'

Feeling wretched, Sara stared into Lia's concerned face. Her only duty aboard this ship was to protect her daughter, but nobody wanted to listen. They seemed hell-bent on sailing into whatever dark water awaited them.

'I'm sorry for this,' said Creesjie, sitting heavily on the chair and putting her head in her hands.

'It's hardly your fault,' said Sara, confused.

'The leper was searching for me, Sara. Don't you see. Old Tom must have sent it.'

Three heavy knocks shuddered the doorframe.

She didn't need to turn around to know it was Arent. Only his hands could be mistaken for battering rams.

'Anything?' asked Sara.

'No sign,' he said, still standing in the corridor, shy of entering. 'I've been up and down the weather decks.'

'Weather decks?'

'Those the sky can get at. The leper wouldn't have had time to get by me into the guts of the ship.' He held out a dagger in its sheath to her. 'If it appears again, stab it in the face with this.'

Sara took the present gratefully, weighing it in her hand.

'I swear to you, I saw it,' she said.

'That's why you're holding my dagger.'

'It was him: it was Bosey. I know it.'

Arent nodded.

'We watched him die,' she said, letting her fear out for the first time. 'How is that possible?'

Arent shrugged. 'Sammy once solved a case where a mason's dead wife asked him to build her a church,' he said. 'He investigated a case where two brothers dropped dead of broken hearts at exactly the same time, despite having not spoken to each other for six years. He isn't called unless the problem is impossible. Luckily for us, he's on this ship.'

'He's a prisoner, Arent. What is he going to do?'

'He's going to save us.'

Belief lit those delicate eyes. It was so fierce, it burnt away the arguments brewing within her. Sara had seen the same thing in predikants and mystics, usually before they went marching into harm's way with only the Lord's love for a shield.

Arent Hayes was a zealot.

His religion was Samuel Pipps.

20

'NERVES,' GRUMBLED A FOOTSORE Arent as he crossed the waist, carrying a sack over his shoulder. Van Schooten had given Sara's tale short shrift, but he hadn't seen her kneeling by Bosey's burnt body on the docks. He hadn't heard her voice when she'd asked Arent to give the leper mercy.

Sara Wessel had seen a man's flesh melted and it hadn't made her hysterical. It hadn't clouded her reason. She'd remained calm and clear-eyed, full of sorrow and compassion.

No, Sara wasn't one for nerves.

Arent stared at his scar, wondering why he hadn't told her about his connection to Old Tom. Much as he'd wanted to, the words had refused to pass his lips. Sammy always said to hold on to what you knew until you understood what it meant. It was a fig leaf for Arent's pride, but he accepted it gratefully.

The bell was ringing for midnight watch, hatches clattering open as sailors came grumbling on to the deck, bleary-eyed and bad-tempered from their bunks. Finding Arent abroad after dark, they glared and cursed under their breath, but they weren't any more inclined to interrupt him than they had been this afternoon.

Finally he arrived at the compartment under the forecastle, where the crew took their recreation. From inside, he heard a young voice whimpering for mercy.

'I never, I swear I didn't, it wasn't –'

'Go spilling ship business to strangers, will you?' responded an angry voice. 'How much did she pay you?'

There was a thud and a howl of pain.

Squeezing himself inside, Arent entered a room that was low-ceilinged and cheerless, lit by a swaying lantern belching out more smoke than light. Sailors were sitting against the walls, smoking their pipes and watching a young boy being beaten senseless by the slab of gut and shoulders that was Johannes Wyck.

The boy was on the floor, Wyck looming over him, his fists clenched, blood running off his knuckles.

'No, Mister Wyck, I didn't, I never –'

'You're a damned liar, Henri,' said Wyck, kicking the boy in the stomach. 'Where've you hid the coin? Where is it?'

This must have been the boy Sara spoke to this morning, Arent realised. She'd paid him three guilders for information on the leper's true identity.

'That's enough of that,' said Arent in a threatening rumble.

Johannes Wyck glanced over his shoulder, squinting at Arent's presence.

'This is ship business,' he sneered, revealing the rotten teeth in his mouth. 'Get yourself back where you belong.'

'And what happens to *him* when I do?' said Arent, nodding at the boy.

Wyck reached into his boot, withdrawing a small, rusty dagger. 'Whatever I damn well please.'

Arent showed no reaction. 'Is that the same dagger you used to cut out Bosey's tongue?'

That gave Wyck pause, but only briefly. 'It is at that,' he said, pressing his fingertip against the blade. 'Not the sharpest thing, so I had to saw rather than slice. Took a bit of sweat, but it was a nice enough job in the end.'

'Was that ship business, as well?'

Wyck spread his arms wide, indicating the breadth of his kingdom. 'Everything I do is ship business, isn't it, lads?' The crew murmured their agreement. Some grudgingly. Others with more enthusiasm. Evidently, ship's business wasn't always popular.

Wyck leered at him. 'And I'll tell you what else is ship's business. The disappearance of a passenger who wanders past the mainmast and is cut to ribbons by the crew.'

Steps approached from behind, half a dozen sailors slinking out of the dark, faces full of murder. 'Nothing but misfortune on a ship like this,' said Wyck.

Arent stared at him, meeting his one good eye. It seemed to glitter with the remembrance of every dreadful thing it had witnessed.

'What does Laxagarr mean?' asked Arent. 'I heard it was Nornish. They say you speak the language.'

'Run along now, soldier,' said Wyck.

'Not without the boy.'

Wyck squatted next to the stricken lad, driving his dagger into the floorboards beside his head. 'Did you hear that, young Henri? This nice soldier's fretting over you; fears for you in nasty Mr Wyck's company. What do you say to that?'

Wyck's eye lingered on Arent, as Henri lifted his beaten head from the floor.

'Cark off, soldier,' gasped Henri, through bloody teeth. 'Better dead than …' He swallowed painfully, '… be helped … by you.'

Exhausted, his head thudded back on to the floorboards.

Wyck tapped boy's cheek. 'You're not welcome here, soldier,' he said in a low, dangerous voice. 'And this is the only warning you'll get.'

'No,' said Arent in a flat voice. 'This is the only warning *you*'ll get. I've business at this end of the ship, which means I'll be passing through this time every night. If any of you bastards makes me lose a single step, I'll slit your throat and throw you overboard.'

Something savage showed itself in his eyes, and the sailors took a half step back. But, as quickly as it had come, it was gone. Arent lifted the hatch and started down the ladder into the sailmaker's cabin.

The sailmaker himself was snoring in his hammock, and he didn't stir as Arent lifted the second hatch, descending into the compartment housing Sammy's cell. The ladder was as awkward to navigate as it had been that morning, but eventually he managed to wriggle himself down.

As promised, Drecht had stationed a musketeer in the room. To Arent's surprise, it was Thyman, the one Sammy had accused of cheating his friend that morning. Eggert was guarding the passengers and Thyman was guarding Sammy. Evidently, Drecht wanted the bickering pair as far apart as possible.

Thyman leapt up as Arent entered, but quickly settled back down when he saw who it was.

A tiny hatch led into the cargo hold behind them, the smell of spices scratching Arent's throat as he struggled to work the locking peg to Sammy's cell free. Finally, it creaked open, the acrid smell of vomit and excrement elbowing its way into the open air.

'Sammy?' coughed Arent, covering his mouth as he peered into the cell.

Shards of moonlight struck through the hatch above, revealing three empty hooks on the wall, and the lower corner of a pillar, but everything else was ink.

Something thumped and Sammy came scrambling out in a mad panic of arms and legs, desperately sucking in air. Moonlight touched his face and he hissed in pain, shielding his eyes from the glare.

Arent knelt beside him, laying a reassuring hand on his arm. Sammy's body was quivering, and he was terribly pale, his whiskers coated in vomit.

Arent balled his fists in rage. He couldn't leave his friend to this torment.

Sammy squinted at him through his fingers, bewildered. 'Arent?'

'I'm sorry I couldn't come sooner,' he said, handing over the jug of wine.

'I didn't expect you to come at all,' replied Sammy, ripping the cork out of the jug and gulping the wine, the red liquid spilling down his chin. 'I thought I was trapped in there for ever.' He stopped, suddenly agitated. 'You shouldn't be here, Arent. If the governor general finds out –'

'He knows,' interrupted Arent. 'He's agreed to allow midnight walks, so long as I accompany you. I'm going to work on getting you daylight.'

'How did you make him …' Sammy frowned, confounded. 'What did he want from you? What did you have to barter for this boon?' His voice was rising. 'Tell him you don't want it. I'll not have you indebted to a man like Jan Haan. I'd rather rot in the dark.'

'Nothing was bartered,' said Arent, trying to calm him. 'There's no debt. It was a favour.'

'Why would he grant you such a thing?'

Arent glanced at Thyman uncomfortably, then lowered his voice. 'Does it matter?'

Sammy stared at him suspiciously, those keen eyes narrowing as he began to burrow for Arent's secrets.

Shaking his head, he turned his face away. Out of courtesy, he didn't use his gifts on Arent.

From above them, the sailmaker stamped on the floor, shaking dust down from the ceiling.

'Take your sweet nothings outside,' he barked. 'I'm trying to sleep.'

Still perturbed, Sammy climbed the ladders, eventually finding his way into the open air. The sailors had scattered to their duties, and Arent joined his friend outside without incident. He was staring at the moonlight running down the rigging and the sails like molten silver.

'It's beautiful,' he said in awe. He lingered on the view a moment, then walked over to the railing. 'Turn your back, please,' he said.

'Why?'

'I must attend my ablutions.'

'Just go, it's nothing I haven't –'

'Arent, please,' he exclaimed. 'I have very little dignity left, and I'd like to keep hold of what remains.'

Sighing, Arent turned his back.

Sammy yanked down his breeches, sticking his arse over the water.

'The governor general is a dangerous man,' he groaned as excrement poured out of him, splashing in the sea. 'I've tried to spare you his scrutiny, so tell me, for my own peace of mind, why would he agree to let me out of that cell?'

'Because he's as family to me,' admitted Arent, taking a step away from the smell. 'I call him uncle, but father would be nearer to it.'

'Father?' replied Sammy, in a strangled voice.

'He's my grandfather's best friend,' explained Arent. 'Their lands are next to each other in Frisia, the province where I grew up. I spent weekends at his estate when I was a boy. He taught me how to fence and ride, among other things.'

'Forgive me, Arent,' said Sammy, wiping his arse on a piece of rope, before hitching up his breeches. 'I know your manners aren't those of a soldier born, but how did your grandfather come to befriend somebody as powerful as Governor General Jan Haan.'

Arent hesitated, struggling to make the words fit. The answer had been buried in him so long, it had grown roots.

'My grandfather is Casper van den Berg,' he said, at last.

'You're a Berg!?' Sammy took a half step back, as if the information had been tossed into his arms. 'The Van den Bergs are the wealthiest family in the Provinces. Casper van den Berg is one of the Gentlemen 17. Your family practically run the Company.'

'Really? I wish somebody had told me that before I left home,' said Arent wryly.

Sammy's mouth opened and closed. Then opened and closed again.

'Why the hell are you on this ship?' he exploded. 'Your family could buy you a ship of your own. They could buy you a fleet!'

'What would I do with a fleet?'

'Anything you damn well please.'

Arent couldn't deny the logic of it, but he didn't have an answer that wouldn't embarrass them both. He'd left home at twenty because after seven years of studying under the Gentlemen 17, he'd seen the breadth of the life on offer and realised how small it was. The rich mistakenly believed their wealth was a servant, delivering them whatever they wanted.

They were wrong.

Wealth was their master and it was the only voice they heeded. Friendships were sacrificed at its behest, principles trampled to protect it. No matter how much they had, it was never enough. They went mad chasing more until they sat lonely atop their hoard, despised and afraid.

Arent had wanted more. Having turned his back on power and wealth, he found himself immune to their lure. Instead, he sought a place where honour mattered. Where strength was used to protect the weak, and thrones weren't automatically handed from one madman to the next.

But every land was the same. Strength was the only currency of merit, and power was the only goal. Kindness, compassion and empathy were trampled, exploited as weakness.

Then he'd met Sammy.

Here was a commoner, born with nothing, who'd upended the natural order by virtue of his cleverness. In pursuit of his goal, he'd accuse a noble as readily as a peasant. Here was somebody for whom the old rules didn't apply. Through Sammy, Arent saw the world he aspired to, like a distant land spied through a smudged glass. Sammy was what Arent had left home to find, but their friendship would never allow him to admit it. He'd never hear the end of it.

'This is the life I chose,' he shrugged, his tone ending the conversation.

Sammy gave in with a sigh and collected a pail from a peg. A long piece of rope was tied to the handle and he cast the pail over the side of the ship into the ocean, before dragging it back up, water sloshing out. The pails were normally used for washing clothes, or cooling wood that was threatening to warp, but he upended it over his head, revealing the pink skin behind the filth.

Twice more he cast the pail over the side, washing his arms and legs, then stripping off his shirt to scrub his scrawny body. It was a week since he'd last eaten more than a fist's worth of food, a fact screamed by every rib now on display.

When he was bathed, he adjusted his sodden clothing and smoothed his breeches, even drawing his fingers through his oily, tangled hair.

Arent watched him wordlessly. From any other man, this would seem pointless vanity, but Sammy was renowned for his beautiful comportment as much as his cleverness. He dressed, danced and dined exactingly, his manners exquisite in all things. If that pride still burnt within him, then he hadn't given up hope.

'How do I look?' asked Sammy, turning on the spot.

'Like you spent the night with an ox.'

'I didn't want your mother to be the only one.'

Arent laughed and gave Sammy the sleeping draught from the pouch at his hip. 'This is from Sara Wessel,' he said. 'It will help you sleep. Hopefully, it will make you more comfortable while I work out a way to free you.'

'This is a wonderful gift,' said Sammy, tearing out the cork to sniff the tincture. 'Please, pass along my thanks. I saw her quality on the docks, but this is … I've never met a woman to match her.'

Arent agreed but said nothing, for fear of giving himself away. Instead, he handed Sammy a hunk of bread he'd stolen from the galley.

'Know who's trying to sink us yet?' he asked.

'That's your job, Arent. I've been imprisoned in a dark room all day.' He bit into the loaf, savouring the taste. Arent had tried some at dinner. It was hard as a moneylender's heart, but Sammy looked as though he'd never had anything better.

'Only difference between today and most other days is that you don't have good wine and a pipe,' countered Arent.

Finishing the bread, Sammy linked his arm into his friend's. 'I'll concede the compliment in the insult,' he said. 'Shall we walk? My legs are stiff.'

As they had a hundred nights before, the bear and sparrow strolled together in amiable silence. They walked across the waist, past the two yawls strapped to the deck, and up the stairs to the quarterdeck. Shadows shifted around them, piles of rope revealing themselves to be sailors curled up on deck, while lurking bodies were exposed as buckets hanging from poles.

Step by step, Arent wasn't sure whether he should be laughing at his own jitteriness, or swinging punches into the air, just to be safe. He didn't relax until they arrived on the quarterdeck, where the first mate was tending the sniffling young carpenter beaten by Wyck. He was speaking to him in a comforting voice. Whatever Larme's words, they seemed to be pouring some iron into the boy's bones.

Another staircase brought them to the poop deck, where the animal pens were kept. Hearing their footsteps on the boards, the sows began grunting and sniffling at the wooden bars, believing they were about to be let out, while the chickens scratched at the wood.

Arent peered over the railing. The passenger cabins were directly below, candlelight spilling out of their portholes. Only Sara and Creesjie's were dim, their deadlights closed in case the leper should return in the night.

'What troubles you?' asked Sammy, noticing his inspection.

'Sara Wessel saw the leper at her porthole this evening,' replied Arent.

'The leper from the docks? The one you put your sword through?'

'His real name was Bosey,' explained Arent, delivering the information that Sara had uncovered about this man's mysterious bargain with Old Tom, and how his tongue had been cut out by Johannes Wyck.

'Tormented and returning to torment, eh?' said Sammy, who was kneeling on the ground, running his fingertips across the rough planks, searching for any sign of the leper's passing. 'Do you think she imagined it?'

'No,' replied Arent.

'Then she didn't, which raises a rather particular question.' Sammy paused his search. 'Well, two actually.' He considered it. 'Three,' he corrected himself.

'Who's pretending to be the dead man at her porthole?' ventured Arent.

'That's one.' Sammy leapt to his feet and peered intently at the dark water below. 'It's a sheer drop with no handholds, so how did he arrive there? And how did he get away once seen?'

'Well, he didn't come this way,' said Arent. 'I was up here in less than a minute after she screamed. He would have had to run by me to get away.'

'Could he have hidden in the animal pens?'

'I'd have seen him through the bars.'

Sammy ran his hand along the railing. 'He would have needed ropes to lower himself down and he wouldn't have had time to climb back up, then untie them.'

'And if he'd dropped into the water, Sara would have heard a splash.'

Sammy walked towards the mizzenmast, which rose up between the poop and quarterdecks, then tugged on the rigging that disappeared over the side of the ship. The ropes were attached to a thick beam that jutted out of the *Saardam*'s hull.

'That beam down there is the only place he could have stood, and it's much too far away from the porthole.' Abruptly Sammy licked the wood, but the disappointment on his face suggested it yielded no answers. 'Tell me about this Old Tom.'

'It's some sort of devil, apparently.'

There was nobody quite like Sammy for a diminishing glare, and the one he threw at Arent could have stripped the bark off a tree.

'I didn't say I believed it,' protested Arent, who'd known his entire life what was waiting for him in the dark. As a boy his father had caught him yawning during one of his sermons, beating him so severely it was feared he might never wake again. His mother had wept for three days, until his father gathered the servants, dragged her down the staircase and slapped her back and forth across the Great Hall, bellowing in righteous fury.

Her grief represented a lack of faith, he'd said. Arent had been delivered before God to apologise for his heresy in person. If his regret was sincere, he'd be returned. Should he die, then it must surely reveal his lack of devotion. Prayer, not tears, he'd argued, was the only tonic now.

Arent had been returned two days later. Devotion had nothing to do with it.

Most people woke up from something like that with a hole in their memory. They felt like they'd been asleep, they said.

Arent remembered everything.

He'd travelled into the afterlife, hollering for help and hearing nothing back. He knew there was no God waiting. No devil. No saints or sinners. There were only people and the stories they told themselves. He'd seen it himself. People gave the heavens a voice, so they had something to ask for: a better harvest, a healthy child or a milder winter. God was hope, and mankind needed hope the way it needed warmth, food and ale.

But with hope came disappointment.

The downtrodden yearned for stories to explain their misfortunes, though what they really wanted was somebody to blame for their misery. It was impossible to set fire to the blight that had ruined your crops, but a blight was easily summoned by a witch, at which point any poor woman would do.

Old Tom wasn't a devil, thought Arent. He was an old man within kicking distance.

'My uncle told me Old Tom devastated the Provinces thirty years ago, destroying villages and noble families,' explained Arent. 'Apparently, it offers people their heart's desire in return for terrible favours. It left a strange sign wherever it went – an eye with a tail. That same mark was on the sail when we set off from Batavia, and it's also on my wrist,' he said candidly.

'Your wrist?' Sammy was taken aback. 'Why would it be on your wrist?'

'When I was a boy, I went hunting with my father,' replied Arent. 'Three days later I returned with this scar and he didn't return at all, and I don't know what happened.'

Sammy blinked at Arent in surprise. 'So you got the scar around the same time this Old Tom was splashing its mark across the Provinces?'

'I think I was the first person to carry it. Or one of them, my uncle wasn't sure.'

'Show me,' demanded Sammy, pulling Arent over to a lantern on the mizzenmast. 'And tell me everything you know about it.'

'I don't know anything, except that I drew this mark on a few doors in a nearby village out of spite,' explained Arent, as Sammy inspected it. 'I didn't realise the harm it would do. An old beggar called Old Tom ended up being beaten to death by some scared villagers.'

'Old Tom?' repeated Sammy. 'So this mark got free of you, then spread like a plague wearing your dead beggar's name. Heaven's sake, this isn't just a demon. It's *your* demon.'

'It was an accident.'

'The worst things often are.'

Sammy's small fingers probed Arent's huge hand, but even with the extra light, there was nothing new to be learned about the scar. It was barely even visible, any more. The problematary didn't bother to hide his disappointment.

'You make for a very poor clue,' he chided, releasing Arent's hand. 'Who knows about the scar and the use you put it to?'

'My grandfather and my uncle. My mother did, but she died not long after I was taken away.'

'Broken heart?'

'Pox.'

'What about Sara Wessel?'

'My uncle may have told her, but I don't think so. She hasn't mentioned it. Otherwise, nobody. My grandfather ordered me to keep it under my tongue. He said the past was poisoned ground and those who lingered there died. I thought he was trying to keep me from thinking about it, but my uncle told me an English witchfinder had been hunting for anybody afflicted by the mark, so they hid me away. I didn't know that at the time, though.'

Sammy murmured appreciatively. 'Your grandfather sounds like a wise man. What do you remember about the day your father disappeared?'

'Very little. We were a few hours into the woods, tracking some boar. We didn't speak. I was only there to carry my father's pack. A man called to us for help.'

'Somebody you knew?'

'I don't think so.'

'And then?'

'We called back, then went to find him. After that …' Arent shrugged. That was his last memory of that day. For years, he'd tried to break through it, but it was like scrambling up a cliff face. 'I woke up on the road, shivering wet with this scar on my wrist.'

Sammy became watchful, his next question tentative. 'Was your father's body ever found?'

Arent shook his head.

'Then he could be alive?'

'Only if the devil has a sense of humour,' grunted Arent. 'My father was a predikant and his congregation was the only thing he loved. If he'd survived, he would have come back for them. You can't believe my father's involved in this! You said to rule out ghosts.'

'Ghosts are God's problem. The living must deal with me,' declared Sammy, ideas hammering themselves together behind his eyes 'But to call him a ghost, there'd have to be a body. It's not like we haven't seen this before, Arent. Remember The Case of the Empty Spire, where the –'

'Long dead sister was living in the walls,' shuddered Arent. He'd been the one tasked with dragging her into the daylight. He'd spent a week washing the stink off his body.

'What else do you know about this Old Tom?' asked Sammy, his thoughts still clearly on Arent's father.

'It was driven out of the Provinces by an English witch-finder named Pieter Fletcher, who was the second husband of Creesjie Jens.'

'Your uncle's mistress?'

Arent nodded. 'Four years ago, Old Tom found him in Amsterdam. Fletcher packed his family into a carriage and fled to Lille, but it followed and murdered him. It left its mark above his body. Creesjie Jens believes it's raised Bosey from the dead to kill the rest of his family on the *Saardam*.'

Sammy ran a hand across his face, trying to disguise the worry washing across it. 'Arent, *you* were in Lille four years ago.'

Arent didn't need reminding. The shame blotted him like a wax stamp.

It had been the first case he'd been trusted to untangle alone. Sammy had sent him to recover a jewel stolen from the

Gentlemen 17. After four days of investigation, he accused a clerk named Edward Coil of the crime. They were putting the noose around his neck when Sammy arrived on the back of an exhausted horse, holding a handful of splinters that proved Arent had got it wrong. He'd been in such a hurry to accuse Coil that he'd missed them.

Sammy had been kind, kinder than Arent had any right to expect. Time and again, he'd offered Arent another case, another chance to prove himself capable, but the mercenary knew his limitations. He'd seen them up close. That was Sammy's gift to everybody who met him. An instant under-standing of what they could never be.

'You can't believe I slaughtered Creesjie Jens's husband,' protested Arent. 'I didn't even know him.'

'I know you didn't, you damn fool, but either somebody's keen to make us think otherwise, or it's a coincidence. Did Creesjie give any reason the demon might have waited so long to enact is revenge?'

'She fled. She's been moving from country to country ever since.'

'She was moved, or she was ushered?'

'Ushered?'

'There are three people on this boat connected to Old Tom. Fate rarely reveals itself so nakedly.'

'Three?'

'You, Creesjie and your uncle,' explained Sammy impatiently. 'How did you all come to be here?'

'I'm here because you're here,' pointed out Arent.

'And I'm here, because the governor general ordered it so.'

'As is Creesjie Jens. My uncle forced her to depart Batavia earlier than she was intending.'

'Why?'

'She's beautiful and he enjoys her company?'

Sammy seemed sceptical. 'So am I, and I'm in a cell,' he grumbled. 'What about your uncle? Why is he here?'

'He's sailing back to join the Gentlemen 17 and deliver The Folly.'

'Yes, but why is he on *this* ship? Surely your uncle could have chosen any ship in the fleet. Why did he pick the *Saardam*?'

'Captain Crauwels is the best sailor in the Company. They've sailed together in the past and he trusts him.'

Sammy blew out a long, troubled breath. 'It all comes back to your uncle, doesn't it? He's like a damn whirlpool and we're all caught in the churning water.' He considered Arent. 'If your uncle had ordered you to board this ship, would you have done it?'

'Not without you.'

'And if he'd tried to order me to board the *Saardam*, I'd have asked him why he was so keen for me to be here.'

'What are you thinking?'

'That imprisoning me was the only way to ensure *you'd* be on the *Saardam*.'

Arent bristled. 'My uncle can be brusque, and even cruel, but he loves me, Sammy. He'd never do anything to put me in danger.'

Sammy looked out at the bright lanterns of the fleet. 'We're losing sight of the dead,' he chided himself. 'For all the strangeness aboard this ship, we only have one actual crime to investigate. Bosey didn't ignite his own robes and it wasn't his voice that threatened the ship. Until we understand more, I'm treating his death as murder. Have you talked to his friends?'

'I've tried, but it's like trying to pry open traps.'

'Then try harder. He must have told somebody about this bargain he struck. Somehow you two are connected, so let's see if he knew you. Or your family. Find out where Bosey's from. Perhaps he suffered in the village where Old Tom died.'

Arent nodded, but Sammy wasn't finished with his labours. 'And it would be worth understanding what Laxagarr means.'

'Sara's already tried,' responded Arent. 'We think it's Nornish, and the only person who speaks the language is the man who cut Bosey's tongue out.'

'That's useful, because we need an explanation for that, as well.'

'Okay,' agreed Arent doubtfully, remembering his earlier encounter with Wyck. 'What else?'

'Rags and bandages aren't hard to find. Convince Captain Crauwels to search the ship, if you can. Otherwise appeal to your uncle. If we're lucky, the leper's costume will reveal itself in the company of the man who's been wearing it.'

Sammy stared at the lanterns on the water again, frowning. 'Our second avenue of investigation is simpler. If this leper is the threat, how does he mean to assail a ship this size? Did you talk to the constable in the gunpowder store?'

'He reckons blowing the gunpowder wouldn't do it,' said Arent. 'The constable believed the quickest way to sink the *Saardam* was to kill the captain. By his thinking, Crauwels is the only thing keeping this crew from mutiny.'

'He's got a fine head on his shoulders has our constable,' said Sammy with admiration. 'What else did he say?'

'That the threat could come from the fleet.'

Sammy mulled it over. 'Another ship turning its cannons on us, perhaps?'

'It's an idea,' replied Arent.

'A bold one,' agreed Sammy. 'And a troubling one.'

'Why's that?'

Sammy gestured to the lanterns on the water. 'Do you remember how many ships left Batavia?' he asked.

Arent shrugged. He hadn't troubled himself to count.

'Seven,' supplied Sammy.

'Okay, seven,' said Arent, confused. 'So what?'

'So why are there eight lights on the water?'

Four men stood at the railing, water lapping beneath them. Three of them were staring at the Eighth Lantern in the distance, while Sammy stared down at the first mate. Feeling the itch of scrutiny, Isaack Larme peered up at him, that familiar scowl twisting his face.

'What you looking at, prisoner?'

'A dwarf,' replied Sammy bluntly. 'I've never seen a dwarf in the Company before. Mostly, your kind are –'

'Fools,' finished Larme. 'It's our job to call nobles like you cun—'

'Isaack,' growled Crauwels.

Arent had alerted the first mate to the mysterious light, and he'd fetched the captain in turn. Crauwels was more than halfway drunk still, irritable and missing his bed, but the last thing he wanted was Sammy's blood on Isaack Larme's dagger, which was usually the way arguments with his first mate finished.

'I'm the first mate of the ship,' spat Isaack Larme. 'I'll not be looked down on by a prisoner.'

'That wasn't my intent,' said Sammy, as if surprised he'd given offence.

'Isaack's the best first mate I've ever had,' said the captain, still staring at the lanterns. 'And the only other person I know who can keep our bastard of a boatswain in line,' he added darkly.

'What do you think of the lights, Captain?' asked Arent, hoping to change the topic before Sammy vexed Isaack Larme any further.

'Well, it aint pirates,' he said, scratching at his ginger whiskers. 'Whoever it is wants us to know they're there. Pirates come quiet and they don't attack convoys. They pick off solitary ships.'

'Could be a straggler out of Batavia,' suggested Larme, fingering the half-face charm around his neck.

'Could be,' said Crauwels, running a hand through his hair, flexing the muscles in his arm.

Crauwels was clearly a man who admired himself a great deal and wanted others to do likewise, thought Arent.

'Keep a watch on the fleet,' continued Crauwels. 'Just you, Isaack. I don't want word of this getting around and spooking the crew. Might be nothing, but if anything changes tonight, I want to know.'

'Aye, Captain.'

'And first thing tomorrow, have a lookout lay eyes on her,' he said. 'Let's see whose colours she's flying.'

'Captain,' agreed Larme.

The four men dispersed, Arent accompanying Sammy back across the waist towards the bow of the ship.

Once they were out of earshot, Sammy nudged Arent. 'Did you notice the charm Larme wore around his neck?'

'I saw it this afternoon,' said Arent. 'Bit of cracked wood on a piece of string, isn't it?'

'It's half a face, Arent. The matching half of the piece Bosey clung to for comfort on the docks. The edges married up.'

Sammy couldn't have caught more than a glimpse of Bosey's charm, but Arent didn't doubt his recollection. Never forgetting was another of Sammy's gifts. Maybe the most unfortunate of them. He could recall every conversation he'd ever had, every mystery he'd solved, every lunch and when he'd eaten it.

Arent would have envied him, except Sammy wasn't somebody who wanted envying.

The past was filled with sharp things, he'd said.

The pain he'd felt when a thorn scratched him as a child was the same pain he felt remembering it. He couldn't reach for a memory without drawing blood doing it. No wonder he was the way he was. Never looking back, always running forward.

A shriek came from behind them and turning around, they saw Isaack Larme trying to drag a young woman out of the shadows. She was broad and strong and taller than the dwarf, who was struggling to hold on to her.

Growling, he punched her in the stomach ending her resistance, then hurled her gasping on to the ground in front of Crauwels.

Arent moved to help her, but Sammy caught his arm and shook his head in warning.

'You're the predikant's ward, aren't you?' said Crauwels, taken aback. 'What are you doing out here after curfew? It's dangerous.'

'My name's Isabel,' she snapped, glowering at the dwarf as she tried to draw breath.

'And it's a fine name, but not an explanation,' said Crauwels, crouching in front of her. 'What are you doing lurking in the shadows, Isabel?'

'Was just out walking and got startled,' she gasped, rubbing her stomach. 'That was all.'

'Eavesdropping more like,' snarled Larme, earning a filthy glare from Isabel.

Crauwels let out a long breath through his nose. 'Ship's rules are for your safety, and ours.' He smiled a bright, dangerous smile. 'Mainly *your* safety, though. This conversation was private and it needs to be kept that way. If word gets out, I'll know exactly who needs talking to, understand?'

She nodded, somehow marrying simple acceptance with a burning fury.

'Get away then,' he said. 'And don't let me catch you skulking around the deck any more.'

Shooting a glance of misgiving at the forecastle, Isabel got to her feet and headed back towards the compartment under the half deck.

In the darkness, a figure slipped away unseen.

21

THE EIGHTH LANTERN VANISHED a few hours before dawn.

Fearing an impending attack, Isaack Larme summoned Captain Crauwels, who ordered all hands to battle stations. Signals were passed across the fleet to make ready, while Johannes Wyck kicked the crew out of their hammocks, manhandling them up the stairs in whatever they were wearing.

As the anchors were raised and the sails lowered for manoeuvring, hemp was yanked out of the cannon barrels and the wedges pulled from beneath their wheels. The gunpowder store was flung open, sailors rolling dozens of kegs through the ship, then pouring their contents into the cannons and ramming them solid.

Useless among the commotion, the passengers on the orlop deck huddled together, waiting for that first volley of cannon fire. In the cabins, Sara clutched Lia's shaking body, whispering courage. Creesjie hugged Marcus and Osbert, soothing her two young sons with songs.

The predikant and Isabel prayed together, while Arent watched from the quarterdeck. He wasn't one to turn his back on the enemy, no matter what size it was.

Governor General Haan woke early, as was his custom, then worked at his desk, issuing instructions to Chamberlain Vos as normal. Only the slight tremble of his hand suggested something was amiss.

In the darkness, the *Saardam* bristled like a cat. For two hours, they braced themselves, fear becoming confusion, then boredom. Dawn broke, the night turning to ash, before crumbling away entirely.

Climbing the rigging, the lookout shaded his eyes and peered at every point on the compass.

'She's not out there,' he called down to Crauwels and the first mate. 'She's disappeared, Captain.'

22

A KNOCK ON HER door brought Sara lurching awake, her fingers immediately tightening around the dagger under her hand. She'd fallen asleep in her chair at the writing desk, staring at the porthole, waiting for the leper to reappear. She was in her nightgown, her red hair unpinned, curls falling around her shoulders. Freckles blossomed on her nose and cheeks.

Lia was sleeping in her bunk, her breaths whistling ever so slightly.

The knock came again.

'Come,' said Sara.

Holding a cup of berry tea, Dorothea made her way inside, taking in the scene before her with a disapproving glance.

'Odd noises coming from Viscountess Dalvhain's cabin this morning,' said Dorothea, laying the tea before Sara. Red and purple berries bobbed on the surface. They were a particular favourite of the family, so Sara had asked her to bring some for the journey.

'Odd?' said Sara, her thoughts moving slowly. It wasn't uncommon for Dorothea to begin a conversation with gossip, but it was rare Sara had to deal with it this early in the morning. Normally, the devil himself couldn't have roused her at this hour. Batavia was so hot nothing could be achieved by day, which left her hosting midnight banquets and balls for the city's damp nobility. For the last thirteen years, she'd been late to bed and late to rise, considering dawn something that only truly unfortunate people had to suffer through.

Unfortunately, the predikant had decided his sermon should be heard without sailors shouting curses over him.

'Sort of a scraping noise,' continued Dorothea. 'Went on for a few seconds, then stopped and started again. I couldn't quite place it, but it was familiar …' She trailed off.

Sara took a sip of the sweet tea. It was one of the many things she'd miss in France.

'Did you manage to sleep?' she asked Dorothea.

'Enough,' she replied, obviously still troubled by the strange noise. 'You?'

Sara's eyes were raw, with dark pouches beneath. She didn't look like she'd ever slept. She didn't look like she'd ever learned how. 'A little,' she replied, still staring at the porthole.

'Should I wake Lia?' asked Dorothea, glancing at the sleeping miss.

'Let her abide awhile, we've got time before the sermon begins.' Sara stared at her daughter tenderly, then roused herself. 'Did you manage to ask any more of the passengers about that strange word, Laxagarr?'

Dorothea opened a drawer, sorting out her mistress's clothes for the day.

Sara was certain this was to hide the disapproval on her face. From past experience, she knew that Dorothea had very strong views on what a lady should and shouldn't do. The 'shouldn't' column was excessively long, and the 'should' correspondingly short.

She would be thinking that it was unseemly for a woman of Sara's position to be playing thief-taker, but she would have her way, as always. And, as always, her husband would eventually grow tired and put an end to it. Probably violently.

Sara shivered, imagining that day. Dorothea was right. If she carried on like this, eventually her husband would punish her for it, but how could she stop while Lia's life was in danger?

'Asked everybody, but none knew it,' replied Dorothea. 'Might be a few passengers I didn't get to, so I'll catch them during mid-morning exercise.'

'I'd appreciate that.'

Sara finished her tea and Dorothea helped her dress. Lia woke shortly after, but her toilet was half the work of her mama's. Her skin was pale and flawless, requiring no powder, and the brush ran through her dark hair like a carp up a stream.

When all was in readiness, the three of them walked into the humid morning air. It was that strange time when the sun and stars tried to bustle by each another, one coming and the other going. Four bells had yet to be rung for dawn, and the *Saardam* lay at anchor. The ocean was calm and glassy.

Considering the hour, the deck was surprisingly crowded.

The predikant had made it known he would be holding Mass beneath the mainmast, shortly before the day's sailing began. Somehow, he'd wrangled special dispensation for the orlop deck passengers to attend, and they had turned out in great numbers.

Captain Crauwels and his officers were speaking in low concerned voices of last night's mysterious light.

'That lantern belonged to an Indiaman, I'd know it anywhere,' said Isaack Larme.

'Then how did it disappear so quickly?' demanded Van Schooten. 'It was gone a few hours before dawn. Even an Indiaman unladen couldn't have travelled beyond our sight in that time. There wasn't the wind. It's a damn ghost ship, I'm telling you.'

As Sara and Lia approached, the officers fell silent and shuffled aside, allowing them to join the governor general and Chamberlain Vos at the front of the congregation. As in Amsterdam, nobility stood closest to the predikant, hoping to catch his sweeping gaze and, through him, feel God's own eyes upon them.

Dorothea stayed at the back with the other servants.

Sara knelt beside her husband, who didn't acknowledge her in any way. As always, she felt that slight trepidation in his presence.

Craning her neck, she saw Creesjie on the other side of him with Marcus and Osbert fidgeting beside her, restless as ever. They were being watched by that mardijker girl, Isabel, who was smiling slightly.

On the far side of the mainmast, around twenty sailors milled around, waiting for the sermon to start. Sara hadn't expected to see them. She'd heard their language, caught their predatory stares when a woman passed by. If God spoke to them, His was a tiny voice among the catcalls of sin and vice.

'This morning we celebrate our good fortune,' began Sander Kers in a booming voice. 'For aboard this ship, we witness God's glory first-hand. Take a moment, friends, look up at the sails, look at the planks, look at the sea beneath. Sailing isn't a matter of rigging and navigation; it's divinity itself, a hundred blessings showing us God's favour. What is wrought here is impossible, unless He makes it possible. The wind is His breath, the waves His hands. Make no mistake, it is He who guides us across the ocean.'

Sara felt her heart lift. At first glance, she'd thought the predikant a frail old man, likely to give a sermon covered in dust. But channelling God's word had transformed him. That stooped back had straightened and his finger carved through the air energetically, cajoling and invoking.

'Which of you bastards stole the handle of the capstan wheel!'

The sermon stopped, run aground on the furious figure of Johannes Wyck. Sara had never seen the man before, but Arent had described him well enough. He had a dent in his bald head and an eyepatch, a spiderweb of scars surrounding it. A gut and broad shoulders sat atop bowed legs, like they could barely support his weight.

He was stomping through the stinking heap of sailors who'd gathered behind the mainmast to hear the predikant talk, yanking men around by their shoulders to glare at their faces.

'Four handles when battle stations were called and three this morning,' he screamed at them. 'That's ship property, which one of you's got it? Tell me now.'

The sailors wore a mixture of fear and bafflement.

'Capstan makes it easier to raise the anchor, right? If we don't find it, I'm going to pick ten of you every day to haul it up with your bare hands.'

They murmured in dismay, but none dared voice their displeasure too loudly.

'Tell me now, or –'

He stopped mid-threat, staring at the congregation in astonishment.

Sara tried to follow his glare, but Wyck was already backing away. Catching her staring, his eyes snapped to her. They were dirty things, sparkling with menace. He saluted her mockingly, a strange smirk on his lips.

The predikant coughed, regaining their attention.

'As I was saying, we should accuse not, for judgement is the Lord's work.' He seemed to miss the irony. 'Serve Him with compassion. Serve Him with forgiveness and know, that in His love, you are saved! For, as surely, as timbers nailed together keep this ship afloat, so the bonds of brotherhood will keep us safe against what trials are to come,' he finished.

Sara shuddered as the sermon continued. There'd been something oddly threatening in this passage. Others must have felt it too, because they were glancing at each other uncomfortably.

He went on for an hour, until, finally, his voice faded.

The congregation broke apart like lumps of fat in a stew. Sara wanted to speak with the predikant, but he was immediately accosted by Reynier van Schooten, who dragged him off to one side.

'I need to speak with you, privately,' he said, under his breath.

'Of course, of course,' said the predikant. 'What's the matter, my son?'

Van Schooten glanced around furtively. His eyes passed across Sara as if she wasn't even there, then snagged on Guard Captain Drecht, widening in alarm. 'Can we speak in my quarters?'

'I must offer confession to the passengers and crew, but when my duties are settled, I'll seek you out.'

'Confession *is* what I require.'

'For what sin?'

He leant closer, whispering the answer. Alarm showed on the predikant's face. 'How could you not know?' he demanded.

'Just come, please. As soon as you can.' Before Sander could question him any further, he darted away.

Isabel appeared out of the crowd and handed Sander his cane. He was dabbing sweat from his forehead with the sleeve of his tattered robe. He was red-faced and breathless, as if the sermon had taken all his strength.

'Fine sermon, Predikant,' said Sara, nodding a greeting.

Her husband and Vos were heading back towards the great cabin, their heads bowed in conversation.

'It was insufficient.' Sander was visibly annoyed at himself. 'There are many souls to be saved aboard a ship such as this, and I'm afraid stronger words may be necessary.'

Sara shot Dorothea a meaningful glance, and the maid took Marcus and Osbert to see the sniffling sows on the poop deck.

When they were out of earshot, Sara bluntly asked, 'Do you have any knowledge of devils?'

Sander cast an anxious glance at Isabel, who tightened her hands around her satchel. 'What specifically do you speak of?' he asked.

'A leper cursed the ship in Batavia, claiming his master would bring us all to ruin. The same leper appeared at my porthole last night. We think he is connected to the symbol that was drawn on the sail yesterday. This symbol first appeared in the Provinces thirty years ago, and carnage followed in its wake. It's said to herald the arrival of a demon called Old Tom.'

'No, no, I've no knowledge of that,' said Sander, waving his hand, as though Sara were a smudge he was trying to wipe away.

Sara couldn't remember having met a worse liar.

'Please, Predikant,' interjected Creesjie. 'My husband battled this creature and lost his life doing so. Now I think it's come for my family.'

Recognition flickered on the predikant's face. He took a painful step towards her. 'Who was your husband?'

'Pieter Fletcher.'

Sander touched his hand to his mouth, his eyes brimming over. Blinking the tears away, he looked to the heavens, then Isabel. 'Did I not tell you our faith would be rewarded?' he said jubilantly. 'Did I not say that our mission was divine?'

Creesjie peered at him inquisitively. 'Did you know my husband, Predikant?'

'Oh, yes, we were great friends once. He's the reason I'm aboard this ship.' Sander became suddenly fretful, casting around for danger. 'Is there somewhere we might speak privately. I have much to tell you, much that can't be said openly.'

'I'm supposed to breakfast with my husband,' said Sara, gritting her teeth. 'If I'm not there, he'll send Guard Captain Drecht to fetch me. If you tell Creesjie –'

'I'll not do this without you,' said Creesjie, clinging to her arm.

Sara stared at her friend. She was deathly afraid. 'Very well,' she replied hesitantly. 'But we'll have to be quick.' Sara sought Dorothea. 'Would you take a message to Arent Hayes –'

'No!' cried out the predikant. He flushed, embarrassed by his outburst, then lowered his voice conspiratorially. 'There are matters here you do not fully understand. Let me explain, then you may decide whether to deliver the information to Lieutenant Hayes.'

'HOW DID YOU KNOW my husband?' Creesjie asked the predikant, closing the door behind them. 'You called yourself a great friend of his.'

Dorothea had stayed on deck with the boys, but the rest of them had retired to Creesjie's cabin, which was identical in proportions to Sara's, but didn't have a huge harp in the corner, making it seem almost spacious in comparison. A comfortable rug was laid across the floor, wooden toys littering it. Pictures hung on the wall, including one of Creesjie's second husband, Pieter.

He was standing among his hounds in front of their magnificent house in Amsterdam. Aside from his resplendent dress, he was the image of his boys, sharing their prominent ears, mischievous eyes and the half-smile that suggested some mishap was on the horizon.

Something about the picture bothered Sara, but she couldn't immediately say what it was. Perhaps it had to do with the contrasting fates of the witchfinder in the picture and the witchfinder looking up at him. Sander's robes were a few stitches away from being rags, and his frail old limbs were crooked. Everything he did seemed to cause him pain.

'Predikant!' said Creesjie, drawing his attention.

'Oh, yes,' he said, looking away from the picture with a sorrowful expression. 'You'll forgive me, but I haven't put eyes on my friend for a very long time. Seeing him again, even like this, well … it brings back memories.'

'Of what?' asked Lia, who shared her father's impatience for sentiment.

'Pieter was my student for a time,' he replied, 'though I'll freely admit he was far more accomplished than I.' He shook his head, unable to keep his eyes from the painting. 'He was a great man; a hero.'

Creesjie was pouring herself wine, her hand shaking.

She didn't talk about Pieter a great deal, but Sara understood how deep their love had been. Creesjie had been born to prosperous farmers who needed sons for the fields, not daughters for the hearth. They'd married her off young, then forgot about her. Her first husband had been a beast, but as her beauty had blossomed and she began to perceive its power, she realised that she need not suffer.

Fleeing to Rotterdam, she'd become a courtesan.

Officially, she'd met Pieter at a ball. Unofficially, she'd met him in a brothel, the two of them captivating each other from the first. From this unusual soil an unusual life grew. Sara never met him, but by all accounts, Pieter was a generous, good-natured soul, free with his coin and his laughter, and entirely devoted to destroying maleficium wherever he found it.

Sander sighed, running a wrinkled grey hand across his equally grey face.

'It's my admiration for your husband that brings me here,' he said, as Creesjie gulped wine to steady herself. 'Two years ago, I received a letter from him begging for my help. He told me he was being hunted by a demon called Old Tom, which he'd battled across the Provinces. He told me he was fleeing to Batavia and sent funds that I might book passage on a ship and join him. Together, he believed we could finally put an end to this devil.'

Creesjie put her wine down softly, confusion writ plain on her face. 'That's not how it happened,' she said. 'The demon found us, yes. But we fled to Lille. And that was four years ago, not two. My husband was long dead by the time you received that letter.'

Sander was perplexed. 'Perhaps he meant to travel to Batavia afterwards, but –'

'He'd never heard of Batavia,' disagreed Creesjie. 'Neither of us had. The only reason I'm here is because Jan Haan summoned me to Batavia after he heard about my husband's death.'

The predikant's old face wrinkled, his thoughts drifting into unmapped waters. 'But he sent for me,' he repeated stubbornly.

'Are you quite sure of the details?' asked Sara.

'Of course,' he huffed, annoyed at the question. 'I've read that summons a hundred times if I've read it once.' He looked across to Isabel. 'Would you fetch it for me, my dear? It's in my trunk.' She took a step towards the door. 'Please leave the book, we'll have need of it.'

She stared at him with misgiving, earning a reprimanding scowl. Cowed, she lifted the heavy satchel over her head, depositing it with great care on Creesjie's writing desk.

A moment later, she was gone.

'After I received Pieter's letter, I booked passage on a ship to Batavia,' continued Sander, hobbling over to the desk. 'But when I arrived, I learned Mistress Jens was already widowed. I assumed it had happened in the city and tried to see you, but you'd already taken residence in the fort. The guards were unsympathetic, and sent me away. They wouldn't even hear a message, so I set about establishing a small church and asking my congregation to bring me news of the city's infernal happenings. My investigations had reached an impasse, when a carpenter came to my church for confession. He said that he'd heard a whisper in the darkness calling itself Old Tom. It had bargained with him, offering to make him wealthy in exchange for a few small favours. The carpenter wanted to know if God would forgive him.'

The predikant's words were so thick with judgement, Sara was surprised he hadn't choked on them.

'Was the carpenter's name Bosey?' she asked.

'Something along those lines,' he replied vaguely, waving his hand. 'He was lame.'

'That's Bosey,' confirmed Sara. 'Did he have leprosy when you met him?'

'No, but *that* would certainly have been Old Tom's doing.' His eyes gleamed savagely. 'Those who bargain are enthralled to him. If they resist his will, they begin to decay and can only restore themselves by obeying his commands. He uses these blighted creatures as heralds. They're his foot soldiers.'

Lia fidgeted anxiously. 'Mama,' she hissed. 'We can't be late for breakfast, Father will –'

'Did Bosey tell you what favour was asked of him?' interrupted Sara, gesturing for Lia to quieten.

'Apparently, Old Tom planned to sail aboard the *Saardam*, but first it needed to be made ready.'

'Made ready how?' wondered Creesjie.

'He didn't say. He only told me that Old Tom planned to feast on suffering so great it would nourish him for years, though the carpenter knew nothing more about it.'

Unlatching the satchel, he carefully slid a leather-bound book out of its sheepskin wrapping.

'That's a daemonologica,' said Creesjie, in amazement.

'What's a daemonologica?' asked Lia, approaching the book.

'A taxonomy of devils,' replied Sander, rubbing a spot of dust from the cover with his sleeve. 'It lists their hierarchies, their particular methods of corruption, and how to rid ourselves of them. It's a witchfinder's greatest weapon. Everybody in my order keeps their own copy.'

'I've heard King James has compiled a tome of similar purpose,' said Lia, peering over his bony shoulder nervously.

Sara smiled. Even terrified, her daughter couldn't resist knowledge.

'Incomplete and speculative,' said Sander scornfully. 'Its conclusions are derived from hearsay.' He ran a loving fingertip along the spine of the book. 'Members of my order meet regularly to share what we've learned during our investigations, and we scribe this new information into our own books. Every daemonologica contains the collected wisdom of all witchfinders, obtained from several lifetimes spent investigating maleficium. Only the Bible rivals it for wisdom.'

Sander turned the vellum pages of his daemonologica with trembling fingers. Each one was covered in intricate drawings and framed by ornate Latin script. After finding the one he wanted, he stood aside, so they could see it.

The company shied back. Lia made a small gurgle of disgust, while Creesjie instinctively drew the sign of the cross in the air. Even Sara averted her eyes.

The drawing was horrific.

It showed a naked old man with bat wings, riding a wolf with a bat's head. The wolf was pinning down a young boy and the old man was stroking his cheek with a clawed hand. A ring of cowled lepers surrounded them.

'Is *that* Old Tom?' asked Sara, shivering with disgust.

'Yes,' replied Sander.

'If this thing were aboard the *Saardam*, we'd know it,' said Creesjie disbelievingly.

'This is one of the devil's many forms, but not the one it's using currently,' he said. 'Old Tom walked aboard the *Saardam* looking just like one of us.'

'Are you saying it's –'

'Possessing one of the passengers.'

Stunned silence fell upon them.

'Who?' asked Sara eventually.

The predikant shook his head. 'That is what I'm here to determine.'

24

THERE WAS A KNOCK on the door as Isabel returned with the letter, which she handed to Sander. He immediately gave it to Creesjie, who was staring out of the porthole in thought. Sara's head was bowed with fierce concentration over the picture of Old Tom.

Creesjie unrolled the letter gingerly, as if afraid something sharp would fall out.

Upon reading its contents, her face hardened. 'This is my husband's seal, but not his quillmanship,' she said abruptly. 'Pieter didn't write this summons.'

'What does that mean?' asked Sander Kers.

'That you were lured here.' Sara closed the book with a thump. 'Something wanted you in Batavia, Sander. And the same thing likely lured you on to the *Saardam*. Can you think why?'

Shock caused his legs to buckle, forcing Isabel to rush beneath him.

'I'm the last of them,' he said, running a hand over his face.

'The last of whom?'

'My witchfinding order,' he said. 'After Pieter died, they started ... there were accidents and murders. Some of them disappeared, but … I'm the last now. I've been hiding for years. I changed my name and abandoned my vocation to become a predikant.'

'If you were hiding, how did this summons find you?' wondered Creesjie.

'My order travelled extensively, so we'd send all our messages to a church in Axel. We knew to stop by there every few months to check them. That's where I found the missive from Pieter, but only those in my order would have known to leave it there.'

'My husband was tortured before he died,' said Creesjie painfully. 'It's possible he relinquished the name of the church.'

'Then I'm being hunted by Old Tom,' said Sander. Fire came into his eyes, and he glanced at Isabel. 'The demon has made a grave miscalculation by delivering itself to God's judgement.'

'You have to find it first,' murmured Sara, unnerved by his zeal. 'If Old Tom could be possessing anybody on this ship, why do you trust us?'

Sander peered at her. 'You're unimportant,' he said bluntly. 'Old Tom is prideful. Those he possesses are powerful, or strong. They have influence enough to go where he wishes, and that influence grows in power the longer he controls them. Rancour and ruin emanate from Old Tom the way shadows follow us across the deck. I've heard the stories about you, Sara. Your husband beats you, isn't it so?'

She flushed. Sander continued relentlessly. 'Old Tom would never have allowed such a thing to persist. Mistress Jens is absolved of suspicion because of her husband. He was the foremost expert on Old Tom, and would not have been fooled.'

'Is it not conceivable Old Tom took control of Creesjie after Pieter was murdered?' asked Lia, who had taken a seat on the bunk.

Creesjie shot her a glance, but Lia shrugged. 'I don't believe you're a devil, but *somebody* had to ask the question,' she said seriously.

'Only a soul that bargains with Old Tom can be possessed by it, and I can see little in your personal circumstances to suggest you've acquired that kind of power,' he said. 'The same reasoning absolves Isabel, who was a beggar when I apprenticed her into my order.'

'And you, Sander Kers?' asked Sara. 'Why should we trust you?'

She'd expected him to become angry, but he laughed merrily. 'A question worthy of a witchfinder,' he said. 'If I were Old Tom, I would have little reason to divulge what I have, and besides' – he plucked at his tatty robes – 'witchfinding offers few rewards. I had to beg alms enough for our berths from my congregation in Batavia.'

Lia fidgeted. 'Mama, we have to go, we're going to be late for breakfast.'

'We've a few minutes yet,' said Sara. 'If you don't know who Old Tom's possessing, why did you react so badly when I suggested Arent accompany us?' asked Sara. 'He's strong, I'll grant you, but a servant nonetheless. Besides, I've seen little from him that wasn't honourable, courageous or kind.'

Her stout defence of him earned a glance from Creesjie. Even Sara was surprised by her own words. They'd only known each other a day. They'd met over a burning body. He was the loving nephew of the most dreadful man she knew. Truth was, aside from his loyalty to Samuel Pipps, his ability to play a song she'd enjoyed as a girl, and his refusal to take payment for helping her on the docks, she didn't know anything about him at all.

'You mustn't be fooled by Arent's demeanour,' Sander said, rebuking her. 'Demons disguise themselves in all sorts of ways. I've seen it time and again. It's their skill to make themselves as appealing as possible, so we follow them willingly into damnation.' He pinched the bridge of his nose. 'I don't know if Arent is the demon, only that he could be. Any of the wealthier passengers or the senior crew could be. Any soul that bargains with Old Tom can shelter it. Thirty years ago in the Provinces, Pieter chased it from noble to noble and was constantly surprised by the petty trifles they agreed to give their souls away for. Arent Hayes is a famous soldier, with a life lived entirely in bloodshed. Through Samuel Pipps he has access to any king in the land. He cannot be discounted.'

'And how do you think we three powerless creatures unworthy of Old Tom's attention can help you?' asked Creesjie mischievously.

'We need to uncover the demon's identity.'

'How?'

'Questioning. This devil is a capricious creature, malevolent and spiteful, intent on spreading suffering wherever it goes. Even when hiding, it cannot conceal its true nature for long. If pressed, the devil will reveal itself.'

'And then?'

'I kill it,' said Isabel.

Sander demurred. 'Once Old Tom takes possession of a body, it does not give it up, even in death. Look to Bosey, if you doubt me. To save the soul, we need to slay the body, then perform a banishing ritual contained in the daemonologica.

Old Tom will be sent back to hell until some fool chooses to summon it again.'

Sander flipped through the book, then called Sara over.

The page was split into a triptych of tragedies: the first showed a village filled with mothers wailing at empty cots while lepers carried their babies into the forest, where Old Tom was waiting for them. Next to this was a picture of their river burning, and, finally, a picture of men tending fields, where the crops had turned to snakes.

'Close it, close it!' demanded Creesjie in disgust, whipping her head away.

Sander ignored her. 'After Old Tom's herald announces its presence – as it did on the sail – three unholy miracles always follow, each carrying its mark. They're different every time, but they're meant to convince us of its power.'

'Like the burning bush that appeared to Moses,' supplied Isabel.

'Once the unholy miracles begin, that's when we'll hear Old Tom's voice offering our heart's desire in return for some terrible deed.'

He turned over the page.

The village burnt, bodies piled up on the ground. The villagers were attacking one another with hoes and pitchforks, setting fire to their own homes with torches. Lepers circled them, holding hands, watching the carnage in delight. And behind them the demon prowled, its tongue lolling.

'After the third unholy miracle is performed, anybody who didn't bargain with Old Tom is slaughtered by those who did,' said Sander. 'And those who survive are dispatched to sow the seed of his malevolence elsewhere. This is what awaits the *Saardam*, if we don't act.'

Sara reached out a hand to touch the drawing. Unbidden, her imagination painted those she loved among the dead. Tears pricked her eyes.

'When will these unholy miracles start?' she demanded, dashing them away.

'I'm not certain,' he said. 'That's why we cannot tarry. Old Tom is on this boat, and the longer he goes undiscovered, the closer to ruin we come.'

25

'Tell me!' Jan Haan banged the table, rattling his plate.
'Uncle –' protested Arent.

'Say it,' demanded Jan, laughing. 'Say I was wrong.'

Sitting beside her, Sara felt Lia lean forward to stare at her father. Confusion was plain on her face. As usual, they had gathered to eat breakfast, it being the one meal of the day they shared. Most mornings, she and Lia talked while her husband ate silently, rushing through his food as quickly as decorum would allow, so he could be free of them.

This morning was different. They were the ones who were distracted; their thoughts still trying to make sense of what Sander Kers had told them. In contrast, her husband was full of cheer.

Unlike the dining hall in the fort, which smelt of stone and dust, they were eating in the great cabin, with sunlight streaming through the four lattice windows. The ocean was turquoise, the ship's wake forming a foamy trail all the way back to Batavia – or so Sara liked to imagine.

But the real reason her husband was so cheerful was Arent. He was seated on the opposite side of the table, taking up the space of two ordinary-sized people.

Oblivious to family etiquette, he had immediately started joking with her husband, speaking to him in a way she'd never heard anybody else dare. Her husband was typically a distant, formal presence at breakfast, but he had responded in boisterous fashion, reminiscing about Frisia, where he and Arent had grown up. He'd told stories about fighting the war of independence against the Spanish, then more stories about becoming a merchant and after that the governor general of Batavia.

In Arent's company, he was transformed.

'How would you have handled the dispute differently?' pushed her husband. 'Come now, Arent. You're known as an honourable man. And your grandfather thought you more than passingly clever. What would you have done?'

'I don't want –'

'Husband,' interjected Sara warily.

'Fear not, *Arent*,' he said, flashing her an irritated glance. 'This is a friendly conversation and I'm asking you plain.'

'Blood is a poor way to settle a dispute,' said Arent quietly. 'Every man has the right to eat what he grows and be paid proper when he barters it. I don't understand why the Company didn't honour that.'

The governor general took another sip of wine. As promised, he didn't seem offended. If anything, he appeared contemplative.

'But you've killed before,' he said. 'Obeyed orders to kill?'

'Aye, men marching under banners,' responded Arent, clearly uncomfortable. 'Men who meant to kill me first.'

'Men you were paid to kill. That's mercenary work, isn't it? Coin and contract.'

'Yes.'

'The people of the Banda Islands broke the contract,' said her husband, leaning forward and clasping his hands. 'We paid them to cultivate and deliver mace. When the boat arrived to collect the cargo, they killed two of our men and drove the boat away.'

Sara's lips moved in silent argument, her words never touching the air. She knew better than to voice her outrage. Her husband brought up the Banda Islands frequently in conversation. He bullied people into agreeing with what he'd done, horrific as it had been.

For some reason, he seemed to enjoy seeing them buckle.

'Because the contract wasn't fair,' refuted Arent. 'They were being paid poorly and feared for their future under such terms. Your men tried to take the crop by force.'

The governor general shrugged. 'They signed the same contract I did. They knew the terms.'

'You could have paid them fair,' ventured Sara, appalled by her boldness.

'The Banda Islands are a wretched hovel,' said her husband contemptuously. 'What use is wealth if they waste it buying beads from the English? They have no art, they have no culture, no debate. They exist as we must have first existed when God brought us forth from clay.' He shook his head sorrowfully, intent upon Arent, as if it were the mercenary who'd made the point. 'Are we to leave them that way? The Company doesn't simply bring wealth, it brings civilisation. It's a light in the darkness.

'Society is built upon contracts, upon the promises we make to each other and the coin we pay for them. There are bad ones, of course. But they must be honoured and learnt from.

That's what I did; it's what your grandfather did. The people of the Banda Islands met ink with blood, and I could not allow that to stand. If I did, other tribes would have followed. The contract – the Company's word – would have meant nothing, and its future would have been imperilled.'

'You wiped out an entire island,' stated Arent, clearly unable to comprehend his uncle's coldness.

'Every man, woman and child, yes.' He banged a fist on the table at each word. 'One slaughter, so there would never be a need for another. And there hasn't been.'

Arent could only stare at him.

The conversation slipped into a familiar silence and Sara turned her attention to her plate. She'd been given salted fish and cheese, along with bread and a little wine. She hated the taste of the drink, much preferring the jambu juice they served in Batavia.

Jan shook his head, glancing at Sara.

'My wife, you were correct,' he said graciously. 'This was too blighted a topic for such a jolly gathering, but I so rarely get to speak with anybody whose opinion I favour.' He inclined his head. 'Nephew, my apologies and my thanks.'

Sara almost choked on her wine. Her husband didn't apologise. He didn't praise. He didn't compliment, or acquiesce.

Under the table, she squeezed Lia's hand. Upon Lieutenant Hayes was lavished the affection her daughter had spent her life craving.

'How goes the investigation?' asked the governor general, tearing a piece of chicken from the bone. 'Have you learned why a demon stalks this ship?'

'Not yet,' admitted Arent, glancing instinctively at Sara. 'We know the leper's name was Bosey and that he was part of the *Saardam*'s crew before his tongue was cut out by the boatswain Johannes Wyck. We know he dealt with Old Tom, who offered a great deal of wealth in return for a dangerous favour. Sammy believes if we make sense of his death, we'll make sense of everything else.'

'Do not mistake this monster for your typical foes,' warned her husband, watching as a loaf of bread was placed on the table and a huge knife laid beside it. 'When it attacked the Provinces, it used people's desires against them. Anybody who has ever held a grudge or coveted the possessions of another. Anybody who ever believed themselves wronged or overlooked. These people are its prey, which makes this ship a feast.' He chewed the chicken as he spoke. 'Believe me, Arent, it's a creature far more subtle and far more cunning than any you've faced before.'

Sara exchanged a wary glance with Lia. *Were these the words of Old Tom? Was the creature playing with them?*

'Then I must plead with you once again to free Sammy from his cell,' said Arent, as a bowl of Batavian fruit banged down in front of him. 'I'm not capable of overcoming this threat alone.'

His uncle swallowed his food. 'I have no desire to repeat yesterday's argument,' he warned. 'You know my feelings.'

Disquiet settled over the rest of the breakfast, which drifted towards its conclusion. Arent reluctantly agreed to attend again tomorrow and the governor general departed to his cabin, obviously annoyed at their manner of parting.

No sooner was he out of the room than Sara strode around the table to speak with Arent, who was staring at his uncle's chair, as if it were some impossible riddle.

'He really didn't care,' said Arent, as she arrived at his side. 'He slaughtered all those people, and he thinks it was the right thing to do.'

Sara and Lia exchanged a look. Nobody they knew would have been surprised by the governor general's callousness. 'My husband has never been unduly troubled by matters of conscience,' ventured Sara.

'He was when I was a boy,' said Arent, lost in memory. 'He was the kindest person in my life. How long has he been like this?'

'From the first day we met fifteen years ago,' said Sara.

'Then something's changed in him,' replied Arent distantly. 'That's not the man I remember from my childhood.'

26

ARENT, SARA AND LIA walked together through the compartment under the half deck and into the sunlight beyond. The heat was a warm, wet blanket, blue sky unfurling in every direction. The *Saardam* was making fine headway, the wind keeping steady and strong, filling the sails as if it were a pleasure to do so.

Guard Captain Drecht was lining up his musketeers on the waist of the ship and handing out their weapons from straw-filled boxes. He planned to drill them daily, Sara understood. More to keep them occupied than to keep them sharp. Boredom in the tight confines of the ship was a spark that could burn the entire thing down.

'What happened last night?' asked Lia. 'Nobody would tell us anything.'

'Another ship appeared,' said Arent, his thoughts obviously still on his uncle. 'Then it disappeared again before dawn.'

'Old Tom?' responded Lia.

'Nobody knows. It was too distant to make out what colours it was flying.'

'It would have to be Old Tom,' she murmured, her brow knotted in thought. 'The wind was southerly last night, and a fully laden Indiaman weighs –'

'Lia!' warned her mother.

'I just meant there's no way it could have sailed beyond our sight in the time it had,' said Lia, abashed.

Arent glanced between them, registering the discomfort, but politely saying nothing. Sara tried to keep the fear from her face. It was muttered comments like this, betraying the cleverness lurking within, that had caused her husband to trap Lia inside the fort. More than once as a little girl, she'd been accused of witchcraft, an accusation that could easily taint their good name if it was allowed to catch hold.

Sara took the opportunity to change subject. 'Did you tell Pipps what you'd discovered?'

'What *we* discovered,' corrected Arent. 'He has some questions he wants us to find answers to.'

'Us?' she said, surprised.

Arent became flustered. 'Sorry, I assumed you wanted to …' He trailed off uncertainly.

'I do,' she interjected quickly, touching his arm reassuringly. 'Of course I do. I'm just not used to …' Her green eyes scoured his face, searching for the lie behind it. 'Nobody's trusted me with anything more pressing than small talk for a very long time.'

'I can't do this alone,' said Arent, unable to meet her gaze. 'I don't know how, and you have a knack for asking the right questions. I'd like your help, if you'll give it?'

'Most men would say this isn't women's work.' There was no mistaking the challenge in her tone.

'My father was one of them,' admitted Arent. 'He taught me that women were frail creatures, purposely crippled by God that men might prove their virtue by protecting them. Sounded right enough, until I went to war and saw men pleading for their lives while women swung hoes at the knights trying to take their land.' His tone hardened. 'Strong is strong and weak is weak, and it doesn't matter if you wear breeches or skirts if you're the latter. Life will hammer you flat.'

His words fell on Sara like the first touch of sun hitting a plant after a long winter. Her back straightened. She lifted her chin. Her eyes glittered and her skin flushed with colour. So often in the fort, she had had woken up feeling empty, as though she'd left her soul in bed. On days like that she'd wander the corridors endlessly, peering into rooms and out of the windows, yearning desperately for the world beyond the walls.

Usually, she'd find a way to sneak past the guards into town, accepting the inevitable beating from her husband when she returned after dark. But speaking with Arent, she felt the opposite of empty. She had so much life, it was bursting through the seams of her.

'How can I help?' she asked.

'A few ways. We need to find out more about Bosey. Where he's from, who his people are, his friends and what Old Tom asked of him. Sammy's treating him as a victim in all this.'

'I'll talk to the senior officers at dinner,' said Sara. 'Their tongues will be loose with wine. Anything else?'

'Sammy wants us to know why so many people connected to Old Tom are on this boat, starting with my uncle. Do you know why he chose to sail aboard the *Saardam* rather than another ship?'

'He admires Captain Crauwels a great deal.' She fidgeted with her cap, which was being tugged at by the wind. 'He mentioned something to Reynier van Schooten about having cargo onboard. He went to check on it the moment we boarded.'

'The Folly?'

'Something else. Something bigger.'

'I heard Captain Crauwels grumbling about that. We're short of food because of the space it's taken. Do you know what it is?'

'I don't, but I'll endeavour to find out. What will you be doing?'

'Trying to find out if Bosey had any friends onboard who can tell us about this bargain he struck, and who he struck it with. Then I have to find some way of convincing Johannes Wyck to tell me what Laxagarr means.'

'You could try bribing him, I have plenty more jewellery to give away.'

She smiled at him conspiratorially and he laughed in spite of himself. 'I'll make sure to mention it. Can you come up to the quarterdeck after dinner again, tonight?' He coughed, suddenly realising the implications of what he was asking. 'I meant we can share what we've learnt.'

'I understood,' she said. 'I'll be there.'

Sara nodded, and Arent departed with the stride of somebody chased away by his own embarrassment.

'He doesn't seem like a devil to me,' said Lia, watching him duck through the arch and disappear down the stairs on to the orlop deck.

'Nor me,' admitted Sara.

'I actually rather like him.'

'Yes,' said Sara. 'So do I.'

'Do you think we should tell him about our plan to –'

'No,' snapped her mother. Then, more gently, 'No, that's ours alone. Ours and Creesjie's.' The sharpness of Sara's tone rose between them like a mountain range. 'I'm sorry, dear heart,' she said, putting her head on Lia's shoulder. 'I've shouldn't have barked at you.'

'No, that's Father's job.'

Sara smiled at her sadly. 'Not for much longer.' The smile fell from her face. 'Do you have everything you need?'

'I do. It's a simple enough task.'

'Only for you.' Sara stroked her daughter's black hair, her hands strangely cold in the humid air. 'We'll start tonight.'

They climbed on to the quarterdeck, where Eggert, the musketeer guarding the passenger cabins, was busy picking scabs from his scalp. He didn't notice them until the last minute, almost dropping his pike when he did. He fumbled a clumsy salute while trying to prevent his pike from falling, nearly impaling himself.

From the poop deck, they heard Creesjie and Dorothea talking. By unspoken agreement, they climbed the stairs and found their friends sitting with their backs against the animal pens. Creesjie had a crochet ring on her lap and a parasol over her head, while Dorothea was darning one of Osbert's jackets.

'Is Arent our demon?' asked Creesjie, as they appeared.

'If he is, he's doing a fine job of hiding it,' said Sara. 'Where are the boys?'

'Vos is showing them the cargo hold,' said Creesjie, in that dismissive tone of voice she always used for the chamberlain.

'Vos? Does he even like the boys?'

'I don't think so, but he's trying to impress me. Anyway, they wanted to go, and it's funny watching him bark commands at them like they're dogs.'

'I think Father's the demon,' decided Lia, who'd clearly carried on their earlier discussion in her head.

'Your father?' said Creesjie, whose surprise at the statement lasted only as long as it took her to consider it.

'It's not your father,' interrupted Dorothea sagely, sucking a thumb she'd pricked on her needle. 'I've lived with his malice a long time. It's his and only his. Believe me.'

'Arent said he'd changed,' said Sara thoughtfully. 'Do you remember him being different, Dorothea?'

'Different?'

'Kinder.'

'I was taken on after the boy had already gone to war,' said Dorothea. 'If there was kindness in him, it went with Arent.'

'Why couldn't Father be the devil?' demanded Lia petulantly. 'The predikant said Old Tom was malevolent and wouldn't be able to hide it.'

'Truth is, it could be anybody,' said Sara, staring at the water. 'Or nobody. For all we know, Sander Kers is lying. If I were Old Tom, I'd be cunning enough to point the finger elsewhere. Or it could all be a deceit in service of some greater evil.'

A reflected *Saardam* skimmed along the surface of the ocean, occupied by phantom sailors and even a phantom Sara. From this angle, she was a beautiful ship, the green and red paint looking as fresh as the day it was applied. If anything, the illusion made the real *Saardam* – with its warped planks and flaking paint – seem like the ghost ship.

'I'll vouch for his daemonologica,' said Creesjie, who leant gently against Sara. 'My husband had one just like it. And, if Sander was lying, why present us with the letter that lured him here? Surely, he'd know I'd see through it.'

'He's not lying,' said Dorothea firmly. 'Lies only come two ways. Too sharp or too soft. He spoke firm. He was being honest. Besides, he's a predikant.' For her, at least, that seemed all the proof anybody should need.

'Or so he says,' murmured Sara.

'Now you really do sound like Pipps,' laughed Lia. 'He's always saying things like that in his stories.'

Creesjie touched Sara's shoulder. 'What do you want us to do?'

Sara turned to find the eager faces of her friends intent upon her. They were like candles, she realised, ready for a flame. Heaven help her, but it was a thrill. Here was the life she'd always dreamed about, the life denied her because she was a woman.

A tingle of fear ran along her spine. Old Tom wouldn't work hard to add her to his ledger, she thought. If he could promise her this, she'd pay almost anything.

'It could be dangerous,' she warned.

'We're on a boat populated by wicked men,' sniffed Creesjie, glancing at the other three for confirmation of her feeling. 'It would be dangerous even if there wasn't a devil stalking it. If we do nothing, we're doomed. Now, Sara, where do we start?'

27

S ARA AND LIA MADE their way towards their cabins, the solitary candle at the end of the corridor guttering miserably. Sara hated the gloom on the *Saardam*. It was filthy and thick, as if the thousands of dirty bodies who'd walked through it had somehow left it stained.

She was about to tell this to Lia when the rattling cough of the mysterious Viscountess Dalvhain drifted through her door.

'Do you think Dalvhain could be Old Tom?' speculated Lia.

Sara stared at the cabin speculatively. Dorothea claimed to have heard a strange noise in there this morning, and, after two days, nobody had laid eyes on her. Apparently, she was suffering some debilitating malady, but there wasn't a soul onboard who knew what it was. Afire with curiosity, Creesjie had tried to interrogate Captain Crauwels at dinner, but even mentioning Dalvhain's name had cast a pall across the conversation. Hearing her cabin number, the other officers had clung to their charms and grimaced, claiming it was cursed. Two people had already died in there, went the tale. Footsteps paced the floorboards, even when it was empty. Every ship had a room like this, they said. It was where somebody fell badly or burnt worse; where a servant had gone mad and cut his master's throat.

The only thing to do was board it up and leave it be, let evil lie where it may, like a hound in its favourite chair.

Sara impulsively rapped on her door. 'Viscountess Dalvhain? My name's Sara Wessel, I'm a healer. I was wondering if there was anything –'

'No!' The voice was old and brittle. 'And I'd ask you not to bother me again.'

Sara shared a surprised look with Lia, then retreated from the door. 'Any ideas?' she asked her daughter.

'Sander Kers gives her confession every night. Maybe he can help.'

'I'll talk to him about it,' said Sara.

After saying their goodbyes, Lia entered her cabin, leaving her mother alone at her door. Sara's hand hovered uncertainly over the latch. The terrible memory of the leper peering in was still fresh.

'Oh, for heaven's sake,' she said to herself, lifting it and stepping inside.

Sun poured through the porthole, illuminating the dust motes in the air. Walking over, she tried to peer outside, but the writing desk was in the way. Pulling the heavy folds of her dress up to her thighs, she clambered clumsily on to its surface, then put her head through the porthole, searching for anything to prove what she'd seen.

Green-painted planks curved down towards her husband's cabin directly below, which bulged out of the hull like a moth's cocoon. From above, she heard three women talking on deck. They called after their children and wondered what it must be like in the cabins, or if anybody had seen the governor general and Sara Wessel since boarding.

She was a wild one, one of them said. A torment to her poor husband.

Poor husband, scoffed another. She'd heard from one of the maids in the fort that his temper was ferocious, and when he was in the mood, he'd kick Sara up and down the corridors like a dog. He'd almost killed her more than once.

That's what husbands did, replied the next. What sympathy could you have for the wife of a rich man? Most people endured worse to live under leaky roofs and eat rotten food.

Sara's temper was about to get the better of her when she spotted a dirty handprint just beneath her porthole.

Leaning out further, she saw a second one underneath it, and then a third and fourth.

On closer inspection, she realised it wasn't dirt staining the wood; it was ash. The hull was charred, as if the leper's hand had been aflame. Holes punctured the planks, where he'd dug his fingers in as he'd climbed.

Her eyes followed them all the way down to the roof of her husband's cabin, where they disappeared over the side.

If her guess hit the mark, the leper had climbed out of the ocean and straight up the hull to her porthole.

28

A RENT WAS STILL PREOCCUPIED by breakfast when he descended the staircase into the humid gloom of the orlop deck. For years, his uncle had raised him with as much tenderness as he could manage. He'd taught him how to hunt, to ride, and even how to bargain. He was quick to temper, it was true, but he calmed quickly and rarely raised his hand.

The man he'd known could never have murdered an island full of people, then boasted of the good that would come of it. Arent had seen slaughter like that at war. He knew those who did it, what overcame them and what they became. It was a poison in the soul that ate them hollow.

That couldn't be his uncle. His wise, kind uncle. The man who'd taught him of Charlemagne, and who he'd run to when his grandfather was too demanding, or too cruel.

Empty hammocks swung gently with the motion of the boat, while shoes, needles and thread, ripped clothes, jugs and wooden toys lay discarded on the floor. Most of the passengers were on deck for their morning exercise. In their absence, two toy dancers the size of an adult's finger whirled back and forth across the floor, their wooden skirts spinning. They were impressive creations, perfectly balanced and still moving, despite being abandoned by Marcus and Osbert.

Marcus had a splinter in his finger, which his brother was now clumsily trying to remove.

The younger boy was whimpering and close to tears, his brother shushing him lest Vos should discover where they'd slunk off to.

Seeing the boys by the boxes, Arent called them over. Osbert came brightly, while Marcus trudged over, holding his injured finger. Their likeness was remarkable, thought Arent. Sandy hair fell across large, round ears, their eyes blue as the ocean outside.

'Let me see your hand,' said Arent, kneeling down to inspect the splinter in Marcus's finger.

Arent felt around gently, wincing in sympathy at his discomfort.

'I think we can save it,' he said earnestly. 'You'll need to be strong for a minute. Can you do that?'

The boy nodded, his brother leaning closer to better see the gruesome work.

Very carefully, Arent squeezed the splinter between his thick fingers, forcing it up through the skin. The hardest part was tempering his strength, so as not to hurt him. The splinter came loose in a few seconds and Arent handed it to Marcus as a trophy.

'I thought there'd be blood,' complained Osbert grumpily.

'If I remove a splinter from your hand, I'll make sure there is,' warned Arent, standing with a groan. There was a lot of him to lift and most of it ached.

'Are those yours?' he said, nodding to the toy dancers, still whirling back and forth across the floor. 'They're clever little things.'

'Yes, Lia made –' Marcus was cut off by his brother nudging him in the ribs. 'We're not allowed to say,' he finished.

'Why?'

'It's a secret.'

'Then keep it under your tongue,' responded Arent, who had enough questions to answer without adding unnecessary ones to the pile. 'Reckon you boys best be off now. I'm about to do something foolish, and it might get sharp quicker than I can control it.'

The boys' faces immediately lit up with the thought of a grand adventure, but the grim, scarred expression of Arent Hayes was enough to change their minds.

Hunching under the low roof, Arent went to the folding wooden screen dividing the deck in two and pushed it aside, entering the crew's side of the ship. It had been partitioned down the middle by a piece of sailcloth strung on rope, with musketeers on one side and sailors on the other. Mats had been slid beneath hammocks to provide additional berths for everybody, their possessions kept in sacks that hung from the ceiling like spider nests.

The half of the deck belonging to the musketeers was empty. They were training on the waist with Drecht, slashing at the air and firing rounds at the horizon. There weren't many sailors to be seen, as they were scattered between the weather decks and workshops. What few men remained were playing dice or talking with their mates. Others snored on their mats. The air was thick with the stench of their unwashed bodies. Somebody was trying to wring a tune from a fiddle with only three strings.

They stopped everything as Arent approached, narrowing their eyes.

Arent raised his coin purse and his voice. 'Anybody know Bosey?' he asked. 'There's a chance he, or somebody he knew, is running around this ship dressed like a leper. Apparently, he struck a bargain with somebody called Old Tom in Batavia to do a few favours.' Arent jangled his coin purse. 'Anybody hear him say anything about that? Anybody mates with him?'

The sailors stared, their lips clamped shut.

The galley fire crackled and popped; steps thudded back and forth across the deck above them, dust falling from the ceiling.

Somewhere distant a drumbeat kept time.

'Does anybody know where he was from, or what brought him aboard the *Saardam*?' pressed Arent, looking from stony face to stony face. 'I'll pay well for gossip.'

One of the sailors stood up. 'We'll have no words with a pig-groping soldier like you,' he spat.

The others muttered their agreement.

From the portside, somebody hurled a jug, forcing Arent to duck. A second narrowly missed him, shattering against the wall.

Strong fingers clamped themselves around his arm. Arent spun to hit whoever had grabbed him, but it was the one-armed constable from the gunpowder store. As yesterday, he was bent almost double, his legs bowed, like God had brought a cannon to life.

He raised his stump in supplication.

'Come away now, before there's blood on the floor,' he said, trying to tug Arent out of the compartment.

Sailors advanced on him with their fists clenched.

Seeing the futility of staying, he allowed himself to be led back beyond the wooden divide, which shook as the sailors beat their hands against it, hurling insults after him.

'You're a silly bastard and no mistake,' said the constable, somehow making it sound like a compliment. Without another word, he crossed the deck to the gunpowder store, which he unlocked with a key kept around his neck.

Dozens of kegs of gunpowder were stacked on the floor, leaving almost no room to walk. The old constable snorted at them in disgust. 'Hundred men carried them out of here when the captain called battle stations last night, and now they expect me to put them back by myself.' He gestured to the empty racks on the walls with the stump of his arm. 'Isn't a damn sensible thought anywhere on this boat.'

He waited, then sighed meaningfully when Arent didn't catch the hint. 'Lot of work for an old man with one arm,' he said slyly.

Arent picked up two kegs effortlessly, slinging them into their racks. 'Is this why you dragged me out of there?'

'Partly,' said the constable, dropping heavily on to his stool. 'But I saw something last night I thought you'd want to hear about, being as how the ship's in danger. Not a leper or nothing, so don't go thinking –'

'Just tell me,' said Arent, heaving another two kegs into their racks.

'Well, it was after the two bells, before Captain sounded battle stations. I went down to the cargo hold for my piss. Always do it down there, near the bottom of the staircase, you know, where there's still some light. Don't like going –'

'Constable!' said Arent. 'What did you see?'

'All right, all right, I was just trying to offer a little extra colour,' he protested. 'A woman came creeping down. Broad-shouldered and curly-haired. Mistook me for somebody else in the shadows, because she dashed down, saying she'd almost got them caught.' The constable chewed the inside of his lip thoughtfully. 'Gave me a bit of a fright, so I popped my carrot back in the sack and stepped into the light. That was that. She took off like a rabbit seen a fox.'

Broad-shouldered and curly-haired sounded like the predikant's ward, Isabel. She must have come down to the cargo hold after Larme spied her eavesdropping on their conversation last night. Evidently, she had a knack for show-ing up where she wasn't supposed to.

'I'll ask around,' said Arent, as he pushed a few kegs across the rack to make space. 'Thank you, Constable.'

The constable nodded, clearly happy to have made this somebody else's problem.

Feeling a twinge in his back, Arent wrapped his arms around another keg. It came off the ground effortlessly.

'This is empty,' he said.

'Toss it over there,' said the constable, waving towards the corner where three others had been discarded. 'Likely, one of the boys panicked and packed his cannon before the order came to make ready.' He chortled. 'Would have been up at first light, trying to tip the gunpowder into the sea before anybody realised. Worth a flogging, if he's caught.'

Arent threw the keg away, as the constable swung his bare feet on to the box containing The Folly, causing two dice to jump into the air.

'Know what it is?' asked the constable. 'Didn't feel as I could ask yesterday with that Vos in the room. Makes me think of something dead and dug up, he does.'

Arent eyed it, then nodded knowledgeably.

'It's a box,' he concluded.

'A box that Chamberlain Vos has made excuses to visit twice,' said the constable shrewdly. 'Reckon whatever's inside must be important.' His eyes twinkled. 'And valuable.'

'You telling me you haven't tried to open it,' said Arent, the ship tilting ever so slightly as they changed course.

'It's locked, and my lock-picking days are long behind me,' said the constable, scratching his stump.

Arent shrugged. 'You're asking the wrong man. Nobody ever told me what it was, and I never asked. I'll tell you this, though, the governor general thought it important enough to call Sammy Pipps all the way from Amsterdam when it was stolen.'

'Aren't you curious what's inside?'

'Curiosity's Sammy's job,' replied Arent. 'Up until yesterday, I just punched the things he was curious about. Speaking of which, have you ever heard the word Laxagarr?'

'Nope.'

'In that case, do you know what it means when two sailors carry two halves of the same charm?' he asked, recalling how Sammy had noticed that Isaack Larme's half-face charm fitted perfectly into Bosey's.

'Oh, aye,' he said. 'Means they're married.'

'Married?' exclaimed Arent, his eyebrows shooting up.

'Not land married, sailor married,' he said. 'If one dies on the voyage, the other gets his pay, any booty he's earned and his death pouch. Doesn't mean they share a hammock or anything, though I dare say it's happened.'

'Then they'd be close.'

'Have to be,' he agreed. 'You don't make that sort of pledge without being certain. Get it wrong, and you're liable to end up with your blood on their hands and your coin in their pocket.'

Arent paused in his work to wipe the sweat from his forehead. 'Why are you so loose-lipped? The rest of the crew would rather spit in my face than talk to me.'

'Good question, that.' He grinned toothlessly. 'Seems like you're getting the hang of being on an Indiaman. Soldiers and sailors are fire and fuses. Been that way since the first boat, and it aint going to change on this voyage. These boys hate you, Hayes.' He touched the twist of hair he kept on a string around his neck. 'Now me, I'm old. Too old to be told who to hate. I just want to get home to my daughters, play with my grandchildren and live with the dirt under my feet a little while. If some bastard's trying to sink this boat, then I'm with the man who's trying to stop them, whether he's a sailor or a damn soldier.'

'Then tell me how I get Wyck to talk. He knows what Laxagarr means, and he cut out Bosey's tongue for some reason.'

'Wyck.' The constable clicked his tongue in thought. 'Funnily enough, Wyck I might be able to help you with. Open that door for me.'

Arent pulled it open, and the constable leant his head forward.

'Is there a cabin boy out there?' he hollered, tipping his ear, listening for a response. None came. 'I know there is. There's always one of you little bastards shirking your duty in the gloom. Get in here now.'

Tentative footsteps sounded on the wood, a young, nervous face appearing at the door.

'Go fetch Wyck for me,' commanded the constable. 'He'll be in his cabin. Tell him the constable needs him, urgent business.'

'What's your notion?' asked Arent, while they waited, but the constable shook his head, practising what he was going to say when Wyck arrived.

They didn't have to wait long.

'What do you think you're doing,' screamed Wyck, from halfway along the orlop deck, his steps thudding through the wood. 'You don't ever summon me! You don't –'

Wyck stormed into the gunpowder store in a towering fury, his fists clenched and shoulders heaving. When Arent had confronted Wyck last night, the gloom had helped conceal his size, but in the light of the orlop deck, he was enormous. While not Arent's height, he was about his width, with thick arms and legs, a bald head and round body. He was a rockslide in piss-stained slops.

Taking fright, the constable leapt up from his stool and scrambled backwards into the wall, holding his hands up defensively.

Before Wyck could wring the poor man's throat, Arent slammed the door shut behind him.

'He didn't summon you,' he said. 'I did.'

Wyck spun, withdrawing a dagger quicker than a wolf could bare its teeth.

'There's no need of that, Johannes,' implored the constable, who was still trying to put as much distance as he could between himself and the enraged boatswain.

Arent's eyes travelled from Wyck's pitted face, down to the dagger, then back again. 'What does Laxagarr mean?' he asked. 'And why did you cut out Bosey's tongue?'

Wyck blinked at him, then at the constable in confusion. 'You woke me up for this?'

'I woke you up, because I've got an idea,' said the constable.

'You're wasting my time.'

'You're going to fight and Arent's going to lose.'

Arent's eyes narrowed in surprise. The constable finally came away from the wall, trying to soothe Wyck like he was a bull gone mad in the field.

'Boatswain's a position you take by force, not promotion and I've heard there's a couple of lads with an eye on your throat.' The constable licked his lips nervously. 'What you need is a show of force. Lay Arent low in a fight, and everybody will fall in line, you know they will.'

Wyck's expression flickered. He was tempted, it was obvious.

'This is your last voyage, you said it yourself,' pressed the constable. 'You've got a family depending on you, and not enough money to keep them.'

'Spill more of my business and your blood will follow,' growled Wyck but it was obvious some internal scale was tilting.

Arent knew the effect his size had on people, and had learned to spot whether somebody would be cowed, or become belligerent, as if offended by his refusal to shrink in their presence.

Wyck's calculating eyes were running him up and down, noticing how he had to hunch to even fit in the room, and how he was so wide, he blocked the door entirely. 'In return for losing our fight, I assume you want your questions answered,' he asked, scratching his ear with a grubby finger.

Arent nodded.

'And what else?'

'Nothing else,' said Arent. 'I'll pay for answers in humiliation.'

Wyck turned his glare on the constable. 'And what do you get out of this, you greedy old sod?'

'I'm going to bet against Arent,' he laughed. 'I guarantee, nobody else will be doing that.'

Wyck grunted, nodding slyly. 'Aint no fights on this ship allowed without a grievance,' he said. 'Otherwise it's a flogging. Give me a few hours and I'll come up with something you can take to Isaack Larme.' He withdrew a blob of wax from his ear and flicked it away. 'If either of you bastards tries to betray me, I'll gut you.'

Wyck stomped out of the store, almost colliding with Dorothea, who was looking around frantically. Upon seeing Arent in the gunpowder store, relief washed over her face. 'Lieutenant Hayes, I've been searching for you. My mistress has news about the leper.'

29

S USPENDED BY A ROPE tied to the mizzenmast, Crauwels emerged on to the roof of the governor general's cabin, foamy water rushing by beneath him. He'd been inspecting the lower half of the hull for any traces of the leper's passing.

'Well, Captain?' Sara Wessel called down to him from the poop deck.

'They run all the way from the railing to the waterline,' he hollered, sticking his fingers into the holes left by the leper's ascent. 'You were right, my lady. For any doubts I harboured last night, I apologise.'

Sara wasn't typically vindictive, but the memory of Reynier van Schooten's sneer rankled still. She spun on him. 'And you, Chief Merchant? Do you still think I imagined the leper at my porthole?'

'No,' he grunted, kicking his own ankle. He was already swaying drunk, and though his clothes were on the right body parts, that was the best that could be said for them.

Last night Creesjie had claimed the chief merchant was in pain. Sara wondered what was causing it.

He was coming apart at the seams.

'You accused my wife of hysteria, Van Schooten,' said the governor general sternly, earning a sharp glance from

Sara, who remembered her husband agreeing with the chief merchant's assessment. 'And now you can't even stand here sober. An apology is in order.'

Van Schooten shifted miserably.

'I apologise, my lady,' he mumbled.

Feeling ashamed of her pettiness, Sara looked towards the taffrail, where Arent was helping Crauwels over the side. The captain immediately inspected his beautiful clothes for marks and smudges, tutting at a tar blot on his shirt with profound regret.

'Your apology is welcome, Chief Merchant,' she said. 'But, of greater concern, is what you plan to do next.'

'This isn't a matter for you, Sara,' interrupted the governor general, waving her away with those sharp fingernails. 'I'm certain you have other duties to attend.'

'Husband –'

The governor general gestured to Guard Captain Drecht. 'Escort my wife back to her cabin,' he commanded.

'Come, my lady,' said Drecht, adjusting his sword.

Frustrated, Sara reluctantly fell in step behind the guard captain. She'd only bothered calling everybody on to the deck because she wanted to watch their reaction to the handprints being discovered.

Her husband had been startled, while Vos had waited quietly by the animal pens, obviously annoyed at being dragged from his work. If the handprints disturbed him, he didn't show it. Drecht – who had so stridently claimed not to believe in devils – had blanched, but otherwise kept his own counsel.

Arent had loomed over them, listening to her story the way a mountain must listen to the wind howling around it. He'd been impossible to read. He didn't fidget; he didn't pace. His face was as expressive as armour. She supposed that was what happened when you worked with a man who could read your every thought from a twitch of the lips.

Drecht was moving languidly down the steps to the quarterdeck and Sara had to fight the urge to push by him. Instead, she watched as storeyed ranks of his musketeers slashed at the air with their blades. It was a curious sight, like they were beating back an invisible army.

'This is your investigation, Arent,' came the governor general's voice from behind her. 'What do you recommend we do next?'

'We should search the ship for leper's rags,' he responded.

'You saw the handprints,' replied Vos. 'They climbed out of the water, straight up the hull to the porthole. Likely, the leper went back the same way. That's why we didn't catch sight of it.'

'Maybe, but Sammy Pipps suggested we search the ship and he's right more often than he's wrong.'

At the bottom of the steps, Drecht opened the red door to the passenger cabins and politely gestured to Sara to go ahead.

Lifting the hem of her dress, she stepped into the gloom.

A commotion erupted from the ranks of the musketeers, interrupting the conversation above. Two were fighting, the others immediately forming a whistling, jeering circle around them.

'That's Thyman,' snarled Drecht, already taking a step towards them. 'He can't seem to keep himself out of trouble lately. With your permission, my lady?'

'Of course,' she said, glad to watch him rush into the fray.

Sara slipped into her cabin and latched the door, before flying to the porthole. The poop deck was directly above her, and, as she'd expected, she could hear everything they were saying.

'Captain, organise the search for the leper's rags,' said her husband. 'I want this ship shaken out like a pocket.'

'Yes, my lord.' Footsteps carried him away. A moment later he was hollering for Isaack Larme.

'Do you truly believe somebody on this ship is pretending to be a dead leper?' asked Reynier van Schooten doubtfully.

'Sammy does,' corrected Arent. 'And whoever it is, they've put a great deal of effort into the charade.'

'Then how can Pipps be so certain this isn't Bosey returned?' wondered Van Schooten, sounding worried. 'When I was a boy, a witch visited unholy terrors upon my village. Every evening, the children gathered in the woods, singing her name. Tame animals went rabid. Milk soured and crops were blighted.'

There was a contemplative pause, then her husband's voice rang out.

'What's your thinking on this matter, Vos?'

'There are powers upon this earth Samuel Pipps is hardly the equal of, and I'll confess they make more sense to me than his far-flung theory.' There was a tremor in his usually dull monotone. 'Those handprints charred the wood. The leper's fingers were strong enough to puncture the hull. Disguised or nay, that's not a human feat.'

Arent made a sound to object but Vos spoke over him. 'And if it's a disguise, it's a damn poor one,' he added. 'A leper arouses terror and rage wherever it goes. Where's the benefit of dressing like one?'

'Those are the questions Sammy usually asks, and answers,' remarked Arent. 'Whatever his crimes in Batavia, they're of no importance now.'

'An easy assertion for somebody who doesn't know what they are,' replied her husband. She knew this contemplative tone. He'd have closed his eyes and would be massaging his brow, trying to coax his thoughts forward.

When he spoke again, it was with the authority of somebody hearing God's words in his ear. 'I'm calling the fleet to a halt, Chief Merchant,' he ordered. 'Have the captains of every ship scour their hulls for any sign of this leper's passing and tell them to search their vessels for these rags. They will report to me personally at eight bells, is that understood?'

The company murmured its assent.

'Then you're dismissed. Vos, abide a moment, we must speak.'

The wind came blowing into Sara's cabin, the breeze strong enough to urge a note from her harp. Steps thudded across the deck above, the animals making a racket in their pens. The stairs crackled, voices fading.

Sara waited expectantly, her heart racing. She couldn't imagine what her husband would do if he caught her eavesdropping, but the act was thrilling. There were so few ways to defy him safely, but, somehow, she'd managed it twice today.

'You did well back there,' he complimented Vos.

'Thank you, my lord.'

There was a pause. It drew on and on. Sara would have believed they'd left, but she could hear her husband's long fingernails scratching the wood – a sure sign that he was worried.

'Do you know the problem with summoning a devil, Vos?' he said, at last.

Sara's breath lodged in her throat.

'I can imagine one or two, sir,' he responded drily.

'They get loose.' Her husband sighed, troubled. 'Old Tom made me into the man I am' – Sara had to cover her mouth to stifle a gasp of shock – 'and now it appears somebody else on this ship has brought it aboard. The question is who's behind it, and what do they want?'

'Everything is occurring exactly as it did thirty years ago, my lord. I would suggest a bargain will be offered soon. For our part, we must anticipate what it will demand, and what we're willing to pay.'

'I'd prefer not to pay at all. It's been a long time since anybody forced me to do anything. Did you assemble the names I asked for?'

'As far as I could remember them. It's been some time since we set Old Tom loose. They're on your desk, though … if I might be so bold …'

'What is it, Vos?'

'There appears, if I may say, one obvious candidate.'

'Arent,' supplied the governor general.

'It can't be a coincidence that the mark appeared when he returned.'

'I understand the implications, though I struggle to see a reason.'

'Perhaps he finally remembers what happened to him in the forest, and why the mark of Old Tom now scars his wrist. Perhaps, my lord, he knows what price you had to pay to summon your demon.'

T HE SHIP REVERBERATED WITH the sound of the
search for the leper's rags. Crates were being torn open,
the crew complaining as their possessions were upended. The
sails were furled and the anchors dropped, yawls bobbing
near the waist, the fleet captains climbing up the rope ladders.
They were a sour bunch, full of complaint. Larme was making
himself scarce until they were gone.

He hacked at his carving sourly.

He was sitting on the lion figurehead, which stuck out at
the very front of the ship, his short legs swinging in the air as
he whittled a piece of wood with his knife. Nobody else came
up this far. They didn't have his agility.

Also, it stank.

The beakhead was behind him. It was a small grated deck
where the crew relieved themselves into the water below,
smearing the entire prow of the ship. The smell made his eyes
water, but it seemed a small price to pay to be left alone.

He twisted his knife, trying to dislodge a stubborn shard
from the block. He was in a rotten mood. He usually was, but
this one had a cause. It was bad luck to tarry when the seas
were fair, in case the wind got the impression they weren't in
need of it any longer. Even worse than that was the threat

of pirates. They prowled these waters, and they'd make good sport of a heavily laden merchant fleet caught at anchor.

'Lepers,' he spat, tearing the shard loose. 'As if you don't have enough troubles.' He patted the hull, the way somebody would a beloved pet.

The *Saardam* wasn't just nails and wood, no more than an ox was just muscles and sinew. She had a belly full of spice, great white wings on her back and a huge horn pointing them home. Each day, they smoothed her coat with tar and mended her torn flesh. They put stitches in those delicate hemp wings and guided her gently through hazards she was too blind to see.

Wasn't a man aboard who didn't love her. How they could not? She was their home, their livelihood and their protector. It was more than any other bastard had ever given them.

Larme hated the world beyond these decks. On the streets of Amsterdam, he was something to be beaten, robbed and laughed at. He'd been kicked from pillar to post, then told to cartwheel so he'd entertain people while doing it.

The second he'd set foot on an Indiaman, he knew he was home.

Here was a world built to his size. Didn't matter if he was half everybody else's height when he knew how to tack and jib. Aye, the crew laughed at him behind his back, but they laughed at everybody. It was what they did to keep from going mad five months into an ten-month voyage.

If a storm was blowing him overboard, he'd trust any of these lads to put their hand out and catch him. If he was being kicked to death in Amsterdam, he'd trust five others to come and join in.

A chunk of wood fell from his carving. He wasn't sure what it would be yet. He didn't have skill enough to make such bold declarations, but it had legs. Four of them, admittedly, but it was still further than he'd ever got before.

Hearing steps behind him, he turned his head to see Guard Captain Jacobi Drecht pushing a musketeer and a sailor up the staircase to the forecastle deck.

Larme knew the boy to be one of the carpenter's mates, Henri. Johannes Wyck had put some hurt on him after discovering he'd told tales to Sara Wessel. His face was swollen like an old turnip.

The musketeer was Thyman. He'd antagonised Arent Hayes by hurling the thief-taker on to the floor during boarding. He'd got off lightly with it that morning, though not so today. He was growing a black eye. Henri and Thyman had obviously been fighting.

Larme swung himself off the figurehead, then balanced along the smeared edge of the beakhead, before leaping over the railing on to the forecastle deck.

From under the brim of his hat, Drecht's eyes narrowed. He adjusted his sword.

Isaack Larme didn't take fright easily – most of a first mate's job was to be hated in place of the captain – but he gripped his knife a little tighter than he had done. It had been a long time since they'd last met, but most folk didn't forget a dwarf.

'That you, Larme?' asked Guard Captain Drecht.

'Aye, it's me,' he said, not bothering to hide his contempt.

'I never forget a scowl,' said Drecht with a grin, the smile dropping from his face when it wasn't returned.

'They been fighting?' asked Larme, rubbing the half-face charm around his neck. Not that it seemed to do much good.

Or, at least, it hadn't for Bosey, who'd kept the other half. Never did have much sense, but he deserved more than to be incinerated on the docks.

'I heard there's some special way you deal with that on this ship,' replied Drecht.

'Grievances on the *Saardam* are settled by fists on the forecastle deck,' explained Larme. 'What's the trouble?'

'He stole my hand plane,' spat Henri, glaring at Thyman.

Larme ran a professional glance up and down the two men, then sighed. He liked a good fight, but this wasn't going to be one. Squabbles like this nearly always devolved into slaps, and these two gave the air of two overfilled sacks of piss waiting to be flung at each other.

'Is it proven?' asked Larme.

'People saw him,' sniffed Henri.

'Do you deny it?'

'No,' admitted Thyman, kicking the boards. 'I stole it, I was caught. Seems fair enough.'

'Can you give it back?' asked Larme.

'I threw it over the side.'

'Christ's sake, man,' said Drecht. 'Why?'

'He had things to say about musketeers, sir. One of them was going over the side. Thought you'd prefer if it was the hand plane.'

Drecht smiled under his beard.

'Come back here after we drop anchor,' said Larme, in the long-suffering voice of somebody who had seen a lot of hand planes and a lot of Thymans in his time. 'Thyman, you've admitted guilt, so you'll take the penalty. One hand tied behind your back.'

Thyman started. 'Come on now, that's –'

'Those are the rules,' growled Larme. 'You did the cheating, you'll pay for it. You fight until one of you drops. The rest of us will watch and bet, so put on a good show.'

'Good enough,' said Guard Captain Drecht, clapping his hands on the shoulders of the two men. 'Off you go then.'

As they grumbled away, Drecht took a pinch of something rotten from his bandolier. He was about to touch it to his nostril, when he remembered his manners and offered Larme some.

The dwarf waved it away.

'Is it true Crauwels knows when a storm's coming?' asked Drecht, sniffing the mix. It brought tears to his eyes.

'It is,' said Larme.

'And he's saying there's one on the way?'

Larme nodded. Drecht tipped his chin to the blue sky.

'Reckon he's got this one wrong,' snorted Drecht.

'Hasn't happened yet,' disagreed Larme, heading for the staircase. 'I've got to help with the search.'

'You were there as well,' yelled Drecht, flinging the accusation at Larme's back. 'So, you can save your disdain. We've got a long way to go together, you and me. Might as well be friendly about it.'

'Stay on your side of the ship and I'll be friendly as you like,' said Larme, descending the staircase. 'I might even keep my blade out of your back.'

Drecht watched him go, then stooped to collect the carving Larme had dropped in his haste to be away. His brow furrowed as he turned it over in his hands. He clearly couldn't tell what it was supposed to be, but it definitely had a wing.

A bat wing, maybe.

31

S ARA FLUNG OPEN HER door before Isabel had time to knock, having heard her approaching steps.

'Dorothea said you wanted to see me,' said Isabel, her eyes roaming over the opulence of the cabin.

'Is there anything in the daemonologica that describes how Old Tom is summoned?' she asked.

Isabel removed the book from her satchel, then found the page quickly.

'Here,' she said, tapping a block of ornate words.

Sara read it out loud.

'To summon Old Tom three things are required: the blood of a loved one spilled on to a blade. The blade used to sacrifice somebody hated, and a dark prayer read aloud in his honour before the body cools.'

Sara blew out a breath, ruffling the corner of the page.

Arent's father must have been the hated one, she thought. He was the only one who'd died in that forest. Arent had been the loved one. She continued reading.

'Once summoned and bound, Old Tom is compelled to offer a boon in return for his freedom. He will bargain, wheedle and deceive, but those who see through his tricks can ask for anything. The price is knowing that they are releasing a terrible evil on to this world to wreak havoc as it pleases, something they will pay dearly for come Judgement Day. Once this initial boon is granted, the summoner must pay a tithe for any further favours. The cost is usually high. Old Tom does not like being made to look foolish.'

Sara clutched Isabel's hand in thanks. 'You've done me a great service. Have you seen Arent Hayes?'

'He was going down to the orlop deck a few minutes ago.'

Sara darted from her cabin and out into the sunshine, almost colliding with Captain Crauwels who was watching a large sandglass, while Larme let a knotted piece of rope through his hands into the water. It was tied to a log, bobbing behind the ship. The sandglass emptied.

'We're making 10.2 knots, Captain.'

'Let's hope it's enough to put us beyond the reach of this storm.'

Manoeuvring around them, she made her way to the orlop deck, finding the stairs rammed with passengers returning reluctantly from their exercise. Pushing through the throng, she saw Arent disappearing into the cargo hold beneath. Ignoring the strange looks she was given, she went to the edge of the staircase he'd descended, a foul stink rising into her nostrils. It stretched much further down than she would have imagined, the steps disappearing beyond sight. He must have already been at the bottom, because she couldn't see him.

'Arent,' she called out in a hushed voice, wary of being overheard.

There was no reply. Straining her ear, she heard the distant sounds of the search, as trunks were tipped over and casks ripped open. The sailors had already been through the aft of the ship and uncovered nothing; now they'd moved into the bow sections.

She put a foot on the first step down, then hesitated, imagining how her husband would react. Even now, she wasn't sure what had possessed her to sit and drink with Arent and Jacobi Drecht last night. It had been foolish. Drecht wouldn't say anything, but gossip carried itself straight to her husband's ear. Everybody wanted to ingratiate themselves with a powerful man.

If he found out … she shuddered to imagine it. Even so, she couldn't hold on to what she'd heard any longer. She had too many questions.

She gave herself to the darkness of the cargo hold. It was oily on the skin, stinking of bilge water and sawdust, spices and rot. Drops fell from the ceiling, pattering against the crates. It was as if every wretched thought conceived on the decks above was seeping through the ship, collecting here.

She found Arent inspecting a gouge on the bottom step, by the light of a brass lantern. Sara recognised this technique from the reports she'd read. By Pipps's reckoning, every object could tell you a story if you understood its language. A broken cobweb betrayed somebody's passing, while the sticky silk on their shoulder told who it was.

'Arent.'

He squinted at her through the fog pouring out of the lantern. It was burning fish oil. The smell was unmistakable. 'Sara? What are you doing down here?'

'My husband summoned Old Tom, I overheard him telling Vos,' she blurted out. 'He murdered your father as part of the ritual, and gave you that mark on your wrist.'

It took his thoughts a few seconds to absorb what she'd told him, his expression changing from bafflement to disbelief, then anger.

'My uncle ...' He couldn't finish. 'Why would he do that?'

'Power, wealth ... The person who summons Old Tom can ask for *anything*, so long as he agrees to release the demon.'

'Where is my uncle?'

'In the great cabin.'

Arent put a foot on the stair, only for a growl to sound somewhere deeper in the cargo hold. Arent immediately swung his light towards the labyrinth of stacked crates. They rose up like walls, his light clawing vainly at the wood.

'What was that?' asked Sara nervously.

'Wolf?' guessed Arent.

'On an Indiaman?'

'Did you bring your dagger?' he asked.

Sara tugged at her gown. 'My dressmaker hates pockets, remember?'

'Go back to the orlop deck.'

'Where are you going?'

'To see what made that sound.' He strode off towards the maze of crates that filled the cargo hold. His lantern seemed very tiny amidst all that wood and darkness.

Sara turned her body towards the staircase. She was trained to obey. Her entire life she'd been told what to do, and she'd done it. It was part of her conditioning and yet, for some reason, the thought of him going alone felt wrong.

It was as if she were abandoning him.

Instead of departing, she stepped off the staircase, putting her foot straight into the freezing bilge water. It was ankle-deep, already creeping up her skirts, sloshing left and right as the ship listed.

'Arent,' she called out. 'Wait.'

'Go back,' he hissed.

'I'm coming,' she insisted, her tone putting an end to the argument.

Narrow alleys had been left between the stacks to allow sailors to cross the deck, but their arrangement was dictated by the placement of the crates. There were no straight lines, and no obvious paths. The passages narrowed and widened, leaving orientation to their sense of smell. The hold had been packed according to cargo, such that one minute they were sneezing on pepper and the next they were gagging on thick clouds of paprika.

Following Arent through the passages, Sara stared at his huge back and massive slouched shoulders, the lantern light running down them.

Her nerve momentarily deserted her.

He could do anything he wanted to her and she'd have no way of fighting back. If she was wrong and Sander Kers was right, then she had delivered herself to Old Tom without anybody knowing where she was – and she'd have done it thoughtlessly, recklessly, indulging the very qualities her husband so despaired of in her.

'Stay close,' said Arent.

How could she have been so stupid? She didn't know this man. Not underneath. She'd seen his kindness on the docks and assumed that's all there was. Now, she'd allowed herself to be led into this precarious position.

She gritted her teeth and put a rod of iron through her thoughts.

This fear wasn't hers, she realised angrily. It belonged to Sander Kers, but she'd caught it like the plague.

She *did* know Arent. She knew exactly what was underneath. She'd seen it when he rushed to help the leper, while everybody else stood and gawped. She knew him from his fiddle playing, and the pleasure he took from it. She knew him from the dagger he'd given her after the leper appeared. She knew him from his loyalty to Samuel Pipps, and the fire that burnt behind his eyes when he spoke of him. She knew him from this very search. If Arent Hayes was a demon, then he had disguised himself so completely he had accidentally become a good man.

'Arent, do you bear the Mark of Old Tom?'

He flinched as if she'd struck him. The lantern shook in his hand as he turned towards her. 'Aye,' he said. 'Got it after my father disappeared, but I couldn't tell you how. Wish I could.'

'You're connected to our enemy,' she said, her pride wounded. 'Why would you conceal that fact from me?'

'I didn't know how to tell you,' he admitted, staring at his wrist. 'My grandfather asked me to keep this secret when I was a boy, and I've been doing it for as long as I can remember. It doesn't come natural to talk about, even to you.'

Another growl rolled through the passages, causing them to freeze. After a tense minute, all was silent again.

'Lord above, I wish I was your size,' said Sara, blood beating in her ears.

'Most places I've been, it's just made me a target.' He began walking again, swinging his flame left and right, searching for danger. 'Believe me, you don't want to be the biggest man on a battlefield. Every archer in the enemy ranks uses you to get their eye in.'

'Do you ever miss it?'

'Being used as target practice?'

'War.'

He shook his head, watching the darkness cautiously. 'Nobody misses war, Sara. It would be like missing the clap.'

'What about the glory, the honour? Your deeds at the battle of Breda are –'

'Mostly lies.' He sounded almost angry. 'There's no glory, except what the minstrels make up so the nobles can feel good about the slaughter they paid for. A soldier's job is to end up dead far from home, fighting for a king who wouldn't give them the crumbs from his table.'

'Then why do it?'

'I needed a job,' he said. 'I left home without stopping to think what would happen next, then there was just one thing after another, until I was in the mud and blood. I tried being a clerk, but my grandfather kept finding me, so I went looking for work with no connection back to him. But what did I know of the world I went into? Until that first winter on my own, I'd never been cold, not really. Never been hungry. Never even had to fetch my own food. I took the first coin somebody would pay me, which was thief-taking work.'

They were deep in the maze now. Sara's dress had soaked up so much bilge water it was beginning to weary her.

'What was it like being a thief-taker? You never talked about your life before Sammy in the reports.'

'I solved petty squabbles for the most part.' His voice had warmed, filled with fondness. 'My first job was convincing a cordwainer off his barstool so he could keep his promise to the woman he'd spilled his seed in. I talked to that man for an hour, before I realised I was just supposed to punch him, then drag him unconscious in front of the predikant.'

'How did you end up serving Pipps?'

'That's a long story.'

'We're in a long maze.'

He laughed, conceding the point. Considering their situation, Sara was surprised he could manage it. Danger obviously affected them very differently. She was talking to distract herself, knowing that if she stopped, she'd fly back upstairs in fright.

By contrast, Arent's hand was steady. His tone was firm. Anybody who'd stumbled upon them might assume he was out for a pleasant walk.

'I'd been thief-taking for a year, when I was sent to collect a debt owed by an Englishman named Patrick Hayes,' said Arent. 'He ambushed me, and I killed him. I didn't mean to, but' – He examined his huge scarred hands – 'my strength gets away from me when my temper's up.'

'Is that why your temper's never up?'

'You've never seen me try to play The Ballad of Samuel Pipps on my fiddle. Whichever bard came up with that must have had nineteen fingers.'

'Why did you take his name?'

'The bard?'

'Hayes,' she sighed. 'The man you killed.'

'Shame.' He glanced at her over his shoulder. 'I wanted something to remind me how it felt to kill a man.'

'Did it work?'

'Still think of him now.' Oily water fell from the distant ceiling and plinked against the lantern. 'I thought that would be enough. I thought all I had to do was feel guilty and promise never to take another life, and that would be it. Only thing is Hayes had brothers, so they came for revenge. They had friends, and the friends had brothers. Nobody ever tells you that if you take a single life, you have to murder the mob who'll follow after.'

The quantity of his regret made her feel foolish for suspecting him.

'Thing about grief is that every death makes the pile lighter,' he said, peering around a corner. 'One death is heavier than ten and a hundred are weightless. By the time I'd killed everybody who'd tried to kill me, mercenary work seemed an obvious way to make coin. After I rescued my uncle at Breda, he bought my commission, so I didn't have to fight in the melee any more. Then Sammy came calling.' He smiled. 'Truth about Sammy is that once the web's unpicked, he couldn't care less where the spider scurries off to. Unfortunately for him, his clients rarely felt the same way. He hired me to do the chasing and fighting he didn't want to do.'

Sara almost stopped dead. In Arent's reports, Sammy was forever leaping out of windows on to horses to chase down the guilty. He was courageous and brave, striking down the unjust like a bolt out of heaven. More than once, she'd imagined herself alongside the bear and the sparrow, dashing off on a new adventure. To find out Pipps was something entirely different made her feel slightly sad, and a little foolish.

'Then why do you do it?' she asked.

'Because it's righteous work,' he replied, baffled by the question. 'Sammy puts right wrongs others wouldn't bother with, or wouldn't see. Doesn't matter if you're a pauper who lost two coins, or a noble whose children disappeared from their beds. If the case is interesting, Sammy will investigate. Imagine if there were more people like that? Imagine if everybody had somebody to help them when the bad things happened?'

He sounded wistful, conjuring an entire world through the yearning in his voice.

'My grandfather saw most people as disposable, there to be used and tossed away in pursuit of ever more wealth and ever more power. Nobody ever stood up for them, or protected them. If you weren't rich and you weren't strong, he believed you had to take whatever unjustness life saw fit to mete out. I hated that about him. And I truly hated that he was right.'

The growl came again, close enough to prickle the hairs on Sara's neck. The lantern jumped in Arent's hand, briefly illuminating something scratched into the wood. Sara took hold of his forearm, drawing the flame towards the nearest crate. As the light fell upon it, she felt a chill settle in the pit of her stomach.

Scarring the crate was the eye with the tail.

'The Mark of Old Tom,' said Arent in disgust.

He took an involuntary step back, but his light washed towards another one a little further ahead. Creeping closer to it revealed another, then another, and another.

A growl came from the end of the passage.

Spinning towards it, they saw the leper waiting for them, a small candle held in its hands.

It was watching them.

It gave them time to see it, then walked unhurriedly away. Sara grabbed hold of Arent's arm and was relieved to see he finally looked uncertain.

'It wants us to follow,' she said.

'Probably into a trap.'

'Then why not just attack us from behind? Why go through all of this?'

Pressed tight together, they followed the passage to the last spot where they'd seen the leper. Turning a corner, they found it waiting for them again. Closer this time. Its head was bowed, reverentially, over its small candle.

'What do you want?' called out Arent.

It turned and walked away. This time they didn't hesitate, quickening their pace in pursuit. The smell of spices tickled Sara's nose. Rats darted away from the splashing water.

The marks covered every crate this deep into the maze, the lines seeming to shift and crawl, like thousands of spiders scurrying up the walls.

Sara gritted her teeth. She was deathly afraid, but she was deathly afraid most days of her life. At least, she could see an end to this. At least this fear led somewhere.

A light flared, as if the cover had been taken off a candle.

Arent tensed, then went cautiously towards it, with Sara following a little behind.

Expecting an assault, he put his arms up to protect his face, then stepped quickly around the corner. Eight candles were burning on a makeshift altar, the Mark of Old Tom drawn upon it. Hundreds more covered the surrounding walls.

'It's a church,' said Sara, horrified. 'Old Tom's made himself a church.'

'Which means he likely already has followers among the crew,' said Arent.

32

A RENT AND SARA SLOSHED back through the labyrinth in a daze. The cargo hold was still pitch black, the
air was still fetid and the stink still scratched at their skin, but
they both knew the danger had been sapped out of it – at least
for the moment.

The leper had completed its errand.

'What does Old Tom want?' wondered Arent.

'Devotion,' replied Sara. 'What else do you need an altar
for?'

'A sacrifice?' They considered that, then Arent spoke again,
lost in his own musings. 'I wonder if the altar is the reason
Isabel came down here.'

'Isabel?'

Arent told her about Isabel's encounter with the constable
last night.

'"Popped his carrot back in the sack"?' she repeated, giggling.
'That's the phrase he used?'

'Almost brought my breakfast up when I heard it,' said
Arent, grinning. 'But we know Isabel's sneaking around the
ship at night. That altar's as good a reason as any. Could be
that Old Tom's managed to convert the predikant's ward.'

'That would make sense,' said Sara. 'Sander Kers is hunting Old Tom. He believes the demon is possessing somebody on the ship. He told me this morning.'

'Who?'

'You.'

'Me?'

'Possibly. Apparently, we're hunting for somebody with a bloody past.'

'Should narrow it down,' replied Arent sarcastically, blowing a little life back into their flame. 'Does Sander Kers want this demon dead, by any chance? Maybe he's found a good excuse to commit murder.'

'He does, but I don't think he's lying.' From high above them, pinpricks of light shone from the grates that had been used to lower the cargo down. Footsteps were passing back and forth across them. It would have been faster to get out by climbing the stacks of crates and pushing one of the grates open.

Then she remembered how heavy her dress was.

'Sander was lured here as well,' she continued. 'He received a letter from Creesjie's husband asking that he join him in Batavia to fight Old Tom, but Pieter was already dead when the letter was written.'

'We definitely need to know more about Sander and Isabel,' said Arent.

'Leave it to me, I'll ask –'

From somewhere near, they heard a scrape, then a thud. Somebody cursed.

'That sounded like Isaack Larme,' said Sara, raising an eyebrow.

'Larme, is that you?' called out Arent.

'Over here,' he hollered back.

They followed his voice to find him inspecting a Mark of Old Tom by the light of a candle on a tray. There was a knife in his hand, its edge made jagged by rust. He was puffing slightly, as if he'd just completed some labour. Upon seeing them, he tapped the mark. 'Did you see these? Same symbols as on the sail.'

Sara noticed a sliver of wood still clinging to the tip of Larme's blade.

'It's the Mark of Old Tom,' said Arent. 'Wherever it appears, disaster follows. This is what I was trying to warn you about.'

'They're everywhere,' said Sara. She waved towards the heart of the maze. 'The leper built an altar. Old Tom's taking hold of this ship.'

Larme glanced at the marks again, then slipped the knife into his boot. 'Or it's the crew playing silly buggers,' he replied. His gaze travelled Sara up and down, without any apparent concern for her rank. 'You shouldn't be down here. No place for a woman, this.'

'We heard a scraping, then a thump,' said Arent.

Guilt flashed across Larme's face. 'Probably the search,' he said unconvincingly.

'Seemed closer than that,' disagreed Sara.

'I didn't hear anything.'

Sara looked around, trying to make sense of it, but the cargo hold was too dark and the candle too bright. It etched out Larme, but blinded them to everything else.

'Why didn't you tell me you were friends with Bosey?' asked Arent.

'I weren't.'

'You've half a charm each,' said Arent. 'I've heard that means you get his pay at the end of this voyage. You must have meant something to each other.'

'And none of it's your business,' said Larme, the flame falter-ing momentarily as he picked up the tray with the candle on it.

'Don't you want to know who killed him?' tried Sara. 'Don't you want to know who stuck him on those crates, then burnt him alive?'

Larme ran a nervous tongue around his lips.

'Or maybe you already know,' said Arent slowly. 'And you just don't want us to find out.'

'You don't know what you're talking about,' snarled Larme.

'Then tell us,' said Arent.

'Don't you think I want to? Do you reckon I'm happy that something wants to put us on the bottom? I can't talk to you, because you're a soldier.'

'I'm not,' appealed Sara.

'You're a woman. Aint much better.'

'For heaven's sake,' she said, annoyed at his stubbornness. 'There's just us three, down in the dark. What does it matter?'

He shook his head angrily, jabbing a finger at them. 'Everybody thinks sailing is about the wind and waves. It aint. Sailing's about the crew, which means it's about superstition and hate. The men you're depending on to get you home are murderers, cutpurses and malcontents, unfit for anything else. They're only on this ship because they'd be hanged anywhere else. They've got short tempers and violent passions, and we've locked them all together in a space we'd feel bad keep-ing cattle in. Captain Crauwels sails this ship, and I keep the crew from mutiny. If either of us makes a mistake, we're all dead.' His jutted out his chin pugnaciously, like a man ready to spill somebody's drink in a tavern. 'Do you know why the crew hate soldiers so much? It's because we tell them to. If they didn't, they'd realise how much they hate each other, and we'd never get home.' He steadied his light. 'If I answer your questions, if I help either of you in any way, I put myself on your side, not theirs. So, there's my choice: Bosey or this ship. Which would you choose?'

Receiving no answer, he snorted and strode off.

Sara and Arent listened to his footsteps fade, then Arent walked to where Larme had been standing. 'What could have made that scrape and thump we heard? What was Larme doing down here?'

'Moving crates?' suggested Sara.

Arent pushed at a couple, finding them pinned solid by the weight of those stacked on top. 'Any other ideas?'

'Perhaps one of the sides is false?' she ventured.

He thumped some. They all seemed firmly attached.

Sara stamped on the floor, water splashing up her legs. She'd always enjoyed the parts of Pipps's stories where he found a trapdoor, and was hoping to discover one for herself. She was disappointed. If the floorboards had secrets, they were holding them close.

Arent stared at the thick beams of the hull curving down towards them. His fingers roamed across the rough wooden planks.

'What are you looking for?' wondered Sara, joining the search.

'Whatever I'm missing. Whatever Sammy would have —' He slapped his hands together. 'Larme's a dwarf! He wouldn't have been able to reach the section of wall we're searching.'

He knelt in the bilge water, soaking his hose. The stink was dreadful.

Sara eyed the dirty water with distaste, but she was already filthy. With a shudder, she joined him in the muck.

Her smaller fingers soon snagged on a peg.

'Here,' she cried triumphantly.

In truth, it wasn't terribly well hidden. Whoever had built it, had trusted to darkness to conceal it, rather than any great craft. She yanked it out, causing a panel to scrape loose, then thud on to the floor.

There was a compartment behind it.

Arent drew his lantern closer, so they could peer inside.

'Oh!' said Sara in disappointment. It was empty. Whenever Pipps did this, there was always something inside. Usually jewels, though on one particularly gory occasion, it had been a severed head.

'Larme must have moved whatever was in here,' she said. 'He came down here to hide something.'

33

A RENT ARRIVED AT THE great cabin to find the fleet captains sitting around the table, banging their fists and shouting over one another, scolding Adrian Crauwels for calling battle stations. A solitary light appearing on a solitary night could be anything, they'd argued. There had been no need to panic them from their beds.

The only person not shouting was Crauwels himself. He was smoking a pipe and playing with the metal disc he carried, tracing the lines of the double-headed bird crest with his fingernail.

There was wisdom in his silence, thought Arent. It was much easier to annoy his uncle than impress him. Half of these men would be hauling peat on clapped-out scows in a year's time, wondering when their fortunes had soured.

'Gentlemen!' yelled the governor general, at last. 'Gentlemen!' The room quietened. 'Tonight we will extinguish our running lights and give our mysterious vessel no flame to chase. If it returns, the *Saardam* will put a yawl in the water and send it to investigate. Return to your ships and start making preparations. Good day!'

Arent waited for the fleet captains to grumble out, then entered the room. His uncle had remained seated and was discussing something with Vos, who was standing at his side, hands clasped behind his back. Guard Captain Drecht had taken a position by the cabin door. He nodded in friendly fashion to Arent.

A master and his two hounds, thought Arent uncharitably.

Hearing Arent's footfalls, the governor general turned his head, then immediately smiled in delight to see his nephew. 'Ah, Arent, I –'

'How did I come by this mark, Uncle?' demanded Arent, holding up his wrist. 'What happened to my father?'

His tone sent Drecht's hand to his sword hilt, while Vos glowered on his master's behalf. The governor general simply leant back in his chair, steepling his hands.

'If I knew, I'd tell you,' he said calmly.

'I heard you talking to Vos,' said Arent, hoping to protect Sara from any recrimination 'I know *you* summoned Old Tom, and I know my father's life was the price for it.'

The governor general's face fell. He glared at the chamberlain, who shied back under his scrutiny. It was like watching a hawk spot a field mouse far below.

'Is it true?' insisted Arent. 'Did you sacrifice my father to bring Old Tom into this world?'

The governor general considered his nephew, beset by calculations. His ink-blot eyes were impossible to read.

'Your grandfather ordered your father's death,' he said, at last. 'Your father was a zealot and a madman, who believed you were the devil's work from the moment you were born. After he beat you unconscious, your grandfather realised he was going to kill you eventually. Casper could not let that happen. He loved you too much. He asked me to make the arrangements, and I did as he asked.'

Arent's world was spinning. The mystery of his father's disappearance had haunted his entire childhood. It had driven him from his mother's home. His grandfather's servants had whispered about it when they thought he couldn't hear. Their children devised games to torment him, whispering through the door that they were his father's spirit returned to carry him away.

And, always, there had been the question of whether Arent had been the one to fire an arrow into his back. And what that made him, if he had.

That his grandfather and his uncle had known the answer all along was the gravest betrayal he could imagine.

'Why didn't he tell me?' he stammered, still reeling.

'Because ordering the death of your own son is no small thing, Arent.' There was sympathy in his response, though whether it was for Casper van den Berg or for him, Arent couldn't tell. 'Your grandfather was ashamed of what his son had become. He was ashamed of what he had to do, and he was ashamed that he couldn't do it himself. Your grandfather abhors weakness of any sort, especially that which he finds in himself.'

The governor general leant forward into a shaft of sunlight, breathing deeply, as if it were something he could taste. 'The past is poison. He wanted it behind him, and I swore to keep the secret.'

'Then why do I have this mark?'

'The assassin did it.' He pursed his lips. 'The assassin did a number of troubling things. He was supposed to kill your father within sight of your home, not leave you wandering the forest for three days. Truly, we don't know what became of you in that time.'

'What became of the assassin?'

'Gone.' He closed his fist, then opened his fingers. 'Vanished. He delivered your father's rosary to Casper, then took his coin. We never heard from him again.'

'The rosary was proof he was dead?'

'Yes. It was your father's dearest possession. Casper knew he would never have relinquished it willingly.'

'But you summoned Old Tom? I heard you admit it.'

Vos coughed in warning. Such was the intensity of the conversation Arent had entirely forgotten the chamberlain was there. The governor general ignored his counsellor, considering Arent shrewdly. 'Do you believe in demons, Arent?' he asked.

'No,' he responded firmly.

'If you don't believe in something, how could I have summoned it? You're asking me these questions because your life changed in that forest, and you want to know what caused the change. I'll tell you this, every decision that's led you here is your own. Not mine, not your grandfather's. Not God's, or Old Tom's. Believe me, we both wished it otherwise, but you always went your own way.'

'You didn't answer the question.'

'I answered *a* question,' replied his uncle, rubbing his eye with the knuckle of his thumb. 'Sometimes that's the best you can hope for.'

'That's a line from one of my reports.'

'Did you think I lost sight of you these long years?' He rapped the table, as if drawing a marker he daren't pass. 'There's much I can't tell you.'

'Uncle –'

'It's testament to my love for your family that I'm answering the questions I am, with the honesty I have. No other man could demand this of me.'

Arent heard the rebuke in his voice. By his uncle's standards, this was a beating in a back alley. His forbearance wouldn't last much longer.

'Did my grandfather know about Old Tom?' asked Arent.

'I kept nothing from Casper.'

'Why is this happening, Uncle? Who's behind it? Why was the demon's mark on the sail?'

'Because I wanted more than was offered. The rest I've trusted you to uncover on my behalf.' He paused. 'Do you believe I love you, Arent?'

Arent spoke without hesitation. 'Yes.'

The governor general puffed out his chest a little. 'Then know that I keep my secrets to protect you. Not from doubt, or fear. I trust you above anybody else on this ship. I'm proud of what you've become.'

He got to his feet and clapped his hands on Arent's arms fondly. He smiled with a vague air of sadness, then stalked into his cabin without another word. Vos followed him inside, closing the door quietly.

Drecht stared at Arent astonished, but said nothing.

Arent left him, his fury having burnt down to ash. He'd been lied to his entire life, though for the best of reasons. His uncle was right. His father had been a monster who certainly would have killed him. Casper and Jan Haan had murdered him to protect Arent, then lied about it to protect themselves.

Sara was waiting nervously outside.

She flew to him. 'I heard everything,' she said. 'I'm so sorry, Arent.'

'Don't pity me, pity the *Saardam*,' warned Arent, glaring back through the doorway. 'If Old Tom has some sort of hold on my uncle, he has a hold on this ship. This battle may already be lost.'

34

'THE SECRET COMPARTMENT IN the cargo hold was empty?' asked Drecht, who was perched on a stool, buffing the nicks from his sabre with a stone. The guard captain was shirtless, thick whorls of blond hair covering his chest. As always, he was wearing that wide-brimmed hat with the red feather in it.

He had entered the compartment under the half deck an hour ago, finding Arent sitting alone, staring into space. Drecht hadn't mentioned what he'd heard in the great cabin. He'd simply thumped a jug of wine on to the keg they used as a table and asked, seemingly without irony, how Arent's day had gone. The mercenary had told him about the leper's altar – which Crauwels had ordered destroyed – and the compartment he'd found with Sara.

'Completely empty,' confirmed Arent, tearing the cork from a second jug. The afternoon heat was beating at the deck, and most of the sailors were indoors, or else hiding in whatever pitiful scrap of shade they could find. As a result, the *Saardam* – usually so alive with sound – was eerily quiet, aside from the splashing of waves.

'How big was the compartment?' asked Drecht.

'Could probably fit a sack of grain inside.'

'Smuggler's compartment,' confirmed Drecht knowledge-ably, scraping the stone down his blade. 'The *Saardam* will be riddled with them. Every Indiaman is. The senior officers use them so they don't have to pay the Company for shipping space.'

Arent took a swig of the wine, then spluttered. It was boil-ing hot after having sat in his trunk. 'What do they transport?' he asked, wiping his lips.

'Whatever can turn a profit.'

'Bosey and Larme were friends,' said Arent, thoughtfully. 'And Bosey was a carpenter. If Bosey built the smuggler's compartment, maybe Larme used it to transport cargo ille-gally, splitting the profits with his mate. But what did Larme take out of it this morning?'

Drecht grunted, having lost interest.

'Do you know why my uncle threw Sammy Pipps into a cell?' asked Arent abruptly.

'Was a favour to somebody, way I understand it. Though for who, I couldn't tell you. The governor general doesn't tell me things like that,' muttered Drecht, frowning at a problematic chip in the blade. 'Vos keeps his secrets for him. I just kill them who carry them away.'

A favour, thought Arent. Who on earth would his uncle do that kind of favour for? Whoever it was, they clearly had some nefarious purpose in mind.

'I'll trade you a question for a question,' continued Drecht. 'Do you know what this secret cargo is that he brought aboard?'

'The Folly?'

'No, something else. Something much bigger.'

'Never heard of it,' said Arent.

Drecht paused in his work, annoyed. 'Whatever it is, it took three days of moving. He had it snuck out of the fort in the dead of night and now it's taking up half the cargo hold.'

'Why are you concerned about it?'

'I can't protect him if I don't know why people are trying to kill him. Whatever that cargo is, it's important.' He shook his head irritably. 'There's too many damn secrets on this ship, and I swear all of them are marching towards him with swords in their hands.'

'How long have you watched over him?'

'Lost track,' he replied somewhat sourly. 'When did we capture Bahia?'

'About seventeen years ago.'

'That was it, then.' He scowled at the memory. 'Your uncle needed somebody to escort him out of Spain and I still had all of my limbs, unlike most of them that survived the battle. Told my wife I'd be back in six months, but I've been with him ever since. How long have you been with Pipps?'

'Five years,' said Arent, taking another gulp of the terrible wine. 'He heard the songs about me and decided he needed somebody like that standing in front of him when he accused people of murder.'

Drecht laughed. 'You never put *that* in your stories.'

'Good sense sometimes sounds like cowardice when you write it down.' Arent shrugged his massive shoulders.

'What's he really like?' asked Drecht, dragging the stone along his blade again.

'Depends on the day,' replied Arent, carefully. 'He was born with nothing and he's terrified of going back to it. I only write about the interesting cases, but he'll take any puzzle that pays well. Most of them he solves after a few minutes, then he sulks because he's bored, so he spends the money he earned indulging any vice that's near at hand.'

Drecht appeared a little crestfallen. 'The tales make him sound so noble,' he said.

'He can be, when the sun's right, and the wind's at his back.' Arent blew out a long breath. Truth was Sammy was kind infrequently, and nearly always unthinkingly, but such were his talents that the effect was life-changing. Once Sammy had overheard an old woman wailing for her dead husband, who'd been struck down in a street and had his purse stolen. Within the hour, Sammy had solved the murder, found the coins and returned them with a hundred more from his own pocket. He'd claimed the mystery had been so diverting it was worth paying for, but Arent had seen the look on the old woman's face. Sammy had reached out his hand and tipped over the world.

And that was the tricky part. Drecht wanted to know what Sammy was like, but it was too small a question. Arent could say that Sammy was clever, unique or special, or he could say that he was vain, greedy, lazy and, sometimes, cruel. Every word would be true, but none would be adequate.

The sky wasn't merely blue. The ocean wasn't merely wet. And Sammy wasn't like anybody else. Wealth, power and privilege didn't matter to him. If he thought somebody guilty of the crime he was investigating, he'd accuse them.

Sammy was what Arent hoped the entire world could be. If an old woman was wronged, she should have her recompense, whether she was rich or poor, strong or weak. The weak shouldn't have to fear the powerful, and the powerful shouldn't simply take what they wanted without consequence. Power should be a burden, not a shield. It should be used to everybody's betterment, not merely for the person who wielded it.

Arent shook his head. He hated it when his thoughts fell down this hole. It made him maudlin. He'd lived too long and travelled too far to believe in hearth tales, but while Sammy was alive, kings and nobles had somebody to fear. That was a comforting idea.

Arent passed Drecht the jug of wine, then asked, 'How did you end up in Batavia?'

'The alternative was another damn battlefield,' he replied sourly, taking a swig. 'And I've seen too many of them to relish going back to another. Besides, if I get him to Amsterdam in one piece, he's promised to make me rich. I can have servants of my own, my wife could come out of the fields. My children could look forward to something more than their father had. Aye, it'd be a fine thing.'

He lifted his sword, so that he could peer along the edge. Sunlight danced on the blade.

'Did my uncle give you that?' asked Arent.

'Reward for my loyalty these past years.' Drecht's eyes narrowed, coming, at last, to the real point of this visit. 'Your uncle is powerful, and powerful men have more enemies than friends. One in particular, I think.'

'Who?'

'I don't know, but whoever it is, he's been afraid of them for a long time. Got so he stopped leaving the fort. That's the reason every member of his household guard is travelling on this boat, instead of the handful who would actually fit. He's terrified of something. The kind of terror even high walls and a company of soldiers doesn't fix. Now, you tell me what could do that.'

'Old Tom?' guessed Arent.

Drecht grunted, then went back to buffing his sword.

35

As the fleet captains returned to their ships, Sara played her harp. There was no peace in anything else. Her fingers found the strings effortlessly, but she wasn't thinking about the music. It was simply there, all around her, like the sea around the *Saardam*. After a while, she would entirely forget that she had anything to do with it at all.

Atop the music floated dark and dreadful thoughts.

By his own admission, her husband had summoned Old Tom, a creature which had caused untold suffering across the Provinces and had now built an altar to itself on the *Saardam*. She wondered what bargain he'd struck, and how many of the horrors he'd perpetrated these last years had been to pay back his debt.

Sara looked through her harp strings at Creesjie and Lia. Her friend had on the damask silk gown she would be wearing at dinner, while Lia knelt at her feet, with tailor's pins in her mouth and a scrap of material clutched in her hand. An empty scroll case lay next to her.

'Can you walk across the room again?' asked Lia.

'I've walked across the room five times,' pointed out Creesjie testily. 'It's fine.'

'What if the case changes your gait and people notice?' fretted Lia.

'My gait is not what the men of this ship have been noticing.'

'Please,' wheedled Lia.

'Lia!' warned Creesjie, exasperated.

'Mama,' pleaded Lia.

'Creesjie,' interjected Sara. 'Just walk across the room one more time, please. Let her see.'

As they continued with their preparations, Sara's thoughts drifted back to her husband. He was wealthy and powerful and had been for a long time. If that was what he'd asked Old Tom for, how high must the price have been?

Slowly, she sifted over every act of malice he'd perpetrated in their time together. He'd slaughtered the population of the Banda Islands over a contract. Could that have been at Old Tom's insistence? Was his survival at Breda actually the creature's doing? What about the three times he'd almost beaten her to death? Where they scraps thrown to the beast to keep it sated?

Her finger missed a string, the music collapsing like a badly made house. She started again.

'I think I should make the loop bigger,' murmured Lia, staring at Creesjie's dress.

'The loop is quite big enough,' said Creesjie, yanking the hem out of Lia's hand.

'Can you lift it easily? Or is it too heavy?'

'Stop fretting,' demanded Creesjie. 'Sara, will you tell your infernal daughter that everything is perfect and she should stop fretting.'

Sara didn't hear. She too was fretting.

She knew how her husband thought. If his enemy couldn't be undermined, then he'd murder them. If he couldn't murder them, he'd try to buy them. If he couldn't buy them, he'd bargain. If Old Tom was on this boat, and it really was threatening him, his first impulse would be to offer it something.

And he had a great deal to offer.

He was sailing back to become a member of the Gentlemen 17, the most powerful body of men in the world. Through them he would have control of the Company's fleets and armies. He would be able to wreak havoc simply by placing a finger on a map. If it was suffering Old Tom yearned for, her husband would make a perfect herald.

The music became discordant. Her hand was shaking.

In the fort, she'd played at being Samuel Pipps, but always in the assurance that whether she failed or succeeded, the questions would still be answered. The mystery would be solved, the righteous would be victorious and no harm would come to anybody she loved.

But that was no longer the case. Old Tom was hiding in one of the passengers and unless she identified him soon, everybody she loved would be slaughtered.

'Lia?'

'Yes, Mama?'

'How well do you understand the principles keeping this ship afloat?'

'It's really a matter of ballast and –'

'Marvellous,' interrupted Sara, who didn't have time to plumb the depths of Lia's knowledge. 'Would you be able to determine the best place to build secret compartments in the hull?'

'I'd need to build a model,' said Lia, eyes agleam.

'If I find you some wood, how long will it take?'

'A week or more,' said Lia joyfully. 'Why do you need it?'

'If Bosey built one smuggling compartment, he likely built more. Whatever Larme was hiding, maybe he moved into another compartment.'

'Oh, good, you've got a new project,' said Creesjie to Lia. 'Perhaps, now, you'll finally leave me alone.'

36

T HE REST OF THE day passed idly, the heat weighing heavy on the ship.

The search had concluded without any sign of the leper's rags, leaving the crew restless and irritable without anything to show for it.

As the sun grew red and dipped behind the horizon, Crauwels gave the order to drop anchor and furl the sails. Two of the ships in the fleet continued into the dusk. They had lost time and the seas were placid. Evidently, they had decided to carry on through the night.

Crauwels watched them disappear into the red sun.

'Damn fools,' he muttered. 'Those reckless damn fools.'

37

T HE STEWARD WAS LAYING the cutlery for dinner, when Sara entered the great cabin, and knocked on her husband's door with the same trepidation she always felt around this time.

No answer came.

She tried again. No answer.

'Is he in there?' she asked Guard Captain Drecht, who was smoking his pipe while standing watch. Few men could stand watch like Guard Captain Drecht. It was like the air itself had been given a sword and a hat. He barely seemed to breathe.

'If I'm out here, he's in there,' he said simply.

Knocking a third time, she opened the door a crack, peeking inside to find her husband sitting stiff-backed by a guttering candle, staring at a passenger manifest.

'Husband,' she ventured.

She'd always been afraid of him, but it was different now. He'd bargained with devils. For all she knew, he'd given himself over to Old Tom. She would have given almost any price not to enter this room.

'Hmmm.' He roused himself. Blinking away his concerns, he focused on her, then the purple sky beyond the porthole, surprise showing on his face. 'The hours have run away from me,' he said distantly. 'I didn't realise our obligations were upon us.'

Standing, he began to unlace his breeches.

'A moment, pray,' she begged, going to his wine rack and taking down one of the Portuguese bottles he favoured.

'Shall we share a drink first?' she enquired, showing the bottle to him.

He scowled. 'Do you truly find me so repulsive that you need to be numbed by wine to tend your responsibilities?'

Yes. She put the thought aside.

'I'm parched is all,' she lied. 'The ship's humid.'

Keeping her back to him, she plucked the vial of sleeping draught from the small pouch concealed in her sleeve, uncorking it and upturning it over his mug. It was the same substance she'd used to ease Bosey's suffering back on the docks, and with the same agonising slowness, a solitary drop of the liquid gathered along the rim.

Upon the desk, she saw a piece of parchment poking out from behind a passenger manifest. Three names were visible, though it was clear there were others beneath.

Bastiaan Bos – 1604
Tukihiri – 1605
Gillis van de Ceulen – 1607

She frowned. The first two names meant nothing to her, but the Van de Ceulens had been a great family, until disgrace toppled them.

She tried to remember what the disgrace had been, but she wasn't sure she'd ever known. She'd been a girl when it happened, her questions about the incident met with vague answers that were more rumour than fact. The nobility was like that. They gorged on scandal, but quickly forgot what they'd eaten. After all, there was always more coming.

'Is the cork stuck?' asked her husband, the wood creaking as he shifted his feet to stand up.

'No,' she said quickly. 'There's a spider in my mug, that's all. I'm trying to get it out.'

'Crush it and be done.'

'There's no need to hurt it.'

He laughed at her timidity. 'A woman's heart is so easily bruised,' he said. 'No wonder most of your species prefers hearth and home.'

Most. The word was a window into his soul. Through it she could see the blighted landscape of their life together.

She eyed the vial. Arent had asked what one drop would do, then two and three. He'd never asked about five.

Five would kill.

It would be the simplest thing. She need only shake slightly harder and the liquid would pour out. He'd be dead within hours.

She'd wrestled with the insidious tug of it.

If Old Tom did lurk inside her husband, Sander could perform the banishing ritual and the threat would be at an end. Even if Old Tom wasn't possessing him, he had unleashed it on the world. Death was the least he deserved.

Her hand trembled, wanting to do it so badly. It was one tainted life in exchange for Lia's, she told herself. One life to put an end to the fear that had plagued her these last fifteen years.

But she didn't have the courage. What if he noticed and called for Drecht? What if it didn't work? What if it did?

Old Tom would be banished, but who'd believe she'd killed her husband to rid them of a devil? Under Company law, Van Schooten would have the authority to throw her to the crew for the rest of the voyage, then execute her in Amsterdam – assuming they made it that far.

Lia would be alone.

Ashamed of herself, she put the plan aside.

'What were you thinking about when I walked in?' she asked, trying to buy some time while the drop of sleeping draught grew heavy on the rim.

'Why?'

'I knocked three times, but you didn't answer.' Growing frustrated, she gave the vial a shake, causing a second drop of the liquid to dislodge itself.

Her heart stopped.

A single drop would put him in a deep sleep, but for no longer than usual. Two drops would keep him under well past breakfast. For a man who usually rose before dawn that would provoke questions. She considered making some excuse to try again, but he would surely notice the delay. Instead, she poured the wine and hoped he would blame his tiredness on the sea air.

'You seemed distracted,' she continued, bringing it over to him. 'That's rare for you.'

'My solace has never concerned you before,' he said suspiciously, tapping his mug with a long, sharp fingernail.

Feeling the first touch of panic, she realised she'd misplayed the moment. She hadn't acted the dutiful wife for many years, and, even when she had, it had been done from spite.

'It's been an odd day,' she said weakly, unable to summon a better lie.

'I heard,' he said, his eyes narrowing malevolently upon her. 'Or did you believe that your flight into the cargo hold with Arent had gone unnoticed?' He banged his wine down on the table and stood up. 'What was your intent, Sara? To humiliate me? What did you hope to gain?'

Panic rose in her. She flinched, expecting to be hit, but he simply stared.

'Did you think me oblivious to your carousing last night?' His face twisted into a lascivious grin. 'Tell me, how did you enjoy his fiddle?'

'Husband –'

'It's done, Sara,' he spat, waving it away. 'You'll see him no more. Arent's too good for you, and I'll not be embarrassed by your infatuation. We'll have no more breakfasts, no more questions.' He dashed his arm through the air. 'Consider your liberty at an end. You will spend your days in your cabin, except to complete your obligations to me, after which you'll return there immediately.'

Regaining his temper, he drained his wine and put the cup back down again.

'Undress,' he commanded, all traces of his former anger seemingly evaporated.

Having gone ice cold, she lowered her eyes, undoing the knots at her shoulders. Her gown slid to the floor, followed by her corset and stomacher, until she stood naked before him. He studied her with contempt, unhooking the six leather straps that kept his breastplate in place and hanging it on the armour stand in the corner. From the corner of her eye, she noticed a scrap of parchment tucked behind the buckle.

His breeches came off next, revealing those pale, bony legs and his erect penis.

Gesturing for her to lie down on the bunk, he took his position on top of her.

It was a work of moments.

A few grunts, gritted teeth and his seed was spilt.

He panted, his breath rancid on her face.

Humiliated, Sara's hands unclenched from the sheets. She stared at his thin neck, imagining what it would feel like to watch him struggle for his last breath.

Her husband gripped her chin and burrowed into her with those black eyes. 'Bear me a son and these obligations will be at an end.'

'I hate you,' she muttered.

It was reckless, foolish. She shouldn't have said it, but it welled up in her like sickness. She couldn't keep it down.

'I know. Why do you think I chose *you* of all your sisters?' He rolled off her and went to his writing desk, pouring a little more wine. 'Your father made an enemy of me, Sara. I sent pirates to burn his warehouses and raid his ships; then when I'd ruined him, I took one of his precious daughters as a prize. The one who could never love me, the one who would hate it the most.'

He finished the wine in a long gulp, then belched. 'How does it feel, knowing your suffering is secondary, that your torment isn't even your own?' He watched her keenly, awaiting her reaction.

'I know you bargained with Old Tom,' she spat, overcome by her loathing. 'I know you summoned it.'

Something stirred behind his eyes. It wasn't shock, or anger. It wasn't sadness, or surprise.

It was pride.

'I was the fourth son of a beleaguered family headed inevitably to ruin by my father's incompetence,' he said. 'God laid no grand plans for my future, so I wrote them myself with the devil that was to hand. You'll not shame me, Sara. And you'll find no regret. When The Folly is delivered, I will be scribed into history, while *you* – unremarkable and dull – will be forgotten.'

He waved her away.

'Now go. I have no further need of you.'

38

IN THE NARROW CONFINES of his berth, Arent wriggled into his old army uniform, his arms and legs shooting through the curtains. The breeches were tight around his waist and his faded green doublet was proving difficult to fasten.

He was dismayed, though not surprised.

For all the chasing after people he did, it was a softer life he lived now. He ate rich food and drank fine wine, going whole weeks without strain. It wasn't so in the army, where they'd marched or fought almost every day. And when there wasn't an enemy, they'd fought themselves. It had been miserable and uncomfortable and some days he didn't miss it at all.

Finally managing to button the doublet, he tucked the frayed hem of his shirt into his breeches, then examined it for stains, finding a few drops of dry blood near the neck.

It would have to do. Tatty as it was, this uniform remained the finest suit of clothes in his possession and the only one fit for dinner. His uncle had bought it for him, along with his commission. For all his myriad faults, Jan Haan had been the only one who'd understood why Arent wanted to leave his grandfather's home. He was the only one who hadn't shouted or forbidden. The only one who'd looked into Arent's eyes and seen the fear lurking underneath. Loyalty had compelled him to try talking his nephew out of it, but when it was clear he couldn't be dissuaded, he'd done everything he could to set him solidly upon his new path.

Once again, Arent felt that pang for the man he'd known, and the sharp shock of remembering who he'd become. Arent couldn't bring himself to believe in demons, but he understood the temptation. It would be a comfort to have something to blame, something he could banish, and have his uncle – the one who'd raised him – miraculously returned.

Arent rubbed his scar. His uncle claimed the assassin had given it to him, but why? And who else knew about it? Whoever it was who knew about his past had put the Mark of Old Tom on the sail. They had enlisted Bosey for some purpose aboard the ship. They'd dressed him in leper's rags and placed him on those crates to deliver a warning.

That took power and planning and organisation, which seemed a lot of effort to waste on a lowly mercenary.

Straightening his jacket, Arent made his way through the empty helm towards the great cabin. Drinks were being served by surly stewards, the passengers and officers mixing like warm and cold water in a bathtub, so that patches of jocularity sat next to awkward pauses, strained conversations stretching towards inevitable silences.

Sander and Isabel were speaking with Lia and Sara. There was a glassiness to Sara's eyes that suggested recent tears. She saw him at the threshold and offered him an inviting smile.

Arent felt his heart swell.

Vos stalked into view. He was staring at something on the far side of the cabin, his face twisted by misery. Arent followed his gaze, realising it was Creesjie under observation. Of them all, she was the only one who appeared to be having fun. She was standing within gossip's distance of Captain Crauwels, and Arent would have been hard pressed to decide who was better dressed. Creesjie was wearing a damask silk gown, inlaid with beads, lace flowing over her chest as blonde hair spilled down her back. Crauwels wore a leather jerkin and a silk shirt beneath. A burst of feathers hemmed his orange breeches and matching cape.

Creesjie laughed, flashing her fine teeth, then tugged play-fully at the captain's sash. 'Tell me, Captain, what are you truly: an uncouth merchant captain or a gentleman?'

'Can't I be both?'

'Impossible,' she said, tossing her hair. 'One creates wealth and so cares only for its acquisition and preservation. The other spends wealth and cares not how it arrived, only that it keeps doing so. They're incompatible pursuits, and yet here you are.'

He puffed out his chest in pride. It was a fine thing to be complimented by Creesjie Jens.

'Now, Captain, tell me, how did you come to be such a fascinating contradiction?'

Crauwels didn't see it, Arent was certain. He was so charmed, he didn't notice how directly she was digging. Hard questions were best wrapped in soft words, Sammy had once told him. Sammy was a master, but Creesjie was even better.

He wondered what she was after.

'I'll tell you, Mistress Jens, for I think you'll enjoy the story,' he said, leaning daringly close to her. 'My family were nobles once, until my grandfather – curse his soul – squandered our wealth. Growing up, there were traces of our former glory all around us. Mama kept pieces of furniture in rooms much too small to house them. She carried the manners of the class we'd departed, and could occasionally call on a connection not yet wrung dry, or an old debt still to be called in. That's how I got my commission as a captain in the fleet. It was the last favour of a former family friend who wanted nothing more to do with those who could offer nothing back.'

Creesjie covered her mouth with her hand in astonishment.

'As it turned out, I'm a natural seaman,' he bragged, enjoying her reaction. 'There isn't anyone better at navigating or reading the sea and sky; you can ask any of my crew. I won't let anybody else touch a map on the *Saardam*, for fear they'll steer us wrong. Even so, these skills seem a poor trade for everything lost, and so I cling to what I can. My manners, my dress, my education. I hold them close, so that when I finally rebuild my family's fortune, I'll be able to resume the life I lost.'

Creesjie gave him a look of such overwhelming promise that Arent looked away, for fear of intruding. 'You're a remarkable man, my captain,' she said. 'And, pray, how will you rebuild this fortune – and, if I may ask, will it be soon?'

Crauwels lowered his voice. 'Soon enough, I feel. There are always opportunities on a ship like this.' He glanced meaningfully at the governor general's cabin.

Valiantly though Creesjie tried she could get no more out of him, and their conversation drifted into empty wit.

Realising it was time to step through the doorway, Arent took a fortifying breath.

'I did the same,' said a drunken voice behind him.

Arent turned around to find Reynier van Schooten slumped in the corner of the helm, his legs splayed out before him, a bottle nestled by his crotch. Some attempt had been made to dress for dinner, but it had gone awry. After spilling wine on his shirt, he'd clearly pulled on a doublet to cover it, but he'd put the buttons through the wrong loops. Bows trailed by his ankles and his hose were piss-stained. About him hung the smell of alcohol and sweat, long nights and regret.

'What happened to you?' asked Arent.

'I made a mistake,' he said, swallowing. There was something desperate about him. Something terrible and sad. 'I wanted to be like them so badly.'

'Like who?'

'Them!' exclaimed Van Schooten, throwing a hand towards the great cabin. 'The thrice-damned nobility. I wanted what they had. I almost had it too.' His head dropped, so his chin pressed against his chest. 'I didn't realise what they did to get it. How much they ask of you. What it costs.'

Arent took a step towards him. Old Tom offered a person their heart's desire for a favour. He knew from Bosey's warning on the docks that it planned to bring merciless ruin to the *Saardam*, and the ship's master would be a fine ally in that cause.

'What did it cost, Van Schooten?' he demanded.

Van Schooten's head snapped up. 'What do you care? The boy who gave up being a Berg, to be what? What are you now? Pipps's lapdog.'

'What did it cost?' persisted Arent.

Van Schooten laughed, pulling at his soiled clothing, as if seeing it for the first time. 'I hate this Company, you know. Always have. Profit comes before principle, pride and people. My mama would have been ashamed to see me now. Would have been ashamed of what I've done.'

Arent was surprised to find common ground between them. His father would have been the same, he thought. Every

Sunday at Mass, he'd railed against the United East India Company, calling it the 'company of want'. It was his belief that everything needed by mankind had been freely given by God. Food hung on trees, grew in the soil and skipped through the forest. God's bounty, given to them by birthright. It was the devil brought want, he preached. Tempting people with fripperies: sugar, tobacco, alcohol; things that distracted them, that disappeared too quickly, that always needed replacing, things to go mad chasing. In the United East India Company, he saw the devil's hands at work, caging humanity with want, persuading them to buy their manacles new every month.

Arent hated his father, but he'd ended up half agreeing with the mad old bastard. He'd seen farmers work themselves to death in the fields, because they were paid a pittance for what they produced. Those who refused were forced. Those who stood in the way were murdered because progress demanded sacrifice.

Van Schooten was right. People didn't matter to the Company. They were commodities like everything else: free to produce and cheap to replace. Only what they dug out of the ground had value.

'You know what,' slurred Van Schooten. 'Truthfully, I'll be glad when Old Tom pulls this ship to the bottom of the ocean. Isn't anybody aboard worth saving.'

'It's not going to come to that,' argued Arent.

'Because *you're* going to stop it?' There was something almost pitying in his voice. 'Pipps's dancing bear thinks he's the one holding the chain now. That's rich.' His eyes narrowed, his tone becoming sharp. 'I heard a story about you. About the last case you took, something to do with a man named Edward Coil and a missing diamond.'

Arent tensed. 'That was a long time ago,' he said.

'And the jewel was never recovered. Did you steal it, Arent? That's what they say.'

'I arrived in Lille three months after it was stolen. Sammy arrived a month after that. It was long gone. Coil had thousands of guilders in a case under his bed.'

'Family wealth.'

'That's what Sammy discovered.' Arent spoke through gritted teeth. 'I made a mistake.'

'What happened to Coil?'

'I don't know.'

'You ruined his good name, and you don't know,' hooted Van Schooten.

'He fled before Sammy could reveal his innocence. We don't know where he went.'

Arent felt somebody push by him. The overpowering pomander immediately told him it was Captain Crauwels.

'Christ, Reynier,' said Crauwels, looking down at Van Schooten pityingly. 'What's happened to you? You've been a donkey's dick for the last two weeks.'

Van Schooten looked up at him pleadingly, tears welling.

'I –'

He was interrupted by a clatter of footsteps, the door banging open as Isaack Larme burst inside.

'It's back, Captain,' he said, out of breath. 'The Eighth Lantern is back!'

39

N o sooner was the cell door open than Sammy came scrambling out, sucking in the clean air. Despite the humidity, he was clammy. His eyes were large as plates, his hair lank, his breath rancid. He was clutching the vial of sleeping draught Sara had given him.

'By God, it's good to be out of there,' he proclaimed, using Arent's outstretched arm to clamber to his feet.

Arent tried to keep the despair from his face.

His only job was to keep Sammy Pipps from harm, but every hour he was locked in this cell was another hour he failed in that task. Yesterday, he'd been convinced his uncle's affection for him would be enough to win Sammy's freedom. Today, he knew it wouldn't even parlay him a cabin.

As he had the night before, Sammy demanded that Arent turn his back when they reached the weather decks, so he could drop his breeches and relieve himself over the side of the ship.

'Eighth Lantern's back, I see,' he said, counting the flames in the distance.

'They're putting a yawl in the water to investigate,' said Arent. 'If you hurry, we can watch them.'

'Never rush a man while he's on the privy,' scolded Sammy, as a torrent of piss arced over the side of the ship. 'Tell me what you've learned.'

'I met the leper today. It led me to an altar it had built in the *Saardam*'s cargo hold.'

'Is it still there? Can I inspect it?'

'Captain Crauwels ordered it destroyed.'

'Of course he did.' He sighed. 'Anything else?'

'We think Bosey built smuggling compartments around the *Saardam*, and was in business with Isaack Larme, the first mate. We found –'

'Who is we?'

'Sara Wessel.'

'Ah.' His voice became knowing. 'Sara Wessel.'

'Yes, Sara Wessel.'

'Very good.'

Arent blinked. 'What's very good?'

Sammy spread his arms joyfully. 'You're as dense as the mountains you were carved out of.' He peered at his friend, lamenting the lost cause before him. 'What was inside Larme's secret compartment?'

'It was empty. Larme had already got to it by the time we arrived, but he seemed surprised to see the marks of Old Tom around it.'

'Then Old Tom may have used Bosey to smuggle something without Larme's knowledge.'

'And then killed him to keep from talking about it,' agreed Arent. 'Oh, and Reynier van Schooten has a secret that's eating him from the inside out. We almost had it, but ...' He gestured to the Eighth Lantern.

Sammy pulled up his breeches, rejoining his friend. Arent gave him piece of the untouched bird he'd stolen from the dinner table, along with a hunk of bread and a jug of wine.

'And I think I've found a way to make Johannes Wyck tell me why he cut out Bosey's tongue,' he said, as they crossed the waist.

'How?'

'I have to lose a fight.'

Sammy swallowed the bread he'd been eating. 'Have you ever done that before?'

'I think it's like winning, except you fall over at the end.'

They were close enough now to see the yawl being lowered into the water. It was far larger than it had appeared when covered up, and had three benches inside, capable of seating three sailors each, with room enough at the prow for another to crouch. Obviously, Crauwels didn't want to risk that many bodies, because there were only three people climbing down the rope ladder.

They did not look happy to be doing it.

Isaack Larme was clucking like a mother hen. 'Row to within sighting distance, no closer,' he said to them, genuine concern in his voice. 'Take note of its colours and what language you hear being spoken on deck, best you can.'

It, thought Arent. Larme had called the ship *it*. Not 'her', as was usually the case with ships, or even 'their', in reference to the crew. That was the power the Eighth Lantern already held over them.

Vos emerged from the compartment under the half deck. In the moonlight, he appeared ghastly, like he had too much skin on too little skull.

'Where's the governor general?' demanded Crauwels.

'I couldn't wake him,' said Vos.

Sammy prodded Arent's arm, jerking his chin to the quarterdeck where Lia and Sara were watching with Creesjie. Evidently, the ladies weren't interested in staying inside for the post-dinner drinks.

Below them, the yawl hit the water with a soft splash.

'Captain,' cried Isaack Larme. 'Look!'

He was pointing in the direction of the Eighth Lantern. The orange glow had turned blood red.

A second later an agonising scream carved through the air, only to be abruptly cut off.

Everybody covered their ears, but Arent knew better.

A scream was a warning.

You either needed to be running towards it, or away from it. Pretending it wasn't happening wouldn't help anybody.

'Arent!' hollered Sara from the quarterdeck. 'It came from behind us!'

He was up the stairs in a few strides, Sammy running after him. Hindered by her dress, Sara followed them to the poop deck. Lia and Creesjie came clattering behind.

Something squelched under Arent's feet. He reached down to touch it, but Sammy's voice stilled him. 'It's blood,' he said, sounding sick. 'I can smell it.'

He'd always been squeamish.

Pulling open the door to the pens, Arent found every animal dead, their guts spilled across the straw. The poor sow had it the worst, he thought. That must have been what they heard scream.

Creesjie ran to the railing and vomited, while Sara took a step back in horror.

'Arent,' she said.

He turned, expecting her to need comfort, but she was pointing at their feet. Drawn in blood, was an eye with a tail.

'The Mark of Old Tom,' whispered Lia, aghast.

'We were standing twenty paces away,' said Sara, glancing back at where they'd been. 'How could something have slaughtered the animals and drawn this mark without us hearing?'

She stared at Arent, as if hoping he might have the answers she lacked.

He didn't. He was as unnerved as she was. For all the years he'd worked with Sammy – all the impossible things he'd witnessed – he'd never seen anything on this scale, or anything so strange that didn't immediately explain its purpose. A dead body meant somebody wanted that person dead. A theft meant somebody wanted the thing that was stolen. How it was done may have been bewildering, but at least he'd always understood why it was happening.

This was different.

This was chaotic, and spiteful. Strange marks and slaughtered animals weren't clues, they were messages. Whatever was behind this – whether it was a devil or not – wanted them to know how powerless they were. How trapped. It wanted them to know how easily it could strike at them. It was trying to frighten them.

And it was succeeding. Arent's skin was crawling. He wanted to leap off the boat and swim back to Batavia. He just wasn't sure how many people he could carry on his back.

'This is it, isn't it?' said Lia, clinging to her mother. 'This is the first of the unholy miracles. It's happening exactly as the predikant said it would.'

'What's an unholy miracle?' asked Arent.

'Sander warned there would be three of them,' said Sara. 'They're meant to convince us of Old Tom's power, so more people accept his bargains. Each one bears his mark.'

'Why only three?' asked Sammy.

'Because after that, anybody who didn't bargain is slaughtered by those who did.'

Finally shaking off his shock, Captain Crauwels called down to the yawl. 'Get over to that lantern double quick, I want –'

'It's too late, Captain,' said Vos. 'It's already gone.'

Crauwels looked past him.

Where the red glow had been, there was now only darkness.

40

AFTER COLLECTING A LANTERN from the waist, Sammy returned to the animal pens and gestured impatiently for Arent's flint pouch. As Sammy searched for a spark, Captain Crauwels gripped Isaack Larme by the shoulder.

'Get a couple of cabin boys up here with mops,' he said. 'Have them clean all this up.'

His calmness seemed vulgar considering what lay before them.

'Hold that order,' demanded Van Schooten, sobered by the shock. 'We can't risk anybody seeing this. The ship will tear itself apart in panic.'

'Aint no secrets on an Indiaman,' argued Crauwels, casting his gaze towards the rigging. 'You mark me, there's eyes up there. This news will be halfway across the ship already.'

'Maybe they saw what happened,' suggested Sammy, finally putting a spark to the lantern's wick, its light leaping out across the deck.

'We know what happened!' said the chief merchant, on the verge of hysteria. 'We can see what happened! That damn ship killed them. It glowed red and it butchered them. And it'll be after us next.'

'Larme, get up that rigging,' said Crauwels. 'Drag whoever you find down here. We've got questions for them.' He nudged the sow's body with his foot. 'And fetch me the predikant and the cook when you're done. I want this meat blessed, then properly butchered and salted.'

Catching the chief merchant's incredulous stare, he shrugged. 'Dark forces be damned, I'll not waste good meat. We're short of supplies as it is.'

Arent felt a hand on his arm and turned around to see Sara cradling Lia against her breast. The girl was wracked by deep sobs. Of Creesjie and Vos there was no sign. They must have left in the commotion, he realised.

'I'm taking Lia back to her cabin,' said Sara. 'Can we talk afterwards?'

Arent nodded, then returned his attention to Sammy, who had crawled so far into the pens only his arse remained outside.

'Okay, thief-taker,' said Crauwels, addressing Sammy. 'What do you make of all this?'

'I find it curious that the porthole the leper appeared at that first night is directly below us,' said Sammy from inside the pens. 'Did you ever find its rags?'

'Had the ship upside down, but we didn't find a thing.'

'You can't *still* believe this is a knave playing games?' interrupted the chief merchant. 'The lantern turned red the moment the yawl hit the water. The animals were slaughtered seconds after that.' He pointed to the sow. 'We heard this poor creature scream. Unless somebody jumped over the edge, there's no way anybody could have done that and fled without us seeing. And if they had, we'd have heard the splash.'

Sammy wriggled back into the night, holding two objects on the end of a stick.

'What did you find?' asked Crauwels, squinting.

The problematary held them up to the light, revealing a scrap of bloodied bandage and a rosary.

'So it *was* the leper,' proclaimed Van Schooten. 'That is one of its bandages. It must have dropped the rosary when it attacked the animals.'

'Mmmm,' said Sammy doubtfully, as he inspected the rosary. 'This was the property of a rich man who fell into poverty. He was well travelled and devout. A predikant, perhaps?'

Van Schooten started, alarmed. 'How did –'

'The holes in the wooden beads are much too large for the string that threads them, and if you look inside you'll see the scratches caused by metal links. These beads once hung on a chain. Most metal rosaries are owned by the rich and have metal beads, often with jewels, so this began life as something far grander. Those beads were more than likely sold and replaced by cheaper alternatives as the owner fell into hardship, then finally the metal chain went, replaced by string. A poor person would have sold the metal rosary immediately or bought a cheap one with the proceeds. Poverty came upon this person slowly. But see how smooth the wooden beads are. They've been worn by repeated rubbing as the prayers were spoken, indicating devoutness. And the beads are made from different woods. At a glance, I can see hard and soft woods from a variety of trees across the Provinces, Germany and France. As I said, they were well travelled.' Coming out of his reverie, he examined their astonished faces. 'Our entire civilisation is built from wood, stone and a few types of metal,' he explained. 'If you can identify them, you'd be surprised at how evident many things become. Who normally tends the animals, Captain Crauwels?'

'Cabin boys for the most part,' he stammered, awed by the display. 'Steward comes up some nights and feeds them any scraps left over from dinner.'

'Can you ask whether any of them were bandaged, or have lost a rosary?'

'This is ludicrous,' exclaimed the chief merchant, throwing his hands up in the air. 'The truth is obvious, and yet you won't have it.'

Sammy ignored him and continued his conversation with the captain. 'Who knows the ship's route back to Amsterdam?'

'I plot it once I've got the stars above me,' he said proudly. 'The other ships take their lead from us, best they can.'

'You're not worried about becoming separated?'

'Aint no way to keep a convoy together for eight months, wind and waves won't allow it. Even in calm weather, we have to keep our distance for safety. Two ships carried on without us this evening, and we'll lose the others eventually, there's no help for it.'

'And yet our mysterious pursuer keeps finding us,' said Sammy, glaring at the spot where the Eighth Lantern had disappeared. 'It's an impressive feat.'

'It's devilry,' repeated the chief merchant stubbornly. 'And I'll not stand by and let it consume us. Captain, I'm ordering you to return us to Batavia at first light.'

Crauwels fixed his jaw for an argument, but it was instinct rather than good sense. With a sigh, he relented. 'Aye, I reckon that's the best way. I'll put a message out to the fleet at dawn, but we'll need the governor general's wave.'

'You'll have it,' said Van Schooten, departing.

As they settled the details, Arent pulled Sammy away. 'We don't need to seek the owner of this rosary,' he said, under his breath. 'I already know who it belongs to.'

'That's marvellous!' exclaimed Sammy. 'Did you see somebody holding it?'

'Yes,' said Arent. 'My father. The day he disappeared.'

41

CREESJIE JENS SNIFFED HER pomander, trying to banish the memory of the slaughtered animals. It was the blood that tormented her. Not the sight, but the smell. It was in her hair and on her skin. She felt it trickling down her dress, even though she hadn't touched it. It was as if she'd bathed in it.

'You're shivering,' said Vos solicitously.

'It's shock,' said Creesjie, descending the staircase on to the quarterdeck. 'I've never been that close to death before.'

She'd left to attend the governor general, as was her duty, only to find Vos trailing behind her silently. This was the first time he'd spoken, and, as usual, she found his presence hugely discomfiting.

'May I speak to you about a personal matter?' he asked, in that same bland tone he used for everything else.

He really was made of cogs and springs, she thought. After everything they'd just seen, he spoke as if they were taking a promenade. Why couldn't he see that she was upset and wanted to be left alone?

'Can't it wait until tomorrow, I'm –'

'I'm about to come into a sum that will change my position quite considerably,' he interrupted, watching her face for a reaction.

'How?' responded Creesjie, short of anything better to say.

'I have been making plans for some time,' he said. 'And they'll come to fruition when we reach Amsterdam. Using my newfound wealth, I intend on pressing my suitability to become the next governor general of Batavia to the Gentlemen 17. I'm counting on Jan Haan's support, of course.'

She stared at him, bludgeoned by this new information. 'Why are you telling me this, Vos?'

'Because I would like to ask for your hand in marriage.'

Her mouth fell open.

'I realise you're promised to the Duke of Astor, but my research suggests the duke's accounts are a war away from ruin, and he's never far from a war.'

Creesjie could only stare at him. She was being proposed to by an abacus. Oblivious to her bafflement, he pressed his case.

'The Duke of Astor is a fine match, but what will you do when he dies on the battlefield in three years' time? You are beautiful, but beauty fades. And when that happens, how will you live, how will you eat, where will your money come from? What I propose is a mutually beneficial marriage. I admire you, and would give you rein, while you helped me build the career I consider my destiny.'

'I ... I ...' Creesjie flailed. She couldn't find the words. She wasn't even certain she would recognise them if she did.

'I thought he was a count?' she said, lamely.

'A mere count would be beneath you.'

Creesjie's eyes roamed Vos's bland face, as if seeing it for the first time.

'I didn't realise you had such ambition,' she said, her interest showing itself for the first time.

'The governor general does not tolerate it and I'm not fool enough to displease him.'

'The wealth that you'd require –'

'I have made the calculations. I know what I'm asking, and what is offered. I could show you my figures, if you'd prefer.'

They passed awkwardly through the helm into the great cabin. The candelabrum had been snuffed and put away, along with all the plates and good cheer. The chairs were stacked, the cabin lit solely by moonlight, the lattice windows carving it into a web of shadow.

'You understand how dangerous this proposition is,' said Creesjie, lowering her voice. Candlelight snuck beneath the governor general's door. 'I'm only onboard the *Saardam* because Jan Haan wished it so. He bought my ticket and he pays my allowance.' Vos frowned slightly at this, his fingers doing their strange little dance at his side, as if these were not taboos he'd previously considered. 'If he discovered you're attempting to woo me while I'm still his mistress –'

'I'm not asking for an answer now, but a promise of your consideration would help me sleep easier,' said Vos.

'You have it,' said Creesjie, inclining her head. Vos beamed, returned the nod, then disappeared back the way he'd come.

Creesjie breathed out in relief, his arguments still clattering around her thoughts. It had been a good proposal, she thought. He'd put words around every doubt she'd harboured, then sucked the sting out of them. For the first time since they'd met, she found herself smiling at the memory of him.

Crossing the room, she arrived at the governor general's door.

'Good evening, madam,' said Guard Captain Jacobi Drecht, in that slightly disapproving tone he always adopted with her.

It was Creesjie's power to be desired by every man she met, so when she'd first encountered Drecht's scorn, she'd considered it a challenge. She'd flirted with him, brought him food, invited him to functions, but everything had failed.

The only thing he wanted from Creesjie was a wall between them.

Through one of his men, she'd discovered that he had a wife and daughter in Drenthe, both of whom he loved without reservation. Four years since they'd seen each other last, but he'd never taken his pleasure elsewhere. The soldier – in an incredulous tone – had claimed it wasn't something Drecht boasted of, as he didn't boast of breathing, or being able to speak. It was simply the vow he'd taken.

And that was where Creesjie's campaign had ended. Men such as Guard Captain Drecht were rare and dangerous. They would do their duty no matter how much misery it caused them, or those around them. His wife was welcome to him.

Standing aside, Drecht allowed Creesjie inside.

Once the door shut behind her, Creesjie's face changed. Abandoning the winsome smile, her eyes became coals.

As Sara had promised, her draught had put Jan Haan into a deep sleep, his thin chest rising and falling, every rib showing.

She looked at him distantly, like he was a bluebottle flapping its last on the window ledge. Whatever strength Jan Haan once commanded had long ago left him, but he disguised the fact with his accomplishments, his abrupt manner and the willingness of hounds such as Drecht and Vos to acquiesce to his every whim. She tried to imagine what they'd think if they knew why he really summoned her every night. It wasn't because of his virility, or because of his unquenchable appetites.

It was because he was afraid of the dark.

Most nights, she simply undressed and lay beside him, so that when he woke in fright, he'd have somebody to wrap a thin arm around.

Occasionally there was sex, but Creesjie was convinced Jan only called on her because Sara wouldn't stay the night with him.

The thought of her friend's stubbornness lit a fierce pride in her.

Any other woman would have submitted to his demands without complaint, believing it worth the life offered in return.

Not Sara, though.

Throughout the beatings, scoldings, humiliations and tantrums, she'd held strong, like a block of stone refusing to yield to the sculptor's hammer. Many a night, Creesjie had arrived to find Jan raging against his obstinate wife, revealing a passion he would be mortified to show in public. All these long years, his arrogance had convinced him he was torment- ing her, but Creesjie knew it was the other way around. Sara was the only enemy he'd never been able to best.

Jan murmured in his sleep, rousing her from her thoughts.

Hurrying to the desk, she'd found the list of names Sara had seen earlier that afternoon. Her friend had asked her to copy them, and Creesjie was in the habit of doing nearly everything Sara asked without question. For the truth was, Sara was more like her husband than she would admit, though her authority was built on a foundation of kindness rather than greed.

Picking up the quill, her eye landed on Jan's armour stand. A piece of folded parchment was tucked behind a strap on his breastplate.

'Now, what's that?' she wondered.

42

S ARA DIDN'T HEAR THE whisper at first.
It was almost dawn, but the sleeping draught had drowned her mind. One drop was all she ever took, though some days in Batavia she had itched for more. Bad days, dark days, when the boredom had crushed her and she'd gazed out at the horizon, wishing she could choose any other life than the one that had chosen her.

On those days, she would stare at the vial for what felt like hours, until eventually she had Dorothea hide it. Far away from her longing.

– *Sara* –

The whisper crawled up the walls and along the ceiling, running over her body on a thousand legs.

Blinking, she came awake, unsure at first what had woken her.

The room was still dark, the hour uncertain. With the deadlight across the window, it could have been one hour or seven since she'd fallen asleep.

It was stuffy, her mouth dry. She reached for the jug at her bedside.

– *Sara* –

The whisper caused her to freeze, her skin prickling.

'Who's there?' she demanded, blood thumping in her ears.

– Your heart's desire for a price –

The whisper was jagged, the words raking across her. She slowly felt around her bedside table for the dagger, her fingers curling around its hilt.

Last night it had felt reassuringly heavy, but now it just seemed clumsy.

Summoning her courage, she sprang off her bed, searching the four corners of the cabin. It was empty. Her only company was the moon, the tattered edges of the clouds giving it teeth.

– What do you yearn for? –

She rushed to the door, yanking it open.

A candle guttered in its alcove, revealing an empty corridor.

– What do you yearn for? –

Sara clutched her ears. 'Go away!' she demanded.

– What do you yearn for? –

Freedom. She almost said it out loud. She almost shouted it. She wanted to go where she desired without being told she couldn't. She wanted to decide each day how she wanted to live it. She wanted to pursue her talents without judgement and be the mother she wished to be rather than the mother she had to be.

– What do you yearn for? Tell me and I'll depart –

'I want freedom,' she said quietly.

– And what would you give for it? –

Sara's mouth opened, then shut. Even in the dark. Even terrified, she was a merchant's wife. She knew what bargaining sounded like.

'What would it cost?'

In his nightshirt, Vos clutched his hands to his ears, trying not to listen to the whisper.

– *She'll reject you* –

'She won't,' he hissed through gritted teeth.

– *She's laughing at you* –

'No.'

– *Blood spilt and a bargain sealed, and she'll be yours* –

———

– *I would place the dagger under the bed* –

Eyes wide in the candlelight, Lia held tight the model of the *Saardam* she was carving. It was such a simple offer, she thought. Such little effort for so great a reward.

———

– *What do you yearn for?* –

Johannes Wyck rolled off his mat and spun towards the door with his blade drawn, immediately alert.

A boatswain couldn't afford to sleep deeply. Those that did usually died mid-snore.

Wyck's compartment was below the forecastle, where the crew took their recreation. He could hear the fiddle and the skitter of dice above him.

– *What do you yearn for?* –

'Who's that?' he demanded, throwing open the door to the sailmaker's compartment. That useless sod was snoring in his hammock, as usual.

– *Old Tom* –

'Old Tom,' repeated Wyck, his expression changing. He returned to his compartment. It was pitch black, but he didn't mind the dark. They had an understanding.

'Aye, I know you of old, don't I?' He tapped his eyepatch. 'Was wondering when you'd come find me, though I didn't expect it to be like this.'

Silence met this declaration.

'Did you think I didn't recognise you on deck?' gloated Wyck. 'I kept your secret once and lost an eye for it. That was the last honourable thing I ever did. I know what you're doing on this boat, and I reckon I know what you're doing it for.'

Wyck turned in a circle, searching the cabin. There was a cunning leer on his face. Devils didn't frighten him. Not after the life he'd led. There was no fresh sin to enjoy. No more depravities to tempt him with. He'd tried every terrible thing he could think to try, and he knew hell was waiting for him come what may. Now, he was on a different path.

The silence seemed to shift, gathering itself.

– What do you yearn for? –

'Something you're going to give me.' He touched his eyepatch again. 'Something owed.'

Down on the orlop deck, Isabel rolled over on her mat, finding herself staring directly into Dorothea's sleeping face. She was lit by the full moon, giving her a fey quality, and Isabel half expected the older woman to wake up and offer her a wish.

The maid had moved her mat beside Isabel's that afternoon, telling her she felt safer sleeping near a friendly face. Isabel had recognised the lie immediately. As Dorothea had said yesterday afternoon, there were only two types. This one was too sharp.

Sara must have sent her.

On the deck above, the two bells sounded. From other side of the wooden curtain, she heard sailors shifting, grumbling, coming awake. Footsteps thudded down the steps, as the watch changed.

Keeping her eyes on Dorothea's face, she got up silently. From the hammocks and mats around her, snores issued, a few people spouting words in their sleep. The only light came from under the door to the gunpowder store, where the constable sang softly to himself.

She'd run into him last night and hadn't stopped cursing herself since. That was likely why Dorothea now lay where she lay. Isabel swore to be more careful tonight. She had to be, otherwise she'd have to stop going.

Offering Dorothea one last, cautious look, she disappeared down the staircase into the cargo hold.

———

Sara was stepping into the corridor to check on Lia, when Creesjie flew out of her cabin and into her arms, sobbing.

'Old Tom whispered to me,' she cried in fright, clinging to her friend.

'And me,' said Sara, still shaking. 'What did he promise you?'

'That the boys would be spared if I killed your husband!' She heaved her chest, trying to gather her breath. 'What did it want from you?'

'The same,' said Sara. 'It even told me how to do it.'

'A dagger under his bunk,' repeated Creesjie, horrified. 'If your husband summoned Old Tom, why does it want him dead?'

43

IT WAS DAWN WHEN Arent finally returned to his berth, his father's rosary twisted around his wrist. Reynier van Schooten had argued to throw it into the water, claiming it was cursed, but Sammy had stayed his hand, citing its importance to his investigation. He hadn't offered any theory on how it had come to be on the *Saardam*. According to his uncle, this was the token taken by the assassin to prove he'd completed his contract and killed Arent's father. That would put it in Casper van den Berg's possession last, so how had it come to be in the animal pen?

These sorts of riddles delighted Sammy, but to Arent it was like repeatedly lifting the same boulder, hoping each time to find something new beneath it.

Warmth touched his neck, a solitary ray of sunlight reaching for him. A yawl was being unlashed. Reynier van Schooten had ordered it to row to the nearest ship in the fleet and tell them they were turning back, as soon the governor general gave the go-ahead. That ship would then dispatch its yawl to the next ship and so on, until the message had been passed across the remainder of the fleet.

As sailors untied the knots holding it in place, they gossiped about the ghost ship that had attacked them last night, and how it had branded them with a demonic symbol. The story had already grown in the telling, he noticed. The Eighth Lantern was now an ethereal thing, hazy and indistinct, rather than simply distant, its crew comprised of souls lost at sea. The Mark of Old Tom had been burnt into the *Saardam*, and rather than being static, the eye had blinked, its tail swishing, before it disappeared.

The gossip accompanied Arent back to his berth. Tugging back the curtain, he stared in bewilderment at his hammock.

His surprise swiftly turned to rage. Somebody had used it as a privy.

Laughter echoed across the deck. Wyck and a few other sailors sat in the rigging, their faces gleeful. Here was the grievance he was meant to take to Larme, he realised.

'Could have found something a little cleaner,' mumbled Arent.

Marching out, he accosted Larme on the quarterdeck. 'I've got a grievance,' he said, without any preamble.

Larme blew out of a breath. 'How the hell did you learn about the law of grievance?'

'Does it matter?'

'Not really, but there isn't a man on this ship who's short of one, so what makes yours special?'

'I hear it doesn't have to be special, just a grievance.'

'Sailors only,' said Larme desperately, searching around to see who could hear them.

'A musketeer fought a sailor yesterday,' replied Arent.

'Over a damn hand plane, and a proper farce it was,' said Larme, relenting. 'Who's your grievance with?'

'Johannes Wyck.'

Larme stared at him disbelievingly. 'Of all the men on the ship, you want to pick a fight with Johannes Wyck?'

'Seems he's picking a fight with me.'

'Do you have you any proof of the offence?

'Only his laughter.'

Larme whistled at the rigging, summoning Wyck. The boatswain scurried down with surprising agility, wearing that familiar scowl beneath his eyepatch.

'Did you shit on this giant's hammock?' asked Larme, without preamble.

'Weren't me,' replied Wyck.

'Shake his hand and call this entire thing over with then,' demanded Larme.

'I have a grievance,' repeated Arent stubbornly. 'By ship's law, I'm demanding fists on the forecastle.'

'There'll be no penalty,' warned Larme. 'You've no proof so I can't –'

'No penalty!' exclaimed Wyck incredulously. 'His size is the penalty.'

'Give over, you're not so small,' argued Larme. 'It'll be the mainmast and the mizzenmast swinging punches at each other.'

Wyck took a step back, holding his hands up as if fending off an assault. 'You've heard the stories. He's the hero of bloody Breda. Fought off an entire Spanish army by himself.'

'Should have thought about that when you were using his bunk as a privy. Might have caused you to clench up.'

'I want an equaliser,' demanded Wyck, staring at them stubbornly. 'Otherwise I'm not doing it.'

Larme glared at him. 'He's called the Right of Grievance.'

'And I told you I aint done nothing. You're putting me in a fight with a bear without any proof. Aint fair.'

Larme scratched under his armpit, obviously wishing he'd been a few minutes quicker to his berth.

'What do you want?' he asked.

'Blades.'

Arent's spine turned to ice. Why would Wyck change the bargain? Losing convincingly was a damn sight harder when metal was involved. There was a lot more bleeding, for starters.

The boatswain's soot-coloured eye bored into him. 'What do you say, soldier. Make it fair?'

'Blades is fine,' agreed Arent, uncertain what else he could do. 'When?'

'Dusk, after we've dropped anchor.' Larme shook his head. 'You're daft bastards the both of you. I'll be glad when one of you is dead.'

44

THE CONGREGATION MUTTERED IN confusion. They'd gathered afore the mainmast awaiting a sermon from the predikant, but he hadn't arrived. Isabel had gone to rouse him, but his hammock was empty.

Cold rain was beginning to fall. Cracks of sunshine could be seen here and there, but it couldn't break through the black clouds.

It was an ill omen, they whispered.

Standing next to Creesjie and Lia, Sara watched the congregation become restless. A devil had whispered to her in the night. It had whispered to Sara and Lia, and it had no doubt whispered to these people as well. From the guilty looks on their faces, it was obvious that they'd been tempted.

She wondered if they'd been given the same offer as her, Creesjie and Lia.

I will place the dagger under his bunk. That's what the voice had said.

Her eyes travelled beyond the mainmast. Sailors watched them, their gazes predatory. How many of them had come out this morning, expecting to see the governor general among the congregation? How many of them were thinking of killing him? What had they been offered to do it? Watching their eyes paw Creesjie and Lia, she suspected she knew the answer.

Johannes Wyck was up on the forecastle deck. She didn't know why he'd chosen that spot. He wouldn't have been able to hear the sermon, though it gave him a good view over the passengers.

Had *he* heard Old Tom's voice last night? Part of her assumed Wyck and the devil were in more regular contact than that.

Isabel pushed through the crowd towards Sara. 'I've searched the orlop deck,' she said, flustered. 'I can't find Sander. Nobody's seen him.'

'Arent's berth is beside his,' said Sara. 'Perhaps he knows something.'

Creesjie coughed, gesturing for Sara to delay a moment. 'Before you talk to Arent, I have something you should see. Last night, in your husband's cabin, I spotted a parchment folded up in his breastplate. You know I've been curious as to why Pipps is imprisoned … well.' She handed her a piece of vellum. 'I copied this while Jan slept.'

Sara read, as rain blotted the words.

Put manacles on Samuel Pipps. I've come across accusations that he's a spy for the English. Not only a traitor to our noble enterprise, but our nation. It's not yet common knowledge, but I've verified the claims and will put them before my fellows soon. Execution awaits. Drag him before the Gentlemen 17 and your position will be vastly improved. Do these things and come quickly.

Yours in expectation,
Casper van den Berg

'Pipps is a spy?' gasped Sara.

'You can't show this to Arent,' warned Creesjie. 'If your husband were to find out I was stealing documents from his cabin he'd throw me over the side of the ship.'

'Then I'll devise some other lie to explain it,' said Sara. 'Arent has to know about this, Creesjie. He worships Pipps.'

The four women went to the compartment under the half deck, but Sara found herself hovering on the threshold. Her husband had strictly forbidden her from seeing Arent, or talking to him again. She'd given him a double dose of her draught, which meant he should still be asleep. Even so, it was a risk to defy him so openly.

Vos could be abroad, and his eyes were practically her husband's.

Her heart tugged her forward and her fear backwards. If she were to carry on investigating Old Tom, she'd need a way to go about inconspicuously. She looked at Lia. 'Would you go to the helm, dear heart, and keep watch for your father, Vos or Drecht.'

Lia grinned. 'This is like being in one of Pipps's stories,' she said, taking her position.

The curtain surrounding Arent's berth was open, revealing him snoring on a mat. The floor around him was wet with recent cleaning, but a faint odour still hung in the air.

'Oh my, the fun you'd have,' said Creesjie, eyeing Arent's huge chest and thick arms. Sara blushed.

'Arent,' said Sara softly, trying to wake him.

He didn't stir.

'Arent!' Sara kicked the bottom of his foot impatiently. 'Wake up.'

'Isssss early,' he slurred, moving his leg out of range. 'I only just ... was asleep.'

'Sander Kers is missing. We need your help.'

Arent came around grudgingly, wiping his blurred eyes to peer up at them. The smell of paprika hung thick in the air. Somebody must have broken open a case in the cargo hold.

'Sander went shuffling out of here first thing,' he said, coming up on his elbows. 'I heard his steps on the staircase down to the orlop deck.'

'I've searched the orlop deck,' said Isabel accusingly.

Arent sat up, resting his head in his hands tiredly. 'Maybe he went down to the cargo hold, or past the divide? Have you searched afore the mainmast?'

'I'm not allowed that far,' said Isabel frantically.

'I'll go ask after him,' he said. 'Soon as I work out how to put my boots on.'

Sara gave him the parchment Creesjie had scribed. 'Before you do that, read this,' she said. 'It's a letter from your grandfather to my husband. It explains why Sammy is imprisoned.'

Becoming alert, he took the missive, reading it twice. He laughed, suddenly. 'I don't know how my grandfather came by this information, but it's a lie. Sammy isn't a spy.' Arent's tone was amused. 'He'd be useless at spying. He doesn't care for nations or kings. He cares about coin in his pocket, and interesting puzzles.'

'Ask him about it,' requested Sara. 'And don't tell my husband what you know. I stole it from his cabin.'

Arent dropped the note out of the window, the wind carrying it away. 'Of course not. Thank you Sara,' he said.

Sara, Lia, Isabel and Creesjie returned to the deck, where the rain had grown spiteful enough to wash away the disappointed congregation. 'We still don't know for certain Arent isn't the demon,' said Isabel.

'He isn't,' said Sara, her tone ending any further debate.

Her certainty took them all by surprise, but she faced their doubt down. Two days in Arent's company and she already knew him more deeply than she knew her husband after fifteen years of marriage.

'Trust me, if Sander can be found, Arent will find him,' she said. 'We should talk to Reynier van Schooten, though. He was begging confession from Sander. He may know where the predikant went this morning.'

'Can we send the boys inside first?' said Creesjie, as they were pelted by rain. 'It isn't very welcoming out here any more.'

Marcus and Osbert were on the quarterdeck, chasing each other in circles, playing some variation of tag only they knew the rules to. Dorothea was watching them fretfully, believing they would eventually run straight through the gaps in the railings and over the edge of the ship.

Considering the boys' gift for mishap, it wasn't an unfounded concern.

They were at the foot of the stairs when the boys came running down under instruction from Dorothea. 'Think we best be getting inside, mistress,' she said, her white cap held tight in her hand against the wind.

Sara caught her arm.

'Could you find time today to make me some practical clothes, Dorothea?' She gestured to Isabel's loose cotton shirt and hemp skirt. 'Something like those. And I'd need a hat, a bonnet or something with a brim that covers my face and hair.'

'A disguise, you mean?' said Dorothea, who had experience of such things, having helped Sara sneak out of the fort on more than one occasion.

'Exactly.'

'I'll have to sacrifice a dress or two,' she warned.

'Tear up whatever you need,' said Sara.

After Dorothea had ushered the boys inside, Creesjie cleared her throat awkwardly.

'Sara ...' she began in an enquiring voice.

'Yes.'

'Arent Hayes.'

The name lingered between them.

'Yes,' repeated Sara, but slower this time, more warning than invitation.

'Your defence of him was very ...'

'Spirited,' finished Lia helpfully.

'Yes, spirited,' said Creesjie, brushing her blonde hair from her eyes.

'Was it?'

'And you've been spending a great deal of time with him recently.'

'Not an undue amount,' countered Sara.

'Do you care for him?'

Sara's mouth formed an objection, but then she thought about who was asking the question. 'Yes,' she admitted, grimacing slightly. It was the first time she'd said it out loud, and it felt like pulling a particularly ugly cow into the middle of the market.

Lia smiled, leaving Creesjie to creep tactfully towards her point. 'These feelings you have … you understand they're impossible.'

'Of course, I do,' said Sara, pulling at the neck of her dress irritably. Dorothea was having to wash everything in seawater, making the clothes stiff and itchy. Still, it was better than the sailors. They washed their clothes infrequently, and when they did it was with their own urine. In another five months, the entire ship would smell like a latrine. 'I'm … I like the way I feel around him,' continued Sara. 'He lets me be myself, rather than forcing me to be somebody I'm very bad at being. That's all it is. It's easily put aside.'

'Are you certain you have to?' asked Lia cautiously. 'He makes you happy, I've seen it.'

'There's no hope for Arent and me.' She lowered her voice. 'If our plan is successful, I'll disappear and Arent will …' She trailed off. She didn't know. Where would he go once Samuel Pipps was executed? Back to war? Hope flickered within her.

He was a mercenary. More importantly, he was a man. There were no obligations upon him. No expectations. He could go wherever he wished. Maybe he'd welcome the chance to follow her and begin a new life far away from everything. Perhaps she would be able get word to him when they docked, telling him where she'd gone.

She shook her head angrily. Why was she even thinking about this? She was so close to earning Lia's freedom, and her own. How could she even think about risking that for a childish infatuation?

Eggert saluted, opening the door for them.

Inside, Sara rapped on Reynier van Schooten's cabin.

The chief merchant appeared, wearing a pair of thin cotton slops and little else. As one, they turned their faces in disgust. His room was a tavern, dozens of empty wine jugs scattered across the writing desk and floor.

This was how the desperate drank, thought Sara.

'Old Tom really *was* listening to me last night,' he said, eyeing the ladies before him.

Creesjie snorted in amusement, causing Sara to smile involuntarily. 'Did you go to Sander Kers for confession yesterday?' she asked.

He gestured towards his cabin. 'What would I need to confess for? Governor General's master of this voyage, which makes me just another wealthy passenger with a trunk full of wine.'

'You helped my husband smuggle something onboard secretly,' said Sara, watching his demeanour change. 'Nobody seems to know what it is, but by all accounts, you've been drinking heavily ever since.'

His face was momentarily stricken, overwhelmed by fear and doubt and guilt. For an instant, Sara believed they might hear what they needed, but bile poured out instead.

'Does your husband know you're playing thief-taker with Arent Hayes?' he asked, cocking his head. 'Does he know you're dragging your daughter into these adventures?' He leered at her. 'Maybe I should tell him –'

'Sander Kers is missing,' interrupted Isabel, pushing in front of him. 'If he came to you for confession, you were the last –'

'I don't know anything, and I wouldn't tell it to a damn mardijker if I did.'

He slammed the door shut in their faces.

45

'WHAT DO WE DO next?' asked Isabel, as they trudged away from Van Schooten's cabin.

Sara considered it, then addressed Lia behind her. 'How's the model of the boat and its smuggling compartments progressing?'

'I've only just started. Why?'

'Your father brought something aboard he wanted kept secret, and Reynier van Schooten helped him do so. If he confessed what he'd done to Sander, and your father found out, maybe that's why he's disappeared. That cargo's onboard this ship somewhere and Bosey's smuggling compartments seem a good place to start looking. We just have to know where they are.'

'Don't forget the letter,' warned Creesjie. 'Sander was lured onboard the *Saardam*. If Old Tom was behind that, maybe it's responsible for his disappearance.'

'Either way, there's nothing more we can do for the time being, except wait for Arent to finish his search,' said Sara.

It was clear the answer didn't satisfy Isabel, but there was no other course of action open. As with all the passengers, her freedom was limited.

Creesjie removed another scrap of parchment from her sleeve and handed it to Sara. 'On other matters, this should cheer you up. It's the list of names you saw in your husband's cabin.'

Bastiaan Bos – 1604
Tukihiri – 1605
Gillis van de Ceulen – 1607
Hector Dijksma – 1609
Emily de Haviland – 1610

'I recognise some of these names from the daemonologica,' said Isabel, peering over Sara's shoulder. 'They're all families who fell under Old Tom's thrall and were investigated by Pieter Fletcher.'

The girl smelled faintly of paprika. It wasn't unpleasant. In fact, it made Sara slightly hungry. She wondered why she'd never noticed it before. There were crates of the stuff in the cargo hold. They must have been directly beneath where Isabel slept.

'Do you know why Jan is interested in these names?' wondered Creesjie.

'I heard him talking with Vos yesterday,' replied Sara slowly, trying to answer the question for herself. 'I only caught a little of it, but he admitted to setting Old Tom loose thirty years ago in return for the power he holds. Now, he thinks somebody else has raised the demon against him. Arent confronted him, but he wouldn't say anything more.'

Creesjie blanched, gripping Sara's arm. 'Jan summoned it?'

'That's what he said.' She turned her attention back to Isabel, 'Do you know what became of the names on this list?'

'Pieter Fletcher kept extensive records,' she said, tapping her satchel. 'The daemonologica will have the answers.'

'Then let's go to my cabin and have a look.' Sara peered at Creesjie. 'Did you discover anything about Captain Crauwels last night?'

'I don't think he's our demon, if that's what you're asking,' said Creesjie. 'His family were nobles once, and he's trying to restore their fortune. Somehow, he seems to think Jan can help him.'

'Did you find out how?'

'No, but I'll try again tonight. Oh, and I may be able to get more information from Vos on your husband's connection to Old Tom.'

'He's fiercely loyal,' said Sara sceptically. 'I'm not doubting your fabled charms, but —'

'He asked me to marry him,' interrupted Creesjie, a twinkle coming into her eye.

'Vos proposed!' exclaimed Lia.

'Yes, last night, after we were attacked by the Eighth Lantern.'

'But you're ...' Sara searched for the word. 'You're *you*, and he's ...'

'Him,' agreed Creesjie thoughtfully. 'Yes, but apparently he's coming into great wealth, and then will apply to become the next governor general of Batavia.'

'Wealth?' Sara's face became eager. 'From where?'

'I don't know, he said he'd been planning for some time ... oh ...' Realisation dawned on her. 'Not Vos. Surely not Vos. He's too ...' She struggled for the word, 'dull.'

'He has influence and his circumstances are about to change. If Old Tom is possessing anybody, Vos is as likely a candidate as anybody else. My husband yielded him a great deal of autonomy over the years. He was the second most powerful man in Batavia, and it seems he's reaching for more. We need to investigate this wealth he's coming into.'

'Yes, of course,' said Creesjie. 'I was going to ask anyway. I'll need all the details if I'm to take his proposal seriously.'

'You're not really considering it?' exclaimed Lia.

'Why not?' said Creesjie, lightly. 'He's infatuated, weak and lacking imagination. Consider the life I could build for my boys out of those flaws. Besides, my beauty won't last for ever. I must sell it for the best price I can.'

Sara shot a look at Isabel, trailing behind. 'Would you mind taking the daemonologica to my cabin, while I speak with Creesjie?' she asked sweetly.

Isabel did as she was bid. Once she was away, Sara took hold of Creesjie's arm.

'If you marry Vos, what happens to our plan?' she asked in concern. 'What about France? What about Lia and me?'

'Oh, don't fret, dear heart,' said Creesjie calmly. 'That could be easily arranged. The Folly is much too valuable to be held hostage to my wedding plans, and I'd never abandon either of you.'

Sara stared at her friend. She was beautiful and loyal, but she lived on whatever breeze stirred that day. She wouldn't have weighed Sara and Lia when considering her marriage proposal, not out of selfishness or spite, but simply because she would assume everything would work out in her favour. She wanted their freedom, so she'd have it. In fairness to Creesjie, this was usually how her life worked out.

'Did you manage to get the plans last night?' asked Sara, changing subject.

After ensuring nobody was around, Creesjie lifted her skirt, revealing a scroll case tied to the inside of her dress by three loops of material. 'Of course,' she said, removing it. 'Jan slept soundly throughout. I must applaud you on the efficacy of your tinctures.'

'Heavens Creesjie, why didn't you just leave it in Lia's cabin?' asked Sara.

'What if one of the cabin boys had seen it? Or your husband had visited. No, no. I thought it safer to keep it on me.'

'That's not the dress I altered,' said Lia, taking the scroll case in both hands.

'No, I fixed this one myself,' Creesjie replied, proudly.

'And you've been walking around with the scrollcase strapped to your leg all morning?'

'I was waiting for the right time to give it to you.'

Sara shook her head fondly at her friend.

'I'll start working on the plans immediately,' said Lia. 'I'll need some new candles, though.'

'I'll have the steward fetch them,' said Sara.

'Perhaps get them somewhere else,' warned her daughter. 'Between your model ship and these plans, I'm going to be up late a lot. We don't want him wondering why I'm going through so many.'

Lia disappeared into her cabin, clutching the scroll case, leaving only the two women to enter Sara's cabin.

The daemonologica was already open on the writing desk.

Isabel was examining the harp, her head cocked in wonder. Batavia's taverns made do with flutes, fiddles and drums, most of them played with more enthusiasm than skill.

From her rapt expression, it was obvious she'd never seen an instrument this elegant in her life. The strings were made of sunlight and the wood was so polished, she could see her own reflection swimming on its surface, like a soul caught under its skin.

She reached out a dirty finger to pluck one of the strings, but hearing them, her hands shot behind her back. For the first time since they'd met, Sara thought she looked like the girl she was.

'You're more than welcome to play it,' said Sara kindly. 'I could teach you, if you like.'

Isabel blanched, embarrassed by the offer. 'I don't mean disrespect,' she said, unable to meet Sara's eyes. 'But that's not my place, and it's cruel to offer. Your fingers are perfect for the harp. They're soft and long. I see them and I know God designed one for the other.' She held out her own hands for inspection. They were calloused and tough, dirty from clambering around the boat. 'These hands were designed for the fields, for hard labour and strife. First time I saw Sander, he was being beaten by two footpads in an alley in Batavia. Him being a predikant, I took my knife and slit their throats before they knew I was there. I wasn't looking for reward, but Sander saw providence in my arrival. He took me in and gave me a witchfinder's education.' Pride came into her voice. 'My mission is divine. I'm the one who'll put an end to Old Tom. That's what these hands are for, not fumbling at an instrument I'll never see again once I'm off this boat.'

Sara opened her mouth, unsure whether to protest or apologise, but Isabel spared her the decision by tapping the cover of the daemonologica. 'I brought the book like you asked,' she said.

Sara kept her gaze fixed on Isabel. 'Creesjie, can you see if the daemonologica can help us with those names you took from my husband's desk? I'd like to examine Isabel's baby, if she's willing?'

Isabel gasped, her hands flying straight to her stomach.

'How did you know?'

'I saw the fondness with which you stared at Marcus and Osbert during the sermon yesterday,' replied Sara gently. 'You were dreaming of your own baby being that age. I've had three myself, I know the look. Besides, you can't keep your hands from your stomach.'

As Sara gently felt Isabel's belly, murmuring periodically in satisfaction, Creesjie began flicking through the pages of the daemonologica, murmuring periodically in disgust.

'The names were all people my husband suspected of being possessed by Old Tom.' Creesjie cleared her throat and began reading out loud. 'Bastiaan Bos was a wealthy merchant, but investigation revealed that his fortune had been derived from numerous examples of rare good fortune, each one coinciding with some terrible event in the villages surrounding his lands. The pattern was obvious. We snatched him off the road late one night and after three days of inter-rogation, Old Tom's face was revealed to us. An exorcism was performed, but Bos could not be saved. We cleansed him with …' Creesjie's voice became small. 'Fire,' she finished limply.

'Creesjie?'

'My husband said he'd never …' she faltered. 'He claimed he'd never killed anybody. He said the rituals were enough to drive Old Tom out.'

She took a fortifying breath and plunged on to the next name.

'Tukihiri was a master shipbuilder from foreign lands, whose boats were lighter, swifter, yet stronger than our native Indiamen. An inspection by Christian shipwrights confirmed that only devilry could have kept them afloat, and sure enough we found foul magics inscribed upon the hull. Tukihiri denied our accusations and died under questioning. His soul could not be saved.'

Creesjie got up abruptly and went to the porthole, her hand covering her mouth.

Sara finished her inspection of Isabel. 'This child is lucky to have you as her mother,' she said, smiling at the girl. 'Everything appears to be going well. We'll keep watch on you throughout the voyage, but if you become uncomfortable, I have some tinctures that might help.'

Sara went to the desk and peered at the daemonologica.

The entries were written in English – a clumsy language stitched together from too many disparate parts to be elegant. Sara could speak it, but uncomfortably, and she found herself mouthing certain words out loud.

She struggled to keep her temper, as she read through accounts of interrogations and confessions, dry recitations of the horrors the witchfinder had seen and the horrors he'd perpetrated in response.

'He didn't need a great deal of convincing, did he?' said Creesjie, who was hugging herself by the porthole. 'Have you reached the account of how he convicted Emily de Haviland simply because she denied being a witch? She was just a girl!'

Sara's eyes found the account. 'Naught but duplicity was to be found in her testimony, a lie atop a lie, disguising the devil within,' she read out loud. 'An exorcism was ordered and Emily freed of the demon, but it was too late. Hearing of the de Havilands' dark deeds, a mob of villagers stormed the house, burning and killing, bringing a once great family to ruin.'

Two more names followed: Hector Dijksma and Gillis van de Ceulen. They had apparently survived their ordeals and went on to live happy lives.

Creesjie was shaking, tears rolling down her cheeks.

'I don't recognise my husband in those pages,' she said, when Sara had stopped reading. 'That wasn't the man who came home to me. My Pieter could never have done those things. Not to Bastiaan Bos, or Tukihiri, or Emily de Haviland, or any of the others. My husband wasn't a murderer.'

46

C APTAIN CRAUWELS STARED OUT of one of the great cabin's windows, his hands clasped behind his back, his fingers dancing in impatience. It was mid-morning, but the *Saardam*, along with the rest of the fleet, remained at anchor.

The sea was growing rougher by the minute. Rain was tapping the glass, as lightning danced malevolently on the horizon. They couldn't be at anchor when it fell on them, they'd be torn apart before they could get the sails up.

By rights, they should already had been trying to outrun it, but Van Schooten was adamant they were returning to Batavia. For that they needed the governor general's wave, but he'd evidently decided to sleep in. The situation was so unusual that Chamberlain Vos had poked his head into his bedchamber a few times to make sure there was breath in him still.

The other captains had reacted with predictable fury to the order. Aside from sighting the Eighth Lantern, the rest of the fleet hadn't reported any strange occurrences since departing Batavia, and they were eager to be on their way. They earned what they delivered to Amsterdam and if they returned to Batavia, the cargo would spoil.

From behind him, Crauwels heard Vos cross the great cabin to knock on the governor general's door, but it opened before he got there. Jan Haan emerged, blinking, into the light. He looked awful. Only four of the six leather buckles had been fastened on his breastplate, which hung crookedly over a shirt that hadn't been tucked in. His bows were uneven, his hose rode up and sleep sat in the corners of his red eyes.

'My lord.'

'Governor General …'

'Sir, we need to –'

Holding up a hand, he pointed to Vos groggily.

'Summarise,' he demanded in a voice that still hadn't risen from bed.

'Captain Crauwels and Chief Merchant van Schooten wish to return the ship to Batavia, my lord.'

'No,' said the governor general, yawning. 'Have some breakfast sent up, Vos.'

Vos bowed and left the room.

'My lord,' interjected Van Schooten. 'Last night the Eighth Lantern appeared again. When we tried to put a yawl in the water as you ordered, it slaughtered all our livestock.'

He spoke quickly, but clearly. He was sober for once, realised Crauwels. He couldn't remember the last time he'd seen Van Schooten without a jug in his hand. Must have been about a week before they departed, when Guard Captain Drecht came aboard to do his inspection. Van Schooten was normally a lively sort of soul. Irritating, but often charming. He wondered what had happened to sour his disposition so.

The governor general dropped into a chair, rubbing the bald patch on the top of his head. He was still half asleep. 'How were the livestock killed?' he asked.

'The leper, sir,' said Crauwels. 'It slit their bellies open. Lieutenant Hayes found an altar it had built in the cargo hold yesterday. It's already recruiting followers among the crew.'

'And how does returning to Batavia help us battle it?'

'We need to empty the ship,' said Crauwels. 'Search every part of –'

'If we do as you suggest, our cargo will spoil and this entire voyage will have been for naught,' interjected the governor general. 'I return to Amsterdam to join the Gentlemen 17, and I will do so in triumph. Not with an empty hold and a surplus of excuses.'

'Surely, sir, there are times when –'

'A few dead chickens and you're ready to fly back to the nest?' interrupted the governor general contemptuously. 'From our past exploits together, I would not have believed you so poor-hearted, Captain Crauwels.'

Crauwels bridled, but the governor general tapped the table with his fingernail, ignoring him.

'If there is a demon stalking this ship, Arent will find it.'

The ship lurched beneath their feet, knocking the governor general out of his chair and sending Crauwels and Van Schooten banging into the table. No sooner had they picked themselves up, then it happened again, but Crauwels was already stumbling towards the windows.

The ocean was choppy and white-tipped. The sky was roiling.

'What's happening?' demanded the governor general angrily, as if his authority was being disrespected.

'It's the storm I've been warning you about,' growled Crauwels. 'It's bearing down fast.'

'Then I suggest you raise sails and point us in the opposite direction, Captain,' he said.

Seeing the argument was lost, Crauwels strode out into the helm, snuffing out the candle in the alcove with his thumb and finger.

'Douse every light,' he commanded, as Isaack Larme barrelled through from the opposite direction. 'Last thing we want is a fire needs fighting while we're trying to keep the ship afloat.'

'What's your order, Captain?'

'Full sail. We're going to try and outrun the storm.'

The tempest stalked them like a wolf.

All day long, the *Saardam* tacked and jibbed, before hoisting full sail to career recklessly forward. So erratic was their course Isaack Larme compared their route to a tangle of string carelessly thrown down on a chart. But no matter their efforts, the storm was always at their back, its black mouth agape, lightning crackling.

The seas were rough and the weather foul, and even the sailors struggled to keep their footing. The nobles were ordered into their cabins and told to remain there until they were safely beyond the bad weather. The passengers on the orlop deck were banned from coming on deck, for fear the sea would drag them over the side.

One day became another, and another, and another. Crauwels was skilled enough to keep them just out of the storm's jaws, but he couldn't put it distant.

For two weeks, the tempest chased them with such an unerring fury that the crew began to see malice in it. Exhausted after their exertions, they would slump against the rigging at change of watch, fingering their charms, hoping this was the day they lost sight of the storm, as they'd lost sight of another ship in the fleet.

Their trepidation was felt in every corner of the *Saardam*. In the orlop deck, deadlights blinding the portholes, the passengers pressed themselves together and murmured prayers, while the nobles fretted in their cabins, their chests tight with worry.

On the quarterdeck, Captain Crauwels hurled curses into the wind, his anger growing in proportion to his fear. No matter how reckless the seafaring, no matter how brave the course taken, their pursuer was always at the same distance.

It was as if the storm had their scent, he raged.

The old sailors recognised it as something called down upon them. A curse that wouldn't be satisfied until the whisper had its pound of flesh. No wonder Sander Kers had been taken, they claimed. They had no love of holy men, but it couldn't be a coincidence that he'd vanished moments before the storm hit. Arent Hayes had searched for him for three days, even as the unsteady ship knocked him over and hurled him into walls.

He could find no sign. Kers had disappeared as surely as if he'd never boarded.

The sailors thought the whisper had offered somebody a fortune to hack the predikant into pieces and give him to the ocean. Almost everybody had heard its jagged voice by now, offering its bargains in the night. *Their heart's desire for a favour*, it had promised. They were simple things for some.

More dangerous for others. There seemed no pattern to what was asked, and what was offered.

When they spoke of their offers in the morning, a few gripped tight their charms, warding off evil, but others went thoughtful, their eyes full of dreams. Why not? they wondered under their breath. What cost could be greater than what this life already asked of them? From their duty stations, they stared at the aft of the ship, to the cabins where the nobles slept. What had they done to earn such plenty? They didn't know how to stitch a sail or tack the ship. They were rich because their families were rich. Their children would be rich because they were rich. On and on in an endless loop.

By contrast, they were poor because they'd always been poor. They had nothing to look forward to and nothing to pass along. Wealth was a key and poverty was a prison, and they'd been born shackled through no fault of their own.

It was senseless and unfair, and mankind could withstand almost anything except unfairness.

Back and forth, they complained, stoking each other's ire.

If this was God's plan, then maybe Old Tom was worth listening to, because it couldn't ask a greater sum for less reward than this. Besides, they might not have a choice.

It had called the Eighth Lantern to torment them, and now this storm was roaring at their backs. Even if they could outrun it, a leper roamed the cargo hold endlessly, scratching his mark into the crates. They'd caught glimpses of it. Tattered robes and bloody bandages. A solitary candle that would lead sailors through the labyrinth to an altar at the heart of the ship. No matter how many times the captain ordered it destroyed, the leper would rebuild it.

It was Bosey, they said. Others spat at that. Bosey was dead. They'd seen him on the docks. Watched him catch flame and be run through by Arent Hayes. But didn't he drag his leg and smell of the privy? Didn't he have business with this ship after what they'd done to him? After what Johannes Wyck had done to him?

Bosey or not, everybody was agreed that bad fortune followed in its wake. A cabin boy, an apprentice sailmaker and a hornblower had already died in the dark. The cabin boy tumbled off a ladder and snapped his neck. The sailmaker and hornblower died bloody. Slashed to pieces by each other's daggers. Their hate had simmered for a while but it was all coming out now.

Sailors who spent too long in the cargo hold came back different, they claimed. Distant, somehow. Odd.

Course, some had boarded like that. Not that it mattered. Rumour twisted tight around them, all the same. It said they'd knelt at the altar and spoke their devotions.

Nobody would go near them.

Something was stirring in the dark water, the old sailors claimed. Something that called itself Old Tom.

47

'Two weeks like a damn fish on a hook and now we're being reeled in,' hollered Crauwels, as the storm finally fell upon them.

His crew were exhausted. The fight was over. They'd tried everything, strained every muscle and sinew, but the storm had been unrelenting. He was proud of them, could ask no more. He wanted to say as much, but he couldn't raise his voice above the wind.

Emerging on to the quarterdeck, Crauwels tipped his head to the sky. You'd be hard pressed to tell whether it was day or night. Gusts swirled and the rain battered down, bouncing ankle-high off the decking.

'Can't see a damn thing,' he complained to Larme, squinting through the sheets of rain at the blurred sails of the other ships in the fleet. Only three had managed to stay close to them during their manoeuvres. Now he wished they hadn't.

'Get down to the helm and point us wherever they aint,' he hollered. 'If we hug each other in this storm, the wind's going to smash us together.'

Larme took off like a fox, but as Crauwels tried to follow, the ship bucked beneath him, snatching the ground away. Flinging himself at a nearby railing, he managed to wrap his arms around it, watching as two sailors were tossed into the air, then slammed into the deck.

From amidships the bell rang desperately.

Stumbling forward, Crauwels hauled a scared cabin boy from the nook he'd wedged himself into.

'Get that bell muffled,' he screamed at him, over the crashing waves. It was bad luck to let a bell ring by itself, everybody knew that. Should have been the first thing tended to when the sea got wild.

'Boatswain!' Crauwels yelled over the howling wind.

Johannes Wyck staggered on to the waist, clinging tight to a rope. 'Captain?'

Crauwels put his mouth to his ear. 'Any sailors not on duty are restricted to the orlop deck,' he ordered, wiping away the rain lashing his face.

Nodding, Wyck grabbed the two nearest sailors by the neck, shouting commands at them, then pushing them towards the hatches.

As white-tipped waves pummelled the deck with foamy water, Crauwels staggered into the great cabin where Arent was securing a deadlight that had come loose, revealing the churning water pressed flat against the glass outside. Every other passenger had been confined to their quarters these last two weeks, but that was no use with Hayes. He came and went regardless of what was said. Crauwels knew for a fact he'd been between Sammy's cell and Sara Wessel's cabin with fair regularity, though he didn't have much to say on either matter.

The ship tilted precipitously, crockery smashing.

'Hayes, I've a use for you,' said Crauwels, bracing himself against the wall. 'I need strong arms on the bilge pumps. We're taking on water quicker than we can rid ourselves of it.'

333

'I have to fetch Sammy first,' he hollered.

'The governor general said –'

'If he stays in that cell during the storm, he'll be pulverised and you know it.'

Crauwels tried to stare him down, but there was no use in that.

'He can wait on the orlop deck,' conceded Crauwels grudgingly. 'Keep him out of the governor general's sight. After that, the bilges.'

They departed the great cabin together. They'd only made it into the compartment under the half deck when the ship nearly toppled them. Using a workbench to get back on his feet, Crauwels saw Sara Wessel stagger through the archway that led outside, with Lia close behind.

He blinked, words deserting him. Sara had changed into peasant's garb, her usual finery hacked away, replaced with a simple brown skirt, an apron, linen shirt and waistcoat. A cotton bonnet covered her head, and there was a dagger hanging at her waist. Lia was dressed in similar clothes.

She was soaked through.

For the beautifully attired Crauwels, there could be no greater act of self-harm than dressing like a peasant.

'It's too dangerous for you to be out of your quarters, my lady,' he yelled, having to shout it twice to be heard above the waves pounding against the deadlight.

'It's dangerous everywhere, Captain, and I can help,' said Sara, bracing herself against the archway. 'I'm a skilled healer and people will need that skill before the day's out. I'm going down to the sickbay.'

Arent stumbled towards Sara and handed her the key to his trunk. 'Sammy's alchemy supplies are inside. There's a salve that smells of piss that's good for healing.'

She touched his arm affectionately, tipping her mouth towards his ear. 'Put Pipps in my cabin, if you wish.'

He met her green eyes.

'How did you know I was going for Pipps?'

'Because he's in danger,' she said simply. 'Where else would you be going?'

'Keep your dagger in your hand,' warned Arent, holding her gaze. 'There's always somebody ready to take advantage of confusion.'

'I'll be safe,' she said. 'You try doing the same.'

As Sara went to Arent's berth and the mercenary descended the staircase, Crauwels hurried back outside in time to see a huge wall of water rear up in front of him, then crash down on to the deck.

Sailors screamed, disappearing into the maelstrom.

The sky was ash and fire, green flames shooting off the ends of the yard and masts. Forks of lighting streaked from the sky, sizzling the ocean. Most of the crew were lashing themselves to the masts, bracing themselves for the next wave.

Keeping tight hold of the railing, Crauwels dragged himself up the stairs and took his usual position on the poop deck, finding Governor General Haan exactly where he'd left him. He'd appeared shortly after the first great swell, taking his place silently, offering neither comment nor explanation for his presence.

Water ran down his face, dripping off that long nose and chin. Blinking furiously, he'd watched the black and purple storm clouds swirling overheard with a half-smile on his lips.

Crauwels had seen the look before. The sea had him.

It splashed behind his eyes and carried sour on his breath. Every man on the ship knew that look, when the cold emptiness of the ocean filled you up. There wasn't any rest once the sea got inside you.

People drowned standing up.

One of the ships had capsized off the portside, her crew spilt into the water. They were waving their arms, crying out for help, but Crauwels couldn't hear them over the wail of the storm.

He didn't even consider trying to rescue them; a yawl wouldn't last a minute in these waves. Those lads were dead, but the sea was going to play with them first.

The governor general tapped his shoulder, pointing upwards. Following his finger, Crauwels saw another ship riding the crest of a towering wave. She was being delivered directly on to the stricken vessel.

Crauwels turned his head, unable to watch, but the governor general's face told the story well enough. The second ship had been hurled into the capsized vessel, ploughing straight through her hull, ripping her in half.

Why would he want to see that? wondered Crauwels. It was as if the storm were an enemy he couldn't turn his back upon.

By his calculation, aside from the *Saardam*, only one ship now remained from the fleet that had departed Batavia. Crauwels cast about for her desperately, hoping to see her well, but she was floundering in the distance. Her colours told him it was the *Leeuwarden*. He didn't give her any greater chance of survival than the *Saardam*.

Confronted by waves tall as the mainmast, Crauwels hollered for the *Saardam* to steer directly into them, the ship climbing sheer walls of water before plummeting into the steep valleys on the other side.

Sailors were lashed to the rigging and rails. They survived each assault spluttering, fighting to keep their footing, ever more convinced that the storm had been brought upon them by Old Tom.

Crauwels gave no further orders. Everything that could be done had been done. If the *Saardam* was strong enough, she'd see them safe. If one of her ribs was bent, or the hull had rotted without them noticing, she'd crack open like an egg. Every storm was the same. You lived or died depending on how much care some stranger had taken building her in Amsterdam.

As forks of lightning struck the deck, Crauwels prayed for God to see them through this. And when that got no response, he prayed to Old Tom.

So this is how men go to the devil, he thought bitterly. Cap in hand and short of hope, all their prayers gone unanswered.

48

Flung from handhold to handhold, Arent made his way slowly down to the orlop deck. Deadlights had been smashed loose by the waves, seawater pouring through the portholes, soaking those beneath them. Dazed sailors coated in blood and vomit clung to pillars, as the world upended itself.

Passengers bunched together, cocooning the children or screaming in fear. Away in the corner was Isabel. She was terrified, panting. Sara knelt by her side, comforting her.

The storm had kept them from organising a thorough search for Sander, and Arent knew Sara had become her solace.

Even so, he was surprised by their closeness.

'You carry God's word, Isabel,' Sara was saying 'These people need to hear it. Bring them the comfort Sander would have done.'

Isabel obviously wanted to, but the ship heaved and she screamed, clutching her knees to her chest.

'Courage isn't an absence of fear,' cried out Sara. 'It's the light we find when fear is all there is. You're needed now, so find your courage.'

Hesitantly, Isabel stumbled across the deck, sinking down into a group of passengers, their arms reaching and enveloping her.

As Sara went to the sickberth on the opposite side of the deck, Arent half fell, half staggered past the wooden divide between the two sections of the ship, making his way across the sailors' mats into the sailmaker's cabin. Rolls of sail had tumbled free of the walls, dressing the cabin in white. Heaving up the hatch, he descended the ladder into the storeroom below and hammered the door to the Sammy's cell.

No reply came.

'Sammy!'

In a panic, he tried to rip the locking peg from its hole, but his hands were wet and the rocking of the ship made it hard to get a hold on it.

'Sammy!' he hollered, the silence terrifying.

When he finally ripped the peg out, he was confronted by the pitch-black cabin.

He tried to squeeze inside, but the hole was much too small, accommodating only his shoulders and head. 'Sammy!'

Nothing.

'Sammy!'

He tried to catch his breath and slow his thoughts. He was being overcome by the terror of loss, trying to imagine what he'd do if Sammy were dead inside. Protecting his friend had been the only worthwhile pursuit of his entire life. It had filled him with pride to be associated with Sammy's deeds. For the first time since he'd left his grandfather's side, Arent had felt himself doing good works, rather than killing for coin, or marching into some foreign land to die badly for ignoble purpose. That's why the accusation that Sammy was a spy rang so hollow. Sammy knew the cost of power, and was therefore suspicious of it. Sammy had been baffled at the charge when Arent put it to him, though he didn't find it quite so funny as his friend. Being English had always brought complications while working for the Company, but he'd never expected to end up in a cell for it.

'Arent,' groaned Sammy, stretching a hand into the light.

Arent could have cried in relief. Instead, he grabbed Sammy and dragged him outside, noting the blood trickling from his forehead.

'Are you well?'

'Dazed, but breathing,' said Sammy groggily. 'Is this Old Tom?'

'I thought you didn't believe in demons,' he replied, placing Sammy's hands on the ladder.

'It whispered to me last night, Arent.' He sounded horrified. 'It knew things, secret things. It wanted me to –'

'Kill the governor general?' guessed Arent, pushing him up the ladder. 'It asked the same of Sara and Creesjie.'

'It offered to free me and restore my name. What did it offer you?'

'I haven't heard anything. Seems I'm the only one, the way the crew are talking.'

From above him on the ladder, Sammy managed to crack a weak smile. 'Being a dull conversationalist has some perks then.'

Emerging through the hatch, they heard a howl of misery. The barber-surgeon was sawing off Henri the carpenter's broken leg, while Sara and Lia tended patients in the sick-bay. Surrounded by a curtain, there wasn't much to mark this compartment as special, except for two operating slabs and the oddly shaped drills and blades hanging from pegs on the walls.

'Sara!' Arent called out.

Seeing Sammy, she rushed over. 'It's nothing,' she said, inspecting the injury. 'A bump. Lay him down there, I'll see he's cared for.'

'No need,' said Sammy, making an effort to hold himself upright. 'I have some skills in this area myself. I can be of assistance, if you'll have me?'

'Mr Pipps,' said Lia, rushing forward excitedly. 'I'm a huge admirer –'

Sammy stared past her at his supplies, lying open on the table. 'That's my alchemy kit,' he said, a touch of anger in his voice.

'And we'd be glad of your help making use of it,' said Sara. 'Many of these compounds are lost on me.'

Sammy was still staring.

'I didn't mean to offend you,' said Sara, confounded. 'Arent suggested the kit might be some help in aiding the injured and –'

'Yes, of course,' interrupted Sammy, abashed. 'Please forgive me. Those compounds represent my life's work. They've helped solve more cases than I can count, and I've held their secrets close. My selfish desire to keep my tricks to myself momentarily overwhelmed me. Here, let me show you what will be of practical benefit.'

Arent exchanged an amused glance with Sara, then descended into the cargo hold, where four feet of water was sloshing through the alleys of crates, drowned rats bobbing on the surface. Carpenters were frantically nailing fresh planks over the leaks in the hull, while sailors and musketeers pumped the bilges, their back-breaking work having little effect on the steadily rising water. Drecht was among them, stripped to the waist.

The ship lurched violently, crates tearing free of their netting and falling on to the sailors working below.

Howls of pain were lost to the din of waves smashing into the hull.

Blood blossomed in the water.

'Drecht!' Arent called out, wading towards the bilges. The guard captain looked up in relief. 'You see to them,' said Arent, pointing to the bodies. 'I'll work the bilge.'

Three men were usually needed to pump the long levers, but Arent pushed them away, ordering them to tend their mates.

From somewhere distant, guns fired in distress.

One of the fleet must have been in even worse trouble than the *Saardam*, but it was a futile gesture. They couldn't be helped, not in this storm. And every person on that ship would know it.

He pumped faster, trying to lose himself in the work.

Hour after hour, he kept on, ripping the flesh from his palms. Drecht tried to convince him to rest, but if he stopped, he would never be able to start again.

It wasn't until dusk that exhaustion overcame him, and he fell to his knees.

The *Saardam* had stopped heaving, water no longer rushing through cracks in the hull. Carpenters were slumped against the wall, their hammers clutched by claw-like hands they could no longer unclench.

Most of the water had been pumped out, so now it was only ankle-deep rather than waist-deep.

A hand touched his shoulder, a mug of barley stew and a hunk of bread appearing before his tired eyes. Raising his heavy head, he found Sara in front of him.

'We're safe,' she said. Anticipating his next question, she added. 'Everybody's safe. Sammy, Lia, Creesjie, Dorothea and Isabel. Our friends survived.'

A bruise marred her forehead, her curly red hair sprung loose of its pins, falling across her face and shoulders. Her sleeves were rolled up, her dress and forearms covered in blood.

'Is any of this blood yours?' he asked, taking her hand, too tired to care about the propriety of it.

'Only a little,' she said, smiling at his concern.

'You continue to rise in my esteem, Sara Wessel.'

She laughed, then noticed his palms, made ragged by the hours of working the bilge pumps. 'If you come up to the sickbay, I can treat those,' she said.

'They look worse than they are,' he said.

Guard Captain Drecht dropped down beside Arent, clapping his shoulder.

'You should have seen him,' he said to Sara in awe. 'He worked the bilge pump single-handedly for the entire night without rest. I've never seen its like. It was as if he were heaven-sent.'

Arent was too busy inhaling the sour aroma of the stew to heed the compliment.

'What is that?' asked Sara. 'The cook's handing it out.'

'It's barley stew,' said Drecht, wrinkling his nose. 'It's the vilest substance you'll ever put in your body.'

'It's what being alive tastes like,' corrected Arent, smiling in happiness.

343

Barley stew was what they gave you when you came back from battle, shivering cold, covered in mud and blood, short a friend or two. It was hot and salty and cheering, but, more importantly, it was cheap. Cauldrons of it bubbled in every camp across Company territory. Cooks kept them going day and night, throwing bits of old meat inside, turnip ends and chicken bones; anything foul and unwanted. Everything in that cauldron would likely be rotten, waking a dragon in the guts of anybody brave enough to try it.

Beaming, he took a huge gulp, wiping the oily liquid from his lips.

'Do you want to try it?' he asked Sara.

She took it gingerly, tipping it to her lips. Revulsion overcame her and she immediately spat it out, snatching the jug of wine from his hands to wash it down.

'It's awful,' she spluttered.

'Yes,' said Arent happily. 'But you can only know that if you're alive.'

49

T HE SEA HAD SETTLED and the sky had broken
  into two ragged halves; black behind them, blue in
front. Rain swirled, but it was soft and warm, no longer filled
with thorns. Snapped rigging dangled like vines, slapping
the shredded sails. Cracks riddled the decking, but nobody
was repairing them. Everybody was slumped on the floor
exhausted, their faces blank with shock.

There wasn't a word being spoken.

Crauwels was leaning over the side of the ship, inspecting the damage. His expensive shirt was torn, revealing the
dark chest hair beneath. He was shivering and bleeding from
a gash on his arm, barely able to stand.

'What's the damage?' asked the governor general, striding
towards him. Somehow, he'd come through the experience
with barely a scratch. Chamberlain Vos followed at his
master's heel once again.

'We might as well be a raft,' said Crauwels, gesturing
towards the useless sails. 'Sailmaker reckons he'll have them
patched in two days. About the same for buckled decking.
Hull appears to be intact, mercifully.'

'We survived, though.'

'Aye, but the storm blew us beyond the wagon lines.' He winced as he touched the wound on his arm. 'I have no damn idea where we are and there isn't a single ship out there. We're alone now.'

'Last I saw, the *Leeuwarden* was still afloat,' said the governor general, staring at the empty sea. 'If we can find her, she may be able to render assistance.'

'The lookout hasn't spied her,' argued Crauwels, irritated by such unfounded hope. 'Some of the men say they saw her capsize. Even if she survived, she'll be as badly damaged as us and equally lost. We won't find her, not with our luck.'

The governor general considered him. 'I sense you have a favour to ask of me.'

'We need The Folly.'

'That's more than a favour, Captain.'

'I know its power, I tested it for you,' he replied. 'Without it I've got the stars and nothing else. We'll end up sailing in loops searching for land, so we can take a bearing. And between you and me, we don't have the supplies for this delay, especially now the rest of the fleet is out of sight.'

A trickle of blood ran from the governor general's nose. Vos immediately handed him a handkerchief to wipe it with.

'I'll take you myself,' said the governor general.

The three of them headed for the gunpowder store, meeting Guard Captain Drecht coming up the staircase.

'How goes it, Guard Captain?' asked the governor general.

'We lost four musketeers in the storm,' he said.

The governor general considered this as they emerged into the orlop deck, the severity of the damage bringing them to a shocked halt. Water dripped from the ceiling into puddles of blood and vomit. Cannons lay on their sides, possessions scattered across the deck, including a small boot dangling from a peg on the ceiling – like the storm had come across it during its rampage, then put it out of harm's way.

Bedraggled sailors and passengers hacked and coughed, bringing up seawater. They were sprawled on the floor, cradling broken arms and legs as they waited to be tended by the barber-surgeon, Sara, Lia or Sammy. Arent was talking to his friends.

Crauwels had spotted the two ladies and the prisoner dart out of sight behind the sickbay's curtain when they descended. No doubt they feared the governor general's reaction should he discover them down here. Thankfully, he was fixated on a bone-weary cabin boy, who was laying sheets of hemp across the dead. Crauwels wondered if he'd been ordered to do so, or simply taken it upon himself. Either way, he was going to get an extra ration of ale tonight.

There was a body at the bottom of the staircase. Guard Captain Drecht stepped over it and rapped smartly on the gunpowder store.

'You alive in there, Constable?' he demanded.

The panel slid open, revealing the wild white eyebrows. 'The bits I can feel, which isn't all,' he complained. 'Who are you?'

The governor general stepped in front of Drecht. 'He's with me. Open up. We're here to collect The Folly.'

Fear flashed across the constable's face, but he did as he was asked, slowly withdrawing the bolt and standing aside.

'I don't understand,' said Drecht. 'How does a bloody big box help us?'

'The Folly lets us accurately fix our position while at sea,' explained Crauwels. 'That thing will tell me where Batavia is and what bearing I need to go directly there.'

'I thought it was a weapon,' sniffed Drecht, unimpressed.

'With The Folly, Company ships will be able to sail beyond the wagon lines without fear, exploring the unmapped ocean,' explained Vos.

If anything the unimpressed silence only deepened.

'Don't you see, Guard Captain,' continued Vos. 'With The Folly, our fleets will be able to outmanoeuvre their enemies with ease. They'll be able to accurately chart unmapped oceans and discover people and places nobody's ever set eyes on. The Folly is how the Gentlemen 17 will put their hands around the world.'

The governor general gestured for his men to get on with it. 'Vos, take one end. Drecht, take the other. We'll need to carry it up on deck.'

Grunting, they lifted it, but they'd barely taken a step, before the governor general cried out. 'Put it down!'

They followed his horrified gaze. Burnt on to the planks where The Folly had previously sat was the Mark of Old Tom. Drecht immediately crossed himself, while Vos cursed, taking a hurried step away.

It was a vulgar thing. The eye bulged and the tail twisted away. Under the swaying lantern, it appeared to have a life of its own. Drecht half expected it to dart out of the door.

'Open the box,' demanded the governor general, retrieving a large iron key from around his neck and thrusting it towards the guard captain. 'Open it now!'

The lock was rusted by the humidity, and took a few tries before it opened, and dropped on the ground with a thud.

Drecht lifted the lid, then blew a breath through his lips.

'There's nothing in here,' he said, pushing the empty box round to face the governor general. There were only three empty sections where The Folly's three pieces would have sat.

The governor general grabbed the constable by the chin, levering his face upwards so their eyes met.

'Where is The Folly?' he demanded.

'I don't know,' whimpered the constable.

'Did you think we wouldn't notice?' he was almost shrieking. 'What have you done with it?'

'I don't know, sir. Truly I don't. I didn't know what was inside, sir. It was just a box to me. A box.'

The governor general snarled and pushed him away, sending him sprawling on the floor. 'Twenty lashes will jog your memory, I think.'

'No, please, sir, mercy,' wailed the constable, raising an imploring hand, but Drecht was already hauling him out of the gunpowder store.

Arent had been having a jolly time with Sammy, Sara and Lia before his uncle arrived.

Sara had been telling Sammy everything she'd learned about Old Tom, including Sander Kers's belief that it could be Arent. Sammy had reacted incredulously, listing several of his friend's most boring, and therefore most un-devilish tendencies, with relish. This had set them all to laughing.

By the time, the governor general emerged from the gunpowder store, however, they were cowering in silence, afraid of being caught. Behind him came Drecht, his hand clamped around the constable's solitary arm.

'Uncle, what's happening?' called out Arent, stepping out of the sickbay.

'This man stole The Folly,' the governor general replied without stopping.

'It wasn't me, sir; it was the demon everybody's talking about,' cried the constable, who was still being dragged by Drecht. 'I saw the mark myself, it was the demon.' He looked at Arent with desperate eyes. 'Please help me, Lieutenant Hayes. Please.'

'Uncle, I know this man, he's –'

The governor general gave him a pitying stare. 'I gave you a chance to stop Old Tom, Arent. You told me you weren't up to the task, and I should have listened. It's not your fault, it's mine. Fret not, I'll put an end to this my way.'

Arent tried to protest, but Drecht put a friendly hand on his chest, and shook his head in warning, before pushing the constable up the stairs.

As soon as they were out of sight, Arent grabbed Sammy. 'Come on, that's an innocent man they're dragging away. You need to work out what happened before they put the lash to his back.'

'I've already found the damn thing once,' grumbled Sammy, as Arent pulled him towards the gunpowder store. Despite his words, his eyes already betrayed that dreadful eagerness that always overcame him before a new case. 'How long do I have?'

'Depends on how long it takes them to find a lash amongst all this mess.'

Arent pushed him into the gunpowder store, as if he was a prisoner in a dungeon, then crossed his arms and waited by the door. Sara and Lia peered around him.

'It stinks of ale, farts and sour piss in here,' complained Sammy, sniffing the air. 'Do you have a pomander handy?'

Sara offered him the one dangling from her waist, which he accepted gratefully, before turning to his work.

'What should I do?' asked Sara, rejoining Arent and Lia.

'Just watch,' replied Arent excitedly. Seeing Sammy let loose upon an impossible problem was one of the great pleasures of his life. It was no different now.

Lying on his stomach, Sammy inspected the store's floorboards, then the box, running his hand up and down every piece of wood. Dissatisfied, he darted across the room, examining each of the gunpowder kegs on the racks in turn, rocking them one by one – nodding in satisfaction, as some internal idea presented itself.

Leaping on to the box, he tapped the beam connecting the whipstaffs in the helm to the rudders, then put a beady eye on the ceiling, which was covered in tin.

He murmured something to himself, then jumped down.

'Who had keys to this room and the box, Arent?'

Arent racked his memory for the answer. He'd asked the question when he'd been investigating threats to the ship, but a lot had happened in the last two weeks, and he hadn't slept for most of it.

'Quickly, Arent, quickly, your constable is running out of time,' said Sammy, clicking his fingers impatiently.

'My uncle and Vos had keys to The Folly's box,' said Arent. 'Only Captain Crauwels, Isaack Larme and the constable had keys to this room. There was no overlap.'

'No, but one of the keys to this room would have been much easier to acquire than the keys to The Folly's box.'

For the first time, Sammy noticed the crowd gathered at Arent's back, watching this demonstration. 'Ladies and gentlemen, while I'm, of course, honoured by your interest in my work, the matters under discussion must be tended with the strictest discretion. Lia, would you shut the door, please.'

A disappointed groan met the proclamation, but this was almost immediately drowned out by the sound of a drum beating across the weather decks. The rhythm was slow and steady, as if the *Saardam*'s heartbeat could suddenly be heard.

'They'll bring the constable out soon,' said Arent. 'What do you know?'

'I have two theories, neither satisfactory.' Sammy rubbed his hands together.

Arent noticed Lia flash an excited glance at her mother, who couldn't help but return it. He knew they enjoyed his reports, and he could only imagine how much they were enjoying seeing them come to life.

'The first is that The Folly was stolen in Fort Batavia and only the box was brought onboard,' continued Sammy. 'After we recovered The Folly, it was taken to the treasury in the fort. That treasury guarded the family's most valuable possessions and was accessible only to the governor general, Vos and ...'

Sara, thought Arent, flashing her a glance.

She had told him that she kept her jewelled pins in the treasury and had gone to collect them the morning of their departure. She might easily have taken her husband's key beforehand, used it to remove the pieces of The Folly from its box, then locked it again, while she was doing it.

The theory didn't explain what she'd done with the pieces once she'd stolen them, though. She'd still need to have taken them from the treasury. Could she have had help?

'I was in the treasury the morning we set sail,' said Sara, as if aware of his thoughts. 'The box was opened by ...' The name died on her lips. 'By an expert to ensure The Folly wasn't damaged. It was definitely brought aboard.'

'My second theory is equally flawed, though ingenious given the time you gave me,' said Sammy, unaware that Arent was lost in his own thoughts. 'The room itself is solid, without trapdoors of any kind. So how about this? Vos stole either the captain's key, or Isaack Larme's, then used it to enter the gunpowder store.'

'Vos?' exclaimed Sara. 'Why Vos of all men? I wouldn't have believed he had the imagination, and he knows the damage it will do to my husband. His ascension to the Gentlemen 17 depends on him delivering The Folly.'

'When I was working on recovering the device in Batavia, I noticed that the governor general and Vos never let the keys to the box out of their sight. They kept them on strings around their necks. As the governor general left just then, I noticed he still did. I doubt those keys could be easily obtained. However, the keys to the gunpowder store do not seem to be treated with such care. When we boarded, Isaack Larme certainly didn't have his upon him. His slops have no pockets and he was shirtless.'

Sammy threw himself down on to the constable's stool. 'If we assume – as we must, given the time we have – that it was the key to the gunpowder store that was stolen, our suspects become the governor general and Vos, but the governor general has nothing to gain. The Folly is already in his custody, and would benefit the Company he sails to take command of.'

'But what motive would Vos have for such a crime? He's loyal as a hound,' asked Arent.

From above them, the drumbeat drew faster.

'The Folly is priceless,' remarked Sammy. 'I heard Vos talking. Any nation that owns it can remake the world. They can explore unmapped waters, start new trade routes, strike at their enemies from the fog of a blank map. A king would empty his treasury for such power.'

Sara murmured her assent. 'Vos told Creesjie he was coming into a large sum when he proposed to her. If he'd already stolen The Folly that could explain why he felt bold enough to ask for her hand after so many years.'

'And my uncle ruined his company,' said Arent. 'Vos denies feeling anything about it, but he could have harboured a grudge these last years.'

'Then let's place the theft upon Vos's head for the moment,' concluded Sammy. 'Our second question is, how did he get The Folly out of a locked and guarded room, without being seen by the passengers on the other side?'

'The constable told me he goes for a piss and a walk at the same time every night. If he were watched, that pattern would be easy to spot.'

Sammy sprang from the stool and opened the door to the crowd on the other side. 'Did any of you see a solitary man dragging anything large out of here at' – he glanced at Arent – 'what time does he go for a piss?'

'Two bells,' supplied Arent.

'Two bells!' Sammy told them. 'Could have happened any time since we set sail.'

Glances were exchanged, but there wasn't any knowledge in them. Sammy slammed the door on them once again.

'Then we have Vos's window of time, but not his method. Is Vos friendly with anybody on this ship?'

'Not that I can see,' said Sara.

Sammy paced and thought. 'Three of the kegs were empty when I rocked them,' he muttered.

'The constable told me those kegs were empty because sailors had packed their cannons without orders,' said Arent.

'Three kegs and The Folly comes in three separate pieces.' Going to the racks, he tried to take one of the empty kegs down, failed, then gestured for Arent to do it instead. Tearing the lid free, they inspected the insides.

'Here,' said Sammy, before going to another one. 'And here. You can see the teeth marks where the cogs gouged the wood when they were wedged inside.'

He straightened up, satisfied with his work. 'Vos stole a key to the gunpowder store, then used it to enter while the constable was relieving himself. Using his own key, he stole the three pieces of The Folly from the box, then hid them in three kegs, which he must have emptied of gunpowder ahead of time.' His eyes clouded, then became bright. He snapped his fingers in delight. 'Oh, what a meticulous man he is,' he said admiringly.

'Sammy?'

'Battle stations!' said Sammy, whirling on him. 'An Indiaman on an eight-month voyage will call battle stations at least half a dozen times. Vos knew that, so he planned accordingly. It didn't matter when he retrieved The Folly, as long as it was before we arrived in Amsterdam, so he hid the pieces in the kegs, then waited. The first time battle stations were called, he dressed in a sailor's garb, then followed two accomplices into the gunpowder store. In the confusion, nobody would have noticed him under a hat.'

'Why two accomplices?' wondered Sara. 'Why wouldn't he take all three himself?'

'He couldn't risk somebody taking one of the kegs he wanted before he got it.'

Arent marched towards the door.

'Where are you going?' demanded Sammy.

'To tell my uncle.'

'He won't listen.' Sammy rushed after him. 'Arent, stop! Your uncle won't heed you. Vos is his most trusted servant. He wouldn't believe this of him any more than he'd believe the *Saardam* could grow wings and fly. We need proof.'

'They're about to flog an innocent man,' growled Arent, staring up the staircase. 'A good man.'

'He won't be the last,' said Sammy sorrowfully. 'Besides, our theory doesn't exonerate your friend. If anything, it puts him deeper in the conspiracy. Vos's scheme would have been better served by paying the constable to put aside the kegs he wanted. If you try to tell the governor general what you suspect, it will alert Vos. If you stay quiet and watch, he'll do something foolish. He'll give you what you want.'

'How do you know that?' asked Sara.

'Because murderers can't help but murder. Blackmailers can't help but blackmail and thieves can't help but thieve,' said Sammy. 'It's the itch. The itch is what kills them all.'

Arent sagged.

Sammy was right, as usual.

Guilt was like dirt. It got under the skin and didn't come clean. It made people second guess everything that was done, find fault where there was none and imagine mistakes that weren't made. Soon enough, worries were worming out of them, growing fat on their doubt. Before long they were on their hands and knees at the crime scene, searching for clues they hadn't left.

Sammy had caught a lot of guilty bodies because of the itch.

'So what the hell do I do now?' asked Arent.

'The one thing you're very bad at doing,' said Sammy. 'Nothing. Keep an eye on Vos. If he has accomplices as we suspect, the knowledge of the missing Folly will almost certainly send him scurrying to them, or them to him. Once that happens, you'll have everything you need.'

'Including Old Tom,' added Sara. Seeing their curious faces, she added, 'Sander said there would be three unholy miracles, each identified by the Mark of Old Tom. When the Eighth Lantern slaughtered the cattle, it left the Mark of Old Tom on the ground. That mark's here again. If Vos did it, then maybe we've found our possessed passenger.'

'Or he heard one of the whispers in the dark,' disagreed Arent. 'This could have been the price demanded for –'

From above them, the drums stopped.

50

ARENT TOOK A BOTTLE of wine from his trunk and walked through the compartment under the half deck, shielding his eyes against the sun's glare.

Lia and Sara were still tending the injured on the orlop deck, and Sammy had returned to his cell, fearful of being noticed now the commotion was at an end. Arent had wanted to escort him, but he couldn't let the constable suffer alone. For some reason, he felt responsible for what was happening to the old man.

The crew were packed tight on the waist, waiting silently. Dressed in slops, their torsos bare, it was difficult to pick one sailor from the next. Some were tall, others short, but life at sea had whittled them all down into the same malnourished shape, strong-shouldered and bow-legged, ruined for any other task.

The constable was having the shirt torn from his back, while Drecht waited nearby with the lash coiled in his hand. Evidently, the governor general had decided to give this job to somebody he trusted.

'Please, sirs,' the constable cried out. 'I swear by my five daughters I didn't do this, I didn't –'

Voices urged him to be quiet, worried that his flailing tongue would earn him another dozen lashes.

Arent pushed towards him, whispered threats rising out of the crowd.

This wasn't me, he wanted to tell them. *I objected to this*. But he knew it wouldn't make a difference. By the crew's reckoning, there was only *them* and *us*. Passengers and crew. Rich and poor. Officers and common sailors.

Didn't matter how he dressed or how he spoke, Arent was one of *them*.

The only difference was that the others were gathered on the quarterdeck above, watching the performance below like they were in their boxes at the damn theatre.

His uncle was standing next to Vos, who was watching proceedings without emotion. It would be better if he was malevolent, Arent thought. Better if there were some enjoyment. Hate, malice, anything. But there was none of that. His face was passive. Those luminous green eyes were devoid of any feeling.

Captain Crauwels and the rest of the officers were standing behind, their postures suggesting in the strongest possible terms that they had nothing to do with any of this.

Only Van Schooten was missing. Apparently, the chief merchant had chosen to seclude himself in his cabin with a bottle of wine until it was over.

Emerging from the crowd, Isaack Larme whispered to the constable. 'Courage,' he said. 'I'll see that you get double rations when you're done.'

The constable's eyes caught Arent's approach and became wild with panic.

'Hayes!' pleaded the constable, tears running down his grizzled cheeks. 'Please, sir, don't let 'em do this. I've not the strength.'

'There's nothing I can do,' said Arent gently. He turned around, then lifted the hem of his shirt so the constable could see the scars on his back. 'There's fifty lashes on there and I screamed from the first to the last. You should do the same. Scream as loud as you can, else the pain's got nowhere to go.'

He uncorked the wine and tipped it to the constable's lips, only pulling the jug away when the man spluttered for breath. 'Comes a day for bastards like the governor general and Vos,' said Arent. 'But it isn't today. Today you have to endure them, understand? You've got the strength and you've got five daughters to get home for.'

The constable nodded, seeming to take courage from the thought.

Because of the constable's missing arm, the sailors were unable to tie his hands around the mast, so they were using his waist instead, his belly sagging over the ropes. With each pass around, they apologised under their breath to the help-less old man.

Arent placed the jug of wine on the deck where the consta-ble's eyes could cling to it. 'Rest of this bottle's yours when this is over.'

Arent stepped away, watching as Drecht stuffed the constable's mouth with a mound of dirty hemp. Whatever he thought about this, he didn't let it show. He was just a soldier going about his duty.

Wind snapped the sails. The waves slapped the hull. Everybody was staring at the governor general, waiting for this sharp, thin creature to pass his sentence.

'A heinous crime has been committed,' he said, once the constable was gagged. 'Something of great value has been stolen.' He gave the accusation time to settle. 'I believe the constable to be the culprit, but I do not believe he acted alone. Until the stolen object is returned, a random member of the crew will be lashed every morning, every day.'

The sailors howled in protest.

The governor general has just set fire to the *Saardam*, thought Arent.

'Twenty hard lashes whenever you're ready, Guard Captain,' demanded the governor general, nodding to the drummer to begin again.

Drecht uncoiled the lash and drew back his arm.

He timed his strike to match the beat of the drum. It was a small mercy, but a mercy nonetheless. Knowing when the pain was coming would help the constable brace himself for it.

The whip cracked, ripping into the constable's flesh, bringing a scream of agony and groans of disgust as blood splattered the faces of the nearby sailors.

'Does anybody wish to confess or admit knowledge of this crime?' said the governor general, making the offer of a drawn-out, painful, death sound benevolent.

Meeting no response, Drecht raised the whip again.

Twenty were ordered and twenty were given, despite the constable collapsing unconscious after twelve.

It was a mercy.

When all was done, Drecht dropped the lash on the ground.

A cold breeze was swirling, raising goosebumps on the constable's skin, which was now slick with sweat.

Arent took out his dagger and sawed through the ropes binding the old man to the mast, catching his limp body before it fell. Gentle as he could, he carried him through the crowd and towards the sickberth.

The drumbeat stopped, the crew dispersing back to their duties, carrying their hatred with them.

High up on the quarterdeck, Vos watched them go with his hands clasped behind his back, his face a veil, his thoughts shifting darkly behind it.

51

H<small>UNCHED OVER HER WRITING</small> desk, Lia hummed happily as she copied the artificer's instructions from one parchment to another. The original was by her left hand and it was covered in odd sketches of cogs and tracks, suns and moons and stars, instructions written in Latin. Most people wouldn't have thought the symbols any less infernal than those in the daemonologica.

Not that Lia let herself be distracted by such thoughts. She concentrated on what was before her, for it was an exacting document, perfect in every detail. It had taken her three weeks to scribe the original in Batavia, each blotted letter, drop of sweat and smear of ink reminding her of that awful period. Despite the terrible heat, her father had confined her to a locked room, refusing to allow her to leave until the work was done.

Lia hadn't been allowed any company, for fear it would distract her into making a mistake, but her mama came anyway, singing softly, cradling her when she was tired, and hiding under the bed when her father came. Even now, the thought of her mother, emerging from under the bed covered in dust, filled her with such an overwhelming love, she almost had no place for it.

There was an insistent knocking.

Lia quickly began covering everything up, but Creesjie's voice quelled her panic. 'It's me, dear heart,' she said, opening the door a crack and slipping through quickly.

Behind her, Lia saw Marcus and Osbert playing with the pair of spinning dancers she'd made for them in Batavia. They were chasing them up and down the corridor under Dorothea's supervision. The boys thought them magic. Lia thought them a nimble piece of woodworking. Sometimes she wished she were young enough to share in their glee. Her mother had tried to occupy her, but the fort had been a lonely place for a little girl to grow up.

Still, it had given her more time to build.

Coming up to the writing desk, Creesjie picked up the almost-finished model of the *Saardam*, turning it around in her hands. It was perfect in every detail. Even the string rigging was in order.

'Is that what Sara asked you to build?' she asked, amazed.

'Yes,' said Lia. She reached over, removing a hidden clasp that allowed the ship to break in half. Within, Creesjie could make out all the decks. Lia tugged open a small door.

'I've calculated the spaces in the hull where a smuggler's compartment could be built and cargo stored without it affecting the ballast of the ship.'

'There are dozens,' said Creesjie.

'Yes,' agreed Lia.

Putting the wooden ship down, Creesjie stared at the plans scattered around her desk, running an affectionate hand through Lia's long black hair. 'You're a wonder to me,' she said. 'You make such miracles.'

Lia blushed, enjoying the compliment.

Smoothing her dress, Creesjie sat down on the edge of bunk. 'I wanted to …' She reconsidered. 'I shall see your father tonight. Should I bring back more plans?'

'Yes, please,' said Lia, sifting through documents. 'I need another hour or more on these, but then I'll be done.'

Creesjie coughed awkwardly. 'I never asked whether you were … I mean, are you comfortable with what we're doing?'

'Comfortable?' asked Lia, tipping her head in almost exactly the same way her mother did when she was uncertain of what was being asked of her.

'Is it what *you* want?' asked Creesjie forthrightly. 'Your mother's been very adamant, but I thought, perhaps, you might have some other ideas.'

'Mama says if I go back to Amsterdam, Father will eventually make me marry somebody I don't want to,' said Lia, struggling to see Creesjie's point.

'Your mother says that,' said Creesjie, leaning forward. 'What do you think? Do you think it's bad to marry somebody chosen for you?'

'I don't know,' said Lia carefully, this entire conversation a labyrinth. 'You've had arranged marriages before, haven't you?'

'My first. The second I chose. And, perhaps, the third if I throw over Count Astor for Vos.'

'He's a duke, Aunt Creesjie.'

'Vos said he was a count.'

'I'm certain he would have said a duke. He's usually quite reliable.'

'Well, then, I'd be tossing away a duke,' continued Creesjie, waving the rank away.

'But I thought you hated Vos?'

'Yes, part of me does,' she acknowledged, her tone suggesting *that* part of her was of little importance. 'He always struck me as the smallest of men, but his proposal is very appealing. And it shows an ambition I didn't think he had, which was the thing I disliked most about him.'

'But you don't love him,' said Lia, puzzled.

'Oh, you truly are your mother's daughter,' said Creesjie, watching her affectionately. 'Love can be feigned, dear heart. You can even convince yourself of it, if you try hard enough, but it's impossible to spend an imaginary fortune. Marriage is an inconvenient convenience. It's the shackle we accept for our safety.'

'Mama says she'd rather be free than wealthy in a cage.'

'An argument we frequently enjoy,' Creesjie snorted. 'Unlike your mother, I don't believe women can be free, not while men are stronger. What use is the freedom to be assaulted in the first dark alley we come across? We can't fight, so we sing, we dance – and we survive. Cornelius Vos adores me, and, if he becomes wealthy, he would make for a fine marriage. My sons will be well educated, protected and heirs to a future worthy of them. If I cast off that protection for some imaginary freedom, what will become of them? Where will they live, how will they eat, what will their future be? And what of myself? I'd be at the mercy of any lustful man who had the strength to put his hands upon me. No, no, no. Marriage is the price I pay for the privilege of nobility and I consider the price well spent. Poverty is the most dangerous thing for a woman. We're not well suited to a life on the streets.'

'But do you *like* being married?'

'Not always,' admitted Creesjie, her blonde hair catching the light.

Lia looked at it enviously. It was like spun gold.

'My first husband was a wretch,' said Creesjie without feeling. 'But my second husband, Pieter, was the love of my life.' Her voice came alive, the way a bush could suddenly be full of birdsong. 'He was charming and eloquent. He could dance and sing, and he made me laugh.'

'You don't speak of him often,' said Lia, saddened by Creesjie's wistfulness.

'It's too painful,' she said. 'Every morning I reach over, expecting to find him in my bed. I hear the door downstairs and think it's him, returning from one of his trips. I miss him so.'

'Do you think he would have been able to stop Old Tom?'

'He didn't think so when he forced us to flee Amsterdam, but he made many mistakes.' There was something bitter in that. 'And, for all my admiration, I must confess that my Pieter wasn't as clever as your mama. Even so, it's not the easiest task finding a demon among these men. There's malice enough on the *Saardam* to bring heaven to ruins.'

The door flew open and Sara bustled in breathlessly.

'Oh, hello,' she said to Creesjie, snatching the model of the ship from the desk. 'Don't mind me, I've had an idea.'

'Sara!' came Arent's voice from the end of the corridor. 'What did you want me to —'

Sara kissed Lia on the forehead. 'Thank you for this, dear heart, it's beautiful.'

And then she was gone, slamming the door shut behind her.

Lia smiled at the place where her mother had been. 'I've never seen Mama this happy.'

'It's lovely, isn't it?' agreed Creesjie, who was obviously glad to change the subject. 'It's a shame. Your mother is wonderful, but she suits your father ill.'

'Why?'

Creesjie took a moment to think about it. 'Because he doesn't need a partner,' she said, at last. 'He needs a wife and your mother doesn't need a husband, she needs a partner.'

'Is that why he beats her?'

Creesjie flinched at the coldness in Lia's voice.

'I think so,' admitted Creesjie.

'Is that why he hurt her so badly she couldn't walk?' pressed Lia, whose face had twisted into something malevolent.

'I'm not trying to persuade you, or dissuade you,' responded Creesjie, obviously uncomfortable. 'I just want you to make your decisions for the best reasons, with all the facts laid before you. It's a terrible thing to betray kin, especially when we don't understand the price. Regret is the worst thing we do to ourselves.'

'I understand,' said Lia, nodding.

And, finally, she did. Creesjie thought Lia was doing all of this because she didn't want to be forced into a marriage once they reached Amsterdam. She thought that Lia hurting her father was simply an unfortunate step along the way. Of course, Creesjie had it the wrong way around.

Arranging her skirts, Creesjie took a step towards the door.

'Do you believe there are some things that can't be forgiven?' asked Lia.

Creesjie's face flickered, as if trying to make sense of the question.

'Yes,' she said hollowly.

'Good,' said Lia. 'So do I.'

And with that, she returned to the plans on her writing desk.

52

Emerging on the quarterdeck, Sara jammed the model of the *Saardam* into Arent's hands. Confusion became wonder as he turned the miniature capstan wheel with his finger. That feature hadn't strictly been necessary, but Lia wove delight into everything she made. It was one of the things Sara loved most about her.

Arent's eyes were wide, a foolish smile on his lips. She saw the boy he must have been.

'This is magnificent,' he said. 'Where did you get it?'

Sara hesitated. She trusted Arent, but Lia's secrets were dangerous. She'd been harbouring them as long as she could remember, ever since that first old man had heard her muttering about adding barrelling to the castle's cannons to extend their range.

Before she'd known what was happening, a crowd had surrounded her. They'd never heard such words before, let alone from an eight-year-old girl. Sara had managed to usher her away without too many more questions, but, it had happened again a few days later, when Lia had idly suggested a stronger design for the fort's walls to the stonemason.

He'd seen the sense of it immediately, but not coming from a young girl.

In fright, he'd marched her to the governor general. That had been the last time Lia had been allowed outside of the fort.

'Lia built it,' said Arent quietly, observing her disquiet. 'Her cleverness is one of those things people keep tripping over themselves trying to hide. Don't worry, I've seen the trouble Sammy's intelligence has brought him. I'll keep it to myself.' He sucked a breath through his teeth. 'Did she invent The Folly?'

Sara opened her mouth to lie, but was defeated by his honest expression. 'How could you know that?'

'I saw The Folly after we retrieved it,' said Arent. 'It was obviously clever, but it was also beautiful, and elegant. There was something playful about it that made me think it was a toy. This has the same quality.'

Arent inspected the model carefully. 'Lia invented The Folly, which makes her the most valuable thing on this ship,' he murmured. 'If Old Tom knows, she could be in danger.'

'I've thought about that,' she said. 'If Old Tom comes for my husband, I don't doubt he'd trade Lia to it in return for his own life.'

Arent stared at her in disbelief. His uncle and his grandfather had been so worried about Arent's father killing him, they'd hired an assassin to murder him in the woods. It was a horrifying act of devotion done from a black-hearted love, but it was love all the same. How could his uncle not be willing to extend that same devotion to his own daughter? How empty must his heart have become to see Lia as nothing more than another breastplate?

'I can't believe we're talking about the same man who raised me,' he said hollowly.

'Power changes people, Arent.'

Arent looked out at the empty ocean, troubled. He still wasn't used to it. For the last few weeks, there had always been the reassuring sight of the other ships. Without them, the sea suddenly looked very large and the sky very threatening, and the Saardam very frail.

Arent changed subject, trying to focus on a fear he could do something about. 'What's the purpose of this model? You said it could help us.'

'I asked Lia to work out the spaces onboard where smuggling compartments could be built.' Sara reached inside the ship and pulled open a tiny door. 'I thought we could check them one by one. Bosey built them, so if Old Tom was involved in the theft of The Folly, perhaps that's where the pieces were hidden.'

'If we return The Folly to my uncle, we may keep him from flogging the crew unnecessarily.'

'And we'd be able to prevent a mutiny.'

They were almost to the compartment under the half deck when Larme's quick, short steps sounded behind them. 'Arent,' he called.

The mercenary met him.

'The crew's in my ear about this fight you organised with Wyck. Now the storm's passed, they're eager to see the blood they were promised.' Before Arent could respond, he wagged a finger. 'I'm asking you to reconsider. Two weeks have passed, and I reckon that's enough time to let wounded pride heal. He soiled your bunk, but no harm was done past that, which is a better end than most men have got out of him. Forget it happened, Hayes. He'll have somebody else to torment by now. I know him.'

'I want to fight him,' said Arent levelly.

'You're being pig-headed and it will get you killed. He's the best man with a blade I've ever seen, and he's got a fierce temper. If you draw blood, he's likely to kill you for it.'

'I need my questions answered,' said Arent. 'Can you think of any other way to get them out of him?'

Larme glared. 'No,' he admitted grudgingly.

'Then I'll see you at dusk.'

Sara eyed him apprehensively, but said nothing. There wasn't any point. They were each going about this investigation in their own fashion, using the tools given to them by God. Sammy observed, Creesjie flirted and Lia invented. Sara asked questions and Arent was going to fight, same as he always had.

He was capable of more, she was sure of it. He'd worked out The Folly's creator after spending a short time in its company, but, for some reason, he didn't trust those skills. She wondered what had happened to make him doubt himself so completely.

They spent the rest of the afternoon in the cargo hold, navigating by candlelight, trying to match the spots on the model to the corresponding places on the ship. It was slow going, and disappointing. Bosey and Larme clearly didn't have as much imagination as Lia, and had only built their smuggling compartments in a few obvious places.

None of them contained The Folly, or anything else.

'This has to be the last one,' said Arent, as they reached a large section of wall. 'I'll have to go up to the forecastle for the fight soon.'

The compartments were always locked with a peg, and she found it easily enough, pulling it free as Arent lifted the panel from the wall.

A stink rolled out of the dark, sending them staggering backwards, covering their mouths.

'What's in there?' coughed Arent, his eyes watering.

Sara crept closer, holding her candle out in front of her. Sealed in the dark, his throat slit, was the body of Sander Kers.

53

DUSK BROUGHT A CHANGE of watch, the second mate ringing the bell amidships. The repairs had been ongoing all day, and the ship looked tidy, if not seaworthy. Under a purple and orange sky, Arent followed the throng of sailors and musketeers to the forecastle deck, with Sara walking behind him.

They'd told the captain about Sander's body and he'd sent sailors to bring it up on deck to be disposed of. Arent had asked him to delay, so Sammy could inspect the corpse that evening, but Crauwels had refused. Everybody knew the dead brought plague if left to rot. Any ship even suspected of being plague-ridden would be held at port for sixty days, the passengers and crew forced to endure onboard until it passed, or killed them.

Crauwels didn't want to risk it.

Sara estimated that Sander had been in there a couple of weeks, which suggested he'd died the night he disappeared. The night the Eighth Lantern had attacked.

They'd told Isabel, who'd taken the news better than they'd expected. Tears filled her eyes, but her back remained straight. After asking where he'd been taken, she'd gone to pray over the body.

'Don't let Wyck nick you here, or here,' said Sara, pointing to spots on Arent's legs and chest. 'You'll bleed and keep bleeding, and there won't be anything I can do.'

'Sara –'

She ignored him. She was speaking quickly and nervously, obviously afraid for him.

The waist was packed with spectators, who parted to let them through, shouting insults or encouragement, depending on which way they'd bet. Ignoring their curfew, passengers from the orlop deck had gathered at the mainmast, craning their necks to see more clearly or standing on the railing for a better view. Creesjie had brought Marcus and Osbert out, and the boys had found some willing shoulders to sit on.

Even the governor general would watch, according to the rumours. Arent was thankful Sara was wearing her peasant clothes, but he was still afraid of her being spotted. He'd begged her not to come but she'd flatly refused his advice.

Arriving on the forecastle deck, Arent saw Wyck at the beakhead, practising with his dagger.

'He's good,' said Sara.

'He's *very* good,' corrected Arent.

His hands were a blur, the point of the attack changing with every swipe and thrust. More importantly, he kept his feet moving.

Arent felt the first touch of nerves. Despite his size, Wyck was fast and nimble. He would be hard to hit, whereas Arent would be hard to avoid. It didn't matter whether this was friendly or not. If that blade nicked him in the wrong spot by accident, he was dead.

Drecht appeared in front of him. His hat was pulled down low, a pipe sticking out of his beard. The guard captain glanced at Sara agitatedly, but he knew better than to argue with her. He took the dagger from his waist and held it out to Arent.

'Guard your body and if you get the chance, put a blade in his throat,' he warned, lifting the brim of his hat to stare at Arent with those pitiless blue eyes. 'Every second this fight drags on is to his advantage.'

'I've told you, I'm going to lose,' argued Arent. 'Nobody needs to die.'

'That's your plan,' said Drecht. 'His plan is to lie to you, then kill you quick, and if that fails, to kill you slow. I know men like this. They can't be trusted.'

Taking the weapon, Arent handed Sara his father's rosary. 'Can you keep this safe for me?'

'I'll have it waiting when you come back.'

Their gaze lingered, but Arent could feel Wyck's eyes upon him. He touched Sara's arm and then stepped into the ring, where Wyck was bouncing from toe to toe.

As the crowd roared for them to start, Arent crouched, putting his arms out in front of him, trying to protect as much of his body as he could. Being tall and wide had its advantages, but not in a knife fight where the key was to make yourself as difficult to hit as possible.

Wyck circled, trying to find an angle.

He thrust quickly, but Arent parried with the edge of his blade, adjusting quickly and slashing back.

Wyck jumped away, laughing at the attempt.

He was as irritating to fight as to talk to, Arent realised.

The sailors howled, urging the boatswain forward, while the musketeers cheered for Arent.

The boatswain came again, slashing and thrusting. Sidestepping the first two strikes, Arent caught the second on his blade, iron scraping along iron as he tried to push Wyck away, but he was strong.

'Old Tom sends his regards,' sneered Wyck.

Taking advantage of Arent's surprise, Wyck punched him in the side, then tried to ram his blade into his belly. Stumbling backwards, Arent avoided the thrust, earning the slightest of nicks.

The crowd roared in appreciation.

Drecht was right. This wasn't a friendly contest. There would be no quarter. No hesitation. Wyck meant to slit his throat, and he was going to do it at Old Tom's behest.

'You have to stop this,' screamed Sara. 'This isn't fake. Wyck's going to kill you.'

Arent wished he could reassure her, but he didn't dare take his eyes off Wyck. Everybody believed he was defending desperately, trying to keep himself alive until Wyck tired, but that wasn't the plan. He wasn't defending, he was watching how Wyck fought, working out his reach and where he left himself open when he attacked.

Wyck was fighting, but Arent was planning.

Seeing Arent distracted, the boatswain charged forward, snarling. This time Arent didn't take a step back and he didn't parry. He twisted slightly, letting Wyck's blade slide past him as he slashed at his opponent's face.

The boatswain caught the strike on his forearm, blood spraying across Arent's clothes.

Rather than falling back, Wyck swung his arm at Arent's eyes, momentarily blinding him with blood.

Arent kicked out desperately, catching Wyck in the stomach, ripping the air from him. As Wyck sucked in breath, Arent wiped as much blood as he could from his eyes. His vision was blurry, but good enough to catch Isaack Larme's nod to somebody in the crowd. Glancing in the same direction, Arent saw the glint of a knife emerging from a sailor's sleeve.

Circling, Wyck thrust suddenly, trying to manoeuvre Arent so his back was to the hidden blade.

Arent gave him what he wanted, but kept a few steps between himself and the assassin.

When Wyck came again, Arent was ready. Rather than parry, he let the first strike catch his arm. Ignoring the searing pain, he yanked Wyck close and caught hold of his wrist. Roaring, he hurled the boatswain at the sailor with the blade, the two of them cracking together.

Arent was on them in two steps, scooping up the fallen knife and jamming it straight through the second sailor's hand, pinning him to the deck. Falling on Wyck's body, he punched him, then leant close to his ear, the overpowering smell of paprika rising into his nostrils.

'What does Laxagarr mean?' he demanded.

Wyck ripped the dagger out of the sailor's hand and drove the point at Arent's hip.

Growling, the mercenary grabbed his arm, banging it against the deck and sending the dagger skittering. Before he could try anything else, Arent elbowed him in the face, dazing him.

'What does Laxagarr mean?' he demanded.

Wyck coughed blood, his eyes unfocused. 'Old Tom take you.'

Arent hit him again, his fist landing like cannon fire. Something cracked in Wyck's face.

Sara screamed for him to stop.

'What does Laxagarr mean?'

'Go to –' Arent hit him again, Wyck's head snapping back. A small, dark, vile part of Arent revelled in it. He'd held his strength for so long, wary of fighting because he knew how it ended. There was a ball of rage held tight at his core that had been there for as long as he could remember. Every insult, every jeer, every slight; that's where he kept them. They were fuel for the dark furnace he normally kept shuttered.

He raised his fist again.

'What does –'

'Trap,' spluttered Wyck. 'It means trap,' he said, coughing blood.

The crowd went silent.

Puffing like a pair of bellows, Arent looked around. The crowd were watching him with the awe of soldiers seeing a bombardment for the first time.

Aside from Old Tom, Wyck was the fiercest, most terrifying thing on the ship. Everybody who'd found themselves on the wrong end of him had suffered, grievously.

Bosey got it worst, but he hadn't been alone. They all had their scars.

Wyck was what these murderers, malcontents and rapists had nightmares about. And Arent had put him down.

Some delicate, but crucial, balance had shifted on the *Saardam*.

As the sailors pondered this, Sara broke through the crowd, hugging Arent fiercely.

'Sara, what will –'

'Shut up,' she said, her face pressed against his chest. Finally, she dashed the tears away. 'I thought you were going to kill him,' she said.

Arent lifted his forearm, inspecting the slice. It was shallow enough, but it would ache for a week. 'Laxagarr means trap in Nornish,' said Arent. 'When the other sailors asked Bosey what he was working on, that's what he was telling them.'

Drecht pushed through the crowd. 'Why didn't you kill him, you damn idiot.'

'The dead don't answer questions,' replied Arent, returning his dagger.

'And they can't ask them,' responded Drecht. 'Strength follows strength. You've made him look weak in front of his lads. He'll be coming for you now. He has to.'

'Somebody's always coming for me,' said Arent, staring at Isaack Larme. 'And they better come damn quick, or I'll find them first.'

54

A RENT STAGGERED INTO THE compartment under the half deck, blood dripping off his fingers. A solitary candle burnt on a cask, discharging thick, foul smoke into the air.

Isabel's laughter came from the shadows at the rear of the compartment. She was sitting on a stool, talking with Dorothea. They stopped the moment they saw him, their eyes widening in alarm.

'Did you win?' asked Dorothea.

'He won,' said Sara, opening the box of healing sundries she'd left there earlier, revealing a collection of rags and unguents, corked vials and bags of powder. From beneath them, she took out a hooked needle and a length of catgut.

Dragging the candle a little closer, Sara inspected the wound.

'You'll need to take your shirt off,' she said to Arent. 'The material's in the way.'

He did as she asked, uncovering a patchwork of scars and burns, stab wounds and musket holes badly healed.

Isabel murmured a prayer. 'God made you pay a high price to get here,' she said devoutly.

'God didn't put a sword in my hand,' he disagreed.

Sara's hand was already slippery with blood and she had to ask Isabel to thread the catgut for her. 'Is healing people something you can teach me?' asked Isabel, frowning at the eye of the needle as she tried to engineer the catgut through it.

'If you've the feel for it, I'd be happy to,' said Sara, taking the needle from her. 'Is there an unopened jug of wine anywhere?'

'I can find one, my lady,' said Isabel.

'It's Sara,' she said. 'If there's none about, ask the steward. Use my name.'

Isabel departed.

Gripping the thread in her teeth, Sara slipped the point of the needle through the edges of Arent's ragged skin, then looped it and started again. The sting was almost enough to make him wish for the days when he would have let the injury alone, then lain down for a week or two and hoped not to die.

That was what he'd been taught by the army's stinking old barber-surgeon, who'd told him the bad humours had to be allowed to seep out. Once they were expunged, the body would do its own work, he'd said.

Sammy hadn't liked that. First time he'd seen Arent injured, he'd stitched him up like a torn jacket. Arent had tried to argue, telling him about the humours and the surgeon's advice, but Sammy didn't take it kindly. He'd even pricked him a couple of extra times with the needle to emphasise his disquiet.

He was surprised to find Sara knew the technique also.

'Where did you learn to do this?' he asked, watching Sara work.

'My mother,' she said distractedly. 'My grandfather was a healer of some renown. He taught her and she taught me.'

'Could your father do this?'

She shook her head. 'He was a merchant.' Her voice frosted over. 'My mother used her gifts to save his life after he became ill passing through her village, and he fell in love with her. She was only three guilders away from being a peasant, but my noble father didn't care. They married and lived happily ever after, except for all the friends he lost because he'd snubbed their well-born daughters.'

She finished another loop.

'Love nearly destroyed my family,' she said drily. 'On the bright side, they had five daughters, so my father had lots of chances to make up for his mistake.'

Sara worked quietly after that, shushing Arent when he tried to talk.

When Isabel returned with the wine, Sara used it to wash the wound, offering the jug to Arent so he could dull the pain.

He hardly touched it.

Having Sara kneeling in front of him like this, even under these circumstances, was proving tricky. Pain was the only thing keeping everything where it ought to be.

Isaack Larme stomped into the compartment, throwing a bag of coins at Arent's feet. 'Your winnings,' he said. Then, leering at Sara, 'But I reckon you've done well enough out of this already.'

'I'm a noblewoman with rank, wealth and a very sharp dagger,' said Sara, squinting at her stitches. 'So a little respect, if you please.'

'Apologies, my lady,' said Larme, lowering his gaze.

'You set those boys in the crowd on me,' said Arent levelly. 'I caught the nod.'

'Would have been more if I could spare them,' said Larme, unabashed.

'Why?'

'Wyck keeps control of the lads for me, which means I need him more than I need you. You went looking for a fight. I tried to warn you off, but you wouldn't have it.' He cleared his throat uncomfortably. 'That's why I'm here. I want to know what your plans are for me.'

'Plans?' said Arent, confused.

'I don't intend on spending the rest of this voyage waiting for you to jam a blade in my back. Do what you're going to do.' The dwarf puffed his chest out, as if expecting Arent to stab him right there.

Sara rolled her eyes and went back to work.

'I'm not going to kill you, Larme,' said Arent wearily. 'If you piled my dead up, you could spit in God's face from the top. I'm done adding to the sum. That lad you sent after me didn't have to die, so I didn't kill him. Same goes for Wyck, same goes for you. Answer my questions and we'll end this day as friends.'

Larme studied him, obviously trying to find the ambush hidden beneath all of his benevolence. It was the same look Eggert had given Arent the day he'd apologised for holding a blade to his neck. Charity was evidently so rare aboard the *Saardam*, nobody recognised it any more.

'You wouldn't survive an hour as a sailor,' said Larme eventually.

'Nicest thing anybody's ever said to me,' said Arent, inviting him to take the stool opposite.

Larme appeared doubtful, but was swayed by the wine Arent pushed towards him.

'What was in the smuggler's compartment in the cargo hold?' asked Arent with a grimace, as Sara completed another loop. 'You emptied it before we got there.'

'A piece of The Folly.' He caught their shocked expressions, then added quickly, 'I didn't steal it, mind. I was searching for Bosey's robes like the captain ordered. Figured he might have hid them in one of the compartments, but I found that instead.'

'Not the entire thing?'

'No, more's the pity.' He sounded like a man who'd been too often on the wrong side of fortune's flipped coin. 'A piece would have fetched a good price, but if I'd been able to sell the whole thing I could have bought a ship of my own.'

'Could have?' asked Arent. 'What happened to it?'

Larme eyed him suspiciously. 'Why?'

'I'm out of patience for the self-interest on this ship,' sighed Sara. 'If you don't answer our questions fully, I'm going to tell my husband you stole The Folly and watch him cut you into quarters.'

'All right, all right,' he said hastily. 'I destroyed it, after you two almost caught me. Smashed it to bits, then tipped them out of the porthole in the cable locker. I thought it was too dangerous to keep.'

Arent shared a glance with Sara. She tilted her head, suggesting it was probably true.

'How did you know it was a piece of The Folly?' she asked

'Governor General tested it on the *Saardam*. Not that I was allowed to use it. Captain Crauwels does all the navigating. Rest of us just sail in the direction he points.'

'Sander Kers was murdered and stuffed into one of your compartments,' said Arent bluntly. 'What do you know about that?'

'Nothing,' he said. 'I've no reason to hurt anybody.'

'Except Bosey,' said Sara. 'You ordered Johannes Wyck to cut out his tongue, didn't you?'

The jug of wine stopped halfway to Larme's lips. Sara wasn't even looking at him. She was still stitching Arent's wound.

'That's how you work, isn't it?' she said, her tongue pressing against her top lip in concentration. 'Wyck does nasty things to people when you think they need doing, and you put an arm around whatever's left of them. That trick with the knife in the crowd showed that. What was Bosey saying that you wanted kept quiet?'

Larme leant forward, lowering his voice. 'The *Saardam*'s my home. Only one I've ever had where I wasn't kicked for sport. It's my job to keep her safe and Bosey put her in danger.'

'How?'

'He was recruiting my lads. Twisting them around.'

'How?' insisted Sara.

'He had coin, too much for a simple sailor. He was buying them, getting them to do strange jobs for him onboard.'

'Your talent for vagueness is both admirable and irritating,' said Sara.

'I don't know what the jobs were specifically, but we caught him and a few of the others in parts of the ship they shouldn't have been in after we docked in Batavia. They were searching for something, I reckon. Tapping the walls and kicking the floorboards. Whatever it was, it was big, judging by the tools they were carrying. I even caught them measuring the aft of the ship, but I couldn't get a word out of them as to why.'

'What happened to these other sailors?' asked Arent eagerly. 'Could we talk to them?'

'They vanished,' said Larme sorrowfully. 'Marched off the ship one morning like they'd heard the devil's whistle.

They never came back. That was Bosey's doing, I'm telling you. Never met a man with fewer principles when coin was flashed before him. He killed those boys, I know he did. That's why I ordered Wyck to cut his tongue out. I didn't want any more of my lads disappearing with that bastard's coin in their hand.'

'I thought he was your friend,' said Arent. 'You built those smuggler's compartments together, didn't you?'

Larme whistled, impressed despite himself. 'Aye, we built those holes together and made fair coin doing it, but that was as far as it went.'

Scratching his belly, Larme hopped off the stool.

He glanced at the arch leading out on to the waist, then sighed, as if losing the tug of war his conscience had been playing with him. 'Be careful of your new friend Jacobi Drecht,' he said.

'Drecht, why?'

'You ever hear of the Banda Islands?'

Arent shared a glance with Sara, remembering their breakfast discussion. His uncle had massacred everybody who lived there when they refused to honour a spice contract that would have left them starving.

'What's that got to do with Drecht?'

'It was the *Saardam* they sent when the population revolted,' said Larme. 'Governor General was aboard; that's how he knows the captain. He gave the order to slaughter everybody and he sent Jacobi Drecht and his musketeers to do it. Your friend butchered his way across those islands, then drank and sang the night away with his friends. Governor General gave him that sword for his loyalty, and he pledged more besides.'

'More?'

'A king's fortune. More wealth than Drecht could ever spend, so long as he got him home safe. Turns out that's how much it costs to convince somebody to slaughter children in their beds.' Fury pulsed through him. 'Old Tom's welcome to the lot of them.'

55

A RENT, SARA AND SAMMY were kneeling on the waist, staring at the body of Sander Kers. The predikant had been laid in a hemp cocoon, which would be stitched tight and dropped over the side at first light. Dozens of the cocoons were lined up on the deck and more were being carried up all the time. Most of them belonged to people who'd succumbed to injuries inflicted during the storm. Sara imagined them settled on the seabed, like one of the dotted lines Crauwels used to mark their course on a chart.

'Are you certain it's safe for me to be out of my cell?' said Sammy, glancing nervously at the crowd of sailors who'd turned out to watch him work.

The sun was sinking behind the horizon and Sammy hadn't seen it for so long that he'd burst into tears when Arent had brought him outside.

'If word reaches your husband that I'm ignoring his commands, he'll toss me back into that cell without any hope of light again,' concluded Sammy.

'My husband has locked himself away to brood,' said Sara. 'He believes the theft of The Folly was part of some grand campaign Old Tom is waging against him.' She could not conceal her delight at his discomfort. 'You have nothing to fear for the next hour, at least. Guard Captain Drecht watches his door, and Vos is inside, listening to him rant. You'll have to go back into your cell when their meeting ends, but you're safe for now. As am I.'

Sammy ran his eyes across her peasant clothing. 'This voyage has changed you a great deal, Sara Wessel,' he said, lifting Sander's shoulder to resume his study of the body. After a moment, he let it drop again. 'This body has nothing more to tell us. His throat was slit approximately two weeks ago, and he was stuffed into a secret compartment.'

'But why was the body hidden?' muttered Sara, who had to repeat herself to be heard over the hammering and chiselling of the repairs. In truth, the sound suggested a greater array of activity than could currently be seen. If she had to guess, she'd have said fewer than ten sailors were actually on deck. After their exertions during the storm, the captain was letting most of them sleep.

'There must be something we're not supposed to find,' said Sammy. He got to his feet, dusting his hands off. It was a futile effort. They were coated in grime and slop, the accumulated filth of two weeks in his cell. 'Did Sander Kers have any enemies?'

'We think Old Tom lured him to Batavia. I saw the letter myself. Our devil wanted him here, and now he's dead. It would seem to me that was its intent all along,' said Sara.

Sammy put an aggravated hand through his hair, dislodging some of the lice that had taken residence there. 'Try as I might, I'm struggling to make any connections between the facts of this case,' he said, pacing the deck.

Sara wished Lia was here to see this. Arent described Sammy's short-legged but energetic walk with great detail in his reports, and when she and Lia play-acted them, they always strode with such vigour they fell about laughing.

'From the first, my concern has been with the murder of Bosey, a carpenter who accepted an offer of great wealth from a voice in the darkness in return for making this boat ready for his passage. Quite what that entailed we're unsure, though Isaack Larme described finding Bosey and his acolytes in strange places around the ship, and said he thought they were searching for something. When asked what he was doing, he told them "trap".'

'Maybe he was building one,' mused Sara.

'Or finding one,' countered Sammy.

'Or disarming one,' added Arent.

Sammy glanced between them, then murmured, 'Both fine ideas. Either way, he was doing his work at the behest of something calling itself Old Tom, which was the name of a beggar Arent inadvertently caused to be beaten to death when he was a child. After Arent was removed to his grandfather's estate, this demon apparently swept across the Provinces, possessing the bodies of a number of wealthy merchants and nobles, causing them to commit unspeakable horrors before leaving their lives in ruins. It announced itself with a mark that resembles an eye with a tail, and that same mark was etched into Arent's wrist after his father disappeared thirty years ago. His father's rosary was found in the animal pens after the Eighth Lantern appeared to us. Those animals were slaughtered without anybody going near them.'

So fierce was his concentration, it was as if he were walking back through the events, thought Sara.

'The slaughter of the animals was the first of three unholy miracles, according to our dead predikant here. The second was the disappearance of The Folly from a locked room, which would appear to have been the work of Cornelius Vos, undertaken in a bid to marry Creesjie Jens. And we're expecting a third, after which anybody who didn't bargain with Old Tom will be slaughtered. Are there any details I've missed?'

'That Old Tom is possessing one of the passengers,' ventured Arent.

'And my husband apparently summoned it all those years ago, but now it wants him dead. It asked me and Creesjie to kill him with a dagger that it would leave in a drawer under his bunk.'

'Ah, yes,' said Sammy happily. 'Have you looked in the drawer?'

'Guard Captain Drecht does every night, but he swears there's only clothes.' She peered at him. 'Tell me, Mr Pipps –'

'Sammy, please.'

'Sammy.' She curtsied, honoured by the offer of familiarity. 'Do you believe there's a devil at work aboard this boat?'

'Of one kind or another.' He smiled grimly. 'The truth is, I find myself facing an opponent beyond any I've encountered before, and it would flatter my ego to believe it was supernatural. Your question is, if I may say without insult, irrelevant, though. Whether this is a devil dressed as a man, or a man dressed as a devil, our course of action remains the same. We must investigate each incident, then follow the clues back to the truth.'

Sara could only marvel at the confidence in his voice. Listening to him, she truly believed they would do it. For the first time, she wondered if maybe the accusation of spying levelled against him by Casper van den Berg was part of all this. Had the charge been intended to put Pipps out of the way, so Old Tom could go about its scheme without inter-ference? If so, did that not suggest Arent's grandfather was somehow bound up in all of this?

'If Old Tom truly is a devil, what will we do then?' wonder-ed Sara.

'I don't know, that's beyond my realm. Though, it would explain why the one man versed in banishing devils was killed.'

'We still have Isabel,' said Sara. 'She's studied the daemon-ologica and is as zealous as Sander in her duty, if not more so.'

'Let's hope she's enough.'

'How do we proceed, Sammy?' asked Arent.

The deference in his tone was strange for Sara to hear. Normally, he was so forthright. Whether he could see the path or not, he charged forward. It was something she admired about him. But speaking to Sammy, it was like he couldn't think for himself, couldn't conceive a way forward without his friend.

But why would that be? Everything they knew about Old Tom they'd learned while Pipps was locked away. Her husband respected Arent, and he'd never respected a stupid man in his life. Arent was the heir to his grandfather's fortune, chosen over five sons.

She examined the slight figure beside him, talking so quickly the words seemed to tumble out of his mouth. It must be hard to stand next to Sammy Pipps and call yourself clever, she thought. Five years they'd worked together. Arent had witnessed one miracle after the next. She could see why you'd start to mistake yourself for stupid.

'Follow Vos and hope he delivers us the next part of this strange puzzle before the third unholy miracle happens. Our only aim now is to prevent a slaughter.'

UNDER THE STARLIGHT, SAILORS carried the last of the bodies on to the waist, laying them in hemp sacks side by side. Mourners were few. The dead were bad luck on an Indiaman. Every sailor on watch had their head turned away. The sailmaker stitched up their sacks with his eyes closed, and even Captain Crauwels and Isaack Larme made sure to peer over the bodies, rather than at them.

Isabel said a prayer for those lost, having taken up many of Sander's duties since his death. Sara, Creesjie and Lia watched with their heads bowed respectfully.

When all was done, Crauwels nodded to the sailors, who lifted the bodies one by one, dropping them over the side with a splash.

Five minutes after the funeral began it was over.

There was no point lingering. They all knew there would be plenty more before the voyage was over.

As Vos DINED WITH the other passengers, Arent crept into his cabin, finding a room that perfectly reflected its owner. There were no decorations, no fripperies of any kind. Upon the desk were a candle on a tray, a quill, an ink pot, and a bag of pounce. Shelves had been built, each one overflowing with scrolls.

Arent wasn't sure if he believed Vos was a demon as well as a thief, but his cabin rejected vice of any sort. It spoke of obsession and order, a towering ambition that would be achieved through hard work. If Sammy had seen this place, he would have hurled himself over the edge of the ship, for nothing could be so antithetical to his own tastes, which veered towards sensuous, distracting, and entirely unworthy.

The desk was tidy except for a ledger and three bills. Unfolding them, Arent discovered they were receipts of passage for Sara, Lia and his uncle, along with their cabin assignments. Apparently, Sara was supposed to have been in Viscountess Dalvhain's cabin, but they'd been switched around. The ledger listed orderly lines of profit and expense, no doubt representing his uncle's wealth and trades.

Abandoning the documents, Arent tapped the floorboards and panels, inspecting them for secret compartments as

Sammy had taught him. He shifted a few scroll cases, but it was pointless. The remaining pieces of The Folly weren't hidden in here. There wasn't the space.

Departing the cabin, he heard a strange sound coming from across the corridor. It sounded like … hissing, perhaps. A long hiss, then silence, then it started again.

He knocked.

'Viscountess Dalvhain.'

'How many times must I tell you people to leave me be?' came a feeble voice.

'I can hear hissing.'

'Then stop eavesdropping,' she snapped.

He considered pressing the matter, for no strange occurrence aboard the Saardam could be overlooked any longer, but he knew he had to keep watch for Vos. Returning to the quarterdeck, he slipped into the shadows near the mainmast and waited for the chamberlain to finish dinner.

Arent was good at waiting. Half of everything he did for Sammy was waiting. Putting his hands in his pockets, he felt the now familiar wooden beads of his father's rosary and tried to imagine how it could have arrived in those animal pens.

Short of his grandfather having snuck aboard without him realising, he couldn't think of a way.

He felt an old warmth in the pit of his stomach.

Right now, he'd have welcomed the old man's gruff advice.

After he'd left his grandfather's business, Arent hadn't returned to Frisia until shortly before boarding the *Saardam*. He'd found his grandfather much older, but far more forgiving of his choice than he once had been.

They'd talked for two days, and departed as friends.

Now, for the first time in years, Arent missed him.

Dinner ended, the passengers emerging into the darkness. They were sombre, speaking in hushed tones. Sara appeared first, clinging to Lia. Vos followed on Creesjie's arm. She was laughing gaily, giving every indication of delight in his company.

After a few awkward words at the door to the passenger cabins, Vos came back down the stairs, his entire demeanour shifting. Becoming furtive, he swept the deck for any observation. Arent stayed perfectly still, trusting to the darkness to disguise him.

Vos darted away.

On soft feet, Arent went after him, following him cautiously on to the staircase leading into the hold.

From beneath him, he heard water sloshing.

Staring down the staircase, he saw Vos remove a candle and striker from his pocket, creating a flame at the fourth try. Of course, he'd come prepared, thought Arent – almost admiringly. He'd have to forgo a light of his own for fear of alerting his quarry.

Arriving at the bottom of the staircase, he found the cargo hold restored, the warrens of crates rebuilt. Most of the bilge water had been pumped out, but it was still higher than it had been before the storm. Dead rats floated on the surface.

Thankfully, Vos moved cautiously. It was obvious he hated being down here. Every drop of water and skittering claw caused him to stop and peer around.

One passage looked much the same as another to Arent, but Vos soon found what he was searching for. Kneeling in the bilge water, he began hammering on one of the crates with the pommel of his dagger, listening for the sound it made.

When one struck hollow, he let out a cry of relief, only to immediately shush himself and place a hand to his lips.

As he pushed the dagger under the edge of the lid, Arent crept forward hoping to better see what was in there.

Vos stopped. Frowned.

He cocked his ear, then sheathed his dagger and took off around the corner with his candle.

Arent considered going after him, but he had what he wanted.

Lacking any sort of light, he felt his way along the passage to the crate Vos had cracked open. All he had to do was scoop up the pieces of The Folly and somehow find his way back before Vos returned.

With proof of his wrongdoing to present to his uncle, he could free the constable and have Drecht shackle the chamberlain.

The jagged edges of the crate arrived beneath his fingers.

Pushing his hand inside, he heard the slightest of noises behind him and realised he'd been tricked.

Half turning, something smacked him in the head, sending him crashing into the water.

58

Arent came awake groggily, waves of pain greeting the smallest movement of his head. He was still in the cargo hold, but he'd been tied to a beam, a gag stuffed in his mouth.

He struggled, but the bonds were knotted tight.

Vos was standing next to him, carving the Mark of Old Tom on to a pillar. He'd already completed three of them, though this one was coming along better. The others were clumsy.

Arent wriggled, trying to loosen the ropes. When that failed, he wondered whether he'd been able to stretch his neck and bite Vos's ear off.

Hearing him struggle, Vos looked over at him. Fear showed on his plain face.

He put the dagger to Arent's throat.

'I'll pull down the gag so we may speak,' he said urgently. 'If you try to call for help, I'll slit your throat, is that understood?'

For all his fear, the threat came easily enough.

Arent nodded.

Tentatively, Vos pulled the gag down, the material scraping across Arent's whiskers.

'Not many men can get behind me,' said Arent. 'I'm impressed.'

'I've learned to go unnoticed in my years of service to the governor general.'

'Handy talent for a thief.'

Vos's eyes widened slightly, then narrowed. He relaxed.

'Then you *do* know,' he said. 'Good, that makes this easier. Who else knows? Who's waiting for me upstairs?'

'Everybody,' said Arent. 'Everybody knows.'

'And yet you came alone,' said Vos, tipping his ear to the air. 'And I hear no steps, no distant chatter, none of the sounds that would indicate anybody else is down here.' A horrifying grin split his face. 'No, you're alone. I think you saw poor, wretched little Vos and mistakenly thought him no threat.' He wagged his dagger at him. 'You're not the first, but one does not rise out of the mud to become the governor general's chamberlain without putting a few rivals out of the way.'

'And now you have The Folly, you won't have to be the governor general's chamberlain any longer.'

Vos became confused. 'The Folly? Is that why –' He burst out laughing. It was a wholly unnatural sound coming from him. 'Oh, my dear Arent. Fate has no love of you, does she? I didn't steal The Folly, though I'm honoured you think I could. I'm afraid you've hit upon the right criminal, but the wrong crime.'

The idea obviously tickled him, for he was still chortling as he tugged the gag back over Arent's mouth, then returned to carving the Mark of Old Tom on the pillar.

'Odd as it may sound, I'm glad of this,' he went on. 'My work requires that I hide myself and pretend to be less than

I am, but I was always thinking about my future. I was never content to be the governor general's favourite hound for ever. It's pleasant to finally be seen, however accidentally.'

A candle appeared in the distance. A tiny spot of light coming steadily closer.

Vos traced the point of his dagger over the Mark of Old Tom. 'Fear not, I haven't succumbed to the creature's whims, if that's what you're thinking. The beautiful thing about fear this large is that nobody will look beyond it. It can explain anything. I'll carve this mark on to your chest, and everybody will believe the demon killed you. They won't even think to question it. They'll want to believe it. People like stories more than they like the truth.'

The candle came closer, rags emerging out of the darkness, the light illuminating the bloody bandages around the leper's face. Vos had his back to it. Enthralled by his own voice, he didn't heed Arent's muffled cries of warning. 'Old Tom whispered to me, you know. Creesjie's hand for the governor general's life. It even offered to leave a dagger under his bunk to use.' He became thoughtful. 'I'll confess I was tempted by its offer, but thankfully I have my own plans.' He sighed, tapping the dagger against the wood ecstatically. 'I knew Creesjie would accept me eventually. It was a matter of patience, that's all.'

The leper was only two paces behind him. Arent strained, jerking his head towards it, screaming through the gag.

Vos furrowed his brow, as if perplexed by a man in Arent's situation making a fuss. 'Calm yourself and you may have your final words,' he said.

The leper was a solitary step away. Arent stopped trying to yell long enough for Vos to tug the gag down.

'Behind you!' roared Arent. 'Behind you, you damn fool!'

Startled by the terror in Arent's voice, Vos spun around, coming face to face with the leper. From somewhere under the bandages, it hissed, driving a dagger into Vos's chest, before twisting it.

The chamberlain screamed in agony, the sound echoing around the cargo hold. His body went limp and the leper slowly withdrew its blade, letting Vos collapse with a splash.

The leper stepped over his body, bringing its bloody bandages within touching distance of Arent's face. It stank of the midden.

Its knife appeared in front of Arent's face, Vos's blood still dripping off the edge. It had a crudely carved wooden handle and a strange thin blade that looked like it would snap the very second it was used.

The leper touched the point of the dagger to Arent's cheek, the metal cold against his flesh.

Arent squirmed trying to pull his head away.

The blade ran down his cheek and along his neck, crossing his stomach. Through its bandages, Arent could hear its rasping breaths. The dead don't breathe, do they, he thought triumphantly.

The dagger pressed against his stomach, then it stopped suddenly. The leper sniffed him. Then again, deeper this time, as if surprised by something. A hand snaked its way into Arent's pocket, slowly pulling out the rosary. Cocking its head, it stared at the beads in fascination, letting out that strange animal growl he'd heard with Sara.

For a second, it considered him.

Hissing, the leper blew out the candle and disappeared.

59

S ARA DIDN'T HAVE TO wait for the knocking to know that Arent was coming down the corridor. His stumbling steps reverberated through the wood, falling heavily enough to be heard over the harp she was playing for Lia, Dorothea, Creesjie and Isabel.

Opening the door, she saw him carrying a heavy sack over his shoulder, every one of his long labours these last days showing. Blood trickled down his forehead and from the slash she'd stitched up on his forearm. His wrists were rubbed raw. He was soaked through with stinking bilge water, his face so weary she couldn't imagine how he'd dragged himself up here.

The other women joined her in the corridor, still holding the wine they'd been drinking.

Arriving in front of them, Arent dropped the sack on the floor.

'Sammy was right about Vos,' he said hoarsely.

'He was a thief?' asked Sara.

'Yes.'

'Is this The Folly?' asked Creesjie, eyeing the sack.

'No,' said Arent. 'Sammy was wrong about that part. Vos didn't steal it. He stole this instead.' Arent kicked the bag over, spilling silver plates and chalices, tiaras and diamonds, gold chains and beautiful jewellery.

Creesjie stared at the jewels sparkling by her feet.

'He told me he was coming into wealth,' she said, kneeling down to sift through the stones covetously. 'This must have been what he meant.'

'This is a fortune,' said Sara, astonished. She peered at Arent. There was a sickly sheen to his skin, and his eyes were unfocused. 'Where did Vos get all this?'

'The leper killed him before he could say.'

'The leper? You saw the leper?'

'It saved my life,' said Arent, resting his weight against the wall. 'It was going to kill me, but then it seemed to sense my father's rosary on me. It stole it and left me to wriggle my way out of the ropes.'

'Vos is dead?' said Creesjie, momentarily stricken. 'Oh, that fool!'

While Lia consoled her, Sara placed a hand against Arent's chest. She could feel his fever through the thin shirt.

'You need a bed, Arent. You're burning up,' she said.

'Some of these pieces are older than me,' said Dorothea, who was gleefully piling ring after ring on to her fingers. 'These suit me, don't you think?'

She held her adorned hand out for Sara to admire.

'Wait,' said Sara, tugging one of the rings off Dorothea's finger. 'I recognise this crest. My father made me memorise reams of pageantry when I was a girl. Every coat of arms, every family name, every piece of genealogy. This is the crest of the Dijksma family.'

'Hector Dijksma was one of the people possessed by Old Tom,' replied Creesjie, surprised. 'He was on that list I stole from Jan's cabin.'

'Yes, I remember reading about him in the daemonologica,' said Sara, struggling to recall the exact passage.

'Dijksma was the second son of a wealthy trading family in the Provinces,' supplied Isabel. 'Sander made me study the daemonologica until I could recite every page. Dijksma was possessed by Old Tom in 1609, and it used him to perform dark rituals in the family home. Maids had been going missing from nearby villages for months, and Pieter discovered they'd all been summoned up to the house. He went to free them, but they'd been butchered. He battled Old Tom and managed to exorcise it from Hector, who fled the Provinces before a mob could build him a pyre.'

'Did the daemonologica ever say what became of him?'

'No,' said Isabel. 'But if this is Hector Dijksma's treasure, perhaps Vos was actually Hector? Once his family name was ruined, maybe he fled with what was left of his family's wealth.'

'Or Vos was Old Tom,' speculated Creesjie. 'Could that have been it?'

'I caught him carving its mark on to the crates,' supplied Arent. The others could barely understand him. His words were running together. 'But he denied being our devil. He said fear was a great cover for a crime.'

'Come with me, Arent,' said Sara, worried. 'We need to get you to your berth.'

'I'm going to see Sammy first. Can somebody tell my uncle about Vos? Let him believe Vos stole The Folly. I don't want another innocent person getting flogged.'

As he staggered off, Sara ran after him. He was having to balance against the wall to stay upright.

'Will you be okay?' she asked.

He laughed grimly. 'It's been a long day and a lot of people have tried to kill me.' He considered it. 'Vos may, or may not, have been Old Tom, a demon which may, or may not, exist. If it does exist, it was summoned by my uncle – a man I loved once, but who now seems to be a vindictive, callous, murdering bastard. Vos has treasure stolen from a family Old Tom destroyed nearly thirty years ago; my newest friend butchered an island full of people; and we're a solitary unholy miracle away from everybody being slaughtered, according to the prophecies of a murdered predikant. Worst of all, the only man who could hammer a beam to this mess is locked away in the dark under false accusation from my grandfather, and there's not a damn thing I can do to help him.'

With that, he collapsed.

60

T HE GOVERNOR GENERAL WAS disturbed by three polite knocks on his cabin door, which he recognised from their swiftness as belonging to Guard Captain Drecht.

'Come, Drecht,' he said.

After two weeks of being pecked at by his own thoughts, the governor general had become whiskery and gaunt, with deep, dark circles under his eyes. What little weight he'd carried from Batavia had fallen away, leaving a body made of bones and will.

He was working by the light of a solitary candle, comparing the list of people Old Tom had possessed and the passenger manifest. An old debt was being called in, and somebody onboard was responsible. The Mark of Old Tom had been daubed on to the sail to let him know his past had swallowed his present, and was now coiling around his future. He'd trusted Arent would put a sword through Old Tom before that happened, but he hadn't given him enough information. Arent was strong and clever, but even he couldn't fight with a hood over his head.

Jan Haan carried few regrets, but lying to Arent all these years was one of them. The past was poisoned ground, that's what Casper van den Berg had taught him. God chose every individual's path, so what use was worrying about those who fell by the wayside, those you hurt or caused to be hurt, those who had to fall so you could climb?

The governor general believed this, but he'd longed to tell Arent the truth about the forest and his father, and the bargain that had been struck. So armed, Arent would surely have discovered who was threatening this ship, but the secret was buried too deep. Try as he might, Jan Haan couldn't tug it loose.

And now Old Tom had stolen The Folly.

His ascension into the ranks of the Gentlemen 17 was predicated on delivering that device to them. It was the only reason they'd looked past their distaste for him in the first place.

He couldn't return to Amsterdam empty-handed.

He wasn't sure if the constable had bargained with the devil or was innocent, as Arent insisted. It didn't matter. Fear was contagious. The crew had seen what he'd done to the constable and they knew it would be one of them tomorrow. In their foul hearts, one of them held the information he needed. After enough of them had bled, they would bring it to him.

In the meantime, he stared at the manifest and the list of possessed souls. Old Tom was on this boat, and Old Tom always bargained. The governor general just had to work out what to tempt him with.

Drecht jangled into the room, dragging a heavy sack behind him. Halfway inside, it tipped over, a cup tumbling across the floor and landing at the governor general's feet. He scooped it up and held it to the light. Turning it over, he saw the crest on the other side.

'Dijksma,' he murmured.

'You know it, sir?'

'From long ago. Where did you come by it?'

Guard Captain Drecht straightened and placed his hand on the hilt of his sword. This was the posture he always adopted before delivering bad news. 'Your nephew recovered it from Cornelius Vos, sir. He identified Vos as The Folly's thief, but Vos tried to kill him.' He puffed out his chest. 'Vos is dead, sir. Killed by the leper.'

'And Arent?' he asked in concern.

'A fever has him, my lord.' Drecht's face twitched beneath his beard. 'He's being tended to.'

The governor general leant back in his chair. 'Poor Vos. Ambition is a burden few can carry. I'm afraid his crushed him.' He shook his head. 'He was an excellent administrator.' And there ended his eulogy, for his thoughts had already moved on.

'Was the Folly recovered?'

'No sir.'

Haan cursed. 'How did he steal it?'

'Apparently, he hid the three pieces in three separate kegs, then had accomplices roll them out when battle stations were called.'

'Three?' he murmured. It had taken three of them to summon Old Tom all those years ago. That couldn't be a coincidence. 'The others must have turned on him. Do we have these accomplices?'

'Not yet, sir.'

'Then flog *two* men at the mainmast each day. I want them found.' He drummed the table with his sharp fingernails.

Vos had betrayed him. Could it really be so simple? It had always struck him as a waste to kill those you'd defeated, for how else would they understand the totality of their loss. Mercy, he believed, was the gravest wound you could inflict, for it was the only one that wouldn't heal. Had that mercy back in the Provinces brought this upon him? Would it also point the way out?

He looked out of his porthole at the full moon, prowling behind tattered white clouds.

'Old Tom,' he muttered, as if he saw the devil's face floating there. 'We should have been more careful,' he said to nobody in particular. 'We should have known that something that powerful would get free of us eventually. That's the problem with summoning demons, you see. Sooner or later somebody else raises them against you.'

Drecht's face moved from bafflement to concern as the governor general's gaze drifted to the names of those the demon had possessed over the years.

Bastiaan Bos
Tukibiri
Gillis van de Ceulen
Hector Dijksma
Emily de Haviland

'Who were his collaborators?' he muttered, comparing the names to those on the passenger manifest. 'Where are you hiding, my devil?'

His eyes widened in surprise, as specific letters swam into focus. For two weeks, he had stared at these two documents, trying to drag out information that was being given to him plain. How had he missed what was so obvious?

'This isn't about The Folly,' he said sickly. His face had gone pale. He ran a trembling hand across his eyes, then looked up at the worried guard captain. 'Come, Drecht, we're going to the passenger cabins.'

Outside, rain tapped the wood, as if trying to get inside. The ship groaned unnervingly. It hadn't been the same since the storm. The creaks had become shrieks, the rigging messier, like a broken cobweb.

Like everything on this ship, the solidity had been an illusion. They'd encased themselves in wood and nails, throwing themselves into the sea, believing their courage would see them safe. And then their enemy had raised its hand and showed them how foolish they'd been.

Rain ran down the governor general's long nose and off his pointed chin. It flew off his eyelids when he blinked. The guard captain could barely keep up.

'Wait here,' demanded the governor general, as they reached the entrance to the passenger cabins.

'Sir, I don't –'

'Wait here! I'll call if you're required.'

Drecht pressed his lips tight, exchanging uncertain looks with Eggert, before taking a place on the opposite side of the red door. Straightening his breastplate formally, the governor general stepped inside and swung it shut behind him. Drecht quickly manoeuvred his sword sheath into the gap, preventing the door from closing fully. He couldn't see what was happening inside, but at least he'd be able to hear.

The governor general rapped on a cabin.

No answer came.

The governor general knocked again, then cleared his throat. 'It's Jan Haan,' he said, in the deferential tone of somebody with rugs to sell. 'You've been waiting for me.'

The door creaked open into gloom, revealing a figure seated in the corner. Its face was hidden behind a bloom of candlelight, but as he entered the cabin, it pushed it away with a long finger, revealing itself.

'Ah,' said the governor general sorrowfully. 'I was right then.'

The door slammed shut behind him.

In the ocean's darkness, the Eighth Lantern opened its eye.

61

STILL GUARDING THE DOOR to the passenger cabins, Drecht stared at the Eighth Lantern off the starboard quarter of the ship, desperation growing within him. He'd lost battles before. He'd been overwhelmed and forced to retreat, but never had he so singularly failed to comprehend the scale of his enemy, its intent or the terms of surrender.

How was he supposed to protect the governor general from something that could appear and vanish at will, speak without a voice, slaughter at distance and pluck things out of locked rooms without leaving a trace?

Isaack Larme came clattering up the stairs and through the red door into the passenger cabins, emerging with Captain Crauwels a few minutes later. The captain had obviously been asleep, for he was just dressed in his breeches. It was the first time Drecht could remember him being dishevelled.

The two of them went to the taffrail a few paces away.

'Even *we* don't know where we are,' cursed Crauwels, staring at it. 'How did it find us?'

'Governor General wanted us to train cannon on it if it appeared again,' replied Isaack Larme.

'It's too far away, and it has the wind gauge,' said Crauwels irritably, glancing at the flag flying above them. 'Even if they didn't, our sails are still in tatters. We can't manoeuvre, which means we can't fight. Not even sure *what* we'd be fighting.'

'What are your orders, Captain?'

'All hands on deck and armed,' he said. 'Until then, we watch.'

Governor General Jan Haan appeared from the passenger cabins after two hours, and silently returned to his own cabin. Guard Captain Drecht took his usual position outside, lit his pipe and waited. After a few minutes, weeping sounded through the door.

62

THEY WEREN'T BOARDED THAT night, or the next, although the Eighth Lantern appeared again. Both times, it disappeared before dawn.

Over the next two days, the sails were repaired and the *Saardam* made seaworthy. In a bid to sight land and take a bearing, Crauwels ordered they sail in arcs, covering the widest area possible.

Where there should have been fresh hope, there was only new fear.

From the second they'd left Batavia, they'd been damned and damned and damned again, and now everybody was waiting to see what catastrophe would come next. The governor general had locked himself in his cabin, refusing to come out. Arent was laid low with fever. Vos was dead. The predikant was dead. The leper stalked the cargo hold freely, and the ship was only barely afloat. Each night, Old Tom whispered to the sailors of unholy miracles. Two had been performed and one remained. Anybody who had not bargained with him when it was revealed would be slaughtered by his other followers. That was his promise.

For most, the temptation was overwhelming. Safe passage for somebody else's blood was too fine a deal to pass up, certainly better than they'd ever received from the Company.

Every morning, there were more charms hanging from the rigging. They tinkled in the wind, discarded. They served no purpose any more. The crew had already shaken hands with the devil they were meant to keep at bay.

63

ARENT WRITHED IN HIS bunk, murmuring. Sara placed a hand over his heart, listening to it thump furiously in his chest. She'd only recently returned from her husband's cabin and had been dismayed to find Arent in exactly the same state she'd left him in.

It wasn't clear whether he'd caught the fever from his knife fight with Wyck, or working the bilge pumps during the storm, but his life hung in the balance. Sara heard wagers had been placed among the sailors and musketeers. The odds were against him. For all his strength, they'd seen men similarly struck down after a battle, and they knew what it meant. What was shattered could be sawn off and bad blood ran clean eventually, but what couldn't be seen couldn't be healed. More men died murmuring than screaming.

For the last three days, she'd tried everything she could to break this fever and there was nothing left, except patience and prayer.

'I've had rations sent to Sammy,' she said, knowing he'd like that. 'The musketeer guarding his door, Thyman I think his name is, offered to walk with him at night, so he's had his exercise. I spoke with him briefly last night. He misses you. He wanted to come up here and tend you himself, my husband be damned. I talked him out of it. I said you'd not thank me for letting him die while you were bedridden. It was hard for him to accept. He loves you a great deal.' She swallowed, annoyed by how difficult this was. 'I suspect he's not the only one.'

She watched his face for any twitch, a suggestion of recognition.

'He tried to comfort me,' she continued, seeing nothing. 'He told me you'd been into the dark before and found your way back.' Sara put her lips to his ear. 'He said you'd called for God, and he hadn't come. He said you believed there was nothing waiting. No God or devil, no saints or sinners. He's in awe of you. He said you're remarkable because you choose to do good, rather than because you're afraid of what's waiting if you don't, like most people.' She struggled for words. 'I don't believe heaven is empty. I think God is waiting for you, but so am I.' Her hand pressed fearfully against his chest. 'I'm waiting for you here, on a blighted boat, stalked by a devil I can't stop alone. I need you to wake up and help me, Arent. I need you.'

Something heavy splashed into the water outside, startling Sara, whose hand leapt away from his chest.

Going to his porthole, she looked outside. A few ripples showed on the ocean's surface, but there was no indication of what had caused them.

The sea was keeping her secrets, as usual.

From behind her, Arent said hoarsely, 'Can't people see I'm trying to sleep.'

64

U NDER THE GREAT CABIN'S swaying lantern, the
diners prodded listlessly at their food.

Many of the seats were empty. The governor general had
barely been seen out of his cabin since Vos's death. They'd
heard him holler for Drecht as they took their places, but he'd
gone quiet now.

The guard captain was stationed outside his door, as usual
at this time. He was smoking a pipe, his face obscured by the
miasma.

On the deck below, Arent Hayes tossed and turned in his
hammock. Sara Wessel had spent every hour at his bedside,
leaving only to complete her obligations to her husband. She
was treating Arent with strange things she burnt in trays.

Viscountess Dalvhain remained secreted in her cabin.
Captain Crauwels had checked on her after the storm, earning the same barked dismissal as Sara and Arent.

That only left Crauwels, Reynier van Schooten, Lia, Creesjie
and Isabel to push around the meagre fare on their plates.
They'd left Batavia with barely enough supplies to reach the
Cape, and that had been assuming they could resupply from
the fleet. But they'd been alone since the storm.

Van Schooten had ordered quarter rations for everybody, leaving them with a few hard bits of tack, a sliver of meat, and a gulp of wine or whiskey.

Unsurprisingly, given everything that had happened, conversation was muted, petering out quickly as it was sucked into the whirlpools of their thoughts. Even Creesjie was quiet, that twinkle of mischievous humour entirely absent from her tired face. The silence was so thick that a few people started in surprise when Isabel coughed her way into a question.

By rights, she shouldn't have been at the table at all, but she'd taken up some of Sander's duties, even offering sermons at the mainmast. Fewer and fewer people came, but it wasn't for a lack of zeal. God burnt in this child brighter than He'd ever burnt in Sander Kers.

'Captain, can you help me with something?' she asked.

Crauwels was midway through chewing a hunk of bread and made no attempt to hide his irritation at suddenly having all eyes upon him. He dabbed crumbs from his lips and reached for his wine.

'I'm at your service,' he said.

'What's the dark water?' she asked. 'I heard the men talking about it on deck.'

The captain grunted, putting his wine down again. 'What were they saying?'

'That Old Tom was swimming in the dark water.'

Crauwels picked up his metal disc from the table, and rolled it around under his hand. 'Did he mention if Old Tom had been whispering to him in the night?'

As one, the passengers gasped, exchanging frightened glances. Everybody had kept the whispers to themselves, treating them as their own secret. Whether invited or not,

Old Tom was a devil. Its presence alone suggested some prior taint, some inclination towards depravity. The whisper exposed the sin they each felt within themselves.

Crauwels looked from face to face, nodding in satisfaction. 'Thought so,' he said. 'That's all of us then. Maybe everybody on this ship.'

'*What do you yearn for?*' repeated Drecht from the governor general's doorway.

'That was it,' agreed Reynier van Schooten, sounding sick to his stomach. Since the rationing had been put in place, he'd managed to keep himself almost sober, though everybody agreed he remained a haunted man. His eyes were empty, red raw from a lack of sleep.

'Captain,' persisted Isabel. 'What's the dark water?'

'It's what old sailors call the soul,' answered Van Schooten, from the opposite end of the table. 'They reckon our sins lie beneath it like wrecks on the ocean bed. Dark water is our soul, and Old Tom is swimming within it.'

As if summoned, out to sea the Eighth Lantern sprang into life, its light splashing through the windows on to their horrified faces.

It was so much closer than it had ever been before.

And it burnt red.

65

JOHANNES WYCK WAS SITTING on one of the slabs in the sickberth, being tended by the barber-surgeon, who was plucking maggots out of a dead rat in a bowl and placing them on the man's wound, where they wriggled and burrowed.

Wyck's stomach was doing something similar, threatening to send his food back up his throat, but he turned his head away and sucked in air, catching the voices of a few sailors discussing his fight with Hayes.

They were laughing at him. He'd promised he was going to humiliate Hayes, then kill him slow. Instead, the mercenary had beaten him so badly it hurt to speak. Even a second knife in the crowd hadn't been enough to help him.

Normally, Wyck's glare would have scattered them, but they were emboldened by his injury. It wouldn't be long before somebody came to slit his throat. That's how you got this job. It was how he'd got it, and it was why he was trying to leave it.

Wyck shook his head. He wanted to settle down, to have a life of toil and quiet, but part of him suspected it would always be like this for him, wherever he went. For as long as he'd been alive, he'd always had enemies. He was a man with a short temper, which meant he found himself endlessly wronged, stewing in perceived slights, and counting his grudges. But within that, he'd always courted a certain nobility. Being surrounded by enemies made him protective of those he loved.

He'd gone to the poop deck every morning to watch the sermon, and while the rest of them sang their prayers, he'd made his promises to the only person he'd ever keep them for.

That's when he'd recognised that liar on deck.

Wyck hadn't been a bit surprised when Old Tom came calling, just as he had in that grand house where he'd worked in the Provinces. Back then, he'd refused to cooperate and lost an eye to that damn witchfinder's torture. And so, when Old Tom had whispered to him the other night, Wyck had agreed, though he'd made his terms clear. He knew who Old Tom was protecting. He knew its purpose on this boat. In return for that secret, he wanted a new life for his family. A home. A decent job. And all his limbs still attached to his body.

Old Tom went one better, whispering of wealth beyond his dreams if he'd kill Arent Hayes when they fought. The devil hadn't mentioned that Hayes could wield a blade better than anybody Wyck had ever seen. It hadn't mentioned that he was faster than any man that size had a right to be, and could predict what you were going to do.

Never bargain with a damn devil. When would he learn?

Screams erupted from the deck beyond the curtain.

Leaping up, and knocking the barber-surgeon aside, Wyck scattered the maggots on to the floor, and strode out of the sickberth. Beyond was pandemonium. Panicked officers were rushing this way and that, screaming orders nobody was heeding. Deadlights were being slotted over the portholes and the wooden screen dividing the deck had been taken down, allowing the kegs rolled out of the gunpowder store to reach the cannons.

It was battle stations. The Eighth Lantern was back, burning that blood-red flame. Last time it'd done that it'd slaughtered their animals without firing a shot.

Striding into the morass, he searched the faces of the passengers, just in case *she* was among them. She often was.

'Fire!' somebody screamed.

Following the sound of the voice, Wyck saw white smoke rising from the floor. People stampeded towards the staircase, crushing one another as they tried to climb into the open air.

'Stand, damn you!' he hollered. 'Stand and raise water!'

They didn't listen. That voice, which had once struck fear into the heart of every bastard down here, was now lost among the cries for help.

The smoke rose quickly, but it wasn't fire. Any bugger could see that. It didn't move right. Didn't feel oily on the skin. This was more like a fog.

And through it came the leper.

The fog twisted and curled, swallowing it.

Wyck staggered back into the sickbay, grabbing a hacksaw off the walls. He'd intended on running, but that seemed senseless when he couldn't see two paces in front of him. Instead, he waved the hacksaw, yelling for the creature to come no closer.

He gagged. The stink of the beakhead wrapping around him.

Something slashed his hand, the pain causing him to drop the saw, as the leper's bloody bandages appeared in front of him.

It raised its dagger to his face.

66

S CREAMS BELOW AND PANIC above.
    Creesjie stopped at the entrance to the great cabin, the hairs standing up on her arms. The burning red light of the Eighth Lantern was spilling through the windows, casting everything in a hellish shade.

'Old Tom,' she muttered.

Part of her wanted to run back upstairs and clutch her sleeping boys, but, even as she considered it, a small glow flared in the darkness. It floated towards her, like a spark come loose from a lantern.

Her heart thudded.

'Reckon you should return to your cabin.' Guard Captain Drecht emerged into the light with a glowing pipe in his mouth. 'Something's afoot.'

'I must see to the governor general,' she said. 'He commands it.'

Drecht considered this, his eyes peering at her from under the brim of his hat. There was something in them, she thought. Some different quality she struggled to name.

He gave no indication of whether he would let her pass, so she simply strode by him and opened the door to the governor general's cabin.

It was dim inside, only the red light seeping through the door to illuminate it. That was unusual for Jan. Due to his fear of the dark, he never went to sleep without a candle burning.

'Jan?'

In that hellish bloom, her imagination immediately made monsters of every shape. A hunched beast revealed itself to be a writing desk, the spikes on its back nothing more than bottles of wine.

Jan's armour stand lurked in the corner, like a footpad in an alley.

A pile of bones on the shelves became scrolls piled clumsily.

Approaching the bunk, she reached out a hand, feeling cold flesh beneath her fingertips.

'Drecht,' she called, alarmed. 'Hurry, something's amiss.'

The guard captain rushed into the room and over to the governor general. It was too dark to see anything, so he took his hand. It fell limp over the side of the bunk.

'He's cold,' he said. 'Fetch a light.'

Creesjie trembled, her eyes fixated on the lifeless hand.

'Fetch a light!' he screamed, but she was frozen by shock. He darted out of the room and collected a candle from the table. It trembled on its tray as he returned to the cabin.

The flame confirmed what they'd feared. The governor general was long dead, a dagger plunged into his chest.

67

C APTAIN CRAUWELS TOOK THE steps two at a time, running towards the panic below decks.

The *Saardam* was paralysed, his orders for naught. The Eighth Lantern had been near enough to board, but it had crippled them without firing a shot. Now it had sailed away, its infernal work at an end.

Arriving at the compartment under the half deck, he found the staircase into the orlop deck jammed tight with bodies, as sailors and passengers fought each other to get out.

White smoke billowed past them and up through the grates.

Those who'd escaped were on their knees coughing.

Isaack Larme was helping the crew at the other end of the ship, while Arent Hayes pulled the passengers from the crush. A sickly gleam of sweat still shone on his pallid skin, but it didn't appear to have diminished his strength.

'We need to get down there and put the fire out,' cried Crauwels over the din, eyeing the passengers spilling up the staircase, like ants from a kicked-over nest.

'Aint fire,' yelled back Hayes, tugging another passenger free. 'Aint no flames, aint no heat. Don't know what it is, but only danger down there is the panic.'

Seeing a small child in the crowd, Arent reached through the press of bodies and scooped him into his arms, delivering him safely on to the deck. His mother leapt forward and clutched the boy tightly, weeping.

'If it isn't fire, what is it?' demanded Crauwels.

'Was the leper,' coughed the constable, battling his way up the staircase.

His eyes were raw with smoke, tears running freely. He was still weak from his flogging, but he'd resumed his duties in the gunpowder store. 'I saw it in the smoke … it killed Wyck and …' He rushed to the railing, vomiting into the ocean.

Arent immediately began pushing past people, heading down the steps.

Seeing a path emerge, Crauwels followed him down. The smoke was already clearing, swirling tendrils snaking out of the portholes.

A few bodies lay on the ground. Some were unconscious, others groaning, clutching bloodied limbs.

'These people need tending,' Crauwels yelled up the stairs, as he pressed further into the chaos.

It didn't take long to spot Johannes Wyck sprawled backwards over a slab, his face contorted into the last expression it would ever have. He'd been gutted, like the animals in the pen.

'Heaven on fire, what is Old Tom doing to my ship?' the captain said, his stomach turning.

He'd seen plenty of dead bodies in the course of his career, but none that had been put to the sword with such relish.

Arent was kneeling by the body, inspecting it thoroughly. He grunted in satisfaction, then got to his feet.

'Have somebody bring Isabel down here,' he ordered.

430

'Why?'

'Because Wyck smells of paprika.'

Crauwels couldn't imagine a more confounding answer, but Arent obviously wasn't in the mood to explain. He was already stalking across the deck to the far door

'Where are you going?' Crauwels called after him.

'To let Sammy out of his cell. This has gone on long enough. He's needed.'

68

S ARA ARRIVED IN THE great cabin to find a solitary candle had been lit in the candelabrum, its sombre flame peeking over the edge of the table. Lia was a few steps behind her, racing down from the quarterdeck above. They'd heard Creesjie screaming, but it was sobbing they followed now, straight into the governor general's cabin.

Their eyes found the body.

He was dressed in the night-shirt Sara had left him in earlier. Only now it was sodden with blood, a wooden-handled dagger protruding from his chest.

She felt nothing. Not even jubilation. There was something pitiful about it all, she realised. In death, without that aura of power cloaking him, he was exposed as a thin, frail old man. All his wealth, all his influence, all his scheming and cruelty, they'd all been for nothing.

Suddenly, she felt very tired.

'Are you okay, dear heart?' Sara asked Lia, but her daughter's face told the story well enough. It glowed with relief; with the knowledge that some terrible ordeal was finally at an end.

This was his legacy, thought Sara. Not his power. Not Batavia. Not a seat among the Gentlemen 17 he would never occupy. His legacy was a family who were glad he was dead. For that, she almost found some pity for him.

Aside from her husband's body, everything else in the cabin was exactly as it had been. Two mugs of wine sat on the table, one empty and the other full. Between them was a jug and a flickering candle. And on the ground was a tatty flag, the Mark of Old Tom smeared across the lion emblem of the Company.

Her husband's murder was the third unholy miracle, she realised.

Seeing her, Creesjie flew into her arms and, for a moment, they simply held each other. Neither knew what to say. Commiserations didn't need to be offered, and there was no hurt to soothe, or tears to wipe away. Their breeding demanded a Christian reverence for the dead, while every memory of the man who'd been murdered demanded they dance and drink.

For Sara, he was simply a victim of the creature terrorising this ship, making him something to be studied, rather than lamented.

'Did you notice the dagger?' asked Creesjie, disgusted. 'I'd wager that's the dagger Old Tom promised to leave under his bunk if we accepted his bargain.'

Sara stared at it. It was an ugly thing with a wooden handle, the sort of blade cutpurses used to steal a handful of coins. Jan's exalted station hadn't even bought him a beautiful weapon to be murdered by.

She wondered if that was the point. Old Tom had stripped him of every piece of dignity he had.

'Do you think somebody accepted Old Tom's offer?' asked Creesjie.

'I don't know. If there's suddenly a king aboard in the next few days, I'd say yes.' She smiled tightly, then felt guilty. 'Has anybody told Arent? They were close.'

'He's awake?' said Creesjie, squeezing her arm.

'An hour ago,' confirmed Sara, smiling.

'There's a fire on the orlop deck,' said Lia. 'I heard he was helping down there.'

'Of course he is,' said Sara, a touch of pride in her voice. 'Well, if he's working down there, I suppose I shall start up here.'

'How?' asked Creesjie.

'In his cases, Pipps always says to look for things that *aren't* there and should be, or *are* there and shouldn't be.'

'Sounds like very unsatisfactory advice to me,' grumbled Creesjie. 'How does he tell one from the other?'

Sara shrugged. 'He never explained that part.'

'Well, I'll tell you one thing,' said Creesjie insistently. 'That candle was snuffed when we entered the cabin.'

She was clearly thinking the same thing Sara was. Her husband didn't sleep without a candle, because he was afraid of the dark. And, more importantly, Sara had tainted his wine with her sleeping draught.

She had watched him drink it.

With that sleeping draught inside him, he wouldn't have been able to wake up until the morning, at the very earliest. Even if he'd had the inclination, there was no way he could have risen to snuff the candle, which meant his murderer must have done it.

She turned to Drecht, who was hovering in the doorway, captain of a guard that had nobody to guard.

'Was I the last person to see my husband alive?' she asked him.

He was lost in thought and didn't immediately respond.

'Guard Captain!' said Sara, her tone of command snapping him out of his despair.

'No, my lady,' he said smartly. 'He called me in just as dinner was being served. He asked me to search the cabin for a dagger. He asked me to do it every night. He said Old Tom had threatened him.'

'Did you?'

'Of course.'

'Did you find one?'

'No.'

The dagger protruding from her husband's chest took on an accusatory air. 'That wasn't in here when I left,' he protested, as everybody glanced at it from the corner of their eyes. 'And even it had been, nobody came or went until Creesjie and I found the body. I was on watch all night. I didn't doze, I didn't wander.'

'I remember hearing him call to you at dinner,' muttered Creesjie thoughtfully. 'He sounded peculiar, I thought.'

'He'd been peculiar ever since visiting the passenger cabins,' agreed the guard captain.

'When was that?'

'The night of Vos's death.' He tugged his beard, summoning the memory. 'He'd spent the afternoon poring over the passenger manifest and that other list of names beside it, rambling about losing control of demons. He must have seen something, because he said this wasn't about The Folly, then leapt up. He went to confront somebody. He sounded afraid.'

'Who was it?'

'I didn't see. I only heard what he said, and the way he said it. "You've been waiting for me, I believe." Those were his words. And he spoke … deferentially. Never heard him sound like that before.'

'Then what happened?' asked Sara eagerly.

Her blood was up. This is what Pipps must feel like all the time, she thought. The thrill of discovery, and the sense of having an enemy just beyond reach. God help her, but this voyage was the most exhilarating thing that had ever happened to her.

'He came out two hours later and asked me to take him back,' continued Drecht. 'He didn't say anything. Once he was inside his cabin, he started sobbing. After that, he didn't come out again.'

'Father was sobbing,' said Lia incredulously.

Sara paced the cabin, trying to make sense of a husband she didn't recognise. He was powerful, which meant he didn't go to see people. He summoned those he needed. Whoever he'd discovered on the passenger manifest had made him deferent. But who could that be? Who would he march to the passenger cabins to see?

Sara went over to the desk and inspected the lists, but could see nothing that would have disturbed her husband. A quill was discarded next to them, a blot of ink dried on the wood.

She felt a strange sense of déjà vu. Only three days ago, she'd done the same thing in Cornelius Vos's cabin, though she couldn't have explained why. There was nothing to be learned beyond what Arent had already observed. Everything had been tidied away, aside from the receipts of passage for the family, suggesting he'd been preoccupied with them before his death. Sara couldn't tell why, though something about it bothered her. Vos was methodical. He wouldn't have taken them out unless there was an irregularity.

'Lia,' she said.

'Yes, Mama.'

'Would you examine the passenger manifest and list of people Old Tom possessed for me? You've a keen eye and a quick mind, perhaps you can see something I've missed.'

Lia beamed at the compliment and sat down at the desk.

The second question was what had they discussed? Whatever it was had made her husband weep. That suggested it had something to do with Arent, she thought. He was the only person her husband obviously loved.

She glanced around the cabin once again, searching for the clue to make sense of everything. Her eyes were dragged back to the candle. The murderer must have snuffed it, but why? And how had they managed to get in and out without Drecht seeing? Drecht could have been lying to them, but Isaack Larme had told them the guard captain had been offered a huge reward for escorting her husband back to Amsterdam safely. Besides, if Drecht had wanted to kill him, he'd had ample opportunities in the past. Why do it here and now, when it would be so obvious he was the killer?

Her eyes prodded at the furnishings, searching for some other explanation. In The Secret of the Midnight Scream, Pipps had deduced that a trapdoor beneath the floorboards had concealed the killer, who'd hidden there until the investigation had concluded, then crept out when the coast was clear.

Sara began stamping on the floorboards, earning strange looks from the others.

They were solid.

'Drecht?'

'My lady?'

'Climb on a chair and start hammering the ceiling will you? My dress is too heavy.'

Drecht raised a bushy eyebrow. 'My lady, I understand you're suffering an ordeal, but –'

'There may be a trapdoor,' she explained, walking over to the writing desk and inspecting her husband's documents. 'Somebody may have dropped down from above.'

'But that's your cabin, my lady.'

'Yes, but I haven't been in it this evening because I was tending Arent.'

As they pondered it, Lia made a small, startled sound, then laughed. 'That's very clever,' she said in amusement. Nobody listening would ever have believed her father lay murdered only a few paces from her.

'I think I know who Father went to see,' she said.

Sara and Creesjie clustered around her, as she took the quill from her father's pot, then underlined the name Viscountess Dalvhain in the passenger manifest and Emily de Haviland in the list of people possessed by Old Tom.

'You see?' she said, though nobody did. 'Dalvhain is Haviland rearranged.'

Without a word, Sara flew out of the cabin as quickly as her dress would allow and on to the quarterdeck. Left flat-footed by her abrupt exit, Drecht, Creesjie and Lia followed her.

Under the star-bright sky, bodies were being hauled up from the crush in the orlop deck, children crying as adults despondently clung to loved ones.

At Dalvhain's cabin, she rapped insistently. No answer came.

'Viscountess Dalvhain!' Still there was no answer.

'Emily de Haviland?' she tried instead.

Creesjie, Lia and Drecht arrived at the end of the corridor, but she ignored them and tried the latch, the door creaking open. By the dim light spilling inside, it was immediately evident the cabin was empty. More than empty, it didn't appear anybody had ever used it. There were no personal possessions she could see; no pictures on the walls, or furs on the bunk. The chamber pot was spotless. The only sign of habitation was the huge red rug covering the floor. She remembered the sailors trying to wedge it through the door that first morning, and it didn't look any smaller unrolled. Its edges climbed the walls.

She crossed the cabin to the writing desk, searching for a candle.

Something crunched unpleasantly underfoot.

'Mama?' asked Lia, from the doorway.

Sara gestured for her to stay back. Drecht gripped his sword, ushering Lia and Creesjie behind him.

Kneeling down, Sara touched something sinuous and curled. She took it into the corridor, where the light could tell her more. It was a single wood shaving. Exactly like the one the carpenter had created when he'd built her a shelf that first morning. Did this have something to do with the sound Dorothea had heard? Was Dalvhain building something in here?

Or Emily de Haviland, as she had been known.

'Laxagarr is Nornish for trap,' she muttered.

'There's an object on the writing desk,' said Drecht, squinting into the gloom. He sounded unnerved, and it was clear he had no intention of setting foot inside.

From her own cabin, Sara quickly retrieved a candle on a tray, then returned to Emily de Haviland's quarters.

The daemonologica waited on her writing desk.

She stopped dead.

Isabel didn't normally let it out of her sight. Did she have some relationship with Dalvhain she hadn't mentioned? And, even then, why would it be the only thing in an empty room? The anagram was clever, but Emily de Haviland had clearly meant it to be unravelled, which meant she wanted somebody to come here and discover this book.

Sara approached it cautiously, reaching out a hand to open the cover.

It wasn't the daemonologica. Not inside.

It had the same cover, the same vellum, even the same style of illustration and writing, but the contents were different. Instead of the reams of Latin script, there were drawings.

Sara turned the first page.

In dark ink, it showed a grand house burning, surrounded by an angry mob who were dragging people outside and slitting their throats. In one corner, the witchfinder Pieter Fletcher watched impassively, while Old Tom giggled in his ear.

She turned the page.

Here was a more detailed drawing of Pieter Fletcher shackled to a wall, screaming. Old Tom was removing the organs from his chest and leaving them in a pile on the ground.

Gagging, Sara turned the page.

This was a picture of them boarding in Batavia. Sara, her husband and Lia were on the quarterdeck, while Samuel Pipps and Arent were being marched through the crowds by Drecht, stalked by Old Tom who was riding a bat-faced wolf.

Her head spinning, she turned another page.

Here was the *Saardam* at sea, surrounded by the fleet. Away in the distance was the Eighth Lantern, except it wasn't a ship; it was Old Tom holding a lantern in one hand.

On the fifth page, the leper slaughtered the *Saardam*'s cattle, while Old Tom danced among the bodies.

On the sixth page, the leper stalked through the fog of the orlop deck, trailed by Old Tom.

'What is it, dear heart?' asked Creesjie, coming up behind her.

'It's a diary of everything that's happened,' said Sara in disgust, turning the page, to reveal a drawing of her husband, dead in his bunk, with a dagger in his chest.

'Mama!' gasped Lia, appearing beside her. 'This is the scene exactly. How could Dalvhain have known what was going to happen?'

Sara's hand felt like stone, but she had to see what came next.

The *Saardam* was aflame, passengers clinging to the gigantic body of Old Tom as he carried them to a nearby island. The devil was staring out of the page at Sara, with a knowing smile on its face. It knew she was reading the book.

Opposite, on the final page, the Mark of Old Tom floated on the ocean, the *Saardam* a tiny speck beneath it.

Something nagged her. The mark was drawn strangely, the familiar lines broken up into rough circles of different sizes, almost like Emily had let the ink simply drip off her quill on to the parchment.

Sara's breath caught in her throat.

This wasn't the Mark of Old Tom, she realised with mounting horror. It was a drawing of an island the Saardam was sailing towards.

This was where the symbol had come from.

The three unholy miracles had come to pass, and now Old Tom was taking them home.

69

ARENT STARED AT ISABEL and Isabel glared back.
'Paprika?' said Captain Crauwels, from behind her.

Sammy laughed weakly. It was the best he could do. For the two days Arent had slept, Sara had asked the musketeer Thyman to attend his exercises. While a surprisingly lively conversationalist, he hadn't been keen on staying up with him all night, as Arent had been. As a result, he'd spent almost two full days in his cramped, dark cell, leaving him twisted and weak, pale as bones, with a wet, hacking cough. He was now investigating Wyck's body, his fingers leaping from place to place like startled flies. 'Imagine how I feel,' said Sammy. 'Four years ago, I tried to train him and got nowhere, yet the moment I disappear for a few weeks, he's working wonders.'

'The constable caught Isabel sneaking around the ship at night,' said Arent, ignoring the jest. 'I've smelled paprika on her these last few days, as I noticed it on Wyck when we were fighting. Paprika is only stored in a particular section of the cargo hold, a place neither of them would have reason to go unless they were meeting there.'

'Is that true?' demanded Crauwels.

'I'd wager that's his babe in your belly,' said Arent, trying to meet her averted eyes. 'Did you make a bargain with Old Tom to kill him for putting it there?'

'Kill him?' Her eyes flashed with fire. 'He was my friend and it weren't his babe, but he had pity for it.'

Crauwels snorted. 'Pity?'

'He knew me of old,' said Isabel, turning her fierce glare on him. 'He'd been sailing to Batavia since I was a little girl, begging on the docks. He'd give me coin for food, for a bed. He came back this time to find me with a babe on the way and no father to raise it. He said he was done with this life and would take care of us in the Provinces, if I'd risk it with him. I couldn't afford a berth on the ship, so I said no, but then Sander told me he'd tracked Old Tom to this boat and we had to give chase. I thought God was smiling on me, at last.'

'Nothing wrong there, so why meet in secret?' wondered Sammy.

'To be boatswain everybody has to be afraid of you, that's what he told me,' she said. 'If anybody knew he cared for something, they'd hurt it to hurt him.'

Crauwels murmured his agreement. 'Boatswain has to keep hold of the crew. When he can't do it any more he turns up dead. Wyck was a damn good one, but that meant he was a damn bad person.'

'We weren't going to talk until Amsterdam, but he sent me a message that he wanted to meet on the forecastle, only I got caught by the dwarf going there,' she said, her voice still simmering with resentment. 'He sent word to meet in the cargo hold instead. He told me he'd spotted somebody on deck, somebody pretending to be somebody else. He said he recognised them from the great house he used to work in.'

'Who was it?' asked Arent.

'He wouldn't tell me, he said it wasn't safe, but they were going to pay dearly to keep the secret, and then we'd have the life he promised.' She stared at his body, bitterly. 'Instead, it ends like this.'

'Which house did he serve?'

'He didn't tell me.'

'It must have been the de Havilands,' announced Sara, coming down the staircase. 'Dalvhain is an anagram of Haviland. One of the people Old Tom possessed in the Provinces thirty years ago was Emily de Haviland. She's been onboard this whole time. Lia spotted it, and so did my husband. He went up there to confront her before ...'

Her voice softened and she looked up at Arent sympathetically.

'He's dead, Arent.'

She took his hand, as Sammy came over. 'I'm sorry, my friend.'

Arent swallowed, then sat himself on a crate.

'I know my uncle was ...' His voice was choked. 'He did ...'

'He loved you,' said Sara gently. 'Despite everything else, there was that.'

As Sara consoled Arent, Sammy reached out a hand to still a swaying lantern overhead. 'Let's put this together,' he said. 'Wyck recognised Emily de Haviland on deck, presumably while she was boarding. He'd served the family back in the Provinces and knew she was once accused of possession, and investigated by Pieter Fletcher. Wyck tried to blackmail her, but she sent her pet leper –'

'My dead carpenter,' interrupted Crauwels belligerently.

'To kill him,' said Sammy.

'But why would Emily de Haviland care so much about protecting a name she knew we'd uncover?' wondered Sara. 'She came aboard using an anagram. She wanted to be found eventually.'

'Maybe it mattered when we uncovered it,' suggested Arent, without any great conviction.

'None of this matters,' shouted Crauwels, shaking his head. 'Old Tom promised three unholy miracles before he slaughtered anybody who hadn't agreed to one of his bargains. Well, we're out of miracles. Way I see it, the only way to stop him now is to find this Emily de Haviland, bind her hands and feet and throw her overboard.'

'Drown the witch,' said Sara wryly. 'How novel.'

70

A GRIM-FACED COMPANY HAD gathered in the great cabin under a swaying lantern, shadows leaping across the walls. The book they'd found in Viscountess Dalvhain's cabin was centred on the table, and everybody was keeping their distance. They'd all seen what was inside and all of them would rather they hadn't.

With the governor general dead, the chief merchant was absolute master of the vessel, though he didn't seem pleased about it. He was ashen-faced, pacing back and forth in front of the windows, while rubbing his hands through his thinning hair. There wasn't any wine left for him to drink, though his fingers obviously itched for it.

Even those jewelled rings had lost their lustre, thought Arent.

'Dozens dead, and the governor general among them,' said Reynier van Schooten. 'We have to put a stop to this before it consumes the ship.' He turned on Arent, pointing an accusing finger. 'Didn't your uncle put you in charge of finding this devil when its mark first appeared on the sail? How did you miss the fact that Viscountess Dalvhain was actually Emily de Haviland?'

'Aye, because the rest of you were probably burning with suspicion,' snorted Sammy sarcastically, his feet on the table.

Despite everything that was happening, he'd taken the time to wash in saltwater and change his clothes for the spare set Arent had brought. He was bathed, powdered and perfumed, which meant for the first time in weeks, he was almost his own self, though there was no disguising the frailness of his body, or the slight tremor in his voice.

'Besides, we don't know the two *are* the same,' he continued. 'We only know that somebody came aboard using an anagram of Haviland's name. It could be Emily de Haviland playing games, or it could be somebody else trying to fool us. Assume nothing, Chief Merchant.' He chortled and rubbed his hands together. 'This really is a wonderful case. If it had been brought to me in Amsterdam, I'd be jumping up and down in glee.'

'Who in the seven hells let you out?' snapped Van Schooten, irritated by his flippant demeanour.

'I did,' said Arent, his arms folded across his massive chest. 'My uncle is dead and with him the only reason to keep Sammy imprisoned. Now that the three unholy miracles have passed, we need him out here investigating, not rotting in some dank cell.'

The room murmured its agreement, forcing Van Schooten to concede defeat, but only grudgingly.

'So where is the passenger who was in that cabin now?' he demanded.

'I don't know,' admitted Sammy. 'Did anybody ever meet her?'

'Once,' said Crauwels, roused from his thoughts for the first time since they'd come up from the orlop deck. The captain was standing at the head of the table, his palms flat on its surface. 'Long grey dress and long grey hair. Resembled Vos in a strange sort of way. Had that odd, blank way of looking at you. She sat in the gloom and barked at me to leave her alone.'

'What about the cabin boys? Did one of them tend her room?' asked Sammy.

'They were forbidden from entering,' replied Van Schooten, ruefully.

'Then who emptied her chamberpots?'

'They were left outside her door each night,' said Creesjie, wrinkling her nose, as if she could still smell them.

'If she was so eager to stay hidden, why would she take the risk of booking a cabin?' wondered Sara.

'When did we start letting women into these meetings?' demanded Van Schooten, freshly outraged as he realised Sara, Lia and Creesjie had taken chairs at the opposite end of the table from Crauwels. 'This isn't women's business.'

'Will it be women's business when Old Tom sinks the ship?' shot back Creesjie.

'It doesn't matter who's here, or not,' said Crauwels in a flat voice. 'It matters what we do next. How do we save the *Saardam*? So far Old Tom's been able to come and go as it pleases, slaughtering at will. I've heard the stories about you, Pipps. I need you to help me ferret out Emily de Haviland from wherever she's hiding.'

'She won't be found, Captain,' scoffed Sammy. 'Emily, Old Tom or whoever is behind all of this, has planned everything meticulously.' He waved his hand to the night sky beyond the windows. 'There's a ship out there that's presumably under her control. She's got a leper doing her bidding, who we haven't been able to find. She stole The Folly without anybody realising, slaughtered our animals while we were standing twenty paces away and has now managed to murder the most powerful man onboard, without needing to enter his cabin. She disappeared because it was time for her to disappear. Do you think we're going to find her hiding in the crow's nest?'

'We have to do something,' yelled Crauwels, who'd grown increasingly irate the longer Sammy spoke.

'And I will,' laughed Sammy. 'But stupidity isn't ever the straight line it first appears. As I see it, there are three important questions, and the location of Emily de Haviland is not one of them. The first is what links the unholy miracles: why did our enemy steal The Folly, slaughter some animals and then murder the governor general?'

'I thought they were random acts,' said Creesjie, fanning herself.

Sammy peered at her, then dragged his feet from the table, stood up and bowed exquisitely. 'I don't believe we've met, madam. I'm Samuel Pipps.'

She inclined her head, laughing prettily. 'Creesjie Jens,' she said. 'You live up to Arent's reports, sir.'

'It grows ever more difficult with each one he writes. A few more years under Arent's quill and I'll be nothing but cleverness and virtue.' They grinned at each other, a friendship having clearly been struck. 'To answer your question, the unholy miracles seem to have been random, but very little else in this case has been. I rather doubt Old Tom's started now. The miracles were planned, which means they were deliberately chosen.'

Now he was standing, he began to pace. His finger stabbed the air as he spoke. 'My second question is how was the governor general murdered? My third is why the leper killed

Cornelius Vos, yet let Arent live? Once I have the answers to those questions, I'm certain the rest of this fascinating puzzle will arrange itself.'

'That's it!?' demanded Crauwels. 'Solve a murder and you think it will end our torment? Every time that damn Eighth Lantern burns red, my ship rips itself apart. The leper climbed up out of the sea to reach Sara's cabin, and now Emily de Haviland's loose on my ship. Sending Arent to fight it was like sending a child to war and now I see you're no better.' He scowled at everyone, then stormed out

'Get to work, Pipps,' said Van Schooten, staring after him. 'I'll calm Crauwels down. Larme, we need to get the lads back to sailing and not worrying about demons. Finding a new boatswain would help.'

'Candidates usually stab each other until there's only one left, but I'll try to hurry it along,' grunted Larme, who was leaning against the doorway into the helm.

Sammy signalled to Arent, the two of them making their way to the governor general's cabin. Sammy strode straight in, but Arent couldn't make it past the threshold. His sense of dread was choking, his eyes lurching away when he tried to look at the bunk.

When he did eventually see his uncle, the pain made him want to howl.

Clamping his jaw shut, he blinked back tears, trying to reason with his grief.

In every way that mattered, this wasn't the uncle he remembered. Cruelty had replaced the kindness. He'd beaten Sara and locked Lia away, and made a deal with Old Tom. He had turned his back on the ideals he'd espoused to Arent as a boy, and yet … Arent had loved him.

451

And that love endured. Whether it was earned, or worthy, or right, it sat at the heart of him, and, try as he might, he couldn't dislodge it.

For fifteen minutes, Arent watched Sammy put his eyes on everything, touching and caressing, lifting and staring, passing through the room like an inquisitive breeze, leaving the objects he inspected precisely in their original place. Once he was satisfied, he tugged the dagger out of the governor general's body with a sickening squelch, then investigated the wound.

'Splinters,' he said, delicately removing a small sliver of wood from the governor general's chest. 'Possibly from the hilt of the murder weapon. See what you make of it, Arent.'

Preoccupied, Sammy pressed the dagger and splinters into Arent's hands. Sammy always asked him to examine the murder weapons in case his insight as a soldier should prove useful, but this was different.

This wasn't a weapon. It was guilt.

His uncle had been murdered two decks from him. How could that be? Arent had once saved him from the entire Spanish army, so why hadn't he been able to protect him from a whisper in the darkness?

Deep down, where his grief became blame, a voice suggested that maybe he hadn't wanted to. Now he was dead, Sara was free of him.

'Stop it,' he said to himself.

'Hmmm?' asked Sammy, who was creeping along the floor on his hands and knees, his eyes almost touching the wood as he searched for clues.

'Nothing,' mumbled Arent embarrassed, examining the dagger. It was shorter than normal, the blade thinner. Much too thin, he realised. It was almost brittle. No smithy would make a weapon this way, it was no good. It would snap when it hit armour.

'I know this weapon,' said Arent, weighing it in his palm. 'The leper threatened me with it in the cargo hold.'

'That's interesting, because the leper's handprints climb up to the porthole, and above it are seven widely spaced hooks. I don't know what their purpose is, but we'll need to find out.'

'Then you're blaming the leper for my uncle's murder?'

'The creature must be considered. By the coldness of the governor general's body and the degree to which his blood has congealed, I would suggest he had been dead some hours by the time Creesjie and Guard Captain Drecht lit the candle.'

'So, you think he was murdered during dinner?' asked Arent. 'That would exonerate all of the passengers. They ate together.'

'We should confirm that none of them left the dinner for any reason. If they didn't, I'm afraid it places Sara Wessel in rather a bad spot.'

Seeing Arent's objection, he held up a placating hand. 'I know you're fond of her, but you were unconscious for a majority of the evening. She could easily have slipped away from your side. For all we know, she saw a chance to murder a devil and blame another devil for the work, and she took it.'

Arent shuddered, remembering how Vos had planned to do the same thing. He would have succeeded had the leper not interrupted them.

'Now, to the matter of the snuffed candle,' said Sammy, peering out of the porthole. 'Sara said her husband never slept without a light. Not a single day in all the years she knew him.

Creesjie confirmed this. Apparently he was afraid of the dark, something only those closest to him would have known. Was there a strong wind tonight?'

'No.'

Sammy placed his body equidistant between the porthole and the writing desk, extending his arms. Even then, he couldn't reach the candle. 'And it would be impossible to lean in and snuff it from outside.'

Sammy plucked a scroll case from behind the netted shelf and tossed it to Arent. 'We'll have to search everything in this room, so start here,' he ordered.

Arent took himself to the writing desk and sat down heavily. Removing the cap from the case, he unrolled the scroll within. It was a plan for The Folly, he realised. Or at least one very small part of it.

'Arent?' said Sammy, who was gazing up at the porthole with his chin pressed to the floor. 'How did Isaack Larme feel about your uncle?'

'He hated the slaughter my uncle ordered at the Banda Islands,' said Arent. 'Other than that, I don't know. Why?'

'Because with a little wriggling, our dwarf could have got through this porthole.'

Arent eyed it, trying to imagine Larme squeezing through.

'The clatter would have woke my uncle and brought Drecht running,' disagreed Arent, picking up the next scroll.

My dearest Jan,

My health is failing. I will not see another summer.
*   Upon my death, my place among the Gentlemen 17 will fall vacant. In keeping with the vow I made you, and in recompense*

*of our great undertaking all those years ago, I have nominated you
for the post and my colleagues have agreed.*

*However, they each have their favourites and the manoeuvring
has begun. Once I die, I cannot guarantee the position.*

*Heed my advice and return to Amsterdam without delay.
Bring your daughter, for she is of marriageable age and will serve
you well when the bartering begins.*

*And put manacles on Samuel Pipps. I've come across accu-
sations that he's a spy for the English. Not only a traitor to our
noble enterprise, but our nation. It's not yet common knowledge,
but I've verified the claims and will put them before my fellows
soon. Execution awaits. Drag him before the Gentlemen 17 and
your position will be vastly improved. Do these things and come
quickly.*

Yours in expectation,
Casper van den Berg

Sammy read the missive over Arent's shoulder, becoming
immediately awkward. Compassion wasn't something he was
versed in, being a man who saw bodies as clues and murder
as an occupation, but he tapped his friend in a vague approx-
imation of sympathy.

'I'm sorry,' he said. 'I know you loved your grandfather.
Hearing about this at the same time as –'

'He's not dying,' interrupted Arent.

Sammy looked down at his impassive face.

'It can be difficult –'

'This parchment is dated a week before we sailed,' he said,
pointing to it. 'It would have arrived in Batavia at the same
time we did. I saw my grandfather a few days before we left
Amsterdam. I was worried I might not survive the journey

and I didn't want him to think …' Arent swallowed. 'He was healthy, Sammy. Old, but not dying. He didn't write this. He didn't accuse you of being a spy.'

Sammy snatched the letter from his hand.

'Then it was somebody who knew his mind intimately,' said Sammy. 'Was your uncle close to Emily de Haviland?'

'He didn't mention her, and far as I know their house fell into ruin long before my uncle's stock rose far enough for them to have met. My grandfather might have known her. He's about the right age.'

'The letter mentions a great undertaking that was done. Any idea what that could be?'

'My grandfather was friends with Jan Haan for years before I was born. They were even in business together briefly, though I don't know what they did. They never told me, but it helped make both of them rich.'

Sammy rolled up the scroll, pressing the broken edges of the seal back together. 'This is the official seal of the Gentlemen 17. Only the highest-ranking officials in the Company even know what it looks like, let alone how to forge the stamp, and even then, it has to be delivered by a trusted representative of the Company.'

'Who could that be?'

Sammy blew a breath through his lips, throwing the ascension order back on the desk and walking over to inspect the wine mugs. 'Vos could have done it, I suppose. Captain Crauwels. Reynier van Schooten. Me. They may not even be on the boat, any longer.'

'Could Viscountess Dalvhain have delivered it?' wondered Arent. 'We know my uncle went to see her before he died.

Maybe she wanted you in a cell, so you couldn't investigate his murder.'

'A fine notion,' Sammy agreed. 'If she had some connection to the Gentlemen 17 she certainly would have been trusted with the seal.'

'My uncle was manoeuvred here, wasn't he?' said Arent suddenly. 'Like Sander Kers. Old Tom wanted them both onboard.'

Sammy was sniffing the mugs again. 'I doubt you're here by accident either. Old Tom was *your* story. The mark is the same as *your* scar. *Your* father's rosary was in the animal pens. The leper left *you* alive in the cargo hold. Everything that's happening on this boat keeps coming back to *you*.'

'But I'm only on this boat because *you* were locked up.'

'Which brings us back to Dalvhain.'

Sammy considered the idea, while tipping the wine jug back and forth, and listening intently to the movement of liquid inside. He then upended the wine into an empty cup, watching the flow of liquid.

'This is tainted,' he said, peering into the cup. 'Come, look.'

At first, Arent saw nothing, but Sammy drew the candle closer, revealing the viscous sediment that had settled on the bottom.

Using his fingertip, Sammy tasted it.

'Can you identify it?' asked Arent.

'It's the sleeping draught Sara gave me.'

'Maybe my uncle took it, as well.'

'And perhaps we should let the lady provide her own explanations,' replied Sammy, opening the door and sauntering back into the great cabin. Everybody remained in the positions where they'd left them. Each was deep in their thoughts, their eyes unfocused. Fingers were tapping and feet jogging.

Sammy walked over to Sara, Lia and Creesjie, unobtrusively running his eyes across Isaack Larme's clothes as he went. He stopped abruptly. 'You have green paint flakes on your slops,' he said, earning a scowl. 'Why is that?'

'None of your –'

'Answer him,' warned Van Schooten, who was standing at the windows with his hands behind his back.

Larme's eyes were daggers. 'I'm up and down this ship, aren't I?'

'The hull outside the governor general's cabin is painted green.'

'Aye, as is the forecastle, which is where I spend most of my time.'

Sammy watched his face for a moment longer than was comfortable, until Larme swore and stormed out of the room. Once he was gone, Sammy turned his attention to Sara. 'Did your husband take a sleeping draught before bed?'

'No,' said Sara, reaching for the hands of Lia and Creesjie. 'I was drugging my husband's wine, so Creesjie could steal the plans to The Folly.'

She spoke as though this was perfectly reasonable. Creesjie picked up the tale.

'Each night, I'd put one sheet in a scroll case attached to the inside of my gown, and then deliver them to Lia who would scribe a copy. I'd return it the next night, and do the same again.'

'Why would Lia –'

'I invented The Folly, Mr Pipps,' said Lia, lowering her eyes, as if ashamed of the fact.

Van Schooten almost fell over.

'I invent lots of things,' shrugged Lia, glancing at him. 'The Folly wasn't my favourite, but my father seemed to like it.'

'I intended on selling the plans to the duke Creesjie is going to marry, in return for sanctuary in France, along with my wealth and freedom,' said Sara, her tone unwavering. 'It seemed a small price to pay. I understand that you must suspect me, but, you see, there was really no reason for me to risk killing my husband.'

Silence descended on the company.

'I thought I was marrying a count,' said Creesjie quietly.

71

B Y A SINGLE CANDLE in his cabin, Reynier van Schooten inspected the revised list of victuals in the hold. His head was in his hands, his temples throbbing. They'd lost most of their supplies to the storm. Even if they could find their way back to charted waters, they wouldn't have enough to reach the Cape. The best they could hope for was a safe return to Batavia, wasting an entire shipment of spice.

The Gentlemen 17 wouldn't care about devils, or storms. They cared only for the number in the ledger, and these numbers would not please them. Chief merchants were responsible for the cargo they delivered, and when it was lost, they were expected to earn back the loss. He was going to spend the rest of his life as an indentured servant to the Company.

Years of experience had taught him to treat a crossing from Batavia to Amsterdam with the utmost caution. He knew the dangers of the voyage, as he'd known the fleet would scatter, making resupply uncertain. Why had he agreed when the governor general demanded the extra cargo space?

Money, he thought with loathing. More than he'd ever seen, with the promise of more to come.

He'd worked his way from clerk to chief merchant without sponsor or favour, doing the work with a competence that couldn't be ignored. His superiors had promoted him regretfully over their second cousins and brothers, allowing him to climb above those who sneered at him when he'd stayed in the counting rooms late, tending his accounts, always believing that one day he'd have his reward.

The governor general's offer had seemed like a shortcut to that. One more voyage, and he'd never have to accept another crossing. There would be no more sleepless nights being harried by pirates. No more tropical maladies. No more arguments with greedy fools like Crauwels.

He could end his career before a wreck ended it for him.

But once he'd agreed to that, it had been easy to agree to the rest. That's how the governor general worked. He handed you a coin covered in honey and before you knew it, you were stuck. Then he put the coin – and the greedy merchant – back in his pocket to be used whenever he needed them.

Van Schooten thumped the ledger, blotting his hand with ink. He was glad the bastard was dead. He was glad Cornelius Vos was dead. He only wished Emily de Haviland – whoever she was – had killed Guard Captain Drecht and completed the set. They'd brought nothing but bad fortune to this ship.

Knocks thudded through his door.

'Go away,' he hollered.

'What was the secret cargo the governor general brought aboard?' yelled Drecht.

Van Schooten slowly put down his quill. His legs were water.

'If you make me break down this door, it will go badly for you,' growled Drecht.

Pushing out his chair, Van Schooten went like a condemned man to the door. It had opened a crack when Drecht's hand shot inside, crushing his throat.

His blue eyes bore into the helpless merchant, his face savage. He looked like a wolf fallen on a hare.

'What was the cargo, Van Schooten? You helped him bring it aboard, and you know where it's kept. What is it? Is it important enough for somebody to kill him for?'

'It was treasure,' gasped Van Schooten, trying in vain to peel Drecht's fingers from his throat. 'More treasure than … than I'd ever seen.'

'Show me,' snarled Drecht.

They went immediately, stopping only once for Drecht to whisper some instructions to Eggert, the musketeer guarding the door to the passenger cabins. Whatever was said sent Eggert scampering off towards the bow of the ship.

Once they were in the cargo hold, Van Schooten took a lantern from the peg at the foot of the staircase and led them through the labyrinth of crates, now almost entirely covered in the Mark of Old Tom. It was obvious they weren't all by the original hand. Many were clumsy, others only half finished. Some were large, some tiny. Evidently, carving a mark had become a way of pledging fealty.

Van Schooten hadn't been down here since boarding, and he was surprised at the change. Normally, a cargo hold was home to crates, rats and whatever stowaways had smuggled themselves onboard. It was unpleasant, but unthreatening.

This place felt damned.

The oily darkness and the rotten stink of spices made the atmosphere infernal.

'This entire place has become Old Tom's church,' remarked Drecht. 'Four bodies and it's got a damn religion.'

By his tone, Van Schooten suspected that Drecht had killed a lot more than that and was beginning to wonder where his reward was.

Reaching the centre of the labyrinth, Van Schooten pointed to a large crate. 'In there,' he said, his voice quivering.

Slipping loose his dagger, Drecht found the edge of a board and pried it open, discovering dozens of hemp sacks inside.

'Cut one open,' said Van Schooten.

Drecht did so, his blade shearing through the material, before snagging on something metallic. Sheathing his dagger, Drecht tugged at the tear with his hands, causing silver chalices and gold plates to spill out, followed by jewel-encrusted necklaces and rings.

'These are the same sorts of objects Vos had in his sack when the leper gutted him,' said Drecht. 'The chamberlain must have been stealing pieces from this stash. Didn't think he had it in him. How much of this is there?'

'There are hundreds of crates. They take up half the cargo hold,' said Van Schooten, sounding sick. 'Most of it's hidden in hemp sacks and disguised as other things.' Something fierce came into his tone. 'This is the secret you murdered those sailors to protect.'

Drecht glanced at him, obviously amused to find a little courage lurking under all that cowardice. The governor general had wanted his cargo kept secret, which meant silencing those who knew about it, including those who'd loaded it on to the *Saardam*.

'I was following orders,' he said, turning one of the chalices over in his hands. 'That's what soldiers do. You're the one who sent them to the warehouse where I was waiting. You're the one they trusted, who took the governor general's coin for doing it.'

He picked up a jewel, the sparkle reflected in his eyes. 'A man with this wealth would never know want again,' he said in wonder. 'He could have servants, a grand house and a future for his children.'

His hand slowly began to unsheathe his sword. 'Thing is, Van Schooten. It wasn't only those sailors who knew about this cargo.' He advanced on the merchant. 'And it wasn't only them I was supposed to kill.'

72

DOROTHEA WAS SCRUBBING CLOTHES on the orlop deck, listening to Isabel sing. All the passengers were listening to her, transfixed by the beauty of her voice. It wasn't a skill she'd mentioned before, nor was it one she seemed to take any great pride in. She just opened her mouth and out it poured. All the games and talk had stopped. The dice had clattered off the wall and lay still. In their hammocks and on their mats, people closed their eyes and savoured the only joy they'd known on this voyage.

'Mistress Dorothea.'

Dorothea turned to find Eggert the musketeer hurrying towards her. She smiled warmly at him, warmer than she smiled at most.

'I'm glad to see you, but it's too early for our evening tea,' she said, confused by his presence.

'Something's happening aboard ship, mistress,' he said in a hush, his fear striking at her heart. 'You need to put a thick door between you and what's coming.'

'What's coming, Eggert?'

He shook his scabby head, terrified. 'There isn't time,' he said. 'Will your mistress shelter you in her cabin?'

'Aye.'

'Good,' he said, grabbing her arm. 'Then stay close to me.'

'And what about these people?' demanded Dorothea, planting her feet and gesturing to the other passengers. 'What are they supposed to hide behind?'

'I've got only one sword, mistress,' he apologised.

'I'll not leave those who need help.'

Eggert looked around him desperately, then rushed over to the gunpowder store, hammering on the door. The panel slid back, a pair of wild white eyebrows on the other side.

'What?' asked the constable. Since his flogging he'd become surly and short-tempered.

'Mutiny,' declared Eggert. 'Can you shelter these passengers in there?'

The constable glanced around the deck suspiciously. Isabel was still singing, and the passengers were watching her. There was no sign of trouble. He addressed Dorothea who was standing at Eggert's shoulder. 'He talking truth?' he demanded.

'Can't see why he'd lie.'

'The orders came from Guard Captain Drecht,' said Eggert. 'The musketeers are already moving. We need to put these people safe.'

A bolt slid back, candlelight pouring into the gloom of the orlop deck. 'Mothers and children inside,' said the constable. 'I can't fit any more, but the rest of the women can barricade themselves in the bread room below. The men better arm themselves. They'll be fighting soon enough.'

73

TWELVE BELLS RANG AMIDSHIPS, summoning the entire crew on to the deck. It was a mournful sound, fit for the mood.

Rain battered down, the cold drops reflecting the change in latitude.

As sailors struggled to find space – their faces strangely angelic in the warm glow of the running lantern – the sails billowed, carrying them forward at a furious pace.

On the quarterdeck, Captain Crauwels gripped the railing and looked down at them, unsure where to start. He knew what had to be said, but he didn't know how. He'd addressed his crew hundreds of times, but only ever with one speech at the start of the voyage. It was good luck and a blessing, the easiest thing in the world to say. This was different. The words were jagged. They'd draw blood.

'The *Saardam* is doomed,' he said, when everybody had gathered. 'We all know what's been happening on this ship, what stalks us in the dark water.'

A rumble of discontent rose up.

'Have you all heard the whispers?' There were nods and murmurs, only a few blank stares. Most had, a few hadn't. It didn't matter. They all knew what was being offered.

Crauwels shifted uncomfortably. He felt like he was trying to build a vase by spitting out bits of broken pottery.

'I've made some mistakes,' he admitted, the faces blurring before him. 'Trusted the wrong people and led you astray, but now we have to make a choice for ourselves. What do *we* want? Not the nobles we carry, or those damnable musketeers. Us, alone. Sailors. We have to choose.'

The agreement was raucous.

'Old Tom walks this boat, aint no denying that. Three miracles were offered to convince us of his power, that's what he told us in the dark. Three chances for us to fly his flag and accept his protection.' The crew watched, their breaths held in their throats. 'There's no more miracles left. Next time he comes, it'll be to sweep away those who didn't take his bargain.'

A great cry of fear went up.

'It's time we made our choice,' boomed Crauwels, holding up that strange metal disc he liked to flip in the air. 'Governor General Jan Haan gave me this for sailing him out to the Banda Islands,' he said. 'And you all know what happened there.'

Butchers, carnage, slaughter, came the cry.

'We've all taken coin for things we aint proud of, but that's the Company, aint it. They ask too much for too little. Them nobles in there are getting richer all the time off the back of our labour, and I'm sick of it.'

Captain, Captain, Captain, they hollered.

He tossed the disc into the crowd, sailors clambering over each to claim it. In its place, he held up his dagger and his palm.

'Old Tom asks a favour and blood to show our devotion,' he said, drawing his blade across his palm. 'The favour is our service. Hold up your daggers if you're ready to become crew to a new master, lads. A master who'll see us clear of all this, who'll ask us to do awful things, but, at least, reward us well for their doing.'

Hundreds of daggers were lifted into the air, slicing hundreds of palms.

Blood ran freely.

'That's it then,' cried Crauwels. 'We fly under Old Tom's banner now, and it's his voice we'll heed.'

His back arched, blood spurting out of his mouth as a sword emerged through his chest.

The crew howled in rage, unsheathing their daggers and surging towards the quarterdeck, as Crauwels's body slumped to the ground, revealing Jacobi Drecht behind him.

'Musketeers, fire,' hollered Drecht. Chaos erupted. Gunfire rang out across the deck, sailors screaming and collapsing.

From the corner of his eye, Drecht saw Isaack Larme charging towards him with his knife in his hand.

He thrust his sword towards Larme's chest, only for Arent to pull the dwarf backwards, away from the blade. Pipps was sheltered behind him, the problematary tiny in his friend's shadow.

'What are you doing, Drecht?' shouted Arent over the noise of the battle.

'I can't give this ship to Old Tom!'

'Those musketeers were in position long before the captain's speech started, before you knew what he was going to do,' spat Arent, seeing him truly for the first time. 'This is a mutiny.'

'I want the fortune that was promised to me by the governor general,' said Drecht. 'I slaughtered children in their beds, so my children could have a better future. I don't sleep any more, Arent. I can't. And now I want what I paid so dearly to have.'

'And who's going to sail the ship when you have it?' demanded Sammy, covering his ears against the clash of metal.

'We'll keep enough sailors alive to take us home.'

'If they let you,' said Sammy, watching the musketeers slashing at the massed ranks below.

Drecht stared at Arent, smearing Crauwels's blood across his face as he tried to wipe it away. 'Do you stand with us, Arent? Tell me now.'

'I stand with the passengers,' hollered Arent. 'Keep your men away from them.'

Arent hauled Sammy off his feet and dropped him on to the deck below, before leaping over the railing after him. Musketeers had taken position near the bottom of the staircase, where they were battling wave after wave of enraged sailors. For the moment, the sailors seemed to have the best of it, but it wouldn't last. The musketeers were capable of fighting two of them at once, and the sailors' strength had been sapped trying to outrun the storm. They would be exhausted long before they ran out of enemies.

The ship lurched, sending them staggering.

The *Saardam* was charging through the water without anybody to guide her. Darting into the empty spaces in the fighting, Arent and Sammy found Larme pressed against the railing, jabbing at the thighs of musketeers with his knife.

Knocking the blade away, Arent grabbed the dwarf's hand and stared at his palm. It was unmarked.

'You're not with Old Tom?' he hollered over the fighting.

'I'm with the *Saardam*,' he said. 'Everything else can go to buggery.'

A musketeer charged towards them, screaming. Arent grabbed him by the shirt and hurled him into the water.

'If we get control of this ship, can you talk this crew back around and get us to Batavia?' demanded Sammy, crouched before Larme.

'Depends how many sailors are left alive,' replied Larme. 'But there aint a better plan I'm considering. Where are your people?'

'Not sure, but I'm heading down to the orlop deck,' said Arent.

He didn't say more, but he didn't need to. Everybody understood what a battle meant for those without the strength to defend themselves. Once blood was spilt, there were no more sins left. It was likely some of these men were already on their way down there, seeking a different sort of entertainment.

A sailor tried climbing over the railing onto the quarter deck, but Drecht put his sabre through his eye, pushing him back into the throng below.

'You won't have a chance of taking this ship while he's still breathing,' said Larme, nodding towards Drecht.

'He'll see reason,' said Arent, 'but –'

Wood shrieked and the deck exploded, a spear of rock shooting upwards, toppling the mainmast and pulverising everybody in its path. Diamonds flew into the air, gold chains and chalices raining down around them.

Dark water surged upwards like a great hand, dragging Arent, Sammy and Larme into the cold sea.

74

T HE ROAR OF THE ocean filled Arent's ears.

Something nudged him and he groaned, his eyes flickering open. It was dawn, the sky a grey slab above him. He tried to move, but his body was made of driftwood. He was dripping wet, crusted with salt.

The musketeers Eggert and Thyman were silhouetted by the glare. One was standing, the other kneeling, rocking him by the shoulder.

'Well?' asked Thyman, who was standing.

'He's breathing,' came Eggert.

Arent lurched on to his side, heaving up seawater until his throat was raw.

Wiping his mouth, he looked around fuzzily.

He'd washed up on a pebble beach strewn with seaweed, white surf advancing and retreating, tugging at his ankles. Fingers of purple and orange coral stretched away into a bay of jagged rocks, the water thrashing between them, throwing up huge plumes of spray.

The *Saardam* was across the bay, run aground on a small island. A pointed rock had speared her underside, ripping through her decks and erupting through the waist.

'Have you seen Sara Wessel?' he asked, knocking the seawater from his ears. 'Or Sammy Pipps?'

He snapped his head left and right desperately, trying to spot them on the shoal. There must have been thirty survivors scattered along the coast, and many more dead floating in the shallow water. They'd been hacked apart by the rocks, red patches showing where they'd been skewered and bludgeoned.

Mothers cradled children, wailing for those they'd lost or hollering for those they hoped to find, while men hurled themselves after the supplies bobbing in the water, grabbing anything they could, scuffling with others for what they couldn't.

Three musketeers held down a struggling sailor, while a fourth jabbed a dagger into his belly. More were prowling the beach, putting their swords through the bodies of any sailors that had washed up, whether they were breathing or not.

Cliffs reared up to Arent's right, the curve of the bay disguising whatever was to his left. The centre of the island appeared to be jungle, a skirting of scraggly red shrub separating it from the shoal.

Of his friends, he could see no sign.

'Aint seen Pipps. If he's alive, he'll be at the camp with Guard Captain Drecht,' said Thyman.

'So Drecht is alive,' said Arent, staggering to his feet. 'Course he is.'

'He gave the order to abandon the *Saardam* and put Sara and her family on the first yawl to the island,' said Eggert. 'They're all up at the camp.'

'Don't expect to see Pipps there,' warned Eggert darkly. 'Old Tom brought his fist down on us. Most everybody is dead.'

This must have been the island that was drawn into Emily de Haviland's daemonologica, thought Arent. The island that was the basis for the Mark of Old Tom scarred on to his wrist. The passengers and crew of the *Saardam* had been slaughtered and delivered here, exactly as she'd promised.

Weak as old bones, he swayed back and forth as his legs reacquainted themselves with dry land after three weeks at sea.

Until now, he thought he'd taken every sort of beating life could mete out, but fate had made a fool of him again. Ragged gashes covered his body and his ribs ached so badly he couldn't straighten up. Teeth wobbled in his jaw.

He felt as if he'd been stamped on by a hundred men and somehow fought his way free.

Water rushed through the rocks, covering and uncovering the sharp coral, the dead and dying. He'd always believed miracles were what happened when you finally ran out of hope. They were bits of luck, polished until they gleamed, delivered exactly as you needed them.

This wasn't a miracle. He felt like a pig that had survived the slaughterhouse only to run straight into the kitchen.

'You really can't be killed, can you?' said Thyman suspiciously. 'All them songs were right.'

'Where's the camp?' he asked hoarsely.

Eggert pointed up the shoal to the left.

Clutching his aching ribs, Arent followed his directions. A grey sky pressed against the grey ocean, the temperature rising steadily, warming the ever-present rain, which hit him like a windborne stream of piss.

At each body, he bent down to examine the face, always in terror of seeing Sara's red curls. He found an unconscious

Sammy in the shadow of some cliffs covered in white scat, with long-beaked seabirds darting in and out of nests built into holes in the rock. He was lying on his side, with his back to Arent. He drew breath yet, though it rattled. Those fine clothes he'd put on last night were tatters, his thin body showing through. Blood oozed from dozens of gashes, the colour alarmingly bright against his pale, quivering skin.

Two musketeers circled him, unsheathing their blades.

Wincing in pain, Arent drew himself upright.

'Away you go, lads,' he called out.

After searching around for help, and finding none, they slunk off. Arent watched them until they were out of sight, then allowed himself to sag again, moving as quickly as he could to Sammy's side, groaning when he saw him.

Half of his face had been shredded by coral, taking his right eye with it.

Grimacing, Arent reached down and heaved him off the shoal. Pain coursed down from his ribs, almost driving him to his knees. For a minute, he fought for each breath, before he finally gritted his teeth and started to walk.

Each step was an agony, but what use was his pain to those who needed his help. Sammy was badly injured, and he had to find Sara and Lia. Barely able to lift his feet, he pressed forward.

A screaming sailor came running towards them, chased by two musketeers who fell on him like wolves, stabbing him a dozen times until he was dead. Bloodied, but laughing, the musketeers got to their feet, eyeing Arent hungrily, before moving off to find more prey.

They'd struggle, thought Arent. The shoal was littered with sailors they'd already bludgeoned, beaten and slaughtered.

Sammy stirred in Arent's arms, swallowing. His solitary eye focused on his friend. 'You look like you spent the night with an ox,' he rasped weakly, bringing a burst of painful laughter from Arent.

'I didn't want your mama to be the only one,' he responded. 'We're going to get you help.'

'What' – he coughed – 'what happened?'

'We ran aground on an island, while everybody was fighting.'

Sammy clutched Arent's shirt. 'Is it a –' he struggled for every word '– is it a nice island, at least?'

'No,' said Arent. 'I think it's where Old Tom lives.'

'Ah,' nodded Sammy in satisfaction. 'At least we won't have to look for him any more.'

Sammy's eye closed, his head falling limp. Arent inspected him fearfully, but he was still breathing.

They came upon a makeshift camp not a minute too soon. Arent's arms were trembling and breaths were getting more difficult to come by.

To his relief, the first thing he saw was Marcus and Osbert skimming stones off the shore, watched by Dorothea. Aside from their ruffled hair, they seemed no worse for wear from the crossing.

Isaack Larme was slumped on a cask, scowling at the supplies bobbing in the water, as if they were insults flung at him by his own treacherous ship. Jacobi Drecht was pointing and barking orders at his musketeers, who were splashing in the surf trying to collect the crates and casks before stacking them under the trees to keep the rain off. Nearby were dozens of cases, overflowing with treasure.

Upon seeing Arent, Isaack Larme stomped over. 'Hundreds dead, and here you are, barely a mark on you. Seems God isn't done with you yet.'

'Sammy got my share of hurt,' he replied.

Drecht tipped his head in greeting. The beard had survived, and so had his hat, though the red feather was lost. A chunk was missing from his right ear and one of his fingers was set an unnatural angle. Unfortunately, it wasn't on his fighting hand.

'I'm glad to see you well, I feared the worst,' he said.

Arent looked between Drecht and Larme. 'Surprised you two aren't trying to kill each other.'

'After we wrecked I called a truce in order to get as many of the passengers into yawls as I could,' said Drecht.

'What about the sailors your men are slaughtering on the beach?' snarled Larme.

'Only the injured ones,' Drecht said candidly. 'We discussed this. I don't have enough supplies for the living. I'll not waste any on the almost dead.' Those blue eyes found Sammy in Arent's arms. 'Does he draw breath?'

'Yes, and you're not having him,' grunted Arent. 'Have you seen Sara?'

'Put her in the boat myself,' said Drecht. 'She's helping the injured. Come, I'll take you.'

Drecht drew him further down the shingle, following the curve of the coast. Larme trailed behind.

'What happened after we ran aground?' asked Arent.

'God took a side,' said Drecht, his lips tightening. He turned towards the wreck of the *Saardam*, speared by the rock. A huge crack was widening down her middle, her timbers shuddering under the sea's endless assault. Arent had watched

477

men suffer the same way, torn open and breathing still, shivering as the heat deserted their bodies. It was an ignoble end, especially for something once so grand.

'Most of the sailors were still on the waist and orlop decks,' continued Drecht. 'The rock that skewered us killed nearly all of them, leaving my men untouched. Old Tom's disciples are decimated.'

'And a lot of good men alongside them,' said Larme, seething at Drecht's victorious tone.

Drecht led them into a large cave, filled with groaning, half-shattered bodies. It ran deep into the island and was surprisingly cool, a salty breeze coming out of the darkness like the breath of a slumbering beast.

There were around twenty people inside, and none of them had survived easy. They cradled broken arms and hobbled on broken legs. They were gashed, gaunt and pale, their faces obscured by dried blood, their eyes misty with confusion and pain.

Arent found a patch of space and laid Sammy down, gently as a babe in its crib, then sought out Sara. She was moving among the injured with a pocketknife, digging wooden shards out of their bodies with no more fuss than if she were picking worms from a bushel of apples.

'I'm going to organise a rescue boat,' said Drecht. 'We're only three weeks out of Batavia. The storm's blown us badly off course, but I'm optimistic we'll be able to find a friendly ship.' Larme snorted his derision for this plan, but Drecht ignored him and carried on talking. 'We're forming a council to make decisions about our survival once we know who's survived. I'd like you two to be part of it.'

'Aye, sounds like a good idea,' said Arent.

'Then come find me when you're finished here.'

'Arent!' He turned into a flurry of arms, legs and red hair, as Sara pulled his face down to hers and kissed him. It was desperate and passionate, and enough to make a man forget he'd ever been kissed before.

Sammy had once told him that love was the easiest thing to spot, because it didn't look like anything else. It couldn't hide itself, it couldn't disguise itself, it couldn't go unnoticed for very long. Arent had never really understood what that had meant until now.

She caressed his cheek. 'I thought you were dead.'

He pulled her close, relieved and ecstatic, feeling the warmth of her body against his own. His ribs screamed, but he cared not.

'Did Lia and Creesjie … are they …' he asked tentatively, searching the cave for them.

'Both came over by boat. They're tending to the injured,' said Sara, pointing to a gloomy corner where they were tearing strips of clothing into bandages with Isabel.

She clutched him tighter.

How long they stayed like that, neither knew, but eventually Sara pulled away, placing both hands flat against his chest, searching his face tenderly, before alighting on Sammy.

Kneeling down, she began to examine his eye and other injuries.

'Will he be okay, Sara?'

'I'll do what I can, but I don't think the wounds are your problem. Drecht is killing the injured to save supplies.'

'He swore to let Sammy be.'

'Aye, and he swore not to jam a sword through Crauwels's chest, but he did it anyway,' said Larme, squinting at the distant figure of the guard captain. 'And don't think he'll stop

479

at the injured. Once he can't feed the living, he'll start killing anybody he thinks isn't useful to him, and I know where a dwarf sits in that pecking order.'

Arent felt a tiredness building inside of him. It was never going to end, was it? They were never going to stop butchering each other. Jacobi Drecht hadn't even paused to wipe the blood off his hands after the mutiny. That first night on the *Saardam*, the guard captain had told them he didn't believe in devils because men didn't need to an excuse to commit evil. Arent had thought it was a lament, but now he realised it was a confession. He'd simply looked inside and told them what he'd found.

Arent could almost laugh. If Old Tom had brought them here to suffer, it need only let them alone. They'd do the work for no pay, and with twice the glee of any other devils.

He sighed. 'What do you want from me, Larme?'

'I want you to kill Drecht, you daft bastard. And I want you to do it quickly.'

'It won't work,' said Arent. 'Drecht's the only one keeping the musketeers from running wild. If he dies, the rest of us won't be long after him.'

'Then we need to get control of his men,' said Sara.

'Aye,' said Arent, staring at the musketeers gathering supplies near the water. 'How hard can that be?'

75

ARENT LEFT THE CAVE and returned to the makeshift camp. Small fires had been lit under the tree
canopy, surrounded by passengers trying to dry off. The rain
was almost mist, but a few minutes in its company was enough
to make everything dripping wet.

Musketeers were dragging bodies into piles, while others
pried the lids off the salvaged casks and crates to make an
inventory of their supplies. They called out what they found
to the constable, who was adding it to a tally. Seeing Arent,
the constable threw him a small salute.

'A crate of cured lamb.'

'Two crates of tack.'

'Three barrels of ale.'

'Four jugs of brandy.'

'Two jars of wine.'

'Tallow wax and twine.'

'Hatchets, hammers and long nails.'

It was a pauper's load, thought Arent. Enough to sustain
them for days, not weeks.

Two yawls were crossing the rough water, returning from
the wreck. Evidently Drecht had sent men out to claim the
last of the *Saardam*'s supplies and whatever treasure was left.

Arent and Larme found Drecht sitting on a piece of driftwood, rain tapping on his hat, his legs crossed at the ankles.

'Where's your council?' Arent asked Drecht.

'We're it, and now you're here, I'll call it convened,' said Drecht, tipping the brim of his hat to dislodge the rain that had built up.

'We should convene everybody,' said Arent, frowning. 'There's few of us left and these matters effect everybody.'

Larme coughed. 'You'll want to hear what he has to say before you decide that.'

Drecht fixed his icy eyes on Arent. 'Most of what we've salvaged will keep us warm and dry, but unless we can eat nails and drink tar, we'll still be going to sleep with empty bellies.' He ran a pink tongue around his salty lips. 'Nineteen musketeers survived. Twenty-two sailors and forty passengers, including yourself. We can't feed them all, which means hard decisions need to be taken about our resources.'

He gave that a moment to sink in, staring meaningfully at them.

'The musketeers under my command are murderers and cutpurses, but they're skilled at surviving, capable of hunting and tracking. These are the men who will keep us alive. My control of them is not absolute, especially when the rations start running low. Sooner or later, they're going to decide to take what they want rather than wait to be given it. The clever move is to offer it to them in return for obedience.'

Drecht flashed a look towards the women, gathering firewood at the tree edge.

'You're offering rape as a reward,' growled Arent.

'Not them as married, or promised,' interrupted Drecht quickly. 'That wouldn't be Christian. Come now, see the good sense before you, Arent. Sara and you have a bond, I've seen it myself. She'd be spared, as would Lia. And you Isaack, take your pick.'

Arent felt sick. Old Tom had won. It had sought to draw out the very worst of everybody on the *Saardam*, and, here, at last, it had succeeded. It didn't even need to bargain any more. They were dreaming up their own sins, and their own rewards.

'What about Creesjie Jens?' he said witheringly. 'I suppose you'll make the sacrifice and wed her yourself?'

'I have a wife in Drenthe. I don't need another,' said Drecht distantly.

'What do you have to say on this, Larme?' demanded Arent.

'Why does that matter?' Larme stared at them balefully. 'I've a handful of sailors left. Most of them are injured, and none of them are armed. It's his musketeers we have to worry about. I'm just here to make this seem fair.'

'But what do you think?' demanded Arent.

'I think it's the vilest thing I've ever heard,' he said, glaring at Drecht. 'And I think he's going to do it whatever we say.'

'He's right,' agreed Drecht, without shame. 'I've got the strength, which means I have the power. And I know it's the right thing to do. These passengers respect you, Arent. It would go easier if I could make the announcement with you at my side.'

'What if I say no? Where will I be standing then?'

'As far away from my sabre as possible, if you're wise.'

They stared at each other, finding themselves right back where they'd started on the *Saardam* that first morning, waiting to see who'd run who through first.

'I want Sara and Lia,' said Arent solemnly. 'And Isaack has to agree to wed Creesjie, though not touch her. She can't be left to your men.'

The former guard captain searched his face for some hint of deception, but Arent had been withstanding the attentions of Sammy for years. He saw only irate compliance.

'On your honour?' He held out his hand.

Arent shook it. 'Aye.'

Drecht blew out a breath in relief, unable to conceal his pleasure. 'I wasn't looking forward to that conversation, Arent, but I'm glad you've seen reason. We need to make sure we have all the supplies secured. Once that's done, we'll tell our plan to the passengers. I recommend tomorrow morning, after a hard night on short rations has made clear to everybody what we face.'

'I'll need one more thing before that happens,' said Arent, as they got ready to depart. 'I want Sammy on the rescue boat.'

Larme sucked his teeth. 'It's a fool's dash that,' he said. 'We have no navigators left worth the name. Whoever goes, they'll have few supplies and no bearing to guide them. They're hoping for fine weather and good fortune, neither of which we've had in abundance.'

'Sammy's injuries are severe. He'll die here, or he'll die out there. I would have him away from this place, with the chance of rescue.'

'If that's your wish, then so be it,' said Drecht. 'I doubt anybody will object. Larme, I'm leaving you in charge of finding a crew for the rescue boat.'

'Oh, aye,' he said witheringly. 'Reckon there'll be a clamour for a berth on a doomed vessel, do you?'

'No, which means you should start thinking about which men you're happy to send to their death.' His face was grave. 'We're in command now, gentlemen. There aren't any easy decisions left.'

76

S ARA EMERGED WEARY FROM the cave, staring at her fingers with a profound sense of satisfaction.

Three weeks ago, she'd boarded the *Saardam*, hidden so deeply under layers of etiquette and hatred that she'd almost forgotten who she was. But somewhere between the horrors of the storm and the torments of Old Tom, she'd discovered herself again, like a dusty mirror under a shroud. Amidst all of this misery she was as happy as she could remember being. For the last several hours, she'd practised her healing without being told it was beneath her station, or an affront to her dignity. She'd kissed Arent openly. She'd been able to go where she wanted, and say what she wanted, and let Lia be as clever as she wanted to be without having to reprimand her.

None of this would be possible once they returned to Amsterdam.

Guard Captain Drecht had seized the plans to The Folly, leaving Sara without anything to trade for her freedom. Lia could probably recreate it, but it would take years of work, and she wouldn't be given time. She was of marriageable age, and Sara's father would immediately seek a good match.

Sara would be chaperoned to the three places she was allowed to go, while her father chose her next husband from a list of suitors she'd never even met. The thought of it made her want to walk into the sea.

'Sara,' whispered Arent urgently, striding down the shoal.

She turned, her smile at his presence quickly banished by the grim expression on his face.

'What's wrong?'

'Fetch Lia and Creesjie,' he said. 'I have some bad news.'

'You never bring me any other kind,' she chided gently. 'Creesjie's trying to coax the boys into napping. Whatever it is I'll tell her later. I'd like Isabel to hear, though.'

'Do you trust her?'

'I do. She's pregnant, Arent. Whatever's happening, she should be part of it.'

He nodded and she quickly delivered Lia and Isabel. After ensuring they went unobserved, he harried them up the verge and into the treeline, out of sight. Once they were ensconced in the jungle, he explained Drecht's plan.

'A brothel?' whispered Sara, in disgust.

The rain was falling hard and the musketeers were busy building shelters for the cargo and sharpening sticks for hunting, but they were also casting hungry glances at a group of women knotting fishing nets on the shoal.

'When will he do it?' asked Lia, wiping wet hair from her eyes. She was sodden and shivering, wearing the shawl she'd left the *Saardam* in. There were no more clothes to give her, forcing Sara to wrap herself around her like blanket.

'They're going tell everybody the plan tomorrow,' said Arent. 'Probably with their hands on their swords while they do it.'

486

Isabel placed her hand to her stomach in horror.

'Then we all need to flee tonight,' said Lia. 'Can we hide in the forest?'

'That's the idea,' said Arent. 'I'm going to scout it this afternoon, and see if we can find some caves to fortify. Can you spread the word among the passengers, tell them to get ready? Drecht's planning to hand out some jugs of wine to reward his men's labours. Once they're drunk, we'll slip away.'

'And then what? Drecht has all the rations and the weapons,' said Sara. 'He'll find us eventually.'

A dangerous, reckless anger burnt in her voice.

'We can't fight, Sara,' warned Arent. 'It would be suicide.'

'Fight today or die tomorrow, what difference does it make?' she said fiercely.

'Because if we flee today, we might find a way to flee tomorrow and the day after, until rescue comes,' said Arent. 'Surviving isn't winning. It's what you do when you've lost. Besides, this is Old Tom's island. We were brought here for a purpose, which means the Eighth Lantern won't be far behind.'

That brought a glint to Sara's eyes. 'You think we can seize a ghost ship?'

'After everything it's done to us, I think a ride back to Batavia is the least it can do.'

Giddy excitement crackled between them.

Somewhere distant, Drecht called Arent's name. He was walking down the shoal, hands cupped to his mouth, searching for the mercenary.

'I have to go,' said Arent.

'You should know, not all the passengers will come with us,' said Sara.

Arent looked stunned. 'What? Why?'

'Some of them will think Drecht's offer is fair, either because it doesn't affect them, or because they think living is worth the price.'

'I don't understand.'

'That's because you've never had to,' said Sara, her hair blowing around her face. 'Don't worry, we'll try to spread the word only amongst the sympathetic. Just know we won't be saving everybody.'

They looked at each other frankly. They had believed they would die on the boat. Now they believed they would die here. There were no barriers any more, no secrets. The *Saardam* had taken much, but at least it had also taken those.

'Then we'll save who we can,' he said.

77

A NCIENT BRANCHES CLAWED AT Arent's cheeks
as he headed into the deep jungle. Nothing stirred,
even the sea breeze couldn't worm its way in here. Arent had
told Drecht he was going hunting, but, secretly, he wanted
to scout out an escape route for the passengers. If all went
well, they'd slip away quietly in the night, but when it all
went wrong, he'd want to know what they were being chased
towards. This was Old Tom's island. Whatever it had planned
for them was in this jungle. He didn't want them stumbling
on it blind.

The interior of the island was a strange, twisted place. Tree
trunks split at the base, the sections reaching into the air like
the fingers of some monstrous beast. There were huge red
flowers standing half his height from the ground, each one
a collection of fleshy threads, sticky enough to catch the flies
that landed on them. Butterflies the size of petals thrashed
inelegantly through the air, while petals the size of plates
shaded him from the worst of the sun's heat.

Unseen creatures were skittering through the under-
growth, claws clambering through the branches. During his
first hour in here, he'd thought every one of those noises had
an empty belly and ideas about his throat. He'd nearly run

back to the shoal, which was reason enough to keep moving forward. Fear was too brittle a material to make good decisions from.

Sweat rolled down his face, the air so humid it seemed to hang from the branches. He sucked breaths in wet lumps, his body in agony.

Sara hadn't wanted him to go by himself. She'd argued and protested, demanding she come along. It had taken every argument he had to convince her he'd be safer alone, moving quickly and quietly.

The last person to care for him like that was his uncle.

Loss grew like a bubble in his gut.

It made no sense, he thought. He wasn't a boy any more, and the man he'd met in Batavia wasn't the same man who'd raised him. He'd beaten Sara. He'd slaughtered the population of the Banda Islands. He'd consorted with a devil. He'd locked Sammy in a cell, which would certainly have killed him.

These were the acts of a monster, and yet … deep down, Arent still loved him. He grieved his death. Why would that be? How could that be?

Wiping the tears from his eyes, he pressed on, noticing a trail of broken branches. Somebody had passed through here. A few steps further on, the trail widened. This hadn't been done recently, thought Arent. The hacked branches had already started healing.

The trail stretched out ahead of him. This was the work of months, by a dozen or more men.

He followed it cautiously, finally entering a large clearing, where three long log huts had been built around a stone well, with a pail lying by its side. Keeping to the treeline, he searched for inhabitants, but there was nobody around. There hadn't been for months, to judge by the huge spiderwebs spun across the doors and shutters.

Arent darted out of the trees and pressed himself to the wall of the nearest hut, working his way around to a set of shutters. He tried tugging them open, but they were latched from the inside.

He carried on to the door, which was in full view of the other huts. There was still nobody around, and the muddy ground didn't show any footprints.

It was deserted.

'Or abandoned,' he muttered, opening the nearest door and stepping into the gloom, disturbing the spiders which skittered into the thatched roof. Inside were thirty double bunks in orderly rows, though they didn't appear to have been slept in for some time.

There was another door at the far end of the hut, which he headed for. On the way, he spotted a mother-of-pearl button on the floor, a piece of thread still tangled in its hole. It was expensive, the sort of thing Crauwels might have worn. 'Someone was living here,' he said to himself, blowing dust from it. He stared at the bunks. 'A lot of somebodies,' he added.

His heart began to thud.

He opened the second door with more confidence. Beyond it was a supply room. Shelves were filled with bulging sacks, crates and clay pots stoppered with corks.

Taking a clay pot down, he jiggled the cork loose and sniffed the contents.

'Wine,' he murmured.

The lid of the crate had been hammered shut, but he drove his elbow into its centre, cracking the wood. Using his fingers, he pried the shards away to find it filled with salted beef. Another contained tack.

His dagger ripped open the top of the nearest sack, revealing the barley within. There was enough food here to feed the survivors of the *Saardam* for weeks.

He let the grains run through his hand.

This was Old Tom's island, so this was likely where it intended to berth his new followers. They'd be warm and well fed, and would likely be grateful.

Arent's fist closed, holding the last of the barley tight. This wasn't right.

Old Tom wouldn't build this. What did a devil care for gratitude? The daemonologica described a creature intent on slaughter and destruction that left nothing behind except depravity. Its followers were sent into the world to cause suffering. Nothing mentioned two solid meals and a good night's sleep first.

No king he'd fought for had ever treated his soldiers this well. They got stinking stew and dirty old blankets in the mud.

Troubled, Arent left the hut and lifted the cover off the well. Aside from a few dead insects, the water was clean. Cupping his hand, he tried it. It was sweet and refreshing. After splashing some on his face to cool down, he inspected the other huts.

Both were equally well provisioned.

There was room for hundreds of people in this camp and the huts must have been stocked recently, because nothing would keep long in this heat. Drecht had butchered the injured for nothing. This food and ale would keep the survivors alive for months, if they required it.

Going back outside, he walked slowly around the buildings, unable to comprehend such benevolence.

Offcuts of wood, chunks of beam and broken crates had been discarded at the treeline and closing the distance, he realised there was more detritus behind. Nails spilled on to the jungle floor from an upturned box and wooden poles had been stacked against the thick trunk of a tree. Picking his way through the mess, he pressed deeper into the jungle, finding sheets of tattered sailcloth and then a badly damaged yawl.

It was concealed by massive leaves, and he would have walked right by it except that a few had fallen away, revealing the wooden hull beneath. Tearing free the remaining leaves, he inspected the boat. The seats had been ripped out to make room for a huge triangular frame, which must have fallen over. Arent could still see the nails where it had wrenched away from the hull, smashing one entire side of the yawl.

The frame had taken up the entire boat, but there was nothing to suggest what its purpose might have been.

He stared at it for a few minutes, before walking back to the huts.

Thirsty, he returned to the well and took another drink, spotting a sword hilt poking out of the mud. It came free with a satisfying plop, revealing a broken blade. He washed it in the pail, finding very little of interest. It was made of steel and had a basket handle, two sharp edges and a pointy end. Like all swords it was great for killing and terrible for shaving. It didn't tell him anything about the people who'd built the huts, except that they didn't take very good care of their weapons. The edges were chipped and rust had eaten through the blade.

That's why it had snapped so cleanly. The best way to kill a man with this would be to hope he tripped on it and hit his head on a rock.

He listened to the jungle rustle. This was the second badly made weapon he'd seen in the last few days. At least this had a proper blade unlike the leper's dagger. That had basically been a shard of thin metal and a wooden handle. It was almost …

'Decorative …' he said slowly, as his thoughts bumped into a very large idea.

Old Tom had told Sara, Creesjie and Lia that it would leave a dagger under the governor general's bunk for them to kill him with, and the leper had made sure Arent got a good look at the blade. Why?

The beautiful thing about fear this large is that nobody will look beyond it. Vos had said that when he tried to kill him. The chamberlain had carved the Mark of Old Tom on the wood knowing there wouldn't be any questions asked once it was found. What if somebody was trusting the same thinking to disguise the dagger's true nature? *Aye, it wasn't much of a weapon, but don't worry about that because it belongs to a demon. You've seen its servant holding it, after all.*

But what if the dagger wasn't the murder weapon?

Realistically, it couldn't be. The cabin had been locked. Nobody had entered after the governor general had gone to bed. The only person who could have done it was Jacobi Drecht, but he was a professional soldier. If he'd killed the governor general, he'd have used a real weapon. He wouldn't have trusted the leper's dagger to do the job. Nobody would have. And they hadn't.

It was decoration.

An idea came, then another, and another, and another. How did you kill somebody without entering their cabin? What weapon could do it? Who'd wield it?

'It can't be ...' he said out loud, as the answers arrived in a dizzying rush. 'It can't be ...'

S ARA PLACED HENRI'S LIFELESS hand on his chest.
This was the carpenter's mate who'd first told her
about Bosey when they boarded. A piece of exploding hull
had smashed into his chest, crushing everything inside. He'd
drawn breath long enough to be placed in a yawl and brought
to the island by his mates, but there was no healing this sort
of injury. The best she could do was offer comfort, as she had
to Bosey on the docks.

Getting to her feet, Sara wiped away the pebbles that had
collected on her skirt and stared around the cave, sorrow
opening a hole in her heart. Nearly everybody who'd been
brought here had died. Those few who survived wailed in
agony, begging for their loved ones. Some would die soon,
others would linger. Neither had anything to do with Sara,
who'd accomplished everything she could with what she had
available.

God had His own plans for these people. She could only
pray they were merciful. After everything they'd been through,
they deserved that much, at least.

Unable to bear the suffering any longer, she stepped
into the grey rain and across the shoal to the water's edge,

standing just beyond the reaching fingers of surf. Behind her, above the ridge, the trees rustled, bringing a shiver of dread.

This was Old Tom's island, and it had brought them here for some terrible purpose. Whatever its secret, it was likely waiting for them in that jungle, and yet Arent had disappeared inside as if taking himself to the market.

She'd never met a braver man. Not that he'd accepted her compliment. There wasn't courage in doing what was necessary, he'd said.

She sighed. It wasn't going to be easy loving a man like that.

Kneeling down, Sara washed her hands in the sea and stared at the distant wreck of the *Saardam*. The huge crack down the middle had widened, exposing the cargo hold within. Planks were tumbling from its sides into the water and seabirds whirled above it, like crows circling a dead cow.

A yawl was returning filled with casks of treasure. They'd been bringing them over for hours, loading them in a pile under the treeline, a little further down from the other supplies. Even from here she could see the chalices and chains, golden plates, jewels and jewellery. Surely, this was the secret cargo her husband had instructed Reynier van Schooten to bring aboard quietly.

Van Schooten, she remembered with a start.

She hadn't seen the chief merchant since the mutiny. He hadn't been in the cave, or on the lifeboat. She looked along the coast anxiously, but the bodies had been piled under a sheet, awaiting burial. Every so often, the ocean would deliver fresh dead, the push and pull of the surf giving their limbs a strange, twitching life. No doubt Van Schooten would wash up eventually.

Sara watched the musketeers drag the yawl up the beach and unload a dozen crates on to the beach, carelessly spilling gold coins, ornate plates, necklaces, diamonds and rubies. The musketeers laughed and left them there. Who would bother stealing them, they jested.

Grunting, they picked up a crate and carried it towards the camp, leaving the rest unguarded.

Sara stared at the piled-high treasure.

This was the same sort of treasure Vos had been trying to hide when Arent confronted him. The chamberlain must have stolen it from her husband – that's why he admitted to been a thief when accused, even though he hadn't stolen The Folly.

But why did her *husband* have it? He was a merchant. He traded spices for gold. He didn't barter for chalices and plates, no matter how valuable they were.

Sara walked over and examined the pile. Picking up plates and cups, she inspected them for markings. Sure enough, she found the crest of the Dijksma family, just as she had on the objects Vos had stolen.

But there were more crests among them.

Tugging an ornate sword from its sheath, she discovered the crest of a lion holding a sword and arrows, a banner flying overhead proclaiming *Honor et Ars* in Latin.

'Honour and cunning,' she muttered. This was the herald of the de Haviland family. Surely, it was no coincidence Emily de Haviland had been aboard the *Saardam*.

She kept digging, finding coats of arms belonging to the Van de Ceulens and the Bos family. These were all families Pieter Fletcher had saved from Old Tom's evil.

Why would her husband have this? He'd admitted to summoning Old Tom – could this have been why? To rob them?

Not rob, she realised with a flash of insight. That wasn't her husband's way. What if he'd done to these families what he'd done to her father, Cornelius Vos and countless others over the course of his life. Ruin them, belittle them, then leave them alive to suffer their fall.

According to the daemonologica, these families had all been traders, merchants and shipbuilders. People her husband would have needed or been in competition with while he was building his business thirty years ago. What if he'd summoned Old Tom and set it loose on them?

Pieter Fletcher had thwarted the scheme, then her husband had Old Tom kill him in revenge.

Except …

A memory grew nails and began scratching at her. The first time she'd seen the picture of Pieter Fletcher in Creesjie's cabin, she'd been bothered by it. He'd been resplendent in his beautiful clothes, standing in front of their manor house. He'd even been able to afford Creesjie, the natural consort of kings.

In contrast, Sander Kers had been dressed in rags and, by his own admission, he'd had to beg his congregation for alms to board the *Saardam*.

Witchfinding wasn't a profession you grew rich doing. Yet, somehow, Pieter Fletcher had.

Creesjie was helping Isabel gather firewood when Sara caught up with her. Sara was breathless, and had to take a minute before asking her question.

'Did Pieter …' she panted. '… Was he … nobility? Did he come from money?'

Creesjie laughed grimly. 'Witchfinders don't come from money,' she said. 'It was a reward for his good works from the families he saved.'

No, it wasn't, Sara thought. Rewards were given willingly. The governor general had set Old Tom loose on these families, destroying the reputations of his competition, and blackmailing those who could be useful to him. Then, when they'd agreed to his terms, he'd dispatched Pieter Fletcher to 'banish' Old Tom and convince everybody the demon was really gone.

But her husband left his enemies alive. He always did. He enjoyed watching them suffer.

And one of them had found him.

When Sara had found the book in Viscountess Dalvhain's cabin, she'd believed it was a mockery of the daemonologica, but what if it had actually been a true account of what had happened all those years ago. Old Tom had destroyed the de Havilands, leaving only Emily alive. She'd grown up seeking revenge. She would have witnessed Pieter Fletcher's actions first-hand and dedicated herself to tracking him down. She had found him in Amsterdam, married to Creesjie and father to two boys. Somehow, he'd recognised her and fled, but she'd followed him to Lille. She'd tortured him, uncovering his conspirators. That would have led her to Sander Kers and the governor general.

No wonder her husband never took off that damn breastplate. No wonder he'd hidden himself away in Batavia, surrounded by high walls and guards.

How did you kill a man that well protected? *By luring him out*, she thought.

The predikant had received the fake letter from Pieter Fletcher two years ago, instructing him to sail for the city. Her husband had received the fake ascension order from Arent's grandfather a month before they boarded the *Saardam*.

'Laxagarr is Nornish for trap,' she muttered, eyeing the wreck again.

Emily had marked the sail so Sara's husband would know his past had found him. She had left the anagram and the book so he'd know exactly who was to blame. Old Tom brought suffering, and Emily had ensured Jan Haan suffered for what he'd done.

Sara darted on to the shoal, searching desperately for Arent. The ideas were so big her head felt like it would collapse under the weight.

She had to tell him what she suspected.

He was walking down the beach, casting frantic glances around. Upon seeing her, relief showed on his face.

They charged towards each other, Sara taking hold of Arent's arms.

'I know why this is happening,' she said frantically.

His eyes went wide. 'Good, because I know who's doing it.'

79

'T HIS IS A VERY bad plan,' said Arent as they approached the *Saardam* in a yawl. The wreck loomed above them, the exposed hull covered in barnacles and seaweed. Fingers of sunlight poked through the cracks in the cargo hold, revealing the seabirds already nesting in her ribs. She was monstrous from this vantage, like some terrible beast laid down to die.

'Well, you didn't have time to come up with a merely bad plan,' responded Sara, who was perched at the bow of the boat, keeping watch for the shallows. 'Besides, we have to make sure we're right. And this is the only place to do it.'

The sea was choppy and Arent was having to work hard at the oars to keep from crashing into the jagged rocks. They'd told Drecht they were recovering Sara's harp, something they couldn't trust anybody else to do. Having listened to her play the instrument for hours every day in the fort, he'd accepted the excuse unquestioningly.

Arent held the boat steady while Sara leapt out. Tugging the oars inside, he scrambled on to the rocks, then dragged the yawl out of the water. The passengers had disembarked here this morning and the rope ladder still hung down from the waist.

Waves crashed against the rocks, throwing sea spray into the air, soaking them both. Struggling to keep his feet, Arent walked towards the aft, looking up at the spot where his uncle's cabin bulged out of the hull.

The leper's handprints were so small, they could easily have been mistaken for dirt, until he was up close. They ran from the waterline to his uncle's cabin and then past Sara's cabin to the poop deck.

'We assumed the leper punched those holes in the hull when it climbed up, but what if they were already there when we boarded?' said Arent. 'Everybody embarked on the other side of the ship, so nobody would have noticed them in the harbour.'

'A ladder, you mean? Do you think Bosey built it?'

'I do,' said Arent. 'He told Sander back in Batavia that he was making the boat ready for his master. I think this is part of what he meant.'

They walked into the cargo hold through a crack in the hull, the sickly sweet smell of rot immediately engulfing them. The spear of rock that had ended the mutiny in Drecht's favour sheared straight up through the hull. It was stained with spices.

A few jewels sparkled here and there in the bilge water, having been missed by Drecht's musketeers.

'Why did my uncle bring the treasure to Batavia?' wondered Arent, picking up an amethyst and shaking the drops from it.

'Where could he have left it without risking it being stolen, or questions being asked?' replied Sara. 'Aside from the jewels, nearly every piece bore the crest of a great family fallen to ruin.'

'He could have sold the gems and melted down the rest.'

'You really didn't know my husband at the end, did you?' There was pity in her voice. 'He probably dipped into his hoard when he needed money for some endeavour, but he wouldn't have seen any of this as treasure. They were trophies. Mementos of his victories, no different to Vos and I. He liked to collect his victims and put us on display.'

As if it were suddenly hot, Arent tipped his palm, letting the amethyst splash back into the dirty water.

Without another word, they took the staircase up to the orlop deck, which was slippery with blood. Seabirds feasted on the remains of the dead.

Sara had expected them to go straight to the passenger cabins, but Arent pushed open the door to the gunpowder store. Kegs had spilled gunpowder across the floor, but it was damp and harmless. The constable's charm lay among some wooden fragments, having evidently been torn from his neck in the panic of the mutiny.

'What are you looking for?' asked Sara.

'Nothing on this voyage happened by accident,' he replied distantly, wiping gunpowder from the charm before pocketing it. He'd return it to the constable later. 'The ship was a trap, designed to murder my uncle. Everything was planned years in advance.'

'Including the three unholy miracles,' said Sara.

'Only crew members could have rolled the kegs containing The Folly out of here,' said Arent.

'Then we're after three people.'

'Two,' he disagreed. 'Captain Crauwels had to be involved. If Emily de Haviland always intended to bring us to this island, then he was the only one who could have ensured that happened. He was the ship's navigator.'

'Maybe The Folly was his payment,' said Sara. 'It was valuable enough. It almost bought Lia and I an entirely new life. Crauwels was obsessed with restoring his family's name. If he sold The Folly, he could have done that.'

'He knew when the Eighth Lantern would appear, so he knew when he'd be calling battle stations. He just needed a couple of trusted hands ready to take the kegs containing The Folly down to the cargo hold, and hide them in the smuggling compartments Bosey had built. If we're right about Emily's identity, she could have easily stolen the key to The Folly's box.'

They stared at each other, feeling the sting of the revelation.

'Do you think Isaack Larme would have been involved?' he asked Sara abruptly.

'Why?'

'Because I've got a plan he could help me with, but he was close to Crauwels. They may have worked together.'

'I don't think so,' said Sara. 'He admitted to finding a piece of The Folly hidden in one of his smuggling compartments, but he said he couldn't find the rest. Remember how disappointed he sounded. If he was working with Crauwels, why would he have confessed any of that?'

The steps upstairs were broken, forcing them to tread cautiously. The compartment under the half deck sloped towards the helm, and the dead were piled up against its wall. Aside from the bodies, the signs of battle were everywhere, from the gouges in the wood, to the swords still stuck in planks.

The rock had torn through the ship's waist, obliterating everything upon it, including the mainmast, which was now in the sea, connected to the ship only by the rigging.

'Reminds me of a severed arm,' said Sara in disgust.

Arent was silent. Here was the battlefield he thought he'd escaped.

'Should we start in the passenger cabins?' said Sara, sounding sick. 'If we're right …'

'I know,' he said sympathetically. 'I feel the same.'

They went silently, almost unwillingly, up the stairs into the passenger cabins. The fighting hadn't reached this part of the ship. Guard Captain Drecht had made sure to station men at the door. Honour had compelled him to protect Sara and Lia, even as a lack of honour had compelled him to start the mutiny that had endangered them.

Arent couldn't imagine being able to think like that. His mind must have been twisted like old rope.

They went into Vos's cabin first, but Arent remained at the threshold. Arms crossed, he watched as Sara searched through the receipts of passage on the writing desk, then picked an expenses ledger off the ground. She flipped through a few pages, then ran her hand down the columns.

Finally, she thumped it shut angrily. The glance she flashed him confirmed everything they'd suspected.

Arent's heart fell like a rock.

Crossing the corridor, they entered Viscountess Dalvhain's cabin, Sara's foot catching on the huge rug covering the ground.

Arent immediately knelt down, touching the weave with his fingers and murmuring. 'So this is how they got it onboard.'

'The wooden stick?'

He blinked at her. 'What?'

'I was in the corridor when they tried to wedge this rug into the cabin. They broke a long, thin wooden stick that was inside.'

'No.' His brow furrowed. 'That wasn't what I meant. Look.'

He ran his hand across the carpet. Squinting, she realised what he'd found. It was sliced, like somebody had dragged a blade across it.

'The damage runs the length of the rug,' he said.

'What caused it?'

'The murder weapon,' he said, struggling to balance the satisfaction of being right with the revulsion it caused in him.

'That's a big blade,' she said, with understatement.

'It had to be,' he said. 'My uncle was a long way away.'

The ship wailed, wood shrieking as the ground shifted beneath their feet. 'She's tearing apart,' said Sara, bracing herself.

Without speaking they hurried into Sara's cabin, where Arent lifted the mattress off her bunk. Something about his presence near her bed caused her to turn slightly red, despite the circumstances.

'The leper's dagger used to kill my uncle made no sense,' he said, searching the base beneath the mattress with his fingertips. 'It was too thin, which meant it was too brittle to be a good weapon. But clever murder weapons are nearly always bad weapons, Sammy showed me that. Nobody going into battle would trust the venom from a snake, or a sharp piece of pottery. Murderers make their own weapons, according to their needs.'

'And our murderer needed a weapon which could be used without anybody entering or leaving the cabin,' said Sara.

'Exactly. My uncle died in his bunk, so I started thinking about weapons that could reach him while he slept.'

He moved away, gesturing to the spot he'd been inspecting. 'Here.'

Barely noticeable in the dark wood was a narrow slit about the size of her little finger.

'Sammy found splinters on my uncle's chest,' said Arent. 'He reckoned they were from the wooden handle of the leper's dagger, but they weren't. They were from this hole. My uncle's cabin is directly beneath us, and I bet this hole appears above his bunk. It had to be thin or he would have noticed it. Even if he spotted this, he would have mistaken it for a crack in the wood. Emily de Haviland had a long, thin blade built to fit through it. She hid it in the rug because that was the only way to get something that unusual onboard without anybody commenting on it. She took the blade out of the rug, pulled the drawers out from underneath the bunk, then drove it down through this slot, killing my uncle. When she was done, she pulled the blade back up, put the drawers back, and threw it out of the porthole.'

'I think I heard it,' said Sara. 'The night my husband –' she reconsidered '– Jan died. I was tending you, and heard a splash outside.'

'She must have been glad you weren't in your cabin,' replied Arent. 'This was originally supposed to be her room, but Reynier van Schooten swapped you around because he thought this place cursed.'

'If all of the passengers were in the great cabin having dinner when Jan was murdered and the doorway to the passenger cabins was guarded by Eggert, how did our murderer even get in here?'

Crauwels's cabin was at the end of the passage and they went there now. His fine clothes were strewn across the floor, floating in the water that had splashed through his porthole during the wreck. Arent kicked through some ribbons, then pushed on the ceiling, which opened into the animal pens above, straw falling onto his shoulders.

'This is how the Eighth Lantern slaughtered the animals, and this is where the leper disappeared when I chased him after he appeared at your porthole,' he said. 'The night of my uncle's murder, the leper climbed out of the water and straight up the side of the ship to the poop deck. He used this hatch to drop in here. He dried off and changed clothes, so he wouldn't leave any trace, then collected the sword and went to your cabin.'

Their final stop was the great cabin, where the huge table had tipped on to its sides. The windows were smashed, the raging sea slate-grey beyond.

The governor general's cabin appeared as comfortable as it ever had, though his scrolls were now scattered across the room. His quill pot was upended, the wall and desk stained with ink.

Sara poked the narrow slit in the wood above her husband's bunk. 'But the handle of the dagger wouldn't fit through here,' she grumbled.

'I know,' he said. 'That's the clever part. That's why the candle's flame had to be snuffed, but I'm still not sure how that was done. There was no way to do it without entering the room, and it couldn't be done from the porthole because the desk was too far away.'

'I do,' said Sara, smiling. 'I saw it. Then I heard it being built.'

'I don't –'

'When were you last in church, Arent?'

'It's been a while,' he admitted.

'Have you ever seen those long-poled snuffers they use to put out the candles on the chandeliers?'

Realisation washed across his face.

'That pole I saw fall out of Viscountess Dalvhain's rug was a candle snuffer.' She went to the porthole, looking up at the three widely spaced hooks above it that Sammy had spotted after her husband died. 'The leper was probably supposed to collect it from Viscountess Dalvhain's room, then lay it on these hooks for when it was needed, but he didn't know our cabins had been swapped. That's why he was there that night.'

'But you said it got broken. Did they repair it?'

'No, they stole one of the handles from the capstan wheel in the cargo hold. I heard Johannes Wyck raging about it during the first sermon. Then they used a carpenter's plane to make it into a manageable size. Dorothea heard the noise when she was passing Dalvhain's cabin, but she couldn't place it. It was probably the only thing they could easily steal that was long enough.'

'To think,' said Arent, glumly. 'If they hadn't got their hands on that damn handle, there's a chance none of this would have happened.'

80

A RENT AND SARA SPENT the afternoon together, walking up and down the beach, making their plans. They held hands and spoke in a hush, frequently glancing at the *Saardam*.

Everybody left them alone.

Most had mistaken their pacing for romance, an idea swiftly put to the sword by their expressions. Such fury they hoped never to see again.

It wasn't until Jacob Drecht told them the rescue boat was ready to depart that they finally separated, each burdened by their dreadful purpose. Arent sought out Isaack Larme, who was sitting alone at the far end of the beach. He had found a new block of wood and restarted his whittling. He'd been trying to make a Pegasus for years, without any success.

Upon seeing the mercenary, he scowled, remembering how easily Arent had gone along with Drecht's brothel proposition, but his dismay evaporated when he listened to Arent's idea. By the time Arent finished talking, he was open-mouthed with surprise.

'I'd have to be insane to do what you ask,' he said, trying to make sense of it.

'If you don't, everybody dies,' argued Arent. He cast a glance towards Drecht, who was growing impatient, waiting by the rescue boat for him.

'And if I do, I likely die.' Larme eyed Drecht with disgust. 'But I would love a chance to piss in his hat.' He nodded. 'And I reckon that's reason enough. Where do you want me?'

'Furthest left,' replied Arent. Seeing Larme's confusion, he tapped his left hand for him. 'Portside, this one,' he said.

As Larme departed, Arent went to the cave where Sammy was murmuring on his mat. Sara had applied a poultice to his injured face and balmed it with the piss-smelling salve from his own alchemy kit.

Arent picked him up from the cave floor and carried him towards the rescue boat, where Thyman and Eggert were being given orders by Drecht.

'Ah, Arent, you no doubt know our volunteers,' he said.

'I do,' said Arent, acknowledging them. 'They brought Sammy onboard the *Saardam*. We had a little disagreement about their treatment of him. Seems fitting they should be the ones taking him home.'

He laid Sammy flat on a bench at the back of the yawl. He hadn't woken up and Arent was glad of it. He didn't know what to say. He was supposed to protect him, but he couldn't think how to do that any more. He felt like he'd failed.

'I've found a hut full of supplies in the forest,' said Arent, addressing Drecht. 'Salted meat, ale, everything. Enough to feed us for a few months, if needs be.'

'Truly!' Drecht's face lit up. 'That's a grand stroke of fortune, my friend. It must be a pirate's store. Not that I'll turn my nose up at provisions.'

Arent looked at the meagre supplies in the boat. 'I think we can spare these men a barrel more of ale, and some bread. Don't you? Their journey will be arduous.'

Drecht considered it, but nodded, happy to have Arent on side.

The supplies had been grouped at the treeline near the woods and Arent heaved a keg over his shoulder and picked up a basket of tack and dried meat, which he placed carefully into the boat.

Satisfied that he'd given them the best chance he could, he placed his large flat hand against the problematary's thin chest.

It was a coward's goodbye, but he had little else to offer.

Wishing Eggert and Thyman good fortune, he gripped the bow of the boat with both hands and single-handedly pushed it into the rough ocean.

Creesjie watched the rescue boat disappear over the horizon, overwhelmed by concern.

Marcus and Osbert were skipping rocks beside her. Being boys, they had recovered quickly from the shock of the mutiny and the wreck, and now believed themselves engaged on some grand adventure. She hoped she could always keep them so sheltered from fear.

513

Away to her left, she noticed Isabel walking towards her, a vacant expression on her face. She didn't know the girl very well, but she liked her. Since Sander's death she'd taken on many of his duties, showing a zeal that would have put her master to shame.

Crossing the slippery shoal, Isabel arrived at her side. She'd been speaking with Sara earlier on, and whatever she'd said had sent Sara away dismayed.

'Are you well, Isabel?' she asked, when the young girl didn't immediately acknowledge her presence. She was simply standing there, staring at the *Saardam*.

'Do you think Emily de Haviland died on that ship?' asked Isabel.

'I don't know,' replied Creesjie, unnerved by the flatness of her voice.

'Sander took me in when nobody else would,' said Isabel. 'He gave me a craft, he taught me how to battle evil, but I've failed him. I allowed him to be murdered, then Old Tom slaughtered everybody, just as Sander said he would.'

'Most of the passengers died in the wreck,' said Creesjie, unsure how to console her. 'I'm certain Emily must have been among them. We certainly haven't seen any old woman with long grey hair among the living.'

'Then Old Tom has found another host.'

'Isabel –'

'Who knows which of these men pledged themselves to its service before we ran aground,' she said ferociously. 'It could be curled up in any of their rotten souls.' Her eyes were wild, frightening. Her voice shook with righteous anger. Staring at her, Creesjie wondered if the wreck had shaken something adrift within the girl.

'I failed Sander on the *Saardam*, because I wasn't willing to do what was necessary,' said Isabel. 'I won't make that mistake again.'

'What are you planning?' said Creesjie fretfully, casting around for Sara.

'I won't let anybody else be hurt. Whatever I have to do, I won't let Old Tom leave this island.'

81

B Y THE TIME EVENING threw its cape across the island, two camps had been established.

Jacobi Drecht and the musketeers surrounded a huge pyre, jesting and drinking jugs of wine they'd looted from the huts Arent had found. The passengers had been invited to join them, but Sara had spread word of Drecht's plan, hardening most of their hearts. As she had predicted, though, a few of the passengers had joined Drecht anyway, and were happily carousing.

The rest of the passengers had built a much smaller camp-fire next to the treeline, sharing ale and roasted fish they'd caught earlier in the day. A ragged bit of sailcloth kept the swirling rain off their backs, but there was no disguising their misery. Chatter was muted, each person looking fearfully at the drunken musketeers, whose desires were revealed by the firelight.

The passengers knew what was coming – what was always coming when the strong were given free rein over the weak.

Only Isabel seemed oblivious.

Much to Creesjie's chagrin, the young woman was singing, dancing and making merry amongst the musketeers, pouring their wine and letting herself be ogled.

Since their talk this afternoon, something had shifted within her. There was a desperation to her actions that struck Creesjie as reckless, but Isabel wouldn't hear her pleas, or allow herself to be tugged away.

She was having fun, she claimed. More fun than she'd had in a long time.

Hugging Marcus, Osbert and Lia by their small fire, Creesjie could only pray she came to her senses soon.

Her eyes caught movement. Dorothea was going to see if Sara wanted any food or ale. Her friend was standing at the water's edge with Arent, her head against his arm. They were staring at the wreckage of the *Saardam* and holding hands.

At least some good has come of all this, she thought.

A series of thuds came from the other camp, followed by groans and cries of alarm. Musketeers stumbled drunkenly, trying to catch hold of Isabel, who skipped away nimbly.

One by one, they began collapsing.

Drecht staggered forward, trying to draw his sword, but he sagged to his knees in front of her, then fell over.

Arent reached the musketeer camp at the same time as Sara and the rest of the survivors. Around the roaring fire lay dozens of unconscious bodies, their mugs spilled from their hands.

'Are they dead?' asked Sara.

'No,' said Isabel, nudging the body of Jacobi Drecht with her foot. 'I poured a vial of Sara's sleeping draught into their wine. Could somebody fetch some rope, so we can tie them up.'

Creesjie hugged Isabel fiercely. 'I thought you'd lost your mind,' she admitted giddily. 'But this is ... you've saved us all.'

'Not yet,' said Isabel sorrowfully. 'But almost.'

She stepped around Creesjie, addressing the passengers. 'Old Tom delivered us to this island thinking to doom us,' she said. 'But while it was the demon's evil that steered our ship on to these rocks, it was God's hand that spared us.'

Arent staggered, then fell. Some of the other passengers were moaning, the ground spinning beneath them.

'What have you done?' cried out Creesjie, as Marcus and Osbert crumpled on to the shoal.

'Old Tom can shelter in any soul that has bargained with it,' she said, as Sara collapsed. 'But I can't be sure which of you that is.'

Creesjie's vision was becoming blurry.

'The daemonologica taught me how to make holy fire,' continued Isabel, smiling the smile of martyrs. 'I'm going to cleanse your souls one by one until there's no hiding place left. I'm going to put an end to the tyranny of Old Tom once and for all.'

───────

Creesjie woke with a groan.

She'd been tied to a piece of the *Saardam*'s wreckage on the shoal. The knots were tight, and the wreckage was too heavy to move. It couldn't have been more than a couple of hours, because the sky was still dark and their fire bright. Everybody else, passengers and musketeers alike, were equally bound.

'Marcus! Osbert!' she called out.

They were nowhere to be seen, though Sara and Lia were tied up nearby. She called to them, watching them stir slowly, blinking away their confusion as they whipped their heads from left to right, trying to make sense of what was happening.

'Marcus! Osbert!' cried Creesjie. 'God, please answer me!'

Slowly, more people began to wake up. Creesjie couldn't tell how many of them believed in Old Tom or not, but she knew they were afraid. An hour ago, they'd been convinced they would be raped or murdered by the musketeers. Now they were about to be burnt to death by a zealot.

It was a bargain worthy of Old Tom himself.

'Isabel!' screamed Sara, whose head was turned towards something Creesjie couldn't see. 'Isabel, stop this!'

A fire roared into life behind them, an agonising scream rolling up the beach. Creesjie craned her neck trying to see who it was, but she couldn't twist far enough. All she could do was listen to Isabel's strange chanting.

'Mama,' cried out Lia, terrified. 'Don't let her do this, please.'

'Be brave, dear heart,' called Sara, straining against her ropes. 'Remember the courage you had on the docks when we comforted the leper. Close your eyes and pray with me. Pray with me!'

The scream cut off and Isabel emerged out of the gloom, wreathed in firelight. She'd made a torch from a tree branch and sailcloth, and it burnt in her hand, dripping flame on to the shoal.

'Isabel, you don't have to do this,' cried Creesjie desperately, tears staining her cheeks. 'Please, please, please, my friends are innocent, my sons are innocent. Let them go!'

'Old Tom can hide anywhere,' replied Isabel in that flat, broken voice. 'This is our only chance to banish him.'

Going to Lia, she knelt down in front of her. 'You may be innocent, and, if so, I'm sorry for what I must do.' Her eyes were empty. 'If it comforts you, know that the mercy God shows you in heaven, will be equal to the torment visited upon me in hell.'

Using her fingertip, Isabel drew a mark in dirt upon Lia's forehead.

'Isabel, please, she's just a girl,' screamed Sara hoarsely.

Isabel ignored her, lowering the burning torch towards the hem of Lia's dress. 'I am truly sorry.'

Lia screamed for mercy, as Sara cried out for Isabel to stop.

'There's no such thing as Old Tom,' yelled Creesjie at the top of her lungs.

Silence fell upon them, as all eyes turned towards her. The burning torch paused on its way to Lia's dress, confusion clear on Isabel's face.

'I made it all up,' cried out Creesjie desperately. 'I did it all. I wanted to kill the governor general and this was the only way. Lia's not a devil. Don't hurt her, please!'

The mania dropped from Isabel's face. She peered at Sara winsomely.

'How was that?' she asked.

'You did wonderfully,' said Sara, pulling her hands out of the loose ropes and helping Lia to her feet.

Creesjie blinked at them in confusion. 'Sara, what's happening?'

'It was a farce,' said Sara coldly. 'The same farce you performed on us. There couldn't be any doubt. I had to know you were guilty.'

T HE CHARADE AT AN end, Lia and Dorothea immediately set about untying the other passengers, while
gently explaining what had happened. It was quite a story,
and most took it in open-mouthed.

'Where are my boys?' asked Creesjie, straining to find them.

'With Arent,' explained Sara. 'We didn't want them to see
this.' She whistled into the dark, receiving one back. 'They're
coming now.'

Creesjie sagged, looking suddenly exhausted. 'Thank you,
Sara.'

'Don't thank me. This isn't over.'

'And when will it be over?'

The light of the Eighth Lantern burst into life, then immediately exploded. Flaming pieces dropped into the ocean.

'When that happens,' said Sara.

Another lantern was lit to its portside, followed by a dozen
more, illuminating the masts and decks, the beakhead and
even the sailors on the waist. From being terrible, the Eighth
Lantern was immediately transformed into something
mundane. It was an Indiaman. Exactly like the *Saardam*. It
had rigging and sails and had clearly been maltreated by the
storm, much as they had.

'It's just a ship,' said somebody behind her. They sounded disappointed.

'It's the *Leeuwarden*,' came another voice. 'I recognise the colours. She was part of the fleet that left Batavia. I thought we lost her in the storm.'

There was a murmur of agreement, then surprise. A second smaller boat was crossing the water, approaching the island.

'The *Leeuwarden* was the Eighth Lantern from the start,' said Arent, emerging from the darkness with Marcus and Osbert. The boys were jogging to keep up with his long strides. Seeing their mother, they immediately ran to her side, becoming confused when they found her tied to a piece of wreckage.

'It's just a game we're playing,' said Creesjie, trying to be reassuring. She cast an appealing glance at Sara, who nodded towards Arent.

The mercenary took a knife out of his boot and severed the ropes tying Creesjie's hands, allowing her to hug her sons.

'But we saw eight lanterns on the water,' argued Lia. 'How was that possible if there were only seven ships?'

'The Eighth Lantern was just a lantern mounted on a specially rigged yawl,' replied Arent, going to the water's edge. 'I saw a broken version of it in the jungle. Creesjie's crew must have built a few on this island, before they got it right and transported it over to the *Leeuwarden*. When they needed the Eighth Lantern to terrify us, they rowed it out on to the water and set it alight. That's how it appeared and disappeared so quickly. It was only ever coming and going from the *Leeuwarden*.'

Closer and closer came the boat, oars splashing. Somebody was holding a lantern at her bow. Arent watched it, a grim expression on his face.

Sara was staring at Creesjie with daggers in her eyes. 'You put my daughter in danger!' she hissed.

'No,' said Creesjie pleadingly. 'No, that was never the intent. Do you think I'd have brought my own boys aboard if I thought to do the ship harm? Old Tom was all theatre, just a shadow playing on the walls. There was never supposed to be a mutiny, or a shipwreck. I planned it so carefully, Sara. Crauwels was paid to sail us here, then disembark everybody by claiming he needed to thoroughly search the ship for Emily de Haviland. I assumed everybody would be so afraid they'd agree willingly. This island isn't dangerous. It doesn't really resemble the Mark of Old Tom, that was just to convince any last doubters that the demon was real, and had killed Jan Haan. There are supplies here, and the *Leeuwarden* was going to stumble upon us in a day or so. It would have taken everybody back to Amsterdam, leaving Crauwels and a skeleton crew to unload the treasure, minus his payment. Once that was done, they were supposed to sail the *Saardam* back safely, delivering the cargo and appeasing the Gentlemen 17. The only people who were supposed to get hurt were Jan Haan and Sander Kers.' Hatred seethed in every word. 'I didn't know Johannes Wyck would be aboard, and I didn't expect Crauwels to betray me. He wanted the treasure and The Folly for himself, and he thought he could get them by inciting his crew to kill the nobles, including me. Believe me, Old Tom was for your husband's benefit alone.'

'What about Bosey? You bu—' Sara's fury was quashed by the sight of Marcus and Osbert, peering up at her wide-eyed.

They were clinging to their mother, firelight playing on their innocent, frightened faces.

'Me and your mama need to settle a few matters,' she said, her heart aching. 'Will you play with Dorothea for a little while?'

They glanced at their mother uncertainly, but Creesjie smiled at them. 'Off you go, boys. I'll be along to collect you soon.'

Dorothea took each boy by the hand, her expression betraying neither dismay nor confusion at the circumstances. She would have questions later, Sara knew, but for the moment Marcus and Osbert were her concern. They usually were.

A crowd of passengers had encircled them, forcing Dorothea to push through. They were curious for the minute, still numb from everything that had happened, but their rage wouldn't keep in its kennel long, thought Sara. Not once they realised they had somebody to blame for their misery.

Sara glanced at Arent near the waterline, wishing he was closer. Though only a few steps away, she felt she might need him soon.

'Why did you kill Bosey?' asked Sara, watching as Creesjie got to her feet.

Seeing the faces around her, Creesjie lifted her chin haughtily, as if they were servants to be stared down. 'I needed somebody to introduce our demon, so I asked Crauwels to recommend the worst man he could. He gave me Bosey. Believe me, murder was the least of his sins. I didn't enjoy what I did to him, but he was drugged insensible. There was mercy in it.'

'I looked into his eyes as he died,' argued Sara, offended by her dismissive tone. 'He was in agony. There was no mercy there.'

'How did you do it?' interrupted Lia, her eagerness betraying her fascination for the mechanics behind the crime. 'Nobody went near him. How did you make him catch flame the way you did?'

'The stack of crates he was standing on had been hollowed out, and a ladder built inside. A confederate of mine was inside. He was responsible for the voice you heard. When the time came, my confederate simply opened a small hatch and lit Bosey's robes from the inside.'

The crowd muttered angrily. Many of them had been on the docks when Bosey caught fire and such suffering wasn't easily forgotten.

'Why did you hide Sander's body?' pressed Lia.

There was something terrible in her eagerness for answers, thought Sara. It was as if this was just another of Sammy Pipps's cases, empty of consequence, existing only for her amusement.

'Sander Kers was the last of his witchfinding order,' said Creesjie, whose expression suggested she felt the same unease as Sara. 'They tortured and butchered without care, and I thought the world best rid of them. By careful planning, I'd managed to slaughter the others, but I wanted to take Sander's life personally. He taught Pieter every vile trick he knew, so I lured him to Batavia. I'd intended to kill him the same night as Jan Haan, but when he heard Reynier van Schooten's confession, he went down to investigate the treasure in the cargo hold. By terrible coincidence, he overheard me talking with …' She faltered, almost tripping over a name,

'… an accomplice. I managed to get behind him and slit his throat, but it was clumsy. In the darkness, I couldn't be certain I hadn't left something incriminating behind, so we dragged the body into one of Bosey's smuggling compartments until we knew what to do with it.'

From beyond the circle of spectators came a muffled howl of pain. Arent darted towards it, Sara's eyes following him.

Drecht was bleeding from a gash on the head made by a rock now sitting innocuously beside him. Somebody had thrown it at him.

Arent's eyes passed across the crowd slowly, causing them to shy back.

'You've got the right to be angry at him,' said Arent. 'After what he did. You've got the right to be angry at her, as well.' He jerked his thumb towards Creesjie. 'But enough blood's been spilt already. There's wrongs need righting and we'll come to that soon enough, but it won't be done from anger. That's how Old Tom got loose in the first place, and real or not, look at the damage was done.' He let the words settle, then crossed the space towards Creesjie. He was grim-faced and huge, and she shrank away from him.

'Do you have my father's rosary?' he demanded.

'I threw it away,' she said, sounding genuinely remorseful. 'It was among Pieter's possessions. Your uncle hired Pieter to kill your father, and your grandfather asked for the rosary as proof he'd completed his contract. Once he'd seen it, Casper ordered Pieter to destroy it, but he kept it for some reason. A trophy, perhaps. It wasn't left in the animal pens to hurt you, Arent.' There was a throb in her throat. 'I wanted Jan Haan to know why this was happening to him. The assassination of your father is what started everything. When Pieter stabbed him, you leapt at Pieter with an arrow, and he had to half drown you in a stream to keep you from killing him. Pieter was so badly injured it was all he could do to drag himself away. He was afraid of you, that's why he left you in the woods alone. A jagged rock made that scar on your wrist as you thrashed in the water. It shouldn't have led to anything, but you drew it on some doors in a village, and when Jan saw the chaos it caused, he realised he had a way to make himself a fortune. He brought the scheme to Casper van den Berg and Pieter. Casper provided the necessary funds and Pieter spun a tale of possession and rituals out of it, using his fellow witchfinders to terrorise the lands of those Jan sent him after. Together, they drove their competitors out of business, including my family.'

'Your family?' queried Drecht, still tied to his rock.

'Creesjie Jens was born Emily de Haviland,' said Sara, examining every twitch of Creesjie's face, trying to find the woman within. For the past two years, she had looked on these features with love, thinking she knew every thought that lay behind them. Now, she realised how foolish she'd been. She'd been used and betrayed.

She felt like she'd lost Creesjie, not her husband.

Creesjie examined her admiringly. 'I knew you were clever,' she said. 'Though I'll admit that innocent girl's name fits ill the sinful woman I became. How did you know I was behind this?'

'Vos's records. Our passage receipts were on his desk after he died, as if they'd been troubling him. There were bills for my cabin, Lia's and even my husband's. I didn't know why, but when Arent told me he suspected you, I had a thought. Vos kept all my husband's accounts, so he knew exactly what my husband had purchased, and what he hadn't. You kept telling us that you were only onboard because my husband had demanded you sail with us, and that he'd paid for your passage. Why then was your receipt of passage not among Vos's records? It was because my husband had made no such demand, and hadn't paid for your cabin. You mistakenly mentioned the lie to Vos, didn't you? And he realised. That's why the leper had to kill him.'

Creesjie murmured her agreement. 'And if he hadn't, Arent very likely would have died at Vos's hands. Strange how fate works, isn't it?' She looked across at Arent, who had returned to the sea edge to watch the yawl approach. He was holding himself tense, his fists clenched.

'What made *you* suspect me?' she asked. 'I thought I'd been so careful.'

Arent was so intent upon the approaching yawl, he didn't notice people were waiting for him to talk until Isabel tugged his sleeve. 'They want to know how you realised Creesjie was responsible for the governor general's death,' she said.

Arent's gaze passed across the expectant faces before him, his thoughts obviously still far afield. 'My uncle was killed in his bunk by a long blade thrust down through the bottom of Sara's bunk, then drawn back up again. I realised the dagger had to have been plunged into the wound *after* my uncle was dead, and there was only one chance to do it – when Creesjie first found the body. That's why the candle had to be snuffed. If the room had been lit, Drecht would have immediately seen that there was no dagger in his chest. It would have taken Sammy minutes to work out how the crime had been committed. After the leper killed my uncle, he climbed down to my uncle's porthole and used a candle snuffer stored above it to extinguish the light. Creesjie forced Drecht to leave the room to get another, then stabbed my uncle in the existing wound.'

'Outlandish, I admit,' sighed Creesjie, rubbing her eyes. 'But there was no other way of killing him without getting caught. Drecht dogged his steps whenever he left the fort, and he wore that damn breastplate everywhere except bed.'

'If Aunt Creesjie wasn't the leper, who was?' demanded Lia, bewildered.

'The answer's in that boat,' said Sara, pointing to the yawl. 'A little patience won't hurt you.'

'It might,' disagreed Lia irritably. 'How did you come to be my father's mistress? I'm assuming it wasn't a coincidence.'

'Without family I had no wealth or influence, so I had to rely on my beauty. My first husband was a holy terror, but I used his wealth to hunt down the witchfinder. Once I found him, I left my husband and reinvented myself as a courtesan. I seduced Pieter, intending to kill him when I had the opportunity, but …' She growled, like an animal in a trap. 'I fell in love with him. He'd given up his work, and he was kind and generous and … he made me feel like somebody new. I allowed myself to believe he'd changed. That *I'd* changed. Then our funds grew short, and he started talking of a scheme that he'd used to make himself rich. He sent a missive to Arent's grandfather, and I knew he was going to start again. He was planning to destroy more families the way he'd destroyed mine. I called –' she almost stumbled into the name again, before recovering – 'an old friend, who tortured Pieter for the names of his associates. We then set about our vengeance.'

There were tears in her eyes. The same tears that had been there every time she'd talked about Pieter in the past. She really had loved him, thought Sara in bewilderment.

'And that brought you to my husband?' she asked.

'I'd met your husband years earlier through Pieter, and knew he had an eye for me. After I killed Pieter, I wrote to him and professed an adoration. He had me on the first boat to Batavia.'

'Then why wait? Why not kill him when you arrived two years ago?'

'Because I would have been caught, and I loved my boys – and now, you and Lia – far too much to be parted from you. I needed to wait for the right moment.'

Arent waded into the water to help pull the yawl up the shoal. Isaack Larme jumped out, holding a lantern. Manning the oars were Eggert and Thyman.

'You were right about everything,' said Larme, shaking Arent's hand. 'He was exactly where you said he'd be. He wants to see you.'

'Who wants to see us?' demanded Lia, vexed. 'Who was helping Aunt Creesjie?'

'You've read all our cases, Lia,' replied Arent. 'Do you know how many things Sammy Pipps has ever overlooked in our history together?'

'None,' she said, as if offended by the notion of fallibility.

'That's right,' he said, sadly. 'And yet, somehow, he missed a simple trapdoor in the animal pens that led down to Captain Crauwels's cabin.'

'What are you saying?'

'He's saying it's time we met Old Tom,' said Sara.

83

THEIR YAWL BUMPED AGAINST the *Leeuwarden's* hull, as Eggert and Thyman pulled in the oars. They hadn't spoken a word during the crossing, and it was clear both were nervous around Arent. He took up the entire rear bench and had barely moved the entire trip. He was silent, glowering at the ship.

Thyman whistled up to the deck and a seat was immediately lowered from above.

'Who goes first?' asked Sara nervously.

'I'll go,' said Creesjie. 'No harm will come to any of you, I swear. You're safe here. Everybody is. Old Tom's work is done. The demon is banished.'

As Creesjie was hoisted into the air, Arent leant closer to Eggert and Thyman.

'How long have you worked for Creesjie,' he asked.

They glanced at each other, uncertain whether to answer. 'You two helped her steal The Folly in Batavia, didn't you? Were you the Portuguese thieves who slipped away from me?'

Eggert grinned, as if reliving an old jest between friends. 'Aye, but if she hadn't told us you were coming –'

Thyman nudged him in the ribs, but Arent seemed satisfied.

'Did you kill the animals, Eggert?' he asked. 'You were guarding the passenger cabins. Would have been easy enough to walk into the captain's cabin and open the hatch in his ceiling.'

'He was supposed to, but I had to do it in the end,' sniffed Thyman. 'Eggert didn't have the stomach to kill the poor little pig, so he kept watch from the captain's porthole for the *Leeuwarden* instead, then called up to me when they lit their lantern.'

'Weren't the way it happened,' replied Eggert angrily, shoving him. 'It was only the sow I couldn't hurt. I'd already killed the chickens a few minutes earlier, and drawn the symbol in the dark. You couldn't have done that quiet as I did. I did most of the work.'

Sara glanced at Arent. His expression mirrored her own thoughts. Who would trust these two fools with anything?

The seat came down again and this time Sara went up. Lia followed, and finally Arent. It took six men to lift him.

The *Leeuwarden* was identical to the *Saardam* in every way, except for the conduct of the crew, who went about their duties quietly and diligently. The captain and his senior officers were talking on the quarter deck, their measured tones a stark contrast to the gruff bickering of Crauwels, Larme and Van Schooten. After the rowdiness of the *Saardam*, it really did feel like a ghost ship, and Lia pressed against Sara's side nervously.

Arent stretched up to his full height, the entire crew pausing in their duties to stare. They'd heard the stories. They just hadn't believed them until now.

'This is not how I intended us to meet again,' came Sammy's familiar voice from behind a lantern.

He lowered the blinding light, bringing a gasp from Lia. Though he was dressed wonderfully in ruffs and ribbons, with a cane and a feathered hat to complement them, his face had been badly injured. Half of it was mangled, an eyepatch covering his lost eye.

'You don't like the hat?' asked Sammy wryly.

'With your permission, Sara, I'd like Dorothea to take the boys to my cabin,' said Creesjie. 'It's the same one I had on the *Saardam*. They can bathe and rest, they've been through a lot.'

Sara nodded, watching as Creesjie kissed the boys good-night. They came to Lia, then her, for the usual hugs before bed. As they went skipping up the staircase to the quarter-deck, Dorothea chasing after them, Sara felt dizzy. It would be so easy to believe nothing had changed at all.

Sammy went to Creesjie, taking both of her hands in his own. Concern was written across his face. 'Are you well? I became worried when you didn't signal.'

'They faked a witch hunt. You'd have been proud, brother.'

'Brother!' exclaimed Arent.

Sammy bowed extravagantly. 'Forgive me this long overdue introduction, my friend. I'm Hugo de Haviland, or I was.' His accent had changed slightly and his expression had become haughtier, as though Hugo had been wearing Sammy the entire time. Then he grinned suddenly, bringing the problematary back to the surface. 'Using the dwarf was genius, I truly didn't expect it.'

'Dwarf?' asked Creesjie, glancing between Arent and Sammy. 'What part did Isaack Larme play in this?'

'Sara and I realised that if the island were the home of Old Tom, it made sense to assume that the Eighth Lantern would be prowling the waters,' said Arent, whose gaze hadn't left Sammy. 'Everybody believed sending a rescue boat was a suicide mission, so we reasoned that if we asked for volunteers they'd likely be those who already knew there was a friendly boat waiting.' He scratched beneath his eye. 'I hid Larme in a cask and put him on the rescue boat with the other supplies. I told him to sneak out once he was aboard and find Pipps in the captain's cabin.'

'How did you know he'd be there?' asked Lia.

'Because I know Sammy.'

Sammy became abashed. 'I've spent three weeks in the stinking darkness, I thought I deserved a little comfort. You can't imagine my surprise when Larme turned up at my door, bold as brass, and told me Arent knew everything, and I should blow up the Eighth Lantern if our friendship held.'

The problematary beamed at Arent, like a proud parent. 'I knew you'd work it out.'

'You did most of it,' grunted Arent, ashamed of the praise.

'A few hints, here and there,' scoffed Sammy, waving them away. 'It's only your second case, I wanted you to enjoy it.'

'People are dead,' said Sara sharply, annoyed by how flippant he was.

'That's how most of our cases start and end,' said Sammy, baffled by the objection. 'If it's any consolation, everybody who died deserved it. Apart from the people who died in the wreck, but that was Crauwels's fault for ignoring the plan.' He ran the back of his fingers down his scarred face. 'And I think you'll agree, I've been punished for my misjudgement.'

A soft wind blew across the deck, the rigging creaking.

'There's no point doing this out here,' said Creesjie, casting a glance at the crew, who were trying hard to make it appear they weren't listening. 'Why don't we go into the great cabin?'

534

'Of course, of course,' said Sammy. 'Everything is arranged.'

Instinctively, he tried to walk alongside Arent, but the mercenary glared at him and he fell back another step, beside Lia and Sara.

'Were you the whisper?' asked Lia, still in awe of her hero, despite everything.

'At various times all four of us were. Myself, Creesjie, Eggert and Thyman. It was actually one of the simpler things to achieve,' he said modestly, as they passed into the compartment under the half deck. Without passengers, it was a neat and tidy space used for storing tools. 'We paid Bosey to drill little holes high up in your walls that we could whisper through. We plugged them with caulking when they weren't used to keep the sound from travelling between cabins.'

A stronger gust clambered over the railing, plucking at their clothes. In the distance, the bonfires on the shoal seemed momentarily to blink out. It was as if the entire island had disappeared.

'What about the crew?' said Lia. 'How did you whisper to them?'

'The crates in the cargo hold almost touch the grates in the floor of the orlop deck, and the sailors slept on the other side of those grates. At night, without any light to see by, a whisper's the easiest thing in the world to make horrifying.'

'But why go to such trouble, Creesjie?' asked Sara, giving voice to the question that had tormented her since the beach. 'If you hated my husband so much, surely you could have found a simpler way of killing him?'

'Where would be the fun in that?' wondered Sammy, confounded.

Creesjie offered him an exasperated glance. 'It wasn't enough to kill him, Sara,' she said. 'We wanted him to know what it felt like to be hounded and haunted, the way we had been as children when the Mark of Old Tom started appearing across our lands and strangers were beating on our gates, accusing us of witchcraft. Samuel and I had always been gifted, and suddenly those gifts became accusations. Servants we'd known our entire lives crept past our rooms, terrified we were going to bewitch them. If we went into the village, rocks would be thrown at us, all because Pieter Fletcher and his witchfinders carved a few symbols in the woods and spread some rumours. We wanted Jan to know he was going to die, and be powerless to prevent it, the way we were when the mob finally stormed our home, butchered our parents and burnt our world to the ground. We wanted him to know our terror.'

'And you wanted him to know it was you,' said Sara, with sudden understanding. 'That's why you put the mark on the sail that very first day. That's why you bought a cabin using an anagram of your own name. You wanted him to find you.'

'I wanted to face him before the end,' affirmed Sammy. 'I wanted him to know who'd done this to him. I was waiting for him in Dalvhain's cabin the night I killed Vos.'

'Reckless, as always,' said Creesjie, rolling her eyes. 'I thought that part of the plan was too dangerous, but he wouldn't listen. He rarely does.' Arent grunted sympathetically, in spite of himself. 'What would you have done if Drecht had seized you?' demanded Creesjie, becoming annoyed at her brother afresh.

'We've spent years studying Jan Haan,' replied Sammy, his weary tone suggesting this was an old argument. 'He was many things, but stupid wasn't one of them. He knew the scale of his enemy, and, in every situation where the odds have been against him, he's tried to negotiate. I knew he'd come with his cap in his hand, hoping to appease us long enough to betray us. Besides, Eggert was guarding the passenger cabins. If Drecht had tried to seize me, Eggert would have stabbed him from behind. The situation was in hand.'

'What did you offer him?' wondered Lia.

'Your father's greatest weakness was thinking that everybody wanted what he wanted, but they lacked the cunning and ruthlessness to take it. I told him we wanted our family's fortune back, and our name restored, something that would be in his power when he joined the Gentlemen 17. We told him that if he betrayed us, we had complete control of the *Saardam* and would kill him, his family and Arent.'

'Weren't you afraid he'd just sail back for Batavia?' asked Sara.

'He had the ascension order in his pocket telling him that any delay would endanger his chances of claiming a seat among the Gentlemen 17. Not to mention a cargo hold full of profit spoiling every day we were at sea.' Sammy smiled darkly. 'Greed is capable of killing even the most cautious of men.'

'That was one of your old orders, wasn't it?' Arent asked him.

'Yes,' he replied. 'I preserved the stamp.'

'How long have you been planning this?' Arent said, stunned.

'Since I recruited you,' he said. 'I only chose you, because I was hoping you'd deliver me to your uncle and grandfather, but, then, to my disgust, it became obvious you were actually an honourable man. Probably the only one I'd ever met. I became your friend in spite of myself. Falling in love with those we believe we're using is actually something of a family trait.'

He looked at Creesjie knowingly.

'Hush, brother.'

They entered a great cabin dressed in candlelight and shadow. A feast had been prepared, with a golden ham, its skin crisp and fat dribbling down its sides. Potatoes were piled high and a cone of sugar sat on the table, the granules sparkling in the candelabrum's warm glow.

Stewards pulled out seats and poured wine.

'What is all this?' said Sara, banging the table in frustration. 'There's an island full of scared people over there, including children, and we're sitting down to dinner? We need to bring them aboard. They need to know they're safe!'

Creesjie glanced at Sammy, then her fingers. 'You're right, dear heart, but we have much to discuss first. How about we send a yawl back with food and wine for them? We only need an hour. By the time they've eaten, we can start bringing them over. Acceptable?'

Sara nodded reluctantly and Sammy called a steward, relaying the order in a hush.

'How did you afford all of this?' wondered Arent, feeling the painted beams in the ceiling. 'You must have bought off the entire crew. I know you charged an extravagant amount for your services, but this scheme would have cost a fortune.'

'Actually, Edward Coil bought all of this,' said Sammy, gesturing for everybody to sit down.

'Coil?' asked Sara, shooting Arent a glance.

'He was a clerk accused of stealing a diamond and fleeing to France,' said Arent, taking a seat. 'I thought he was guilty, but Sammy found proof of his innocence.'

'Only I didn't,' corrected Sammy, laying his napkin on his lap. 'Coil gave me the diamond in return for finding a way to free him, but the reason he'd stolen the diamond was because he was infatuated with …' He gestured towards the woman at his side.

'Creesjie,' finished Lia.

'Exactly like Vos,' said Sara, shaking her head. Creesjie smiled at her hopefully, seeking any tatter of their friendship. She was disappointed.

'You solved that case, Arent,' said Sammy. 'You got everything right and I took it away from you.'

And here, at last, was the apology, thought Arent. Not in the words, which Sammy had never said, but in the tone, and the sorrow. For the wreck and the fear, Sammy felt little responsibility, but he'd lied to Arent about his achievement, rather than celebrating it. It was the only regret Sammy had.

Arent saw him then, truly, for the first time. Not the great man he'd believed in, just a clever one. Callous and cold, like all the others he'd met. Through Sammy, Arent thought he saw a future where strength was subdued by intelligence, making the world safer for everybody, especially the weak. But Sammy believed slaughtering innocents was a fair price to pay to kill a powerful man. He was no different from the kings Arent had fought for.

'The diamond bought us the loyalty of the *Leeuwarden*'s crew,' said Creesjie. 'On its last voyage from Amsterdam, we diverted it to this island to drop the supplies and build the huts and the Eighth Lantern. The *Leeuwarden* arrived in Batavia a few weeks late, but everybody believed a storm had blown it off course.'

'We thought we could convince the governor general to take this ship back to Amsterdam, but he was adamant about sailing on the *Saardam*,' said Sammy, picking up the story. 'So, I paid for the eager services of Bosey and Crauwels instead. Eggert and Thyman had been with us for years, and we knew we could count on their loyalty.'

'Why were you in that cell?' asked Arent.

'Because I wanted to be.'

Creesjie cleared her throat. 'Once my brother delivered the false ascension order to Jan, bearing the accusation of spying, we knew he'd ask Crauwels to recommend somewhere to secure him. We had the captain suggest he be imprisoned at the front of the ship.'

'I couldn't risk being asked to investigate because I knew you'd see through my failures immediately,' said Sammy, pompously. 'But nobody could blame me for not solving a demon's scheme if I was manacled in the worst cell on the ship.'

Sammy placed a sliver of meat into his mouth. 'Once I was in that cell, I had the freedom to come and go as I pleased. We had Bosey build a trapdoor from my cell out on to the beakhead. That allowed me to don my leper's garb and slip into the water, so I could swim over to the ladder leading up to the poop deck. I usually did that after Arent left me. I had only to drop through the trapdoor we'd built from the animal pens into Crauwels's cabin, then dart across the corridor into

Dalvhain's cabin before anybody was up and about. I spent most of my days in there.'

'That's why you had Eggert and Thyman slaughter the animals,' said Lia, with sudden understanding. 'They made such a racket every time anybody went near them. If you were constantly coming and going –'

'It would have been noticed,' finished Sammy. 'As it was that first night when Sara saw me at her porthole. I'd gone to collect the candle snuffer from my sister, but I didn't know your cabin and Dalvhain's had been swapped. Arent nearly caught me, but I managed to get into the animal pens before he did. I dropped into Crauwels's cabin with a chicken in my arms. Thank heavens, everybody was too distracted to hear it.'

'You murdered the governor general while everybody was eating dinner, didn't you?' asked Arent, pushing away a pile of potatoes to lean his elbows on the table.

'Yes.'

'And it was you who saved me from Vos?'

'That hadn't been my intent, though I'm glad I was there.'

'Did you kill Wyck?' asked Sara.

The ship listed slightly, the plates sliding on the table.

'He was a stable hand in our house when we were children,' said Creesjie, taking hold of her wine. 'Pieter tried to coerce the servants into saying they'd seen us performing satanic acts, but Wyck stood by us. He lost an eye for it, and ended up joining the Company after the family was slaughtered. That experience changed him.'

Sammy touched his sister's cheek soothingly.

'When I whispered to him, he told me he'd recognised Creesjie on the deck,' said Sammy. 'And that he'd want paying

541

for his silence. We couldn't let that stand. I actually offered him a fortune to kill Arent during their fight.' Seeing Arent's baleful glare he held his hands up. 'I know he couldn't win. I was hoping Arent would kill him in self defence, sparing me the trouble.'

'How did you make the white smoke everybody mistook for fire?' wondered Lia, with a professional curiosity.

'Something I stumbled on while making philosopher's wool from zinc,' he related happily. 'It's impressive, isn't it? We laced the caulking on the orlop deck with it. I had only to touch a flame to the tar and it burnt away, creating that white smoke, while leaving the wood intact.'

From his voice, Sara might have believed he'd used it for nothing more than conjuring tricks at court. Watching Lia's delighted reaction, she could have believed the same.

'How long have you been doing this?' asked Arent, his voice cracking. 'Committing crimes?'

Sara could hear the rage, barely controlled. She sought out his hand under the table, but his fist was clenched.

'I was planning murders long before I was solving them,' admitted Sammy. 'My family name was destroyed, and we had nobody to support us. Emily and I survived however we could, and it turns out more people want somebody dead than care who killed them. I could tell you I carried on doing it because I was poor and starving, but I've lied enough for today. My gifts demand exercise, and the only thing more thrilling than unravelling a complicated murder is plotting one, then seeing it come off so perfectly nobody even recognises that it was a crime. Kings die peacefully in their beds. Nobles fall off horses while hunting. Beautiful heiresses commit suicide at balls. Good mysteries so rarely come along, but if you've got a little imagination, you can invent as many as you want. It's proved a lucrative venture over the years. I've exported them to France, Germany, the Cape. They're my spices, but unlike sugar and paprika, the nobility will never get sick of murdering each other.'

'You really are Old Tom,' said Arent hollowly.

'There's no such thing as demons, Arent.' Sammy took a sip of wine, the liquid reddening his lips. 'But there are always bargains to be struck.'

Perhaps it *was* the wine, or the dancing shadows, or the flush in his cheeks, but there truly was something devilish about him, thought Sara.

'Bargains,' she repeated slowly, hearing an offer in his tone.

Creesjie clasped her hands and leant across the table, into the candlelight. 'I told you earlier that we did all this because we wanted Jan Haan to know our fear. But we also did it because we didn't want to be caught. Everybody on that island believes a demon killed your husband, which is exactly what we intended. That's the story they'll go back home and tell.' Seeing Sara's doubt, she waved a hand. 'All of this we can explain away, but superstition burrows itself deep. They believe it now. They believe in Old Tom. They'll spend their lives cursing him for things that go wrong in their lives, and rubbing charms to keep themselves safe. Their children will believe, and so will their grandchildren.' She paused, gathering herself. 'I love you, Sara.' Her eyes found Lia. 'I love you, Lia. My boys love you. I want you to come with me to France as you planned. We have Jan's treasure, which means we can live the life we always talked about, free of any obligation to marry.'

Lia shot a quick glance at her mother, but Sara kept her gaze firmly on Creesjie. Lia was sweet and clever, but she cared little for the suffering of strangers. She wanted the life so long promised with Creesjie, and Sara knew those dark eyes would beg her for it.

Sara didn't know if she'd have the strength to resist. Or, even, if she should. For the fifteen years she'd been married to Jan Haan, she'd dreamt only of her freedom. Now, she was being offered exactly what she wanted. Part of her yearned to accept, to snatch at it greedily.

'Whatever your intentions, hundreds of people are dead,' growled Arent. 'Children have lost their mothers and fathers. Husbands have lost their wives. You can't walk away from that. Somebody has to be held to account.' He stared at Sammy fiercely. 'That's what we did, Sammy. We held people to account for doing things like this.'

'Your uncle was held to account,' said Creesjie. 'And my conscience aches for the hurt we've done accomplishing that, but it's assuaged by the knowledge that we prevented the Gentlemen 17 from taking control of The Folly, and, through that, expanding an empire which empowers ruthless men like Jan Haan.'

'Until you sell it to somebody else,' argued Arent.

'We've destroyed it,' said Sammy flatly. 'Or, at least, the two parts we recovered. The Folly was much too powerful for any king or Company to possess.'

Only Sara heard Lia groan, pained by the years of lost work.

Creesjie hung her head. 'We grieve what we set in motion, but it was Crauwels who cost these passengers their lives. We intend to save who we can and return to Amsterdam.'

Sammy leant forward into the light, fixing his attention on Arent. His expression was watchful, but also hopeful – like a child making a request of his father. Sara could only curse herself for missing the resemblance between him and Creesjie earlier. They had the same shape to their eyes, the same chin. The same unnatural beauty. Perhaps that was another reason they'd ensured they were rarely in the same room together.

'I know your nature, my friend,' said Sammy, addressing Arent. 'I know it burns you to let something so unjust go unpunished, but there really was a devil, and we really did banish him from this world. The Folly would have brought untold suffering, and we've destroyed it. There is good in this, as there is ill. Accept our version of this story and we'll split Jan Haan's treasure with you and the passengers. You'll be free, and you can choose whatever life you want. Maybe one day, we'll even solve a puzzle together again.'

Sara looked at Arent, trying to gauge his mood. Normally, his face was a mask, every emotion locked away. Not tonight. Fury showed through his furrowed brow and narrowed eyes. It coursed through his tense shoulders and balled fists. He was ready to sink this ship with his bare hands.

'What's the alternative?' asked Lia, her voice quivering. 'What happens if they say no? Will you kill us?'

'No,' exclaimed Creesjie, horrified. 'No, dear heart, no. If any part of me could let that happen, I wouldn't have confessed when I thought Isabel was going to burn you.'

'If you don't like our bargain, you're free to stay on the island in peace,' said Sammy, sounding genuinely pained by the idea. 'There's food enough for years and the hunting's good.'

Obviously discomfited by Arent's anger, he peered at Sara. 'Old Tom asked you what you most desired, and you said freedom. Now, we're offering it to you. The question is: what will you pay for it?'

Sara looked at Lia, then Arent.

Lia's stare was pleading. This was everything she wanted. By contrast, Arent's huge frame seemed to fill the great cabin, his massive shoulders rising and falling, like a bull pawing the ground. Here was the Arent of the songs, implacable and unstoppable, sent by heaven to topple kingdoms. But the god he'd served had disappointed him. There could be no forgiveness.

Sara knew that whatever she said next would decide whether Arent lived or died, and how many people lost their lives trying to stop him.

What was her heart's desire? And what would she pay for it?

For a second, there was only the creaking of wood as they awaited Sara's decision.

'No,' she said softly. There was an intake of breath from around the table. Arent tensed, ready to spring out of his chair. 'No, I'm sick of being dictated to,' continued Sara. 'There's a third way.'

'I assure you, we've thought of everything,' said Sammy, eyeing Arent warily.

'Hush, Samuel,' rebuked Creesjie. 'What's your third way, dear heart?'

'Atonement,' said Sara. 'These passengers deserve recompense for all they've lost, and you've treasure enough to give them new lives, but you can't saunter away afterwards like nothing happened. Too many innocent people are dead. You have to make amends.'

'And how do you suggest we do it?' queried Creesjie, cautiously.

'By turning Old Tom to noble purpose,' replied Sara excitedly. 'By making sure he whispers to those who deserve to hear his voice.' Sensing their gathering objections, she rushed on. 'We all know there are hundreds of others like my husband who do terrible things, but are so powerful they go unpunished. What if that wasn't the case? What if the next time a noble murdered his maid, Old Tom found him and made him pay God's price? What if the next time a king led an army to slaughter, then fled the battlefield in cowardice, Old Tom was waiting in his castle?'

Sammy and Creesjie exchanged an incredulous glance, but Arent was smiling. As was Lia.

'Look at the lengths you've gone for your revenge,' pressed Sara. 'Four years you planned this and Arent and I solved it in a few weeks. Lia invented The Folly to fend off boredom. Imagine what the five of us could accomplish together. Imagine the good we could do.'

'We can't avenge every act of evil in this world,' protested Sammy, but his words were at odds with the eagerness in his voice. He wanted to be talked around, Sara realised. Here was a challenge that would last the rest of his life. She just needed the right words.

'We don't need to avenge every act of evil,' said Arent in a low rumble. 'But we can make people terrified to commit them.' He stared at Sammy. 'You're a scheming, lying, betraying bastard, Sammy Pipps, but you were my friend until today, and I'd wish it so again. You blew up the Eighth Lantern because I asked you to prove I could still trust you. Now I'm asking for this.'

'Creesjie, please,' begged Lia, reaching for the older woman's hand across the table.

Creesjie looked hopefully at her brother. 'Is it even possible?'

'We've treasure enough,' mused Sammy. 'A ship, an island. Not to mention cleverness and cunning aplenty. It just might be. I'd certainly like to find out for myself.'

Tentative smiles were exchanged, as a strange new contract was signed between them.

'Then maybe it's time a devil did what God will not,' said Creesjie gaily. She turned her inquisitive stare on Sara. 'Where do we begin?'

AN APOLOGY TO HISTORY. AND BOATS.

Hello, friend.

Sorry for barging into your evening uninvited. I wanted to turn up after the plot dust had settled and have a word.

You see, I believe a book is whatever you decide it is. The sights, the smells, the characters – everything you believe about them, you're right! That's why I love books. No two readers are the same, which means no two readings are the same. Your version of Arent isn't my version of Arent, as demonstrated by the amount of people who think Arent's hot. Sexy bodyguard really wasn't my intention, but who cares. If you want sexy Arent, sexy Arent you shall have.

Equally, I don't like pinning a genre to my stories. *Seven Deaths* – my prior book – was variously described as a golden age mystery, a metaphysical sci-fi novel, a modern fantasy, and a horror. In every instance, they were right. It was their book, so it could be whatever they damn well pleased.

I suspect as many genres will be pinned to *Devil*, and that's fine. Except ... I'm a bit worried some people might describe this as a 'boat book', or a piece of historical fiction.

At a glance, they are. *Devil*'s set in 1634, so it's definitely historical. And it's definitely fiction. And it's definitely set on a boat. My concern is that people looking for Hilary Mantel and Patrick O'Brien are going to come looking for detail I wilfully ignored. Not from arrogance, but simply because it got in the way of the story I was trying to tell.

An Indiaman would have had dozens of officers, all vital to the running of the ship. I had three, because I didn't want to bog the story down with that many characters, or subplots. The history that snuck into my book often happened differently, much later, or not at all. The technology is far more advanced than it should be, as are some of the attitudes – and the speech. Definitely the speech. This is all intentional. I did my research, then I threw away the bits that hindered my story. See what I mean? This is historical fiction where the history is the fiction. Hopefully, you don't mind that. But I know lots of people will, because lots of people want chocolate, not coffee. They want the details I tossed overboard.

This is quite a long winded way of saying please don't send me critical letters about proper rigging techniques on galleons, or women's fashion in the 1600s. Unless they're super interesting facts you'd like to share.

I love a good fact.

Right, I've kept you long enough. I truly hope you enjoyed *Devil*, as I've enjoyed our chat. Have a lovely evening. Let's talk again in two years when my next book's out. It's going to be really fun, I promise.

Bye,

Stu

ACKNOWLEDGEMENTS

Buckle in kids, I'm going full Gwyneth. On *Seven Deaths*, I thanked half the people I should have. This time I'm thanking absolutely everybody. Writing *Devil* was hard work, as was having a new-born baby while I was doing it. I moaned a fair bit about both. Sorry everybody. I'm happier now. Come find me, I owe you a pint.

Poor Resa. Aside from all the listening and tea, my wife took care of Ada all alone on many more weekends than was fair. She was also the one who pointed out that my original ending was rubbish. If you have a partner like Resa, 90% of your life is perfect. Thanks, hottie. (Using this nickname in public will definitely get me killed.)

Let's talk a little bit about my editors, Alison Hennessey, Shana Drehs, and Grace Menary-Winefield. *Devil* had to be dug out, word by word. It kicked, and spat, and bit. They had to read so much dross and were nothing but kind and positive. *Devil* wouldn't exist without them.

My agent Harry Illingworth is ... tall, so there's that. In all seriousness, he's my mate who knows a lot about publishing. This is marvellously helpful. He's also brilliant at not crying when I tell him I'm going to miss ANOTHER deadline, and he has to break the news to Alison. These skills can't be taught.

Big Phil's abandoned us, so she's dead to me. I was going to say how brilliant her campaign for *Seven Deaths* was, and how ace the campaign for *Devil* was shaping up to be. I was going to say she's a pal, but she selfishly got pregnant and went on maternity leave, so I'm not going to say any of those things. They're all equally true of Amy, so I'll say them to Amy alone. Amy, you're a miracle worker. Thank you. And Phil, of course. I can't really be mean, because you've got a newborn. That's punishment enough.

Glen brings me brownies whenever I sign books. For that and letting me talk his ear off as we crisscross London bookstores, I thank you. David Mann designs wonderful covers. The two for *Seven Deaths* were his. The *Devil* cover was his. I love them all. Ta, mate. Emily Faccini drew the map you've been ogling. She's supremely talented. She did the *Seven Deaths* one, as well, which is why that's also wonderful.

Caitlin, Valerie, and Genevieve have managed to shove my books in front of so many faces I'm surprised people aren't tripping over them when they leave the house. Thanks guys. And let's not forget Sara Helen, making the production process look effortless, even in the midst of a pandemic. Nice work. Ta!

And, finally, mum, dad, and spud. How do you thank the earth you stand on and the ozone layer for protecting you from incineration? I've been trying to be an author for a long time. They never stopped believing I would be. That still matters.

Queue the music. Queue the tears. I'm out of here.

A NOTE ON THE AUTHOR

STUART TURTON is an English author, living in Hertfordshire. He previously wrote *The Seven Deaths of Evelyn Hardcastle*, which was an international bestseller and won a number of awards, including the Costa Best First Novel Award, despite being absolutely nuts. Before becoming an author, he was a travel journalist, and before that, he did every other job you can possibly imagine. Goat farmer was the best. Cleaning toilets was the worst.

Find him on Twitter @Stu_Turton.

A NOTE ON THE TYPE

The text of this book is set in Adobe Caslon, named after the English punch-cutter and type-founder William Caslon I (1692–1766). Caslon's rather old-fashioned types were modelled on seventeenth-century Dutch designs, but found wide acceptance throughout the English-speaking world for much of the eighteenth century until replaced by newer types towards the end of the century. Used in 1776 to print the Declaration of Independence, they were revived in the nineteenth century and have been popular ever since, particularly amongst fine printers. There are several digital versions, of which Carol Twombly's Adobe Caslon is one.